Maybe in Missoula

ALSO BY THE AUTHOR

Montana Women

Maybe in Missoula

Toni Volk

Published by
Soho Press Inc.
853 Broadway
New York, NY 10003

Library of Congress Cataloging-in-Publication Data

Volk, Toni, 1944–
Maybe in Missoula / Toni Volk.
p.   cm.
ISBN 1–56947–007–3
1. Man-woman relationships—Montana—Fiction.   2. Mothers and
sons—Montana—Fiction.   3. Women—Montana—Fiction.   I. Title.
PS3572.03943M38   1994
813'.54–DC20   93–48027
CIP

Manufactured in the United States
10 9 8 7 6 5 4 3 2 1

*To Jacque,
Marci and Tim
and for Glen,
keeper of
dreams*

Part One

BUTTE

Chapter One

Where the meek waited to inherit the earth Annie didn't know. But the poor in spirit of Butte waited unperturbed for the kingdom of heaven over drinks at Jake's. Most of them were here now and the bar was packed.

"What did you say?" Annie asked her son Sammy over the noise.

"Grandpa says he's leaving this place to me."

It was the last thing Annie wanted for him and she frowned.

"How much is it worth?"

"Oh . . . ," she said. She had never considered it as something that might have value.

"Dad says quite a bit. Just the liquor license alone," Sammy said.

"The what?" Someone had started up the jukebox.

"Yeah, he says to sell the license, tear down the bar, and use the lot for something else."

"Sammy," she said. "Don't ever say that around your grandfather." But he just smiled and she saw that he knew better.

Annie hadn't thought of Jake's as something you could divide up like that. That she would care, that she would feel unsettled by Morton's advice to Sammy, surprised her. Honestly, her husband could be such a snob. He suffered every time he came in here and, during those few visits of his over the years, Annie suffered too.

Once in a while, casual friends or Morton's business associates, after dinner or a movie, would suggest going to Jake's. Sometimes they knew her father owned the place, sometimes they didn't and simply picked it as *the* place to "liven up" or "get depressed" at, implying that Jake's was a joint and appropriate for slumming. There was nothing mean here, it was just a thing the halfway bored, the halfway drunk, might come up with toward the end of a Friday or Saturday night.

"No, it's too late for that," Morton would say. That was always a puzzler. Or, "We're too dressed up." A clean shirt could be dressing up too much for Jake's. "How about the Finlan or the Holiday Inn?" he'd suggest. The Holiday Inn, for God's sake. That alone said something about the differences between them. If where you came from in life determined where you took cocktails—and didn't it usually?—Morton would be found in hotel lounges, and Annie, on the bar stool closest to the door, in places like Jake's.

But Morton never came right out and said that Jake's was a dump or that he didn't want to go there. Never in front of friends anyway. Morton had certain rules that did not allow open disagreement.

So mindful of Morton's feelings, but in deference to her father's, Annie stopped in by herself over the years for an occasional beer at Jake's. She appreciated fully that these two men's antithetical positions represented something in herself. There was a diametral chord, a line down her center, marking the halves of her own duality, her own equally strong but contrary opinions when it came to Jake's—and hers, at least, were based on intimate association. She had a right to hate the place, or not. But what could Morton say about it except it was that thing about her background that troubled him most. It flaunted something he'd rather not look at—maybe less breeding—that placed her at a level of class below the one he assumed himself to be at. She was surprised, in fact, that he'd accompanied them tonight.

"Dad, aren't you coming?" Sammy had asked at dinner.

"Where?"

"To Grandpa's party." It was her father's fortieth year as proprietor of Jake's and, if not all successful years, they'd come close enough to suit him.

"You're going?" Morton asked, taken aback.

"Sure, Grandpa invited me."

Without much resistance then, Morton went off to find a pair of jeans—to dress down from his usual suit and vest.

As if a bargain had been struck between them, she and Morton stayed a safe distance from anyone he thought too strange, like the old-timers who were usually toothless, no longer making much sense, and penniless as ever. Any one of them could talk you to death.

Sammy, to her dismay as well as Morton's, was enjoying himself. She'd expected him to be bored, bored and polite and slightly sullen. She hoped Morton would someday forgive her the place yet she preferred that Sammy stay clear of it. Except for Christmas Eve, when they came for Tom and Jerrys and a buffet supper, or special occasions like her parents' wedding anniversary party last year, she kept him away.

Christmas Eve here, unlike tonight, was quiet. Holiday music and decoration swelled into the corners then and set limits on conduct and no one misbehaved. The difference was now plain to Sammy. He was evidently old enough to be openly dazzled by the spirited and unrestrained state of things: a standing-room crowd, good-natured but loud; people over in the corner singing along to the player piano; the sudden occurrence of laughter. But overriding all that was the sense of a more riotous past having already been accomplished. There was that feeling that much more interesting things had taken place here than anyone would own and, too, that the latter-day patrons had lost some capacity for true decadence. She watched Sammy consider the place, the ancient oak back bar, the top of the front bar, polished not by wax but a century's worth of elbows, the brass railing, the faded pictures of old Butte on the wall hung there by previous owners. The bar itself had been Jake Raymond's last effort to strike it rich. Raymond, a prospector, on becoming too old and crippled to work the placer mines around Silver Bow Creek, had moved to Butte and opened Jake's. In a few years, Butte was bustling with activity as silver, copper and zinc drew an aggregate of miners, speculators and—a regular told her once—not enough whores to go around.

Annie's father, Nicholas, like previous owners of Jake's, had not been one for changing things, not even the name; the place might have been a museum. Many of the storefronts and other businesses of the old neighborhood were gone, swallowed by the once continually expanding copper pit. What remained of the hill supported a maze of old homes, winding porches, faded gables and turrets with outdated trims. Each street had its own collection of ancient brick buildings, unkempt or boarded up, and empty lots where less favored buildings had been dismantled, burned down or, like the Miners' Union Hall on Dakota Street, blown up during labor disputes. And over all was a color only mining towns have, the soot-blackened rusty pall of oxidizing metal.

Over the years most people had abandoned uptown and moved on down to the flats where they lived and worked in structures that, from the hill, resembled small squat packages. Probably the only place on earth where people, to better themselves, moved down the hill instead of up.

Others remodeled. They hid tin ceilings with low, fiberboard ones, covered oak floors with linoleum or indoor-outdoor carpet, modernized storefronts with fake marble and plate glass, even changed the lighting to less appealing fluorescent.

But the old-timers, regulars for fifty years, still hung out here, played checkers or poker on rainy afternoons, came in to cool off on hot summer nights. Not only its own old regulars, but the ones who used to frequent places similar to Jake's, missing something now in the replaced or remodeled, came too. And since it was handy to a whole neighborhood, everyone who drank, no matter what their age over twenty-one, walked over for a drink now and then. Now the younger drinkers were catching on to Jake's. For whatever reason, they were having a good time here among the checker-playing, panhandling old men and women with their outrageous arguments and old stories.

Laborers, miners and railroaders had always stopped here, waitresses preferred it, as did students from the school of mines. There were even two men with long hair and headbands who arrived early Friday afternoons, kept to themselves and left late into the night.

"He could turn this bar into a showplace," Morton was saying into her ear now. "Polish all that wood and brass, raise his prices and get rid of all those . . . those people," he said. She didn't know if he was talking about what her father should do now or what Sammy could one day do. "He could put in some skylights, hang a few ferns, serve hors d'oeuvres, have a two-for-one hour and attract the young professionals. But look at it, would you look at it."

Annie saw what he meant. There were peanut shells all over a floor that very likely had not been sanded or varnished a second time ever. The old captain's chairs were dried out and cracking, missing rungs and corners from the seats. The tabletops were scarred by cigarette burns, by thousands of spills and the sweaty bottoms of glasses and beer bottles. The wallpaper above the oak panels was faded down to its dried paste and, had any one of the many pictures been removed, a dusty outline would have marked its place. The chandeliers were magnificent but darkened with grime and smoke and the old tin ceiling too stained to see. Why hadn't her father ever fixed up the place? Her mother, so fussy with everything else, never pushed for the simplest of improvements and, like Annie, always kept a noticeable distance, if only a psychological one. The distorted attitude prevailed that this was a place of questionable worth but, nevertheless, ought to be let alone. Such was the atmosphere of Jake's.

Even when she was quite young, Annie had felt ambivalent when it came to Jake's. She used to like to lie in the corner booth or on the floor under the table where she could nap or daydream without interruption. She was always an odd child, but how could she be otherwise? Her propensity for daydreaming, coincident with her residence at Jake's, made normalcy nearly impossible. She liked to position herself well out of sight and then, free to imagine things, she might see feet parading or dancing nearby. She would watch those feet: Jake Raymond's and those of miners, long dead, wearing pants cinched at the bottom by leather tied close around dirty work boots. In particular, Annie liked the feet of the girl from the picture above the piano. It was said that this picture had once hung in the parlor of the girl's family. But on her return from some unapproved outing, the girl found (as tradition in the home dictated) that her father had put out her things, and ordered her picture turned to the wall. Nobody was to mention her name again. Then one day the picture made its way to Jake's (that part unexplained) and Annie the child knew, because she saw her there, that the girl had too. The harlot. Annie had overheard the title *harlot* and liked it, thought that she might be one too someday. Looking further than the girl's shoes, Annie saw that, just as in the picture, her dress was white and so were the flowers in her hair. Annie was certain that everyone else could see the harlot too and liked her, for her beauty and the graceful way she moved, as much as Annie did. The harlot took on glorious proportions from Annie's location hidden beneath the table, up until the time Annie— from something more overheard, no doubt—understood that harlot meant *bad* and was a curse. So the harlot went. But Jake's remained the same, its condition escaping Annie's notice until she viewed it through older, more critical eyes. Then, despite her own objections to Jake's, she was at once defensive and protective.

"You want to try to find a seat?" she asked Morton.

"There aren't any," he said and leaned against the jukebox.

There was a large cake on the pool table, on top of a plywood cover that protected the table's felt. Naturally. Wasn't that felt the newest, most cherished and best-cared-for item in the place? Someone had brought in a large coffee urn and it steamed there too, not a foot from the cake, though no one but Morton had helped himself to coffee all night. A beer or a whiskey ditch was now and historically the preferred beverage of the average patron of Jake's.

"Did the first miners used to come here, Grandma?" Annie heard Sammy ask her mother.

"They certainly did," she said. "The owners of the mines themselves, especially come time to buy votes."

"Votes?"

"That's right. They bought whole barrels of whiskey and handed out drinks to swing elections."

"This is how our son learns history," Morton complained to Annie.

"Relax, honey," she said. "As soon as they cut the cake we'll go."

"If someone doesn't fall on it first," he mumbled. "Oh, no," he said. "Here comes Bubba."

An old man, shortened by an arthritic curve to his back and shoulders, was squeezing his way though the crowd toward them.

"Bubba," she said and took his hand and kissed a whiskery cheek.

Arnold Bubnash had been a customer of Jake's and a friend of her father's, as long as Annie could remember. He smelled, as always, of leather and tobacco and whiskey. A shoemaker by trade, he'd once made the finest boots in Montana. But when he retired, he sold his little place to a young couple who now did no more than repair factory-made shoes. Bubba's wife, Fern, had died several years earlier. She had been a pleasant, round-faced woman whose father was one of the men imported from Wales to smelt copper when there turned out to be more of that than silver. She used to sit next to Bubba at the bar, happily, and without too much to say, slowly sipping short bottles of Miller. Now and then she'd brought in fresh baked rolls or cookies and passed them down the bar. It had never occurred to Annie to *not* like Bubba and Fern. But Morton never understood attachments like that. "That's why you liked them?" he would ask. "Because they gave you cookies when you were a kid?"

"Well, not just that but . . . ," she'd begin but by then something else would have caught his attention—the news, the traffic, a phone call.

"Bubba," she said now. "You remember Sammy." Behind him, Morton was scowling at no one in particular and Annie hoped Bubba wouldn't notice.

"How come you hardly ever bring this kid to Jake's?" Bubba asked. "You ashamed of us? Or him?" he said and winked at Sammy. "Practically raised your mother here, boy. Did you know that? Did she tell you?" he said, tobacco juice slipping off his bottom lip. "Tell him," he said to Annie.

"You certainly helped," she laughed, noticing Morton's scowl now bearing down on her.

"She told me," Sammy said graciously. Actually Bubba told him, without exception, every Christmas Eve or any other time he saw him.

"Morton," Bubba said and extended his hand.

"How are you?" Morton said, probably hoping Bubba wouldn't tell him. Bubba could be long-winded and Morton, clearly, had had enough of this whole evening.

"Folks, folks," her mother said. She was standing on a step-stool, waving, and the crowd slowly quieted. "Nicholas, as you know, bought this place forty years ago and we're here tonight to celebrate that. Yes," she said, laughing at something someone in the crowd had said, "Jake's will be open this St. Pat's."

March seventeenth was the biggest bar day of the year in Butte and Jake's filled up minutes after the morning parade was over and didn't empty out until late the morning of the eighteenth—unless something unusual happened as it had last year. A busload of college kids from Missoula on spring break had come to Butte to party and somehow a brawl broke out in front of Jake's and her father closed up. Annie sort of enjoyed the boisterous air of Jake's on St. Patrick's Day and she always came by. Morton had accompanied her—once.

"Say a few words, Nick," Annie's mother said now, getting down from the stool.

Everyone hooted and hollered and applauded. Well almost everyone, not Morton. Her father stood on the stool then and motioned for silence. As was his custom behind the bar, he was wearing a white shirt that strained to cover his broad girth, a western tie and a wide belt with a silver buckle. He nodded his nearly bald head at the crowd.

"I bought this place when I was a kid," he said. "I borrowed every cent I could to do it. I've put my life into this place and it's taken good care of me." The crowd hooted and clapped some more.

"Hey," he said. "This place, because of customers like you, has supported my family and convinced my daughter that she doesn't ever want to work in a crummy dive like this." Everyone laughed and looked her way—her father had pointed directly to where she stood. It was too much for Morton and he flushed darkly and grimaced. Sammy, beside him, well into the spirit of the crowd, grinned appreciatively at his grandfather.

"I have lots to be thankful for," her father continued. "Jake's has kept me off the streets, paid for our home, and best of all, for a trip to Las Vegas." Everyone laughed. Now he raised his hands to quiet his audience. "I have only one more thing to say," he added seriously, pausing. "I love every goddamn one of you!"

At this everyone whistled and stomped their feet; it could have been the rodeo grounds.

"Drinks on the house," her father shouted and sat down.

"Let's get out of here," Morton said, grabbing her arm and signaling to Sammy.

"All right, all right," she said trying to catch her father's eye to wave good-bye. "Good to see you," she told Bubba as Morton pushed her out the door to the street.

"My God," Morton said and sighed.

Jake's brought out the worst in him. Morton could feel himself becoming ill-tempered, critical, sneering—misbehaving as Annie never would. She could be put off by someone, annoyed even, but she would still not get really pissed off. She did not make investments of outrage in the behavior of others.

Take a chance, Annie, he sometimes wanted to shout. Be rude, lose your temper, take a swing. Had she done so, he might not have had to so often, he felt. He couldn't seem to avoid it, especially around Jake's. The thought of Annie growing up back of that bar with Nicholas and Elsa always made him a little sick. He couldn't imagine Nicholas ever sharing Elsa's attention with anyone and he blamed that for this need Annie had to suddenly attend to herself, to go inward, to keep mental inventories of what went on there. She probed that invisible space routinely for causes, effects.

"Most things just happen," he told her time after time. "No relationship to anything else required."

And he was disturbed by the poverty he imagined she had undergone. The apartment back of that bar was a lean-to, an addition to the bar itself, one without even a foundation. It had probably once been a stable with a dirt floor, perhaps later enclosed, insulated, old tar paper and linoleum put down, a little plaster, a few windows put in. Nevertheless, it was still small and drafty, a glorified hovel that now stored broken bar stools, pinball machines, jukeboxes and other junk. He'd helped Annie get some old piece of furniture out of there once, though why she wanted it when he owned a furniture store was anybody's guess.

He had looked around in amazement. Suddenly, Annie, who had been chatting happily was quiet. Morton knew that she had become self-conscious, that she was thinking of the pictures they had recently put into the scrap book on the coffee table, pictures of the house he had grown up in, the grounds he had roamed, the gardens he had taken for granted.

There was one of Morton and his parents at the dining table. "Your brother's not in this picture," Annie had said.

"He probably took that one," he said.

His brother Paul used to have a Brownie camera that everyone in the house helped himself to from time to time without asking permission. Of course, this infuriated Paul and he was certain to get even some way. Getting even was a sporting event in that house.

"Who's that?" Annie had asked, pointing to a similar picture in which a girl stood behind his father holding a tray.

"That was the maid."

"But she looks so young," Annie said.

"I guess she was." All the maids were young, he recalled now. He had been about ten in the picture, his brother Paul about eight, the maid maybe sixteen, seventeen.

"What was her name?"

"I don't remember," he said. "We went through so many of them."

"Good Lord," Annie had said, in awe. "You all look so happy," she added, perhaps wistfully.

Yes, they did look happy. It was interesting what an impression a photograph could make. Everything furnished, everyone poised. No surprises. But where were the picture-takers the rest of the time? Who documented those moments when no one was prepared for the camera? And which times were more real or easier to recall? Had there not been photos of that scene in the dining room, Morton would not have remembered it. It would just never have happened for him.

Annie had gone slowly through the rest of the photos. In one, obviously taken at one of those restaurants they always went to,

Morton was with Paul and his mother. Then there was one of him and Paul taken in the yard, probably after their father had died. Another showed the two boys and one of the maids. Morton might have been fourteen at the time, Paul twelve, the maid seventeen.

Morton remembered that there had been other photos of that maid that he had taken. But these were not in Annie's pile; he'd torn them up. He had shot them on the grounds against a background of green. In the first one she was naked from the waist up; in the next, unbuttoning a pink skirt and smiling. There were more of her—stepping out of the skirt, tugging at her panties and so on. A photo essay to suggest all the disclosure and exposure that took place over that long summer with Gwen. That was her name, Gwen.

Morton watched as Annie placed each picture in the album. In these photos, unbeknownst to her, was the story of his childhood:

Child with mother and father looking happy—mother no doubt drunk and in good mood, father dying and probably glad about it.

Two children in restaurant with mother—father is dead now and family no longer eats in the dining room.

Two children in yard alone because mother off on some trip.

Two children with maid because she is their only friend.

Maid in bushes posing for oldest child—in absence of any other source, someone has to teach children about sex.

And Gwen taught it all, at least to Morton. She began one day by telling him he was dirty and to go take a bath. Then she had peeked in the bathroom door, teasing him.

"I'm going to come in and wash your you-know-what," she'd laughed and then slammed the door. He was dumbfounded.

Now that she had his attention she'd gone on with one astonishing deed after another. She showed him pictures of herself nude, taken by an old boyfriend, she said. She exposed her breasts, sneaked up to his room, got into his bed. And while it was an okay experience for him, he had not wanted it for Paul. That he was sure of, though to this day he was uncertain why that was. Perhaps it had been no more than wanting her all to himself. Or maybe he didn't think Paul was old enough. But maybe you didn't get old enough for Gwen. There was something about her that was scary. She seemed to mock him, to taunt him, to hate him. Morton never felt more awkward or unsure than he had those few hot months with Gwen. Or so completely passive. Once he'd gotten off, he had no further regard for her, as uncaring as if he had just deposited hamburger wrappers or mail into some receptacle. No reciprocity whatsoever.

He didn't recall how he managed it or why but he finally got Gwen fired. She had looked at him in surprise at the time, then fury.

"You little shit," she'd said. "You goddamn stupid little shit. You couldn't even do *it* as good as your old man. And he was dying!"

Morton had struck her then and later threw some of her belongings into the pond. He was horrified at the suggestion that his father had ever been intimate with Gwen.

Chapter Two

Annie was the first one to admit that she lived in a dream world. Things unlikely or impossible appealed to her most. She fantasized about silly things like finding a shaman in the hills of Mexico close to a mercado and a good margarita. And about practical things too. She imagined, for example, redoing every room in the house beginning with the upstairs bath.

Unlike the bathroom upstairs that smelled like the sweats Morton always threw on the floor after running or the one downstairs where Sammy hung wet T-shirts to dry, shirts that said things like MONTANA, BEST OF THE BIG-TIME SPLENDORS, this one would smell like flowers and fresh herbs. She had imagined it so often, she could feel herself stepping across its deep pile rugs, her hand on the oiled wainscoting. In one corner would be a large copper bathtub, in another an old parlor woodstove. She pictured small-print wallpaper, bright framed watercolors and large bunches of gypsy grass and eucalyptus. When the bathroom got all steamy, she would open the windows to spring lilacs or summer roses and to pine all year around. This was a place the family might be invited for meetings, where she could tell them all the things that were on her mind.

Here they would sit—she could see that too—on big pillows in front of the tub where perhaps she'd yell at Sammy about his report card or say to Morton, Honey, I don't like sex.

Annie knew no one had the best of all worlds.

"Hey, what are you doing?" Morton asked. He'd shut off all the lights downstairs, locked the door and flossed. Still she sat on the bed where she'd been for the past hour while Morton watched the late evening news in the den.

"I was just thinking."

"About?"

"Painting the bathroom."

She heard him go into the den and she returned to her thoughts. The room would be hers, a place where she could even sleep on occasion undisturbed, on a pillow or fold-up mat. She might pile books beside her and, if she woke up unable to sleep, she would read. Or take a bath. Intrusion, of course, would be forbidden.

"Annie," she heard Morton call. "This jump rope has been on the bookcase at least a year now. Still unopened." It was a child's rope she'd bought at the dime store, red and yellow braiding and bright blue handles in a clear cellophane package. She was surprised he noticed it anymore. It had been there so long it fit, like a vase of flowers or another book.

"But don't explain," he said, reentering the bedroom. "One day you thought you should start exercising but you haven't been in the mood since."

Sarcasm. Well, he could think what he liked. The truth was she'd been doing aerobics for weeks now, in training for something that might be required of her when anything that might happen did.

"That's right," she said feeling suddenly irritable. "But if I get in the mood the goddamn thing'll be there."

"You don't have to get snotty about it."

Morton took off his robe, set the alarm and settled himself next to her against the pillows. He picked up a magazine, leafed through it, stopped on a couple of pages—an ad for a Cadillac, an article on the Middle East.

"Ready to turn off the light?" he asked.

Here it comes, she thought. She turned on her side waiting,

wondering why she dreaded it. Annie couldn't think of anything she had against sex in general, certainly she didn't think it was evil or anything like that. Most of the time she just couldn't get her mind on it. As far as she could tell, sex was a mindful act, a deliberate directing of attention, not a physical thing at all. At least that's how it worked for her. With Morton, she supposed, it was different.

She liked to think there were other women out there somewhere feeling the same, feigning sleep, feeling guilty too, but nevertheless anxious to get to sleep or back to their own thoughts. Like her, these women would hate interruption. They might consider it a shame that men seemed to like sex so much more than they did, or at least more often. Of course, she couldn't say, they couldn't say, that this was always the case. It was her guess that couples simply matched up wrong. Take Georgia. Georgia was always complaining that her husband was impotent. Not clearly, overtly, but in snide jokes and disagreeable comments. And at the last ball game, Karen said frankly that Allen had no energy when it came to sex. Not Morton, his energy was more than ample.

When Annie considered all the articles about sex, it looked like most women loved it. She always read the covers of women's magazines in checkout lines. There were ones about sexually deprived women, bungling male lovers, straying male lovers, articles on how to keep him, how to get him back if he got away, and how to get him to seduce you. Could that be a problem? And yesterday she saw one on how to make sex new and spicy after twenty years and all those kids.

Just once she'd like to see an article called, "How to Tell Him You Hate It and Why." Well, maybe she didn't exactly hate it. Still, could she be the only woman who didn't especially like it? Or was she guessing correctly that women were out there everywhere bracing themselves with fat and anger and cigarettes, messages that said to men, Keep your distance, I'm tired.

She heard Morton's breathing change and knew it was safe to turn on her back to watch the moon coming up through the weeping willows, its light fragmenting on the print she'd bought for a dollar and paid eighty-five dollars to frame. Annie considered this room the nicest in the house and had worked hard fixing it up.

She had scraped a hundred years of linoleum and tar paper off the floor and the same amount of paint off the woodwork. She liked how early sun striking the trees sent a patterned dispersal of light into the room and how moonlight folded into soft shadows along the east wall. Night or day, summer and winter, Annie enjoyed looking out over the yard onto a tangled maze of lilacs and roses or drifted snow, and beyond that, to the mountains and the cloud forms that caught in their peaks. In many respects her life, their life, was quite satisfying. Would it ever be the same if she told him? How could it be? Morton couldn't live without sex.

Annie wished she knew how priests did it. There just didn't seem to be much in the way of abstinence in the world anymore, not in a long time, maybe never. Look at Tolstoy, for instance. He, more than anyone she could think of, advocated sublimation. Yet his wife complained bitterly about his unwanted advances. Was it that man's brain maintained tight control up until some surprising moment when his penis took over, so that in Tolstoy's case he would forget the treatise on refining sexual energy he might have just written that morning?

"What's wrong?" Morton asked when he heard her sigh. He wasn't asleep after all and he pulled her close.

"I'm depressed," she said. She thought briefly about telling him then. But she knew better; he'd stay awake, troubled, and tramp around the house all night. Tomorrow, at lunch, maybe at some restaurant where the store couldn't call, where Sammy couldn't walk into the middle of it—a neutral ground where Morton would not slam things or do calisthenics while she talked.

Annie asked for a table near the back where their conversation wasn't likely to be overheard. She wished she could think of a single precedent for this among her family or friends. But who would admit to quitting sex? No, there was really nothing to prepare either of them for this lunch.

Someday, she hoped, before she died, in some last survey of things, she would look back on this day, see it like an extravagant alteration to an old garment, startling at first, but in the long run, closer to what suited her. Because once you admitted to yourself how you felt about something and saw no hope of changing it, there was no way to go on with it despite the consequences. Certainly there would be consequences. Most people would think she was a fool, the least of the names she might inspire. But did she give a damn? Yes, she did. She had never gotten over wanting and needing some basic validation, some extensive approval. Yet, here she was risking everything, proving nothing. That was it exactly but she couldn't help it. It was driving her crazy. In some slow process of magnification, it'd become all she could think about, the pretense, the loathing she felt.

The only person Annie knew who might support her position was her neighbor, Barbara, who after a trip abroad said, "The reason American men are such bad lovers is because they think women are responsible for their own orgasms."

"Aren't they?" Annie had said in surprise. Wasn't this among the most recent of the enlightened ideas of the time?

"Hell no!" she'd yelled. "You see where feminism has gotten us? We're not only supposed to do everything we used to do—raise the kids, keep the house, take care of men—now we're supposed to bring home a pay check and take care of our own orgasms. Bullshit!" she'd said and walked out the door of the neighbor's house where they were having coffee. Not long after, Barbara left her husband and ran off with a woman she'd gotten to know in a bowling league.

Annie sighed. This entire predicament reminded her of Patty O'Brien. When she was a child, Patty O'Brien with the auburn sausage curls, whom the teacher liked because she did neat, accurate fractions at the chalkboard and whom the kids liked for no better reason than the curls and her father's ice-cream truck, picked on her. Patty did mean things to her. Once, she cut a snip into Annie's sleeve during art hour; she regularly marked up her *English in Action* and always either stole Annie's lunch or knocked it to the floor and stepped on her sandwich. The prudent course would have been to bear Patty's annoying interest in her silently, the girl might have grown out of it. But no, Annie complained. That action changed her life, at least life as she knew it then. Her mother went to the teacher who could not believe all that about anyone so mathematically inclined and punished Annie by pairing her with Patty at the board in what were clearly demonstrations—how and how not. Of course, the kids believed Annie but didn't care and sniggered and taunted her and generally made her an outcast. Come to think about it, she never got a free Fudgsicle again either. It was clear early on that her character was not judicious by nature.

Annie wished Morton would arrive. She tried to imagine his reaction. He might insist that she come to her senses and see a psychiatrist. That would be just like him, to suspect her of insanity because she didn't like sex. But wasn't it possible that there were some men who didn't like it? That wouldn't matter to Morton. He liked it and believed all normal people did.

He was sure to call her frigid. Was she? No, she didn't think frigid was the right word. After all, she could respond as readily as the next person if her attention was aroused, and not without satisfaction either. But otherwise, she'd just as soon fake it. Didn't he ever notice? Sometimes the whole event stretched out before her like a penance, a litany of Hail Marys, flat, monotonous, hardly a devotion. It gave her a headache thinking about it. No wonder there were all those jokes.

Annie couldn't remember how long she'd felt this way. It had been cumulative, a growing series of impressions that finally added up to something. She had questioned all that Morton would now: her femininity, her sanity, her health. Was she merely punishing herself for her sexually active youth? She had been unbiased toward sex then, not promiscuous. Unbiased because she considered sex neither good nor bad, just something nice to do if you liked a person and were in the mood, a choice marriage rarely allowed. Clearly she had reversed the order of things. When she found sex the most engaging, she was thought too young and it too indecent a thing to indulge in if you were nice. Then in the ensuing years as her interest lagged behind the mores of the times, sex became simultaneously an open topic, accepted, expected, even researched. For Annie it became a concession she made much like being pregnant, unavoidable under certain conditions—for example, when you wanted your own child. Indeed, that's when she especially remembered being aware of her feelings about it, when she was pregnant with Sammy. She recalled the relief when the doctor said, "No marital relations"—that's how he put it—so long before delivery and so long after.

Annie was sure that Morton would ask for a divorce. Oh, maybe not today. But eventually it would come to that. And though there were no doubt other issues having nothing to do with sex that would enter in, because sex was the issue now on her mind—and soon to be on Morton's—*it* would become the reason to divorce. He might even accuse her of taking a lover or being lesbian. Annie's mother would be shocked, puzzled too, if she ever found out. Annie, she could hear her mother saying, life is a series of tradeoffs. Do you think Morton likes going to the boring store every day? Do you think he likes selling furniture? (Her mother could not imagine that someone really picked an occupation of that sort.) You think he likes everything he has to do to get ahead? But Annie knew all about tradeoffs, she'd done it for years and might have kept on except for an affair Morton had had several years earlier. Morton's affair. That, more than anything else, had caused her to begin to see things in a new way. It made her rethink marriage and to feel unwilling to trade sex for a home and security or to pretend a passion she didn't feel. She no longer felt she had to. Really the affair didn't bother her as much as it amazed her— and pointed up the differences between them. To think he managed two physical relationships when she had to work so hard at one. Damn.

Suddenly Annie was tired. She hoped she had the energy for all this. If only he'd get here. She tried to think about something else, how the ferns and pictures should be hung, the colors she would have chosen, how in general she'd change the architecture and decor of the restaurant. The flowers on the table were real and she rearranged them, snapping off a few stems with fingernail clippers she kept in her purse. With those shorter, she was satisfied. A better composition all around. She caught the waiter looking at her. Did he wonder what she might adjust next?

Annie remembered this restaurant, though it was not a place they came to often. One time during dinner here Morton said how nice it would be if sometimes she did the seducing. She had laughed at that, though he failed to see anything humorous about it. When would he allow her an opportunity like that? In fact, once she had even decided to respond to him readily every time he approached her, thinking wrongly that he'd soon become satiated. So much for that experiment. Yet, how nice it would be to go without sex long enough to miss it. To actually feel longing and lust and have to approach him.

At last she saw Morton across the room. He was still quite attractive and, as usual, impeccably dressed except for his tie. Morton loved tacky, bright ties and wore them like flags. Today's suggested how a blood and mustard stain might look on the breast of a penguin. She watched him search about for her and she waved.

She waited patiently while he scanned the menu and then ordered. She was quiet while he talked of his morning, what had annoyed him, of other matters crucial to the business world he lived in. "On a bad day Fuller can't close a deal to save his life," he said. "So he comes over and sits in my office to complain. I finally told him, 'You need a psychiatrist so I can get some work done.'" The waiter rolled a cart up to the table with their food.

"It's a beautiful day," Morton remarked. "Too bad you think exercise is masochistic, we could jog later." She sighed. He was in such good spirits.

"So what's on your mind?" he asked, now remembering that she had something she wanted to talk about.

The direct question confused her. His complete attention was so unexpected that for a minute she didn't know how to begin. So she told him the story she'd read once about a Chinese woman whose approaching fortieth birthday meant her husband would take on a concubine to replace her in the bedroom. (How the woman waited until she was forty was not in the story.)

"It was a custom, you see, and the woman looked forward to it." She was sure he didn't see. She wanted him to understand how the Chinese woman's body was now her own and the rest of her life free to enjoy as she wished. But his blank stare and impatient tapping on his wineglass unnerved her and she decided to be more direct. "I don't feel like having sex anymore, honey," she said.

Morton's stare became surprise. He had a startled look. He might have been a fisherman who'd caught a fish hook in his ear on an otherwise normal outing. Then he laughed. "If you're not going to eat that salad, mind if I do?" he said.

"Did you hear me? I said I don't want to have sex anymore."

"You must be kidding," he said, reaching for the dressing.

This was a statement he always made, a habit he had, either to see if he'd heard correctly or to allow more time to construct a reply.

"No," she said quietly, a little surprised herself. She hadn't quite believed she would ever get the words out.

"If this is a joke, Annie, I don't think it's funny."

"It's not a joke."

"Then if it's a way to get attention, you've picked a bad day because I've got an important client . . ."

"I'm serious," she said.

Morton leaned back. "Let me get this straight. You invited me to lunch to tell me you don't want sex anymore."

"Yes," she said, biting her lip, "I'm giving it up."

Morton shook his head and emptied the bottle of wine into his glass. "No one just gives it up—it's not like going on a diet, damn it." Irritation was plain in his voice. "If there's a problem, go to a doctor."

"I did. He gave me vitamins and said to eat lots of protein."

"And?"

"I feel great but it doesn't help."

The restaurant was quiet now and Morton looked at her. His eyes seemed to be searching hers for something.

"I don't know what to say. What do you want me to say, Annie?"

"I know it's shocking but . . ."

"Are you telling me I don't turn you on, that you want me to go to one of those counselors to learn technique or something?"

"No, Morton, you have plenty of technique." In fact, she often thought sex wouldn't be so bad if he'd just get right to it.

"It's me," she said. "I just can't seem to get into it anymore."

He stared out the window for several minutes before speaking. She had never seen him so still. Not a finger tapped the table nor did he blink.

"Maybe I've known all along," he said with resignation, as if to himself. "At least I know you don't like it as much . . ."

"As much as what's-her-name?" What's-her-name could like it all she wanted, it wouldn't impress her.

"No, Annie," he said sadly. "As much as you used to. Remember in Whitefish? Remember that time we went skiing?" Annie remembered.

"You liked it then. Remember?"

"Maybe I got it all out of my system."

"For God's sake, Annie, you don't need to be sarcastic."

"Well, it's true. I've hardly enjoyed it in years. And I don't even feel guilty about it. I feel like my great-aunt Bertha must have. See . . ."

"What does your great-aunt Bertha have to do with this?" Morton was beginning to gulp his wine.

"She told me once she always made Uncle Harry leave three dollars on the pillow. You see she always used her lipstick down to where it cut her lip. But then she said she got . . ."

"Jesus, you talk like sex is a job or something."

Annie liked that idea. She could put in an ad for a girl to come in to go to bed with Morton every so often. She'd interview the applicants, curious why they'd take a job like this. Would they hate it, or find it pleasurable? Not that she'd ask. No, she'd keep the interviews brief, dignified, proper so as not to arouse any doubts in the applicants' minds or the women might get the wrong idea, that Morton was kinky or sadistic or something like that.

"Are you listening, Annie? I said you always say no when you want, don't you?"

Annie smiled at that and he didn't press for an answer.

"Is this all because I was unfaithful? Is that what's bothering you? And now you're finally going to get even." Morton sighed.

"No," she said. "I felt the same way before all that." In fact she had felt sorry for Morton when she found out about the young woman, an employee from his store. Obviously he had wanted Annie to find out because he left notes from the girl in his shirt pockets that Annie sometimes just laundered instead of reading. He'd appeared openly in public with her so that the neighbors knew about her and he even took her to one of Sammy's ball games! Annie had seen the whole thing as a bid for her, Annie's, attention.

"Maybe it just gave me the push I needed to face things," she told him now. "I don't know."

Too bad they hadn't compromised. And why not, if sex was just sex—and in this case, something he liked and she didn't? He could have kept his girlfriend and they could have worked out a friendship of some sort, had her over for dinner on Sundays or something of that nature. The young woman could have kept her job, bought shares in the store. Like the concubine, it was an idea that appealed to Annie.

"You know you're the only one I want," Morton said as if he knew what she was thinking. "All I can say is I'm sorry."

Annie felt terrible. He looked miserable. And she did love him, if not sexually, as a friend, a companion, the father to her son. Sometimes she wanted just to embrace him, to sit close or to sleep touching him without it inevitably turning into something else. He looked so sad that she stared at her plate to avoid his eyes.

Sex was overrated, she thought. How ironic that a girl used to have to be a virgin. "Save yourself," her mother used to say, like virginity was a prize awarded to grooms, no matter how adept at sex they were themselves.

"Haven't you ever wanted to take a lover?" Morton asked this so gently she almost wanted to tell him about Kenneth, just to make him feel better. Something told her it wouldn't.

Kenneth was the adult-ed teacher she had hustled, intending to find out whether it was sex in general or just sex with Morton she was opposed to. She tried to meet Kenneth on Tuesday, his day off, several times and then again one Friday morning. But something else was always more pressing. One time she'd had to cancel at the last minute when Sammy chipped a tooth at hockey practice. Another time unexpected guests turned up and she had to meet a flight. Things like that. Then his calls stopped, and just as well, she hated that he smoked. His class, introduction to interior decorating, wasn't that good either.

"I've considered it," she said truthfully. "But it's not something an affair would fix. And really, honey, this has nothing to do with you; it's my problem." Even so she understood as soon as the words were out that now it was his too.

Morton stared at her. It was as though he'd never really seen her and was trying to now. Perhaps at some early point in their relationship, they had unconsciously agreed on an idea of themselves and each other—those people they were supposed to be—a mutual deceit that then fashioned their lives. Once she had begun to see who she wasn't, she began to wonder and to fear who she was, who she might turn out to be later. She felt a fear of everything, to be alone, to be a single mother, to try to support herself. Still she'd had to tell him how she felt.

"Don't you see?" she said. "For a long time women weren't free to like sex. Now they are. It's suppose to make all the difference, but maybe it doesn't."

Morton didn't say a word. He stared out the window and Annie wondered if he had even heard. She saw what he was looking at, a couple sitting on a bench across the street, sharing a sandwich the girl had pulled from a backpack. The two leaned toward each other and appeared to be laughing.

"There's one thing I have to ask, Annie," he said, looking at her now. "Are you still in love with my brother?"

"No," she said.

She and Morton resumed their vigil at the window. The couple finished eating and hand in hand walked out of view, leaving only the deserted bench to watch. At length Morton turned to her again.

"Do we have to quit all at once or can we taper off?"

Annie couldn't help laughing and neither could he. But owing to the unusual issue before them and to the reduced circumstances of their union, the laughter between them had changed.

When Morton left the restaurant, he was too distraught to go back to the store. Instead he drove up the hill toward Boulder, wanting another drink. Clouds were gathering now above nearby peaks and he expected that soon there would be a storm. The valley below and behind him was half sunny, half in shadow, and as he neared the top of the hill he could see the copper pit through his rearview mirror as a large black hole. He leaned over and rolled down the passenger window.

Morton didn't know why he'd ever moved to Butte to open a store. At the time he had been so eager to please Annie that he'd rushed into it. He should have gone back to Chicago where his family was connected, where it would have been easier to finance a small business. There would have been more of a population to draw from, the people there were more cultured, more civilized, more into fine things. As it was, he'd had to change his operation here, scale it down to furniture he didn't really care for, low-end stuff that he sold in volume. Not for quality but for its appeal to people who did not wish to invest in things that would last, who went for a certain style—bold patterns, splashy colors and the lowest down payment. But he could give a goddamn.

Back East he could tell people his name, Tomlin, and they would say, Oh, the furniture makers. His forefathers, however, were not furniture makers. They were sellers of high-quality furniture, like the Tomlin line. But no one would connect his name to that brand of furniture around here. It was far too fine a product for these parts. The only good thing about this area, in his opinion, was that his mother didn't live in it.

Morton slowed down now and barely made the left turn into the first roadhouse on the way to Boulder. His tires spun noisily in the gravel and he stopped short of a large pickup with a gun rack. The dog inside the cab growled at him as he got out of the car. "Shut up you bitch," he said and slammed his door.

When he went in, everyone in the place turned to him silently and then back to their drinks. They seemed in no mood for a snarly stranger dressed in a suit. He took a seat at a table and ordered a double Scotch.

He could feel his own rage over everything he now thought of that had ever pissed him off and he wished someone, anyone, would dare to hassle him. But he knew no one would. Odd how people sensed those times when it was to their advantage to leave you the hell alone. And by the same token, they could tell when you were vulnerable and took those opportunities to kick your face in. He glared at the backs of the men he saw sitting there at the bar. They were the backs of the working class, the laborers, the miners, the farmers who tried year after year to make a living off a dry-land crop or a windswept range. You could bet their lives were straightforward, uneventful and uncomplicated. They probably knew women who didn't give them trouble, women who didn't reason everything to death and, likely, women who liked to fuck.

Two men came in and sat at a table near the wall. Morton watched them, despising their dirty jean jackets and muddy boots. One of them reminded him of his brother Paul for some reason, probably because of the way he threw his leg over the back of the chair to sit down as though getting on a horse. He knew the type, cocky, arrogant, no doubt lazy.

Both men looked at him and Morton turned, caught the bartender's eye and ordered another drink. When the bartender brought it over, Morton noticed that the two men in the jean jackets were staring at him and, from the way they nodded at each other, discussing him too. He paid the bartender and glared in their direction. But then the one who reminded him of Paul got up and came toward him. Without being invited, the man pulled out the chair across the table from him, swung his leg over it, and sat down.

"Ain't you the fellow who's got that furniture store in Butte?" he said.

It was not what Morton had expected at all and he was caught off guard.

"Yes," he said. "What of it?"

"Well, my old lady bought some things and one of them—a rug—ain't wearing too good."

Now Morton was really annoyed. "Well for chrissake, man, bring it back. I stand behind what I sell."

"That's all there is to it?" the man asked, apparently in doubt.

"That's it."

"Fine," he said and stuck out his hand. "Skipper Wilmot," he said.

Though he didn't want to, Morton shook his hand. "Morton Tomlin," he said.

"Right," the man said. "You're probably related to the furniture makers."

That was too much. Now Morton felt deflated and suddenly sad. His anger was gone and he was very tired, depressed even.

The man got up as suddenly as he'd sat down and tipped a shabby cowboy hat. "I'll be in tomorrow," he said and returned to his own table. Now that his business with Morton had been concluded, he and his companion did not glance again in Morton's direction.

Morton finished his drink and left a tip for the bartender. By now the clouds he'd seen earlier had accumulated to the east into large and ominous thunderheads. He threw his suit jacket into the backseat and headed back toward town. The sun was setting into more clouds above a range of hills west of town and what was left of the light shone eerily across the valley floor.

Just as it began to pour, Morton felt his left rear tire bouncing in sudden smacks across the roadway. He pulled onto the shoulder, reached into the glove compartment and pulled the trunk latch.

The trunk had some garden tools in it that Annie must have bought over the weekend when she'd used the car. They were still enclosed in their various wrappings and he sorted through them looking for his tire iron and jack. Finally he threw the goddamn garden tools out onto the road.

He was completely soaked by now and his pants slapped his legs as he searched the field beside the highway for a rock to put under his front tire. While he was at it, he peed onto the field, trying to recall if he'd ever peed into a downpour before. Indeed he had, as a kid with some nephew of his mother's gardener who hung around the grounds on weekends. Paco. Sometimes he and Paco played marbles together in the flowerbeds or climbed trees or searched the pond for frogs.

Morton had gotten the rear end jacked up and was trying to get the hubcap off. He saw a truck approaching and knew he was about to get splashed good by the large puddle that covered the road. But the vehicle did not pass him, it pulled over and stopped behind his car. It was a tow truck, he thought, but its headlights were blinding him and he couldn't be sure. He went back to work, ignoring the vehicle. Its driver finally turned off the lights.

Morton looked up as the driver got out and came close. It was the man who was going to bring back a rug and he held something in his hand, though now it was too dark to tell what it was. Suddenly lightning cracked through the clouds and shot down to the ground and the puddle on the road lit up. By the sound of the thunder that followed, Morton knew it was close. He would not have been surprised had it struck him.

"Howdy," the man said and handed him a package. It was a bottle of whiskey and Morton stood up and took a drink and handed it back.

The man took his turn and passed the bottle back to Morton. Then he grabbed the tire iron, made a quick movement in the dark, and the hubcap popped off onto the ground. Now, just as quickly the man had the flat tire off and the spare on. Morton watched him tighten the nuts. He stood up then and Morton handed him the whiskey. While the man took his turn drinking, Morton threw the flat tire into the trunk. The man released the jack and brought it over to put in the trunk too.

Both men looked upward now as jagged strands of lightning reached earthward like a large bony hand. For an instant, Annie's garden tools strewn across the ground shone brightly and caught Morton's eye, maybe the man's also, because he picked up one of them.

"Thanks," Morton said as the man handed it to him. "For everything," he added.

"I guess I'll go home to supper," the man said.

"I guess I'll head on down the road to that whorehouse I've been hearing about," Morton said, shocking himself. He could not imagine why he'd told that to some stranger.

The man laughed. "That would be Molly's place."

"Yes," Morton said, wiping the rain off his face with his sleeve.

"Here," he said, taking out a business card from his pocket. "You give her this and she'll treat you right." He offered Morton the bottle again but Morton declined. The man got into his truck now and Morton closed the trunk. He got into the front seat, not caring that his leather upholstery was getting wet. Morton put the card into his pocket and pulled out onto the roadway and followed not far behind the tow truck. SKIPPER'S TOWING, he read across the back of the truck.

Farther up the road, Morton turned off the road into a driveway. He could see a modest house with a yard light and a small inconspicuous sign that said MOLLY'S. He took out the business card and went in.

Chapter Three

About three months passed before Morton asked for a divorce. Really it was not as straightforward as that sounds. First he had come to Annie's bedroom—they had separate rooms now—and announced that he couldn't live this way.

"I need intimacy," he said. "I want to sleep with a woman," he said—not meaning he had one in mind necessarily, just a statement of his needs. Well, certainly. She wanted the same thing. She wanted warmth and closeness and another body next to hers in the middle of the night if that was what he meant. What she didn't want was an evening rite—late news, brush teeth, sex, sleep. She had let herself become as utilitarian in this ceremony as the toothbrush or television. Morton apparently was missing the point of her protest.

"Whatever you think, dear," she said. He'd turned and left without a word.

The funny thing was that after they had taken separate rooms, Morton had become more thoughtful of her. Why was that? He'd call her from the office daily to ask if it'd be all right if they joined so and so for dinner, or did she want to go to the lake this weekend or the next? Could he stop at the store for her? Did they need something? He talked more at dinner and several times wanted to take her for a walk after. Nevertheless, near the approach of the ten o'clock news, he became silent and stiff, a little edgy.

But after the night he came to her room, his recent thoughtfulness stopped. He did not call again except to say he would not be home for dinner, or that he was going to the lake alone, that is, without her. Or that he would stay home for the weekend alone, that is, without her, if *she* wanted to go to the lake. Whichever way. Her choice. Then finally one night he came home early, made her a drink and paced the kitchen, then the living room, made her another and drank it himself.

"Morton," she said. She often knew his mind as well as he did. "Do you want to discuss the woman?"

So to say he came right out and asked for a divorce is misleading. From that first conversation, through every one thereafter, they sort of advanced toward it the way sand skips into drifts in wind.

Sammy was never an issue. It was expected by both of them that he would live with her. Morton was not the type to suddenly domesticate, to feel comfortable stirring a pot or doing laundry. Imagine Morton sorting through Sammy's dirty socks or scrubbing their heels. He would have more adjustments to make than she would—even though she was moving, unless he simply moved the woman in here to pick up neatly where Annie left off: cooking, housekeeping, organizing—especially that, as Morton always thought of Annie as having a spacey, preoccupied sort of mind, undeveloped you might say, and in need of exercise maybe, to firm it up. Well, should she leave the woman notes? (The dishwasher soap is on the shelf above the basement steps where it keeps from getting damp and hard. Kick dryer on right front corner if it won't start. Forget the vacuum cleaner, it's useless. Tell Morton you need a new one.)

"You're moving out of the house?" Morton said, amazed. "But I can get an apartment or make other plans," he said. "You'll need the house."

No, they wouldn't, she explained. They were moving away. Annie wanted to relocate. She had spent enough of her life here and it was time to see what the rest of the world was like—not the entire thing, of course, just more of it. Because each year, if allowed to be simply typical, had a way of ordaining the years to follow and, before you knew it, of impounding your prospects entirely. Together, the years seduced you, made you stuck. If she were to ever get out, it was now in the freeing rubble of catastrophe.

"But out-of-state?" Morton asked as he packed up a few things—he was staying at a "friend's" for a few days. But it was merely a question. The matter didn't seem to concern him in any tragic sense. Morton had glided right though the crisis of disconnection. Would Sammy do as well? Would she?

"Is that chicken pot pie I smell?" he asked next, sniffing interestedly as he went out the door. Yes, it was. Lately Annie was hungry for things like that: macaroni and cheese, chipped beef on toast, lima beans and ham, corned beef hash. Well, for heaven's sake, she realized. She had just listed an average week's menu from her childhood. She hadn't even left yet and already she missed her mother. Would Sammy someday, missing her, want guacamole dip and artichoke hearts or, missing Morton, crave roast beef or sirloin tip?

What was going on here? For the first time in a long time, she wanted to cry. Everything she knew was disappearing before her eyes. Ending a marriage she wanted ended was still a loss she couldn't help mourn. Then Sammy needed her less and less each year and she had likely accelerated the rate by which he would pull away from her just by the disruption she was now causing. And her own childhood, for no good reason, was on her mind. Who would miss a past like that?

Until she was seven she thought all adults slurred their speech after dark and assumed she did, too, never connecting it to what they might have had to drink and in what quantity. Annie had understood early on about bar stools, how to climb them, balance on them, how to swing them fast. Only twice had she fallen off one, once knocking her chin against the bar as she did. Sometimes her father would prop her up on the end stool and tell her to watch things while he ran across the street for ice; and if someone came in, she knew how to slide off and go around the bar and in which cooler the Budweiser, the Miller, the Hamms were kept. She could open a beer, climb up the step-stool kept there for just such occasions and take the money. But if the customer wanted a draft or a mixed drink he had to do it himself. Soon she could draw a beer without producing a head or identify any number of different liquors by the shape of the bottle or color of the label. She guessed she'd learned to read not from storybooks but from labels.

Annie learned other things at the bar: Irish didleys, Italian proverbs, Cornish swear words. Before she was five she had acquired a taste for finnan haddie, suet pudding, pasties, gnocchi. She knew a Slavic accent from a Finnish one and the social habits and eccentricities of a dozen different cultures.

Many of the people who frequented Jake's in those days liked high school basketball or football or the local baseball team. On game nights, customers who wanted to go would load into station wagons, taking Annie along to cool, lighted ball parks, freezing football fields or hot, sweaty gyms. Then they'd return to the spaghetti or chili her mother might have made or to popcorn if she had been too tired to cook. Best of all were the potlucks, those nights everyone brought everything, from soused mackerel to beef and kidney pie, offerings placed in rows on tablecloths spread over the pinball machines. Not until later when Annie went to her friends' homes did she realize that her own life was exceptional, probably unsuitable, and aroused interest—something inadvisable to mention at another child's dinner table.

She learned quickly not to bring home friends. Or to explain things. "Where do you put the Christmas tree?" Mary Lou Haggerty wanted to know every year. "Same place as everyone else," she'd answer, letting Mary Lou believe she meant the window. They really put it on the pinball machine, or the piano, or on a shelf above the cash register. She didn't recall it in the same place two years in a row. Christmas Eve the regulars came by for Tom and Jerrys and Mama cooked a ham and put it with cheese and crackers and potato chips along the bar. When Christmas carolers were heard outside, one of them—Bubba most likely, as he was the most sentimental of the regulars—would open the door to snow and wind and yell after them to come in for a drink. And Mama would give them free cocoa with whipped cream if they were children or Baptists, and eggnog with rum if they were older and not teetotalers. Usually they were Catholics, Shriners or Elks. Mama could tell the difference, even Annie could. The non-drinkers sort of edged on in, perhaps praying for grace so as to withstand the ways of Jake's. But the Catholics and others sashayed comfortably up to the bar in step to the carol, so that "God Rest Ye, Merry Gentlemen" became a stomp to get in line first, whereas "Oh Holy Night" prompted a dancing glide. The lodge brothers, though, didn't have to be coaxed to come in. They often began their caroling at Jake's and one year finished it there. That year, more decorous lodge members and irate spouses arrived at intervals to collect the drunken carolers, who by ten o'clock had sung themselves out and by ten-thirty had forgotten the words even to "Silent Night." And that, a silent night, was all they should have hoped for after that performance. Then towards midnight, one or two of the regulars, usually Bubba and Fern, would take Annie to Mass. Her own folks weren't religious but might have come along except they had to keep the bar open until two o'clock as always, they said. Annie realized later that it was then, on Christmas Eve, while she was sitting awed by Latin, flowing robes, flickering candles, the aroma of holy water—this parish always put fresh rose petals in it—that her folks and any stragglers at the bar were filling her stocking, wrapping her presents, assembling her trike, bike, sled or whatever.

But not every day was a holiday around Jake's. Sometimes Annie was distracted from her homework or awakened in the night by disturbances out at the bar. Until she was in high school they lived in the tiny apartment in back, its windows to the alley, and only a thin wall between it and the bar, between it and patrons who often told loud jokes or yelled at each other. One night she woke up to a fight two women were having over a man. An amazing occurrence was what she thought, as the bar was always full of men, plenty to go around. But, no, these two wanted the same one. The next day she found simulated pearls all over the floor, three bone buttons and a clump of blond hair. Annie vowed then to never fight over anything. She saw, in those few items strewn across the bar floor, debasement of some kind; she heard again the discordant timbre of their voices, felt the ruptures that had taken place. Not to mention how impractical it turned out to be. Hadn't the man just fled out the back during the fracas anyway? Annie gave in easily for years after in disputes over anything: the larger donut, which movie, whose turn it was.

But if she spent half her time then at the bar, the other half she lived at the Civic Center. Annie had wanted to be a skater. She got up every morning at five o'clock to catch the bus to the rink, riding with the smeltermen and miners, the only child, the only female. They all sat silently, her skates beside her, their black metal lunch pails beside them, as they quietly smoked or nodded off or stared out the window at a town in darkness, its inhabitants wisely or luckily still in bed.

Annie was the only child not delivered to the rink by a mother. Hers did not drive or get up early. The other kids ate cinnamon buns and drank hot chocolate. She could see them in the bleachers above the rink as she warmed up. After a frenzied workout at figures, she'd change, get back on the bus and go to school, then return that afternoon to free-style skating, her favorite. She took a private lesson a week, rented a patch of ice to do figures on and went to any open session, all of this paid for out of the tips her mother saved in a Prince Albert tobacco can at the bar. She was an awkward skater who had little chance of being great. Others leaped more easily through waltz jumps and loop jumps, glided smoothly into spins and figure eights. Annie might have done better to have played hockey. She was not so graceful and accomplished as speedy and light, and she loved the feeling of cutting the air with her body, the disturbed currents around her like the wind and wake she imagined across a cold, smooth sea. While she knew her deficiencies, she wanted it still and would not give it up. She mastered no jumps to anyone's satisfaction but not because she didn't try and keep on trying. She'd leap recklessly into any position without fear for how she might land just as summers she would attempt any dive into any pool, lake or river. She preferred, and was best at, the jackknife.

Annie's life put her on the fringes of normal experience. For example, something as simple as not having had dinner in a dining room on any regular basis—they ate at the bar—put her at a disadvantage. Though she tried to duplicate any procedure she observed, her alertness was often impaired by her fascination with the lace, the gleaming china and crystal, the abundance of utensils all specially arranged, and by how precisely the diners blotted their lips with linen, knew which direction to pass food, automatically assessed who should begin the passing and at what point to actually start eating and then stop. Not only that but they were not confused or surprised by salad forks, dessert spoons, demitasse cups or water goblets. As a child the whole dining experience was as mysterious and impressive as Christmas Eve Mass. There too, despite her willingness to kneel, to get back up, to cross herself, to recite with the others, everyone else was always a syllable, a movement, a step ahead.

Morton, bless his heart, understood the dining room and other social arenas—poolside, cocktail parties, the country club. And so would Sammy. What could she say to that? That they would never know as much as she'd known at five about other things: the ways of old men, the anger of a cuckolded spouse, the pain of a grieving drunk, the methods some use to deal with the perplexities, the hardships, the routines of unremarkable lives. And were those things worth knowing? Not that Annie had realized at the time that she was picking all that up. Like dining, it was an osmotic process she now appreciated in retrospect.

Sammy's boyhood, though less stressful maybe, was pinioned too tightly perhaps to regulations and measured experience. Couldn't that be as bad? It was what she supposed had happened to Morton. She guessed he suffered from an adequate but uneventful childhood that led him to expect all matters—household, financial, sexual—to be neatly agreed to and unsurprising. More exposure might develop a spontaneity in Sammy, an independent point of view, a capacity for flexibility, maybe something in between her father's sloppiness and the tight order Morton required for his mental health. Morton had no appreciation for the extraordinary or the calamitous. If a water pipe broke, he took it personally; if it rained on his golf day, he sulked and blamed himself.

"It's my own fault," he said once when the temperature rose to seventy degrees the week they went to ski at Big Mountain. "Why didn't we go in February like I'd first planned," he moaned.

Annie thought it was wonderful, went hiking, dragged a chair from the room outside to sit on in the sun, cut off her slacks.

"Morton, come on, enjoy yourself," she told him. "I'll cut off your pants for you."

"God, no," he said.

37

And he got even more upset when people misbehaved than when things did. Morton was not the type who could have weathered a bank failure or a death in the family. Their divorce was certainly one of the more creative and adaptive decisions of his life to date.

But unlike Annie, Morton made profound commitments to his personal belongings, to trust indentures, payments due. Annie believed that everyone would feel much better if they were to burn their possessions every seven years, trade lives with distant strangers, change occupations. It might extend the worth of a thing. One could appreciate something more knowing it was make-do, provisional, about to disappear. Not that Annie didn't enjoy things herself, but only if she could pay cash for them, then leave them when it pleased her.

"Where's our bureau?" Morton had asked after searching the new house the last time they moved.

"I gave it away," she answered.

"You what?"

"It wouldn't quite fit into the moving van," she explained.

The movers were going to unload and rearrange, tie something else on top. No, she said. *Free to good home,* she wrote on a piece of paper and taped it to one of the drawers. Then she got in the car and followed the van, the mahogany dresser still at the curb, its mirror packed in blankets inside her trunk. The mirror might have looked out of place by itself in their new home and been stuck away in a closet or the garage, but she took off the mahogany arms that once attached it to the bureau and hung it in the bathroom.

Annie could adopt belongings just as easily and people learned where to discharge their junk. They cleaned out their attics and basements and delivered any old discard to her.

"You are overrunning my garage," Morton would complain until she agreed to have a rummage sale.

Now, however, Morton would have to go through the entire house and garage and decide what he wanted because she was calling Goodwill.

"You're not taking anything?" he said, worried.

"No."

"But you're going to need things. Samuel will need things," he protested.

"I'll pick up some items when we get there." Acquiring material goods was even less difficult for Annie than casting them aside.

Sammy sccmed interested in all the proceedings, as if great adventure were just ahead. Annie's parents, though, did not see it that way.

"Are you out of your mind?" her father wanted to know. "A good home, security, a good man. You must be crazy. Tell her," he said to her mother. But her mother was at that point at which she could only cry. She would have plenty to say later but, for now, only tears.

To Sammy she explained as fully as possible about the divorce, not the reasons for it, but what it would mean for all of them—change, adjustment, patience. "Honey," she told him. "We were nice people together, we'll be nice people apart—maybe nicer. Love us both, please."

A few days before they were to depart they packed up a few essentials.

"Mom, will we ever come back here?" he said. They were sitting on his bed going through his socks and underwear.

"Of course. We'll visit every chance."

"I mean to live."

"One day when you're old enough and if you want, you can move back. You can raise your own kids here, maybe go into business with your father." She would not say, *Or run the bar.*

"I'd rather live by the ocean," he said.

Good, she thought, as either the furniture store or the bar seemed a sorry choice to her. Think of it. From the dank, dark cave of primitive man, to the dim, foul air of Jake's. From the comfortable easy-to-launder loincloth to the three-piece suit, tight collar and decorative tie. Had man evolved, or not?

Morton put down the phone and then picked it up again to call Annie.

"How's everything?"

"Fine," she said. "Will you be home for dinner?"

"No, not tonight."

"Oh. Will you be late?"

"Probably."

There was a pause then. Neither of them knew what to say to end this awkward conversation. Morton knew that she knew that he was seeing someone. He hadn't tried to hide it and, after all, he had asked for a divorce, hadn't he? The marriage was over, for God's sake.

"Well, good-bye," he said abruptly and hung up. This was so difficult, ending one thing, beginning another, all at the same time. He hadn't expected to get involved so soon. Generally a woman just looked at him when he tried to explain that he was getting a divorce but he and his wife were still living in the same house. She lost interest right away. It was "too iffy," one woman told him right out.

But then he ran into Marge, a woman he'd actually known for years. She had been married to someone he played golf with. She'd come in to buy lamps and he recognized her. She made it easy for him to approach her; she already knew he wasn't a bigamist or a child molester—or whatever women were afraid of when you first met them. She believed him when he said he and Annie were through.

"I'm sorry," she said, smiling at him as though really tickled to death, which pleased him. He needed some unbiased feminine attention.

And so they had proceeded to have a few drinks, then went on to her house for a quiet dinner, which he didn't recall having. She made it easy for him to seduce her, perhaps she seduced him because they fell easily into a very pleasant, ongoing sexual affair. The only problem was that once Annie left for good, Marge would want to get serious. And he wasn't ready for that, not with her, not with anyone.

"Mr. Tomlin?" It was Jardine, the boy who helped him out around the store, looking for him. "There you are," he said, opening the door without knocking. "The truck's here."

"Thanks, Jardine," Morton said. "I'm coming."

Morton followed the boy out back to receiving and watched from the platform as the delivery men unloaded the truck.

"I want all those loungers brought up front," he told his sales manager. "We'll run a special on them over the weekend." The man looked up from his pad and nodded.

Morton liked to think of himself as having one hand up on things. He tried to instill that in his employees and in his son. "Don't let things get away from you," he'd say. "Keep a sharp eye." It annoyed him how someone like Jardine could fart around all day at work the way he did. He could forget whose couch he had on the truck on the way to deliver it. And if a customer wanted to know something as simple as the location of sale items, instead of pointing out the area—sale items were always put in the same area— he'd offer to go get someone to help them. Then he might forget to or take so long the customer would leave. Jardine was exasperating. Morton really ought to let him go. It was just that the kid had no father and Morton felt sorry for him. He supposed Jardine reminded him of himself at a certain age, a much younger age of course. Except that even at Jardine's age, Morton had not been *that* uninterested in work. But at least Jardine was honest, which was more than he could say for other employees he'd had over the years.

Once he'd said, "Jardine, is it that you just don't give a damn?"

Jardine had looked up at him in surprise. "Oh, no. Mrs. Tomlin told me I was trying too hard. 'Don't work so hard at it,' she said. 'Let the customer be and she'll sell herself.'"

Morton had turned then and walked out. He was too enraged to say anything just then. But he straightened it out the next day with Jardine and as soon as he got home with Annie. He found her out in the yard weeding flowerbeds.

"Did you tell Jardine he could just sit on his ass and ignore the customers?"

"Oh, Morton! You startled me," she said, turning to him then. She had a sunburn and her hands were dirty because she refused to wear gloves.

"Did you?"

She'd sighed and got up, taking a last look at her work before quitting. "What I told Jardine was to stop being so uptight. He was so nervous with Mrs. Petrovich the last time I was in that he was stammering."

"Leave my employees alone," he told her. "I'll handle them."

She said nothing more and he went inside and made himself a drink.

He could not stand the idea of a woman undermining a man. He didn't think Annie did it on purpose, she was not the manipulative type. But still he knew it happened sometimes between couples without either party being aware of it.

Now Annie's mother was the sort who could pull the rug out from under someone with a comment. Nicholas, Annie's father, would say one thing and Annie's mother would correct him. Luckily for Nicholas, he was impossible to undermine. No woman had ever managed to get the best of him, Morton guessed. Morton didn't especially like him. He was too coarse, too unrefined for his taste. And that so-called bar? A real dump. Depressing as hell, what with all those old derelicts hanging out there, drinking up their pension money, talking about a Butte long gone. He had never liked Sammy to spend a lot of time with Nicholas.

"Why not?" Annie had asked when he told her that. Her feelings were not hurt as he'd expected. She was just curious, he thought.

"I don't want Sammy to get the idea that a real man has to be so, you know, macho."

She'd nodded.

"What was your dad like?" she'd asked him once.

He'd had to think. "He was quiet. He didn't like confrontation. He was serious." And, Morton thought, maybe sad.

"How do you know he didn't like confrontation?" she'd wanted to know.

He'd had to think again. "Because he never fought back. He never even raised his voice."

"Not even when he was mad?"

"Not even then," he'd said, trying to remember. Not even when his mother made fun of him or went into one of her rages. She could be such a bitch. Sometimes Morton had wanted to scream, "Hit her, Daddy, hit her. Make her shut up!" But instead he'd leave the house or go to his room where he couldn't hear her, where he couldn't see her face—it would be red except for her forehead, which would be white with a blue vein now visible at each temple. And most of all he'd go so he couldn't see his father's face, which would be drawn and ashen. And sad.

One time, he'd come in and found his mother berating Paul, who was no more than six years old at the time. Morton had run out to the garage to find his father, to get him to stop it. But he couldn't find him and he'd run back into the house through the back hall to the kitchen where he could see his father in the adjoining dining room, listening. He had stopped in surprise and then his father saw him, too. That time his father wore a tragic expression, one of helplessness, weakness, confusion even. It so unnerved Morton that he'd stared at his father in disbelief, in horror that this man would not come to the rescue of a small child, his own son. It was at that moment that Morton, an eight-year-old, understood that there was no father there to keep him safe either. It would be forever up to him, Morton, to manage his own boogeymen and probably also Paul's.

He'd run into the kitchen where his mother was still interrogating a silent, stricken Paul.

"I hate a liar," she was saying. "Why did you lie to me? Say something, damn you. Are you an imbecile?" She was pacing around, slamming things into cupboards as she talked.

Morton had grabbed the first thing he saw, a bowl of fruit on the table. He threw it to the floor and then kicked a bright red apple that rolled his way. His mother and Paul both turned to him in amazement. He thought he saw the merest flicker of hope then in Paul's young frightened eyes before he, Morton, ran out the door, his mother screaming not far behind him, all the way to the alley. Once there he was safe as she never chased Morton farther than the back gate.

The funny thing was that it seemed to calm his mother down. She seemed relieved to have someone stop her tantrum, as though tired of it herself but unable to quit. He found her humming when he returned as though nothing had happened—unaware that in an extraordinary earlier moment her eight-year-old son had just taken charge of something. Of everything. It had gone right over her head. She had missed it. She had not seen what her firstborn had—that what had always terrified him about her never would again. And, too, that what terrified him about his father would terrify him forever.

His father understood what had just taken place, though. Morton saw it in his face. But Paul didn't. He only concluded that his mother liked Morton best. Which, of course, was in error. Their mother just found comfort in the knowledge that she had one less male to torture, as torture, Morton believed, was a lot of work for her. It was just one more thing she thought she had to do.

Everyone said that you always married your mother. But it was not necessarily true. Annie was nothing like his mother. If anything, she was more like his dad.

Chapter Four

Annie's mother's kitchen was hot and by now Annie's beer was too. She and Sammy had come to say good-bye. They were leaving in the morning, though her mother still acted like the departure was just being considered. Her mother, a short, stout woman of Norwegian descent, had ceased to cry some weeks ago but ever since had plenty to say.

"I don't care what your reasons are, they're not good enough," she said, snapping green beans into a colander across the table. Annie's father and Sammy were off somewhere, maybe in the basement or garage, looking for binoculars or a compass or something.

"Don't tell me, it doesn't matter. There's no reason good enough to break up a family. But I would like to know why you want to leave Montana. Darling, this is your home, this is where your roots are. It's clean, it's beautiful, it's not crowded. There are no perverts, no sex maniacs here, no religious fanatics." (Her mother was afraid they'd go off to Salt Lake City and become Mormons.) "No pollution like so many places. Why would you leave a place like this?" She was at the sink rinsing the beans now and, because she talked with her hands, she was spattering water over the tile around the sink and across the floor.

"Mama," Annie began. "Haven't you ever done something because you felt you had to and that it didn't necessarily make
sense?"

Her mother sighed. She patted the beans dry with paper towel
and put them into a plastic sack, then managed to pull a twisty out
of a cluttered drawer to secure it. "I have," she said at last, stopping
to look Annie directly in the eyes, her way of making sure Annie
was listening. "Come out to the garden with me," she said. She
grabbed a paring knife and bucket and turned on the back porch
light.

It was a relief to be out in the cool air. There was a wonderful
smell back here of newly turned earth and fresh cut grass. Annie
could hear a sprinkler clacking in the next yard and crickets in the
maple tree.

"Here," her mother said, walking a small path of boards between the various crops of vegetables to the carrots. "Samuel will
love these," she said. "Very tender." She knelt down and began to
pull the leafy tops and Annie heard soft thuds into the bucket as the
tops hit first. "Sit down," she said and they moved to the damp
grass that bordered the garden.

"When you were very small, your father came to me one night
and said he was in love with someone else and that he wanted a
divorce."

"I don't believe it!" Annie said.

"It's true. Oh, I knew who it was. It was the barmaid across the
street at Juliano's. I cried for days and then I thought it all over. The
bar, you know, was his business, so I would be the one to have to
leave. I'd have to take a young child, find a job, maybe be a
barmaid myself. Who'd take care of you? What would happen to
us? I was worried to death and angry too. But it didn't take me long
to decide what to do. A couple of days later I went across the street
to Juliano's; it was late in the afternoon, just as that woman was
getting to work. Oh, she was a pretty thing, and surprised to see
me. She had her hand on her hip, and that hip sticking out as far as
it would go. Real sure of herself. And I carried you with me and
you were all dirty from playing, your nose was runny, your hair
was tangled, you had no shoes on."

"Mama, you never let me get dirty in my life!"

"This time I did. And I didn't look too good either. 'Naomi,' I said. That was her name, Naomi. 'If you want my husband, you can have him,' I said. 'But the bar and the kid go too,' and I held you out to her and she almost leaped back to keep your muddy feet from touching her skirt. 'Get out of here!' she screamed."

Annie started to laugh. "Mama, how could you?" She didn't know whether to believe her mother or not. The story was preposterous.

"Well, I wasn't so easy with your father. I couldn't be. It wouldn't have worked." Annie wished she could see her mother's face as she talked but it was too dark.

"Of course we cleaned up and I put on a nice dress, put one on you too. We looked beautiful and when your father came back from the liquor store, I said to him, 'Nicholas, sit down a minute.' He was getting ready to relieve the fellow who worked part-time then and was rushing around. But he thought I was ready to give in, so he sat. 'Take a good look at us,' I said, 'because we'll be gone soon. But before I go, I promise on my mother's grave that I will burn this bar to the ground. If I can start over, so can you,' I said."

"Mama, for God's sake."

"Don't interrupt now," she said. "So then he says, 'Elsa, what are you saying?' Well he knew darn well what. Anyway, I didn't stick around the bar that night. I took you and we went out to dinner and to a movie—you slept." She paused here.

"So then what?"

"I was in bed by the time your father closed the bar. I waited until I heard him lock up and go out the back door. I knew where he was going. I got up, went to the cellar and brought up all the old rags I could find, all the turpentine, paint thinner, kerosene—anything I could think of, and I made a mess sloshing it around behind the bar, in front of the bar, on top of it, the rags too. Then I went back to bed."

"Mama, you didn't!" Annie was frankly horrified. (And to think that she had once thought a broken strand of pearls and a handful of hair on the floor at Jake's was dramatic.)

"Oh, yes, and when I got up the next morning your father had already cleaned it all up."

"What did he say?"

47

"Nothing. Not one word, ever. I never heard any more about another woman or divorce."

"What about the barmaid?"

"Naomi? I don't know, I guess she left. And to my knowledge, your father never went across the street to Juliano's again."

"Mama, would you really have burned down the bar?"

"I don't know, dear. I felt crazy at the time. I might have. The important thing is your father thought so."

"How could you threaten him like that?"

"Family is everything," her mother said, getting up now. "Think about it. Go ahead, take a vacation, get it out of your system, but for God's sake, come to your senses."

By the time they escaped her parents' house it was ten-thirty and Annie was exhausted. After they had loaded up a sack of carrots, tuna fish sandwiches, peanut butter cookies, a cooler they might need, an atlas, the compass and binoculars, and the AAA card in Annie's name—a surprise gift for the journey—they were able to at last start the car and back out of the driveway. After all that, Annie couldn't have changed her mind if she wanted to. In some weird way her folks, though they would deny it, were counting on her to make it as far away as Alaska or Mexico maybe. She sighed. She still had some packing to do and so did Sammy. He was already asleep in the front seat, his head planted against the door lock.

Annie could think of nothing else but what her mother had told her. The story had to be true. Or did it? She had never known her mother to lie. On the other hand, she had never known her to make threats. Maybe one great ultimatum was enough for a lifetime. In a way it was a marvelous story, both amusing and frightening. On a certain level she envied her mother's daring—to bluff a man twice her size, with half her good nature. But on another, Annie was astonished at the lengths her mother had gone to, to bind her father to them. Still he'd always seemed quite happy. Had he been like the naughty child who is so bratty that even he comes to hope someone will put a stop to his tirades and is relieved to be spanked? Even so . . .

"Sammy, we're home," she said, pulling in their own drive. "Wake up, honey."

Annie helped him out his door and bothered only to take in the food. Sammy, still half-asleep, said good-night to his father and disappeared up the stairs. Morton stood in the kitchen in his robe. "Listen," he said after Sammy went up, "if you ever want to come back, you can have the house and I'll get an apartment."

"That's sweet of you, Morton," she said. "Thanks."

"I'll miss you both," he said.

"We'll be in close touch," she promised and went upstairs too.

It was one of life's better tricks, Annie decided as she threw underwear from the clean laundry into her overnight bag, that her mother's courage had been the result of her fear—she'd said as much. Fear of doing exactly what Annie was now doing. Had she and her mother left Nicholas, how might that have changed their lives? Would her father, free then, in a new life with the woman Naomi, have forgotten her, his daughter?

It was disturbing that a decision incidental to a state of mind, however flawed or temporary, could determine the course of events to come. Had she the right to change Sammy's life like that, to put further distance between him and Morton? For it seemed to her, for reasons Morton never talked about, there occurred some mutual avoidance of intimacy between them, an occurrence now so natural neither questioned it, though surely Sammy would someday. Had they been close, she might have stayed.

It was her father, not Morton, who'd played on the floor with Sammy the infant, her father who had thrown the young boy baseballs until he could catch one and pitch it back. It was her father who'd taken Sammy hunting and camping over the years, returning him hungry and tired, the joy of both as visible as sunburn and insect bites. Likewise, it had been Bubba who'd had time for her, for things like a chess game after school at the bar or a trip across town to the circuses she didn't like; there was something too sad in those tents, some weariness she felt there, some brave pretense she suspected behind the makeup and thin, worn costumes. Bubba was the one who drove Annie through the mountains on a Sunday afternoon, sometimes to his cabin over Pipestone Pass where large rocks rose from their granite beds like gravestones in a churchyard. Here, near the cabin, they fished the creek for the dinner Fern would cook over an open fire. Why was that? Why had Morton and her father relinquished some parental rights to others? And why had she, ungraciously, abandoned Bubba and Fern in the ensuing years? Was it because of all the time that passed between visits with them or was it due more to Morton's prejudices and possibly, shamefully, her own?

Annie closed up her bags. She had packed all she wanted. There was a picture on Morton's desk that he'd recently had framed and, as she passed it, she turned it face down. She didn't like that he had chosen this one, of her and Sammy unposed and laughing unexpectedly over something at a party in her parents' yard. Of all the pictures he might have chosen of himself and Sammy, he'd insisted on this one, a memorial to the way he liked to see them, together, a unit, one he held apart from himself, relegating them to a wall or pocket where he could better manage them.

Had anything been accomplished here? Was there any meaning to the life she had squandered or to the one she might soon acquire? Or would she merely collect the years like trophies for endurance?

As a child Annie had wondered about things—why did she have a bar owner for a father and not a piano teacher like Mary Lou Haggerty, or an architect or a fireman or any number of other father types. Were these matches random or was some choice involved? If there was an afterlife of heaven and hell as Bubba used to tell her, why not, she wanted to ask, a "before" life too? Maybe cycles to it all, with heaven or hell getting as monotonous as everything else, so one dropped on up or down (though direction would hardly seem relevant out in space) to some planet to enjoy a change of scene. More than likely there were cosmic parents who made you go, just as they forced you to go to school when you were six. Perhaps, she used to think, you got to select your planet parents along with anything else you might like or need, so just as you might choose chemistry or biology in high school, you could choose Elsa and Nicholas and their bar for a useful and interesting experience. That was how Annie, lying in the corner booth of Jake's on a slow night, had accounted for the circumstances of her birth.

Did Sammy do that too? Did he think he had chosen—from computer printouts, say, of likely compatible types—the parents he might enjoy? Would he be sorry he had not foreseen that his mother would suddenly alter the basic plan? Or was that information on the sheet too and part of the choice?

Annie went down to the dining room and made herself a drink and took two aspirin. She still thought in circular patterns, everything some repetition of things she had thought before, no new input, just a rehash of things she didn't understand, caught in her brain like a recording, certain to repeat itself until she could fall asleep.

She checked on Sammy on the way to her room. He had left the light on above his study table where a map of the western states lay open. There marked by a red felt-tip pen were side trips and alternate roads near Interstate 90, their westward route out of Montana. She felt better just seeing it. Perhaps even Samuel, young as he was, was anticipating all manner of disaster and good fortune ahead, enjoying that mixture of distress and excitement that accompanies the uncertain. West as a direction was all they'd decided so far, though they let everyone believe Idaho was the target. They hadn't planned to be deceptive, it came about quite innocently, just a private joke. With her, Sammy talked about the Seattle Seahawks or the San Francisco Forty-Niners when locations were discussed just as she considered the Pike Street Market or the Golden Gate Bridge. But at dinner one night when Morton pressed them for details, Sammy grinned at her and said, "Well, Mom's set on Boise." To his grandfather, under similar circumstances, he said Idaho Falls.

Annie turned off the light and closed his door. In her own bed, surrounded by the photographic history of a lifetime of family events, Fourth of July picnics, birthday parties, her folks' thirty-fifth wedding anniversary, her mother's story seemed more fantastic, less believable. Could most of their marriage have really been based on intimidation? If she could only recall anything about it. All she could remember was that Juliano's was always off-limits to her. Annie had never questioned it, assuming rightly that it was just one of those places that was not a good place for children. Funny that it had never occurred to her, or anyone else at that time, that her father's bar was just like it and not a good place for children either.

Morton was restless and, after Annie went to bed, he walked a few blocks, then sat on a bench at the park down the street. There were few lights on in the neighborhood and the dogs who usually barked at him didn't even bother. It was a cloudless night and barely a thread of the new moon was visible over the range of mountains east of the valley below.

When he got back to the house Morton sat in the living room, then rummaged around in the downstairs medicine cabinet for sleeping pills. Finally he went upstairs.

Marge was a little mad at him, he thought. She didn't see why he wouldn't spend at least the early evening with her. She had baked something special for him, anticipating that he might be a little depressed about Sammy leaving in the morning. She was going to bring it over to the store that afternoon but when she found out there was not some big farewell deal going on, she wanted to see him.

"So tomorrow they leave," she'd said.

"Uh-huh," he said.

"So do you have plans with your son tonight?" she'd asked.

"No."

"With your . . . ?"

"No."

"No plans at all?"

"No."

"Well, then, why don't you come for dinner?"

"I thought I should stick around the house. You know . . ."

"For appearance' sake?"

Then they had argued. She accused him of being hypocritical and he didn't dare tell her that Annie and Sammy wouldn't even be home. Maybe Marge was right. He just didn't want Sammy to ever say that his father wasn't there for him his last night in Butte. In any case, he felt better being home.

He knew Annie thought he didn't give a damn that they were leaving. He did, but, on the other hand, he wanted to get the separation over with. He was troubled, feeling there was something he had failed to give her, something she needed from him. And he had a hunch that had he given it, Annie would not be leaving him. He had no idea what this was and it probably wasn't as complicated as he was making it. He thought it might be something simple. But getting that close to someone in order to find out what was needed was impossible for him. Not that he'd known this. He'd always thought that he and Annie were close, not lately maybe but at some earlier point in their marriage. That is, until the Ingebritsons came into the picture.

The Ingebritsons were an older couple who had come to the store looking for a couch a few days before. He had watched them absentmindedly at first but then with real attention. There was something about how they talked to each other that interested him. Not that it had been anything outside the usual. They went from one couch to another, discussing what he liked, what she liked, colors and sizes, the various styles and the room where they would put it. It was how they talked that impressed him. How they talked and how they laughed. Their appreciation for each other was deep and rich, and affecting. It was a stunning example of a lifelong bond, the ultimate in human union. It suggested a history behind them, a future before them. Unity and permanence.

Unexpectedly tears had come to Morton's eyes and he had to excuse himself and go blow his nose. The experience had so unnerved him that he began a series of projects that took up the rest of the day and pushed the incident out of his mind. But now he wanted to take a look at it. He wanted to know what had so intrigued him about what he'd seen. But instead of figuring anything out, his mind had gone on a rampage, bringing up old memories and new feelings.

Just that evening he'd noticed Sammy's baby picture missing from the wall. He supposed Annie or Sammy had packed it that day. He was surprised to find that the picture was now more real and more detailed missing than it had ever been on the wall—he recalled the blue sweater with hood that Sammy had on, that what hair he had was curly and slightly red, that he had two front bottom teeth and that he was leaning on a large white stuffed bear that had no right ear because the dog they'd had then had chewed it off. But had someone asked Morton yesterday to describe the picture of Sammy on the wall in the hall, he would have said, *What picture?*

And the missing picture reminded him of an incident he probably hadn't thought of since it happened. One Sunday afternoon Annie left him to baby-sit. She had to work a shift at Jake's because the bartender hadn't shown up. So she'd left him in charge and someone had come by the house, he didn't even remember who, maybe a neighbor or someone he played golf with. Anyway the two men packed up the baby, maybe put that same blue sweater on him and went off to run an errand. But then they'd stopped at some pool hall and, Sammy, then old enough to stand up and take a few steps, was asleep in the backseat. They didn't have car seats for kids then and the baby had the whole backseat to himself.

Just the thought of it now horrified him, the two of them leaving that baby alone in the car and going into that bar to play pool. He'd looked out the door every few minutes and run out when he saw the baby standing up at the window. Sammy grinned at him and batted the window with his fist and Morton talked to him as he looked for his car keys.

"Hi there, Boom Chew. Daddy's going to take you for ice cream. Whoops, Daddy will be right back." And he'd run back into the bar to look for his jacket where the keys were. But it turned out they weren't in his pocket and he'd run back to the car and sure enough they were in the ignition. But Sammy was still smiling and now investigating some old sun hats in the back window.

So he'd run in again and got a coat hanger from the barmaid, who located some in a closet where uniforms hung.

"We don't have an extra," she'd said staring into the closet.

He gave her five bucks and she took a uniform off its hanger and handed him the hanger. Out of the corner of his eye, he saw her throw the uniform on the floor.

By the time he got back, Sammy wasn't so happy anymore. He now stood at the window with the most pathetic look Morton had ever seen—as though he'd just realized that the adults outside the car were idiots and had put him in jeopardy.

The coat hanger, it turned out, was the thick metal kind that was not very pliable and all he managed was to tear the rubber seal around the window. And Wesley—that's who was with him, Wesley who'd sold him life insurance—kept insisting that Morton just tell the baby to pull up the lock. But when Morton ignored him, concentrating on the coat hanger he had wedged through above the window, Wesley began talking to the baby.

"Here Sammy. See this," and he'd tap on the window near the lock. "Pull this up for Wesley, come on, pull this up." Morton looked over once to see Sammy ignoring Wesley too. Finally Wesley started yelling at the baby and Sammy began to cry and then Morton swore at Wesley and the baby really got excited then and he stepped off the seat and fell on the floor.

Morton had the most sickening feelings of helplessness and shame he'd ever had as he saw that child fall from sight. He was so upset that he'd run into the bar, grabbed a stool and used it to break the car's front window.

"You're going to spray the kid with glass," he heard Wesley yell. But he was afraid Sammy had broken his neck and he couldn't think of a faster way to get into that car. The baby was so upset by now that Morton drove over to Jake's and rushed in with him and thrust him at Annie.

"What's wrong?" she softly asked of the baby, who quieted immediately as she walked up and down behind the bar with him in her arms while Morton stared stupidly at them. He was relieved that the baby was okay and, too, that he could not report the events of the afternoon. Annie then handed Sammy to Elsa, who held him on her lap at the bar.

"Dad's coming in so I can leave in an hour or so if you want to wait for me," she said.

No, he told her. He had to take Wesley home and run a few errands.

"Well, leave the baby, huh?" she suggested as he'd hoped. He then went out and paid Melvin Strickland, the body man he and Wesley had just beaten at pool, over three times the normal cost to put a new window in the car that afternoon.

"Christ, it's Sunday," Melvin said, putting chalk on his cue. Morton had waited for him to shoot. Not surprisingly, he missed. He was drunk.

"C'mon," Morton said.

He'd had to drag Melvin out and drive him around to the salvage yards looking for a window. Morton had then stood over him as he worked, an act of intimidation that more effectively sobered him than the promise of more money.

He never did tell Annie what had happened and never planned to. It was one of those mistakes that made him wince to think about. Sometimes he thought that Sammy had never forgiven him for it. He felt that this tiny child had blamed him for abandonment and neglect. For months after the incident the child seemed wary of him, he thought, and it had been Morton's opinion since that young children knew a hell of a lot more about what went on than anyone ever suspected.

Still unable to sleep, Morton went back downstairs for a double Scotch.

Chapter Five

Annie had pictured a departure in the dark, the sun rising an hour or so later at their backs. As it was, they didn't leave until the afternoon and the sun would be in their eyes soon. Morton had stuck around, despite his busy schedule, to help them load and say good-bye. He followed behind them with odds and ends, reminding them of things. He had a list: Check oil and battery every stop, watch temperature gauge, stop the minute you get tired, windows must be open a crack even if cold, seat belts fastened at all times. This list, for the most part, was the reason for the delay. She wanted to ask him why none of this had occurred to him to worry about earlier, but since it was their official parting, so to speak, she quietly allowed him to double-check what the mechanic had just done the day before. Morton had stayed home a lot the past week, out of consideration maybe or just so their last memories of the house would include him. The woman with whom he had spent most of the last few months likely understood this.

"This is it," she said.

"Well, good-bye," he said and hugged Sammy. He kissed her on the cheek. "Are we crazy?" he asked her. "No," she told him. "Only a little frightened." He nodded.

Did he know what she meant? She was so scared she had to quiet her stomach and heart by breathing slow, deep breaths. She patiently reminded herself that it was only fear and that she was on her way in spite of it. The fear would pass. She hoped.

Once out of town Samuel was content. He read comics and tapped his knees to music that came though his earphones to her as a slight buzz. Then he napped or talked. He told her the entire plot to three movies. She was surprised at how much like Morton he sounded, that same precise attention to detail. Who else would mention that the hero's down vest was almost the same except for the pocket as his friend Clifford's, or draw her pictures of the boat and helicopter the cops used? Only Morton. Certainly not her. She didn't see movies visually. She felt scenes. She didn't recall seeing, say, a murder, or a love scene or the woman in the white summer hat. She experienced and remembered only the terror or joy or whatever, so it was pointless for someone to insist she describe the murder weapon or the bedspread. She missed ball gowns and hairdos and the interiors of New York apartments. It was only when she was not manipulated by emotion that she could see details and then, liking them, show appreciation, or if not, contemplate changing them. How that confused Morton, who knew her as a room changer, a person who saw the value of odd and questionable things, surprising everybody with their eventual perfect placement somewhere. "So with your eye for detail, how do you miss everything in the movie?" Morton might ask during an intermission.

"So then," Sammy was saying, "the helicopter came this close and . . ."

"Uh huh," she said.

"And that's how they were captured."

There was something missing here. Her mind had wandered so that the plots didn't make sense. "You say this guy was sent to find the POWs but wasn't supposed to?" This was not her first question and Sammy was getting irritated.

"Mom, just go see the movie. Maybe you'll pay more attention," he said, refusing to explain it again.

They had to stop for road construction not far from the top of Flint Creek Pass. A twenty-minute delay, a young sunburned girl told all the drivers headed west.

"You want to eat?" Annie asked Sammy, turning off the engine. The earth and her head were both still all at once, more so after the other motorists down the line turned off their engines too. She could hear the breeze moving though the large pines. They got out of the car and walked down a short, steep incline with their sandwiches and pop and sat down a few feet off the shoulder on a squatty boulder. They could smell pine and now their tuna fish and something else in the thick underbrush—damp grass, fresh water, wild mint. She thought she could hear a stream running somewhere, though she couldn't see one. The tops of the pine below them were so dense they made a dark steep sweep of rich color down to a deep canyon where a faint break in the timber indicated a river or perhaps a road. Each range of mountains before them was backed up by another and another into a fine blue haze of infinity.

"Pretty, huh?" she said.

He nodded. They were both quiet, sort of drugged by the cool breeze and warm sun, by the stillness and a sudden awareness of vast distance and extraordinary beauty and how the many sounds—running water, wind, an occasional snap of twig, maybe a small animal somewhere—combined to create a vacuum of stillness. But more than the quiet was the sense that something for the moment had stopped and lay suspended in some great time warp.

"Hey," she said, handing Sammy the map when they were back in the car. "How about if we drop down 395 after Spokane, pick up I-84 and go straight to Portland?"

"We'll miss Seattle," he said.

"Your decision," she said. They had agreed to take turns.

"I'll think about it," he said.

Annie slowed down. She liked driving fast but she no longer felt in a hurry. The sun was low in the sky, still bright and pinkish, reflecting on something that appeared silver along the sides of the road, like old unmelted snow pack.

"It's ash. Look, ash," Sammy said.

"It can't be."

"From Mt. St. Helens," he said.

"But that was several years ago."

"Clifford's dad says it stays around for years and years. Improves crops and everything."

"Do you remember that day?" she asked him.

"We were barbecuing."

And she and Morton were arguing heatedly about something—she didn't recall what, only that it interested Morton more than a volcanic eruption. He'd continued to argue even when, without warning, thick gray-white stuff started filling the sky, covering the newly blossomed lilacs and freshly painted fence. They brought in the food, Morton still at her, and in no time they were unable to see either the barbecue or the house across the alley. To Morton's disgust she got out the car and drove to her parents—a very stupid thing to do and hard on the motor, he said. It wasn't that she wanted to end the argument particularly or was worried about her folks. It was just this need to be out in it, though there was no visibility whatsoever. It was like a storm had struck, and she was sneaking out of bed like she had as a child, eager for the first snow of a moonlit night, when all the earth altered. And thus transformed, demanded to be seen from a new perspective. But Mt. St. Helens erupting as far as her backyard was not quite like that. It was more disquieting than that. It made her consider for the first time that the earth itself was a living thing, not just a series of rocks that held things up, or lake or ocean beds or the dirt that held groundwater and allowed things to grow. No, the earth was not just some handy thing that supported life, it was an organism itself, that boiled and moved and changed and had its say. Its inhabitants could pollute it all they cared to, rob it, scorn it, disdain it, but the earth, when all was said and done, would have the last word.

"What did you decide?" she asked Sammy.

"Seattle," he said, sleepily.

What did it matter? It was just that this trip was too much like one she'd made years before. Even the road construction seemed the same. Only on that trip, she hadn't left Morton, she'd left his brother, Paul.

If Annie were to make a graph of her life, some instructive analysis of events, decisions and errors made, she would start with her years at Jake's. Next to those, she'd put the three years in Missoula with Paul, pointing out highs and lows in the extreme.

The low she would chart first was the first time he didn't come home. Four days later he still hadn't and she withdrew a little cash, put gas in her car and went home to Butte to visit her folks. She was not in a good mood when she got there. She didn't enjoy these visits much, especially since she had to lie about living with Paul. Cohabitation was not an accepted thing then, at least not by her parents.

"You'll be here for Fern's birthday party Friday night, won't you?" her father said.

"No, I can only stay two days. I have to get back to work," she said.

"I thought maybe you'd bring your roommate. Pauline, or whatever her name is," her mother said suspiciously.

"She had to work," Annie lied.

"Does Paula, or whatever her name is, still work at the café too?" her father wanted to know.

"No, now she works at another place."

"I thought she was going to college," her mother said. She was listening from the kitchen.

"School's out for the summer," Annie said. At some invisible point, the lies she had told had begun to have substance.

"Some people go summers," her mother said, bringing her father a beer. "Calvin's boy Mark is going to summer school."

"Well, not Paula," Annie said and headed for her room.

Once when her folks had visited, she had made Paul go stay with a friend. Then she shoved everything of his into the closet so it looked like only girls lived there. Luckily, at the time, the apartment she and Paul had was too small to accommodate overnight guests or Elsa and Nicholas would have wanted to stay.

"Where's your roommate?" her father had asked.

"On a date," Annie said. "But maybe she'll get home before you have to go." They had a room in a motel nearby.

"I'm going to be in bed by ten," her father said. "Is she going to get home before then?"

"Probably not," Annie said.

"I didn't think so," he said.

. . .

The whole time Annie was at her parents' she'd wondered where Paul was and whether he'd ever gotten home. When Paul had first moved to Montana, he'd made friends with someone named Joannie. Annie didn't really know what their relationship was—just friends, occasional lovers, former lovers or friends with a strong desire to be lovers. "We are just friends," was all Paul would say. Annie was half-expecting Joannie to be there in her place when she got home. Two days later she headed back to Missoula to find out.

When she pulled up to the curb Paul and his brother Morton were sitting on the porch in the dark.

"Hey, nice to meet you," Morton said, looking at her with interest. When she thought about it now, Morton had liked her best of all when she was attached to Paul.

"I can explain everything," Paul said cheerfully as they made a late supper a few hours later. He was frying ham and eggs at the stove. "She was good-looking, intelligent, and had a great body."

"However?" Annie said, thinking of her own body, which was a little overweight.

"She wasn't any fun. You," he said, reaching for Annie, "you are fun."

"No, tell me really." She handed a plate of toast to Morton, who was sitting at the table. "How come you disappeared like that?"

Now he grew serious. "I don't have to explain anything to you. You're not my mother."

Morton had looked up at her sympathetically. She was quiet then, embarrassed because a third person was there. She did not bring it up again, not ever, but it was always there between them. She could still see her feelings of that summer, like stops on a bus tour—hope at one juncture, longing at another, even certainty that things would work.

Like they had the two summers before, Annie and Paul spent every chance they got fishing or rafting, with a cooler of beer and sandwiches, usually on the Blackfoot River far above where it entered the Clark Fork.

Paul had a passion for fishing, and Annie, one for that river. They both knew its banks and pools, its tree-shrouded beaches and the best places to camp. Too lazy to backpack, they took Paul's van. They made a bed in the back of it on two old cushions. So now, when Morton came along, they threw in a ragged pup tent too. He'd bring Scotch, real glasses and a cooler of ice. They tied the raft on top of the jeep and either Paul or Morton drove slowly in fear of losing it.

In June the river would be high from spring runoff and full of sediment and debris. By August, it would be shallow and in places they'd be forced to get out of the raft and carry it over the rocks. But that first time out each summer was always the best, Annie thought. Typically, they loaded the raft with fishing gear, paddles, life jackets, sweaters, suntan lotion. When everything was organized, she'd get in and Paul would push off from shore. Once on their way, he'd sit back satisfied, open a beer for her and play with the rim of an old straw hat he liked to wear. "Nice, huh?" he always said, tipping the hat to the river, which was perfect or imperfect that day, it didn't matter to him.

When they were through rafting and had found a place to camp, Paul or Morton would walk to the highway and hitch a ride back to the van while she got things ready for dinner. There was always something basic and promising about cleaning the fish, gathering the firewood, digging out the cooking gear. The sun at that time of day softened and a slight chill from the woods cooled the riverbank. Later Paul cooked and they sipped the Scotch, watching the sun go down and maybe the moon come up over the water.

The times Morton came along, there were usually discussions after dinner that went on long after Annie's participation in them. She'd crawl into bed dog-tired and listen to the night. She felt comforted by the glow of embers in dark woods, the flow of the river, a slight breeze through the trees, and she'd hear their voices like visible things, rather like strings and clots, clusters of jewels, the small words no less precious than the larger ones, like connections to some golden chain. Those words recalled and polished past good times and suggested more in the future; they considered everything—a year in Australia, homesteading in Alaska, the proper way to build log cabins. But sometimes the words arrested her, awakened her, kept her alert: "You have to search alone for life's meaning"; "Ties are distractions"; "When a relationship gets in the way, it's time to end it." (Was that really what Paul used to say or just how she remembered it now?) Nevertheless, his humorless insistence that he not get too involved always chilled her. Those words, or some like them, repeated themselves in her head long after the embers were cold and Paul slept, repeated themselves in the creaking of the trees, the low howl of wind over water—when a relationship gets in the way, gets in the way, gets in the way . . .

Mornings were pretty much alike, the air fresh with pine and the smell of river, cut at a certain point by the aroma of coffee brewing. They loved to wrap up in blankets and sit in any spot of sun coming through the trees to wait for the first cup, too lazy to move until then. After breakfast, they drove back to town. Paul usually dropped her and Morton at the house and went on to the garage where he worked.

One morning that summer there was a bill in the mail from a florist. She couldn't help looking at it after Paul opened it and threw it into a pile on the desk. It was for roses sent during the time he'd been gone.

When Paul came home from work that night, he was riding a motorcycle, trying it out, he said.

"What's the matter?" he asked.

"You sent someone roses. You've never sent me flowers, let alone roses."

"It was Joannie's birthday and I had to get her something. Come on, don't be mad. If you want, I'll send you roses."

"Never mind," she said, wounded. "It wouldn't be the same now."

"C'mon," he said. "I want to take you for a ride."

That ride was the first of many they took on that beat-up Harley, not only to cool off hot evenings but as something to do that couldn't include Morton. That night they rode out to a little tavern in Frenchtown and then to another one in Alberton to play pinball and pool.

"Forget the roses, will you?" Paul said, putting down his pool cue to dance. They circled the pool table to the music, a conciliatory measure as Paul hated to dance.

"Okay, all's forgotten," she said after a reasonable delay.

Then they sat at the bar and ordered a sandwich. The best sandwiches in those days were grilled at that roadhouse by a bartender named Al who wore a butcher apron, which he used like a towel—to dry a glass, shine the bar or to wipe his hands. It didn't matter, she told herself as she watched Al throw pickles on their buns. Joannie's roses were dead by now but Annie had Paul. That night she got drunk.

There had never been a summer since quite so green in Annie's mind, or so eventful. Though they never discussed it, she and Morton, in silent agreement over the years, had given up doing the things they had done with Paul: rafting, camping, gardening. But that summer all three of them had worked to keep up a small garden and watered it in the twilight and were surprised when things grew. Like the surprise she had felt as a child upon seeing that the stuff in the oven, stuff she had thrown together in a bowl not an hour before, had now become cake. That first garden was like that. Not an act of faith so much as one of absurdity, when she thought about it, to bury seeds in the hope the product of their imagined development would one day grace a plate.

And Morton, to all appearances, was staying for good. "When's Morton going to get his own place?" Paul would say to her but as far as she knew, only to her. Paul did not talk to Morton as he did to her. The two of them, Annie and Paul, talked everywhere, at the grocery store, sitting on the front steps after Morton went to bed, lying in the hassock between the large maples. They discussed their parents and psychoanalyzed their childhoods. Paul thought growing up in a tavern sounded, well, sort of interesting. He thought it was why he could never beat her at pool or poker—two skills she'd picked up at Jake's. Together, they talked about Vietnam, draft dodgers and ways to protest the war—Paul feared that he would be drafted any day though his feet, he said, were as flat as Morton's. They considered the male-female role in society and the effects of the sixties, women's lib and divorce. They worried over problems; there were hundreds—Morton's, their friends', the country's. They talked about McGovern, good sources of drugs, and going to college. They read Updike and argued about what he really meant, for example, in the ending to *Couples*.

"It's simply an ending, nothing more," Paul said.

"No, he's suggesting that the cycle will be repeated." Those days Annie saw patterns in everything. She could see that the new couple couldn't last, that there would be distractions and considerations greater than their ability or desire to endure them.

By the end of that summer, Annie had accumulated some savings. She made a budget one afternoon, sitting on the bank of the Clark Fork opposite a fisherman trying to help some guy get a kite out of a tree. She still remembered that day clearly: The air was brilliant and blue and the sun like a last sentinel before the autumn rains. In the way she saw things then it looked like roots were being put down and real commitment possible.

When she got home, Morton was opening a bottle of wine.

"Let's watch the news," Paul said, poking wood into the small woodstove in the corner. The three of them sat in front of the television with their drinks, Paul's arm around her, their feet propped upon a common and worn hassock, its plastic pieces only frayed and random connections to the cord that fringed it. After the news, she sat with Morton facing the stove, like it was a window onto something special, and silently planned a future while he read and Paul cooked. Paul was crazy about cooking though she was better at it. He sometimes did strange things to food in her opinion, like adding hash to spaghetti sauce.

"You put hash in the spaghetti sauce?" Morton asked astonished, and got up to peer into the pot. He had finicky eating habits even then.

"Corned beef. You'll like it," Paul assured him, though Morton didn't and made a sandwich.

After dinner she showed Paul her new budget, which included the usual sum for general distribution in the household and an additional larger one.

"What's this?" he said.

"My share for the down payment."

Paul wanted to buy a small house with a garage big enough to tear apart an engine in.

"I don't want your money for that."

"Why not?" she wanted to know.

"Because if we split up, we won't know whose house it is."

She didn't say any more about it and tried to get into a novel. The house felt hot but she was too tired to get up and open a window. Paul and Morton were doing the dishes.

"If relationships are to have meaning, they have to stay open," Paul said to Morton as he meticulously dried a plate.

"Open to what?" Morton asked.

"To possibilities," Paul said.

"What possibilities?" she asked, putting down the novel. Possibility was never defined, never clarified. That word and the way he used it always hung above her like a suspension bridge to something perilous.

"Possibilities for change. Relationships aren't something one can close off." What did he mean? That he wanted an open marriage kind of thing or the convenience of someone always around but without any restrictions? Well, there had to be perimeters, Morton told him. "Perimeters or parameters?" Paul wanted to know. Morton said that it didn't matter, either would do. Was that true? For all these years, she had neglected to look up the exact meaning of those two words.

"It's boundaries that make everything inflexible," Paul said glumly.

"Annie," he asked, "what do you think?" At the time she hadn't enough confidence to donate her own opinion or maybe she hadn't had one.

"It's too warm for a fire," she said, closing down the damper on the stove.

One night several weeks later after an especially bad day at work—the other waitress had walked out right during the lunch rush—she'd come home to an empty house. Soon Morton came in and she started dinner though it was Paul's turn to cook. By 8:00 Paul still wasn't home and by now the rice was mushy so she and

Morton went ahead and ate. After dinner they had a few glasses of wine in front of the woodstove. Morton was quiet, perhaps contemplating the warmth and noise of the fire, oblivious to the fact that the night was in any way momentous. Annie was thoughtful too.

At ten o'clock, Annie looked through Paul's desk for clues. Among coupons for deodorant and laundry tickets and other clutter, she found an envelope with two phone numbers on it. Around midnight, Annie called them both.

The first one was the Eastgate Bar and she hung up. The second number was answered by a girl. "Is Joannie there?" she asked.

"This is Joannie," the voice said.

Annie hung up. She had wanted to dial her back and ask if Paul were there. Instead she shut the windows on the late autumn chill and went to bed.

It might have been that night or one like it when Annie began to consider the mistake she'd made by wasting three years on a relationship that wasn't going to develop. When she'd met Paul she thought she wanted an open relationship too. She had just moved to Missoula after graduating from high school and did not want any more oppressive household rules like the ones Nicholas and Elsa had had at home. Then as time went on, in their circle of friends an open relationship, as it was termed, was expected. It made sense to give the one you loved his freedom. Wouldn't he just chafe and blister under ropes of containment until the bonds eventually broke anyway? No, she decided, true love did not tie down or strangle.

Still, this philosophy did not deter Annie from feeling jealous. Instead of appreciating her own freedom to come and go and using it to some advantage, she fixated on how Paul might be using his. Annie thought she was cognizant at the time, at least in some fashion, of how absorbed she had become by the sleuthing, the possibilities, real or imagined, and her own misery. She became determined to stop.

She would not become like her mother's neurotic friend Julia. Julia had gone on like this, worrying about her boyfriend's fidelity or lack of it, for years. Sometimes when drunk and not morose, Julia told funny stories about her dilemma at Jake's, like the one time she waited up half the night to make sure her lover was soundly sleeping so she could read his mail. Julia got up, found the keys to his locked toolbox and extracted a letter addressed to a woman, a letter she'd had only a glimpse of earlier that day. What had alerted her about this letter, Julia was never sure, as the envelope was the usual one her boyfriend used when he sent out plumbing bills. (That by the way was part of a theory Annie's mother had, about some unheralded ability women have to detect unfaithfulness as it happens. Whether a woman chose to believe what she knew, according to Elsa, was something else entirely.)

So Julia held the envelope over a pot of boiling water to steam it open. Julia was a good storyteller and at this point became comical and quite animated. The envelope became smudged and her face and hands got sweaty and hot. At last Julia thought to hold it with tongs but, as they were awkward, she dropped the letter into the pot. Now she didn't know what to do—type a new envelope, insert a blank paper, seal it and put it into the tool box and let the woman wonder? Or simply destroy the letter and let her lover wonder, hoping he'd conclude he'd already mailed it. As Annie recalled, Julia thought letting the woman wonder was less risky, even though there was a chance the woman might say to Julia's boy-friend, Why did you send me blank paper?—in which case they could both ponder it.

Annie could see herself becoming like Julia and didn't want to.

All September and October of that last year with Paul, Annie felt on the verge of change, waiting for something to happen. Simply waiting, waiting out days and weeks, impatient to get it over with, yet dreading it, fearing irrecoverable loss. Worse than that, she became morbidly thoughtful and critical.

But did he notice? Not that she could tell. And in her worst moments, there he'd be curled in a chair or on the couch with a book, his hair falling over his dark eyes, eyes that for Annie always had a quiet but disturbing appeal. And she'd know he was ab-sorbed in something beyond her.

Sometimes she found herself irritated by both Paul and Morton, provoked into depression by the least thing—a familiar grin, a too-often repeated opinion, the rounding of Paul's shoulder, the merest whine in Morton's voice. It was all it would take to make her sit alone for hours staring at a fly speck on a wall or at a dot on the horizon, catatonic and sullen. Annie didn't want to be either depressed like that or paranoid like Julia.

She decided she had to leave. And she had to do it before she was asked to or before she was deserted. Or before she really did run into Paul in some bar or café with another woman. She had thought she could handle it but she couldn't.

Annie got up then and turned on the lamp beside the bed. She found a piece of paper and wrote, *This open relationship is now closed.*

The next morning Paul had still not come home and Annie loaded her car. She pulled onto a near-empty highway just as the sun hurdled Mt. Sentinel and struck the Clark Fork River. In that light, she headed south.

She traveled for a month across Montana but did not cross a state line. She stayed in dozens of shapeless motels where doors always leaned into the rooms, where odors were all unpleasantly the same, the bedspreads too, and where tiny plug-in coffeepots either didn't work or were missing, the remaining round hot plates extending from the wall suggesting some permanent emptiness.

Then one morning she got up broke, realized she had lost weight and traced that and all the unpleasant odors to the cause— pregnancy—then threw up water, the only thing on her stomach thus far that morning, and headed home. Home this time: Butte, Montana, and Jake's.

She worked at the bar through the Christmas holidays, her mother fussing over her, her father silent and worried. No one *knew* she was pregnant. Everyone suspected it and pretended they didn't. Bubba, or anyone at the bar, jumped up every time she needed a case of beer or bucket of ice from the basement. The old regulars treated her like she carried some fragile treasure and she did.

She hated being there. She hated everyone's anxious mothering. The smell of smoke and spilled beer and dead ashes made her feel faint. But mostly she hated the stories. They made her think she didn't want to bring a child into a world where such things so easily occurred. The same stories that she had hidden in cupboards to hear as a child—she loved them then—were now imposed upon her and she was sick of them. There was the one about someone named Abraham planting dynamite in the Grand Dame Mine during a labor dispute. The dynamite never ignited, but Abraham was beaten and fired. Then there was Chunky Jovanovich who, after three shots of Cabin Still, which was all she would allow him, told how someone, in another labor dispute, let loose railroad cars parked at the top of a hill. They gained momentum as they sped down the tracks and crushed recently arrived boxcars at the bottom as easily as someone might smash aluminum beer cans. Chunky, the only survivor, was just stepping off the last car, on his way home, and was thrown free. Though most of his bones were broken and his face smashed, he lived to collect the workmen's comp due him. It took him three years and all of his savings to do so. That story and the way he drank to kill his pain increased the desolation she was becoming accustomed to. The senseless violence around that strong union town, in almost a century of battles between management and labor, was appalling. Then even laborers fought among themselves at Jake's and there were always disagreements to referee.

"One day when they've gotten everything out of us and that pit that they want, they'll close it down and we'll all die hungry," someone would say.

"Bullshit," another would counter. "They'll never close that thing. The whole town will be in the pit before that happens."

That would start the argument that everyone at the bar would contribute to. Of course, had they not gotten too drunk, too old, or too stoved up to swing at each other, there would have been that too.

Then there were fifty years of romantic intrigues and liaisons to keep track of.

"That boy's father was really John Sullivan but he never knew that, not even the day he died," Fern, Bubba's wife, would tell her. "That boy" was someone who had just died of old age himself. Fern kept neat accounts of the least-known details of everybody's life.

And Bubba depressed her further with the little talks he addressed to her across the bar.

"See," he'd say, showing her a diagram he'd made on a napkin.

"Notches," he said. "Everyone in their life is trying to go up one or more notches at least from where they are. But you can never go down a notch, because you earned that spot no matter how bad you are. Which just means you're not too high up and certainly not progressing a hell of a lot. God forgives all this." When her father overheard, he'd say, "Bubba, your turn to buy a drink." He didn't like people to talk about God at Jake's. A bad omen, he said, meaning he feared what he called a "guilt effect," that is, that some customers might start feeling guilty and go home.

Then one night, who should walk into all this, the only time he ever came to Jake's on his own accord, but Morton. How much like Paul he looked. Not that Annie had ever considered them to look alike before. Sure, there were particulars: the same dark eyes; Morton arched his eyebrows in the same way in emphasis over a point he wanted to make; and there was always something reminiscent of Paul about his chin. But these similarities seemed coincidental. Now, though, he looked like Paul, that is, if she were remembering Paul reliably. For after only this short time, he had become a faded image and, like movie scenes, only strong emotion remained—in this case, confusion.

"My God," she said and hugged Morton. She was delighted to see him. He was fresh gardens, camping fires, clean riverbanks—all that emanated from him at his sudden entrance into the ugly air at Jake's.

"Marry me," he said, like Paul had never existed between them.

So she did. And as luck would have it, they never moved to Spokane as they had planned. Morton opened a furniture store ten blocks east of Jake's.

Then one day, maybe a year or so later, Morton said he'd written to Paul.

"Oh," is all Annie said.

Then a few weeks later Paul wrote back. "So what did he have to say?" she asked Morton after putting Sammy to bed in his crib the night of the morning that the postcard came. "Is he still with the same girl?" she blurted out.

"What girl?"

"Joannie."

"Who?"

"You know, the girl he liked before I left."

"That's why you left Paul? Because you thought he was seeing someone?"

Annie didn't answer.

"My God, and I thought . . ." He didn't finish the sentence and Annie didn't want to hear it now anyway.

So over the years Paul continued to write to Morton, but at the store, as though he'd forgotten the name of Morton's wife and didn't want to embarrass himself by not putting her name on the card too. Morton wrote back immediately, about Sammy, his business and whatever was the particular news of that year.

She read one of Morton's answers to Paul's cards once. "Samuel will start peewee baseball this summer. I sold the Olds and bought a Lincoln. Had a bad winter this year, and the farmers are bitching like hell. The Anaconda Company is laying off but I'm doing okay. Sounds like you really like having your own garage."

All that would have fit on a postcard too, but he preferred to scrawl luxuriously across a piece of stationery and stuff it into an envelope. A close friendship between brothers reduced to small pitiful notes. It was her greatest guilt.

How would she graph all that? Like an obsolete road map, some great and necessary directions had failed her over the years at all the critical intersections of her life.

What she wanted her graph to show her now was how that had happened. She wanted it to gauge even a hairline's difference between forgiveness and masochism, between what had really been fun those years with Paul and what had ceased to be. She wanted it to explain the ratio of self-love and self-protection proper in matters of intimate exchange, what measure to give and what, as a survival factor, to save back. She would like it to assure her that, with the right procedures, the elements of a good life could be as exact as those for gardens or cakes.

"Samuel," she said. "Wake up, we're almost to Missoula."

Sammy looked up at the road. "But we already passed Missoula hours ago!"

"I know," she said. "I turned around."

"What?" he said. "Mom, you're crazy!"

"I know," she said again.

When she'd gotten to the sign on Lookout Pass that said WELCOME TO IDAHO, she panicked. For some reason she could not cross a state line.

Chapter Six

The day Annie left him, Paul fought with Morton. He'd come home before noon to an empty house. He could see Morton from the window out in the yard raking up maple leaves as though it was his tree to clean up after. Paul had gone out finally.

"How long are you staying anyway?" he'd asked irritably.

"I didn't know it was a problem," Morton said just as irritably.

"It's not. I'm just asking. I thought I might take a little trip."

"You just got back from a little trip," Morton said.

"Well I might take another one if it's all right with you."

"Suits me," Morton said.

But Paul hadn't gone anywhere. Instead he stayed right there with Morton in the backyard, drinking what was left of the cold beer, then warm beer with ice, then Morton's Scotch, the two of them dancing around what was most on their minds—that Annie had gone. There were other things on Paul's mind besides that. That Morton had been in the way was one. Who could have a normal relationship with a third person, an older brother no less, always under foot? There was even some old stuff on Paul's mind dating back to their teenage years and even before: Why had Morton sold his Hudson to Willie Pokarny instead of to him? Why had Morton told Cecile Throckmorton that he wasn't home the night she'd come for him in her brother's car? Why didn't Morton tell him that Mother was drunk that time he'd called home to see if the other Cub Scouts could come for a barbecue? And why was he, Paul, the last one in the household to know that their father was dying?

Paul had heard about it from Martha, the housekeeper. He was acting up one day and she'd taken him aside.

"Shame on you for being such a big baby when your father is dying," she said as though he already knew all about it.

He did not believe her but still he tried to behave after that and did not complain about his father's frequent trips to the hospital or doctor. And the housekeeper began whispering messages to him as he passed through the kitchen. Martha was fond of his father, and of him too, and she worked at putting them together.

"Your father needs someone to talk to," she might say, or, "Your father is more important than school today." So he began spending more time with him, strolling around the gardens or sitting with him in the sun.

"Go play," his father would say. "A boy your age should be out playing ball."

"I don't like to play ball," he said once.

"What do you like to do?" his father asked, concerned about a son who was not like the other kids.

"I like to fish." Paul hadn't the slightest notion why he'd said that. It was just the first thing that came to his mind that sounded like what men liked to do.

"Well in that case, I can teach you to fly-fish," his father had said, brightening. "Go into the garage and on the wall over the fuse box you'll see a fishing rod."

After that his father taught him to tie flies and to cast them expertly into the middle of the birdbath or the center of a rose.

The day his father died, Paul had been sitting with him. All of them, his mother too, had been waiting nearby for the death that was now expected. But his mother and Morton left the room for some reason that Paul had forgotten. Paul, sitting in the window seat looking out over the grounds, heard his father's breathing change. He knew that this was the moment and he went to his father's side and watched as something disappeared from the man. Paul even looked up and around the room to see if he could catch a glimpse of that something that moments before had been breath and days before a voice and weeks before movement and life. He'd looked for it as dispassionately as an unrelated spectator might have, in utter and complete amazement. But that thing took its leave without a trace and by the time Paul looked back to his father's face again, the face had changed. It had gone hard and gray and empty and Paul sat there for some time with the body, feeling a crazy mixture of grief and awe—and shame for having let awe distract him from his grief. Certainly he hadn't seen it that clearly at the time, he had just been the troubled child who now had the onerous duty of informing all the others of the occurrence in the household of death. He chose to find Martha to tell her first.

Paul had wanted to talk about the death, to describe to someone this most mysterious of events but of course no one wanted to hear about it. And he wanted, too, to tell someone how angry he'd been with the doctor, how condescending and impatient this man had been, as though his father's illness was just one more annoyance in his life.

One day the doctor had gotten irritated when his father tried to talk to him.

"I can't understand what he wants," the doctor complained to a maid, who shrugged. But Paul had understood his words perfectly. His father, a meticulous man, was horrified because he couldn't control his bladder or bowels and was too ashamed to tell Martha or any other woman.

"He says he needs his sheets changed," Paul told him, holding back tears.

Paul hated that doctor and after his father died, when the doctor came to sign the death certificate, he let all the air out of the tires of his Cadillac.

But for months after that Paul continued to go over the details of the illness and death in his mind, the frantic periods of worry and dread, the long vigils, the indignities his father suffered with tubes and bedpans and baths. He'd watched helplessly as his father declined and went in and out of consciousness. Paul had prayed for his father as Martha had taught him but at one point he saw that something was radically wrong and that it was not fixable, not by medicine nor, despite Martha's faith, by divine intervention.

Then after the death, the confusion and activity bewildered him. People swept in and out of the house, the hospital equipment disappeared, the body was sent away, and funeral arrangements were made. Food and flowers appeared repeatedly at the front and back doors and old people were always in the garden where he wanted to go but couldn't, without a big fuss, because of them.

And his wonder and respect for death increased; he wanted to know what it was, yet was terrified of finding out. He felt alone and unimportant to anyone. And several times he dreamed the same thing—that he was on the road out in front of the drive, on his way home. Sometimes he was anxious to get there but not always, in fact he had gone back to where he had come from several times and had even taken a few side roads too—but always with home somewhere in mind. Finally he would come to a river, which he knew he must cross to reach the entrance to the driveway. Stripping off his clothes and laying down the few things he had collected in his travels on the riverbank, he'd dive into the water. Sometimes he hurried to cross, sometimes he played, always aware of the fish; and these fish at times regarded him with interest and sometimes did not. Occasionally light would work its way through the thickness of large trees that hung over the river and strike the water. The light blinded him at first, then enabled him to see more clearly. Now and then he tried new strokes, felt his slender, agile body working with the water. Other times he fought the rapids and the current, trying hard not to be carried downstream. He even gave up a few times and let himself go until the rapids reached deeper, still water where he could swim once again. And finally he'd reach the other side where the fish, curiously, watched him climb out. There on the opposite bank he would rest before going on. Then before he'd start off again, he'd wake, puzzled and exhausted from all that swimming.

He finally told the dream to Martha. "Think about the fish," she told him. "They see you get in the water and they see you get out. To them that is all there is of your existence, that short time with them in the water. They don't know you came from somewhere and you're on your way somewhere else. Do you see now?"

And because she wanted so badly for him to understand and he didn't want to disappoint her, he said yes and went away even more puzzled. She said more things about a soul and he'd gone out into the garden to think. Where was his soul? If he had one, wouldn't he be able to feel it or talk to it? And for several days he tried. He got as still as he could and tried to make contact with it. But if his soul was ignoring him, the gardener wasn't.

"What are you doing there, boy? Can't you see I just reseeded that lawn?"

"Sorry," Paul said.

"I don't understand it. Acres of house and grounds to run around in and you damn kids have to get into the four square feet I'm working on."

Paul gave it up then, deciding that Martha had been mistaken and that not everybody had one of these souls she talked about.

Then and now, Paul had no memory of Morton being anywhere around. It was as though he alone had had a father who died. Sometimes he wanted to ask him—Morton, where in the hell were you? But the day Annie left, no mention was made of their father's death or anything else. Instead he and Morton had argued about whose turn it was to go to the store and Morton had said he'd gone last.

"But you're the big brother so it must be your turn again. Big boys always get all the turns," Paul told him.

"Always the spoiled little turd who can't do anything for himself," Morton said, dropping with Paul to the same level of immaturity.

As they had never done as children, suddenly they were at each other's throats, down on the ground, wrestling drunkenly. When Paul broke free he struck Morton on the jaw. "Mama's boy!" he shouted.

Morton struck him back. "You big baby," he shouted. "Running off as soon as the money's gone."

They had continued to fight but only halfheartedly.

The money was all gone? Paul had always thought that there was plenty of it and that Morton had access to it. He didn't remember how the fight ended, only that Morton left and that there was a familiar bend to his back as he strode across the front yard. Morton's attempt to look menacing only looked sad. Very sad, like their father had looked. Then Morton had gotten into his car and driven off. Paul, thinking he'd be back in an hour or so, had gone in to shower.

He'd stood under the water for some time then, still thinking about what Morton had said about the money, about it being gone. When Paul had left Chicago, it was partly because he hadn't wanted anything to do with the family business. He had left, a failure in everyone's eyes, with no direction, showing no promise. But it had nothing to do with money, except that in thinking there was plenty of it, he'd felt free to leave. Had he known otherwise, he might have felt obligated to stay.

At the time he knew that he wanted to work with his hands, to live in the West, to not have a maid or housekeeper around every time he turned around. He wanted a small house where he could hear everything going on within it, not some museum where anything could be happening at the far end. He wanted to be free from his mother's moods and his brother's watchful eye. He'd known this long before he actually left. But then one night he had come home drunk with a friend. They had gone to the kitchen and were scrambling eggs, singing something they had brought from the bar—*Jesus puts his money in the First National Bank, Jesus saves, Jesus saves.* At that moment Martha came in. She was indignant.

"Shame on you, Paul Arthur, making fun of the Lord." And she threw them out of the house and their eggs too.

"Martha, I didn't mean to offend you," he was saying when the frying pan came flying out the door. He laughed then and took it as an omen. It was time to go. He stayed at his friend's that night and left the next day.

Paul got out of the shower intending to apologize to Morton as soon as he returned. He planned to talk it all out and to see if Morton needed some money. But Morton never returned. And Annie never returned either. Like Father, neither one had ever come back.

Part Two

MISSOULA

Chapter Seven

That first night in Missoula Annie and Sammy stayed in a hotel downtown.

"This place is crummy," Sammy said.

It was. It was old, not elegantly old but old and patched up, barely held together, like the old men who lived there, who walked tentatively down the hallways holding onto walls and who coughed in the elevator and through adjoining rooms. But it was cheap and had a parking lot across the street and a view of the river if you leaned out the window just right.

"You can hear the train whistle," she told him.

He didn't seem to think of that as any sort of compensation for what he liked, slick and polished Holiday Inns. In the morning, thinking to cheer him up, she led him a few blocks toward the river in search of a place to eat breakfast. They stopped for a minute and watched strollers walking across a foot bridge to the university. She guessed that the foreignness of fog and water or the angle of the old bridge with its pitch and creosote-darkened beams low over the riverbank did not excite Sammy as they did her. Rather it made him uneasy, maybe afraid. She should have taken him to some homogeneous shopping center, where in its typical anonymous gaiety he would feel safe, secure. Odd, but that was what she thought Sammy felt in such places.

It was a sunny morning, gently warm, and the river fog was lifting. Sammy appeared happier than he had the night before. They walked a block or so along the bank, not far from a woman who pulled a box behind her full of what looked like clothes or bedding. Annie watched her take a pint of something, maybe gin or vodka, from a corner of the box and slip it into a deep pocket in her long skirt. Was she old or not? It was hard to tell, as she was dressed entirely in gray, heavy loose gray clothes, except for a bright yellow scarf around her head that had the effect of washing out all color in her face and eyes, so that they disappeared into the clay gray of her bulky sweater. What had reduced this woman to stony grayness and one battered box? Annie shuddered.

They bought cinnamon rolls, coffee and juice from a bakery and took them outside to a patio where sunlight broke through the trees in varying arrangements of light and shadow against the bricks. It was very quiet there and they watched as an old man rolled up a bedroll from a park bench, whistling as he did.

Why was he so happy? Annie wanted to run after the raggedy figure moving down the street, whistling still, and ask.

"Mom," Sammy said. "This place is full of bums."

"But isn't it beautiful?"

"They should tear it all down," he said. "Can we go now?"

They walked back to the car and drove across the Orange Street Bridge to a residential neighborhood of older houses with porches and thick shrubs and maples and weeping willows that all glistened from the early morning dew.

"Let's live here," Sammy said, relieved to find something familiar-looking.

Annie found a gas station and got directions to a motel—one Sammy consented to after first looking around the room and sniffing the air. The hotel, he said, had smelled funny and from now on he would check any place first. Later they bought a newspaper and map and boxed chicken and sat on the bed in the motel, watching television and reading all the FOR RENT and HELP WANTED ads. Shouldn't she get a place first, settle them and then look for a job?

Finding a place to rent was not easy. They rode around for hours at a time, arguing over directions and how to read a map. Sammy thought only the male brain could handle the complexities of a map. They looked at all kinds of houses and apartments before they found one she thought she could afford, in a neighborhood that would do for schools and that didn't give Sammy the creeps. The house they finally agreed on was a bungalow with two bedrooms, a living room and a dining room. It had built-in bookshelves and a fireplace. She thought it was rather charming. He said it was too old. "Why can't we just get a new mobile home if you like woodwork so much?" he asked. He didn't mind that kind of panelling, he said.

She hadn't realized before that her son had developed such definite opinions about what felt good or not in his surroundings. When had it happened? He was stubborn about the smallest things he'd never before noticed.

"Mom," he said one day not long after they had moved in. "You're not going to put those ugly, old jars on the counter, are you?"

She'd found some lead glass jars in an antique store and had filled the large ones with beans and macaroni and brown rice, and the smaller with fresh bulk spices and herbs from a health food store. He finally bargained with her. He'd tolerate the jars and the primitive pine desk and the art deco-era sofa she'd found at a garage sale if he could cover the oak floors in his room with carpet and have the brown, black and white, large-checked pillow furniture he saw at another garage sale. In her opinion, Sammy, definitely, had lousy taste.

They began going to all the garage sales. The town was full of them. They didn't bother to read the ads, had only to drive in any direction and watch for garage sale, patio sale, yard sale and estate sale signs that were tacked on light poles at some intersections. She didn't know one place could be so full of buyers and sellers and by the time school started they had furnished the entire house with low-cost items, compromising as best they could their likes and dislikes.

The neighborhood, thank God, was full of kids and Annie would come home from job-hunting to yards littered with ten-speeds and basketballs, her own porch messy with pop bottles and potato chips. Sammy joined a soccer team, got a paper route and looked forward, she hoped, to starting sixth grade at a nearby school.

Finding a job was much harder than finding a home. Early every morning Annie put on her one good suit and, leaving Sammy in front of the television, went out to look for work. She applied for anything she thought she could do, until finally when her blouse began to drip with perspiration and her hair fell limp in the heat, she gave up for the day. She'd return home, put on shorts, depressed now, and sit in the backyard on a rusty chaise lounge she'd got at an auction for fifty cents. After days of this, Annie was ready to panic. She'd applied at dozens of restaurants, grocery stores and retail shops, even at a dentist's office.

"This is a college town, dear," the woman at the employment office told her. "No one hires until the students return and then they take a lot of the jobs."

Annie had even gone to a department store and applied for a job titled Interior Decorator Assistant. But a specialist was wanted, a certain degree, a portfolio and experience. God only knew all the experience she'd had, trial and error all the way, beginning with the first time she had painted Sammy's room when he was a toddler. First she'd bought fabric for his window, a splashy and colorful print full of large, purple, rounded shapes—elephants, tigers and dancing bears—on a turquoise background. Then with a sample of this material, she'd gone to the paint store and had paint mixed that matched the turquoise exactly. It was an expensive enamel, guaranteed for wear and washability. It would take the harsh abuse of toddlers with crayons and wagons and dirty fingers. And she painted the woodwork and closet doors and window frames and then did the walls in a soft, pale yellow. But the yellow turned mustard and made the room look like it was collapsing under shiny, crooked angles in a nasty shade of green. And at the falling windows, garish and psychedelic animals, in screaming tones of their former manageable hues, now tried to enter, maybe to attack. Sammy, coming into his room to this, began to cry.

She'd rushed back to the store and bought a safe white, ignoring for the third day the laundry, housework and meals. But when she'd tried to apply it over the special enamel, the new paint smeared and wouldn't dry even after another twenty-four hours. Meanwhile, she had to keep Morton out of the room while she ran fans to dry the paint. It took another week of surreptitious applications until, after the fourth coat of white paint, there was no trace of the yellow and just a shadow of turquoise on the woodwork. She threw the fabric away and bought curtains already made of a conservative blue-and-white pinstripe that reminded her of the shirts Morton wore. Morton raved and Sammy calmly spread his toys around and played quietly until nap time.

But Annie kept at it over the years even though, at first, silence was the usual reaction to her work. Sometimes she saw the slight arch of an eyebrow or a rapid series of blinks. No one ever appreciated the lengths she had gone to, the suffering she put herself through in these strenuous acts of creation. Then she improved, even became good.

Morton, however, never saw it that way. She suggested to Morton that he create rooms at the store to show people how the furniture might look in their homes. But Morton liked things grouped in neat rows. So if someone liked a table, for instance, they had to search for matching chairs over in another area where chairs were lined up or stacked. It was a lot of work to shop at Morton's store, she thought.

In any case, like Morton, the department store did not think her qualified to decorate anything. So Annie continued to job-hunt. Finally one day, after putting on her freshly aired suit and clean blouse, she took one look in the mirror, a clear look, and collapsed on the bed with sudden knowledge about herself—that she was too old to start over, that she would never be younger, smarter, more adaptable or even slimmer. The latter made her cry; it somehow was a more important realization than all the rest. She was on her way down, headed for an unknown place of failure and despair. It was what had happened to that gray bag lady by the river, she knew it. Annie would have to send Sammy to Morton and find a box.

After she had finally quit crying she got up from the bed and took off her now-rumpled clothes and put on shorts. She went out into the backyard and pulled weeds from the beds of wild roses until she was exhausted.

The soft earth comforted her in a way nothing else could, though her fingernails were grimy, her hands scratched and bleeding from violent tugging and digging at deep-rooted thistles. If nothing turned up soon, she decided, she would find a job in a bar. For that, at least, she was qualified.

The next morning she went back to the department store.

"Have you filled that assistant display position yet?" she asked the man in personnel.

"Not yet."

"Hire me until you find someone qualified."

He stared at her, undecided. "I'll start you out in housewares," he said. "Sales."

So she agreed reluctantly to the low salary and went home and took Sammy out for pizza to celebrate.

When Annie wasn't busy with customers, she arranged little displays, borrowing things from other departments to set off what she wanted to sell. From one end of the store to the other she borrowed and signed for bright towels, sheets, baskets, mirrors, lamps, plants, furniture. She got young kids from the stockroom to lug the heavier things and the manager, Mr. Perry, grumbled but seemed pleased with the results. She even brought in garage sale purchases from home. Once she took an old mahogany chest—in beautiful shape—and filled it with towels of soft shades of ivory, navy blue and burgundy, which—spilling onto the ivory flokati rug beneath it—brought out the deep cherry of the mahogany. She put navy blue baby's breath beside it and a cheval mirror behind it. Another time she brought in a small antique store case with little drawers. She placed it and a small stained-glass lamp—a reproduction from decorative accessories—on top of an old Great Falls Select Brewery box. Then she added brilliantly patterned scarves the colors of the glass in the lamp—browns, greens, violets, tans, black—various shades of each, "much nicer than it sounds," she told Sammy, and arranged and displayed wineglasses. "It may sound gross to you but it looks good," she told him when he laughed.

"People will steal the stuff," Mr. Perry complained—she hadn't considered that. "But it looks nice," he said.

But everyone wanted to buy the old things she brought in, so after a week or so on display, she took them home. She bought *Decorating Today* and *Home Arts* and copied the rooms they featured.

Soon she started helping out, unasked, in the furniture department. She kept the salesmen busy making groupings for her. She begged for carpeting and area rugs and the chance to choose the colors and accessories and insisted that people didn't want couches and beds balanced with matching lamp tables anymore, that a room could be enhanced by a variety of periods and asymmetrical compositions. The only reason she got away with all this was that the store's interior decorator, Bernard, was overworked, underpaid and often out of the store on consultations. Then, too, several romantic affairs kept him too busy to worry about her. "Just don't embarrass me with something tasteless," he said. "Or I'll have you fired."

Finally she was actually placed permanently in furniture but, unfortunately, the job still didn't pay well. Her salary and the child support payments Morton sent on the first of each month did not quite cover rent, car repair, utilities, phone bills, Sammy's braces, parking downtown and the price—even with her discount—of the nice clothes she had to wear to work. She constantly took money out of her savings, then worried for days after each withdrawal.

She decided to buy a good camera and start putting together her own portfolio. But it took her a long time before she could take pictures that satisfied her, though she spent hours each night studying the finer points of light meters, f-stops, shutter speeds and film. Still the lighting was often dark or glaring, the photo would be grainy or slightly out of focus—did she need glasses too? She was finally able to get one out of ten the way she wanted and she taught herself to mat them on top of a large light table in the advertising department after hours.

Sammy said he liked school but he wasn't doing as well as he should have been, according to his teachers. He was somewhat of a class clown, is how they put it. That shocked her. As far as she could tell, he was usually humorless, too serious. "He's so quiet," she told them. They might have been discussing two completely different sixth-graders. Well, parents don't always know their kids as well as they should, is what they said.

"You're divorced, right?" a balding gym teacher asked her. "You're probably not home much," he said.

Annie felt suddenly that charges were being made and she was at once guilty and defensive.

"Maybe you don't have time to fix breakfast," another said, this one a handsome woman of fifty.

"We have breakfast together every day," Annie explained.

"Of course," the woman said doubtfully. "But Sammy always eats at the free breakfast program."

"Breakfast program?" She'd never heard of such a thing.

"Yes, but we don't check incomes," the teacher—English and language arts—said, too kindly. "We'd rather just make sure hungry children eat." And Annie had thought teachers were suppose to be intimidated by parents—she'd read that somewhere. She left the parent-teacher conferences wearily.

"Why do you goof off like that?" she asked Sammy when she got home.

"Well," he said. He took a full minute to think. "I get more attention." What could she say to a straightforward admission like that?

"Find a better way," she said, too tired to fight with him.

"Wait a minute," she said. He was leaving the kitchen. "Why do you eat a second breakfast?"

"Everyone does," he said.

"Damn it, Sammy. Leave the food for the really poor kids."

She had other problems with Sammy. One day the patient man who supervised all the paper boys called. He sounded tired.

"You say no one got their paper this afternoon?" she asked. "He should be home any minute, I'll call you back," she promised.

Now she was worried. Had something happened to him like that poor boy in Des Moines she'd read about who mysteriously disappeared one early morning from his route? By the time Sammy did get home, two hours later, she was frantic and angry.

His explanation: Bobby Somebody said he'd help him, but then Bobby said he had to go, and Sammy should come with him. Besides he was sick and tired of delivering papers anyway. So he dumped them in the garbage and went with Bobby but Bobby lived a lot farther away than he'd thought.

"Go get the papers," she said. "You're going to deliver them now."

"But it's dark."

"I'll drive you," she said.

It turned out Sammy had to pay for twelve garbage-damaged papers and for the replacements seventeen customers had gone to the store and bought. The patient newsboy supervisor went over everything with them on a note pad in his little office on Higgins Avenue the next day. He fired Sammy—he seemed used to doing it—and she made Sammy take money out of his savings to pay for the papers. Sammy seemed relieved.

He did other things that surprised her too. Once he called her at the store and said a dog had followed him home and could he keep it? She said, No, it was in the lease—no pets.

"Find out who owns the dog," she said. "Someone will be worried."

She had to work late, she told him, but there was food in the refrigerator.

When she got home there was a note on the kitchen table. "I'm in bed. My dog is on the back step. His name is Pal. I love you, Sammy."

She went to the back door and opened it to a large ragged-looking German shepherd dog asleep on her antique Oriental throw rug. She sighed. Did this mean Sammy was still just a kid after all? The next few weeks Pal dug up the yard, chewed up shoes and table legs and filled the house with old bones, carcasses of long-dead birds and unidentified odds and ends.

Chapter Eight

"Hey, Paulo," his foreman said. "How about this weather?" He stamped the snow from his feet and shook off his parka. "I couldn't see three feet out there."

Paul nodded. He'd had trouble himself and noticed that the truck stop was full. Drivers were staying off the road until either it quit snowing or the wind quit blowing it around. It was early in the year for this kind of weather and no one was prepared. Paul had never seen a ground blizzard this bad, not even in the Midwest where there was nothing to block the wind.

He wondered how many would make it in to work but it didn't matter, the work could wait. No one was going anywhere today. Now someone else came in, admitting a bitterly cold gust of air. Paul shivered. He couldn't seem to warm up this morning. Even the garage, which was usually a little too warm, felt chilly. It was a large building that reminded people of an airline hangar; it could hold up to four complete rigs at a time and usually did. And there were ten work stations for tractors alone.

"You must be some mechanic," a girlfriend had said once, looking in at all the trucks. Actually he wasn't that good at all, especially with diesels. What he was good at was finding men who were. And he did that by hanging out where mechanics drank and listening to them. Because like any other craftsmen, good machinists knew and admired the best of their kind. Paul guessed that the more they admired someone good, the better they were themselves. Lousy mechanics did not know their own limitations. They blamed any failure on the engine, the parts, the driver or what the wife had laid on them that morning.

But finding them wasn't all there was to it, he had to make sure that they stuck around. And he didn't do that by pulling any *I am the boss* crap on them or by trying to save money on their salary or benefits. He paid them so well they couldn't afford to leave or not be good. He didn't interfere with their little rituals around the garage like their lavish betting, their playful comradery, their constant jokes. He let them hang up all the nude calendars they wished to, though a few visiting wives complained and the secretary didn't think too much of them. But the guys always knew to put the most outrageous of these in the men's toilet—a grimy place that even after the janitor left showed the wear and tear of oil and grease.

Paul was proud of his crew. Sometimes he would come into the garage to a lull in the overall din of men and motors. And he'd wonder where everyone was and then discover that his men were simply silent and absorbed by the various tasks at hand—thinking, like the geniuses he knew good machinists to be. They were creative, sensitive and intuitive. They respected the machines they worked on, could tune into them, perhaps they even loved them. If a mechanic ever demonstrated impatience or played loud music while he worked, Paul got rid of him. There was nothing worse than a stupid mechanic. They were the ruin of anything they touched.

The garage had taken up most of his time since he opened it, but Paul was thinking of expanding it to include heavy equipment like cranes and road tractors. At present it was an operation that catered mainly to semis as Missoula had become a large port for trucking over the years. He'd seen that the day he'd broken down near a truck stop west of town on I-90. While waiting for a tow, he'd seen more trucks all in one spot than he'd seen the whole trip west. He and his friend Max had driven out of Chicago on a cold spring day, headed for the coast. They drove through Iowa to the

Missouri River. Because Max wanted to see Mt. Rushmore, they'd detoured north instead of crossing the river into Nebraska. They spent a couple days in South Dakota and took I-90 into Montana, through Billings, Bozeman, Butte and Missoula. It was impressive to come off the plains into suddenly awesome landscape, to drive into higher elevations of passes, forests and peaks. The Rocky Mountains. Paul had never seen anything like them. And when he got to Hell Gate Canyon outside of Missoula, a narrow corridor between densely forested mountains still capped with snow, he pulled off onto the shoulder and got out.

"What's wrong?" Max said. Stopping had awakened him and he'd opened the back door of the van.

"Nothing," Paul said.

"Well then, on to the coast," Max said in jest, perhaps sensing that something unplanned was about to happen.

And it did, just a few miles west of Missoula. Much to their annoyance, the van's engine blew up. They pushed it into the truck stop and agreed there, outside of the men's can, to part company. Max climbed into a semi with a trucker they had been talking to and Paul went to call for a tow. In the café where he waited, he watched the large trucks coming and going. What a town, he thought. Someday he'd open a garage right there just for diesels.

By the time he had all the parts he needed to rebuild the engine in the van, he also had an apartment and a job. It was only a short time after that that he met Annie. She said it was destiny—the way they both came to Missoula from somewhere else in time to meet at the Top Hat Bar that first weekend in town for both of them. He said there were probably five hundred other newcomers in town that same weekend.

"Maybe," she'd said. "So how many of them did you meet?" That was so typical of Annie—to think, because he had not answered that silly question, that he, therefore, had agreed to the probability that, first of all, there was such a thing as fate and, too, that they might have one in common. The only thing he'd wanted in common with this odd girl that night was a bed.

But she had grown on him and soon the two of them were embroiled in this full-blown relationship. And by the time she walked out on him, he didn't know what to think. At first he thought he was glad. Then, after a few months, he became determined to find her.

He began the search in Butte, looking for Jake's. He had no address and just began driving around the downtown area, up one street and down another, until he found it. Jake's was old even then, but solid. He could see that driving by. He'd parked and walked down the street amazed at the view of mountains available because a building on the block across the street had evidently burned down recently. There were still piles of rubble and half-burned timbers on the blackened foundation.

The entrance to Jake's, he recalled, had sunken slightly and for some reason he'd measured the depth of the doorway with his hand. He figured it was about eight inches, a funny thing to remember after all these years. It was dark in Jake's after driving in the bright sun and it felt cool there. He'd stood in the entrance and looked around, expecting to see Annie sitting at the bar waiting for him—that's how foolish the whole trip had been. A nightmare.

There was a seat at the bar and he sat down between two old men. The one on his left appeared to be sleeping and his head was on his arms on the bar. An old blue cap covered his head. Paul ordered a beer and asked the bartender if he was the owner.

"No, but he'll be back pretty soon," he said and wiped the bar, his rag skirting around the blue-capped head on Paul's left.

"You want to see Nicholas?" the man on his right asked.

"Yes," he'd said. The man waited for more.

"I know some people he knows here in town," Paul said finally. Some people hell. He knew Annie.

"So you're not from Butte?" the man asked next.

"No," he said. How the conversation had gotten so personal, Paul didn't know. But soon enough he was telling this old guy how he'd lost his girl and that now he was going to find her and take her home if she'd still have him and so on. Of course, he didn't mention any names. The man had listened, saying little while Paul drank several more ice-cold beers.

"So what do you think my chances are?" Paul said.

"Depends," he said.

"On what?"

"Maybe your girl has another life by now."

95

"In a few short months, I doubt it."

The old man shrugged.

"Nah, she wouldn't have had time."

The man said nothing more and Paul nodded to the bartender to get them another round. "Not for me," the old man said and got up. "I'm on my way home."

Then, not long after the old man had gone, Nicholas came in. Paul didn't know it was Nicholas but he guessed it had to be, the way he slammed things around as only someone who owned the place would dare. No one said anything to him because there was a ball game on the TV over the bar and now everyone was involved in it, though Paul didn't recall if it were baseball, football or what—only that no one cheered or commented as guys usually did in bars around Missoula. They were quiet, brooding, with eyes fixed on the screen, maybe their minds elsewhere.

And Paul had sat there wondering how to ask Nicholas where he could find Annie. Then a woman came in and sat at the end of the bar and most of the men turned their attention to her. She looked a lot like Annie and Paul guessed this woman was Annie's mother. It had felt so strange observing these two people, knowing who they were. And he felt foolish too so he just sat there waiting for some cue perhaps, some indication it was time to step forward. Both of them, maybe everyone there, noticed Paul though. Because, certainly, he stood out here. Annie's mother had even looked at him curiously. But she'd only smiled briefly, concentrating on something she was sewing, needlepoint he thought they called it.

Then a couple came in and stood behind Annie's mother and Nicholas suddenly turned off the TV, which made everyone start at the sudden quiet. Now the woman began a discussion of the recent fire across the street. Paul couldn't quite hear it all. "Arson, my ass!" the man with her said, pointing his finger toward the door. Soon it was quiet again and the man brought a stool over for the woman.

Paul was considering how to introduce himself when the old man with the blue cap sitting to his left suddenly lifted his head from the bar.

"Son, go home now," he said. "Annie's married."

"What!" Paul said in disbelief.

"Go ahead, ask her father," the man said, removing the cap. His hair was thin and cut raggedly as though he had taken scissors to it himself.

And that's how Paul had found out that Annie was married—from an old man with shaggy hair and a blue cap. But hadn't that been what she'd always wanted? What had made him think she'd be waiting around for him? It wasn't until another six months or so that he'd found out that she'd married Morton.

But anyway that day, stunned, he'd finished his beer and gotten up to go when the peculiar old man with the cap next said, "Don't worry, son. I won't tell anyone you were looking for her."

"I don't know what you're talking about," Paul had said. He was flabbergasted. Defensive. Embarrassed. He didn't know what all.

"Certainly not," the man said. "Wouldn't do no good to be looking for anyone in here now."

Paul felt every eye at the bar on him as he stumbled out into the bright sun.

When Paul got home it was to a draft notice. Not long after, he left for Vietnam. That was another thing he never talked about. Not that there was much to say, as he was there only a short time before the war ended, but long enough to see, as everyone said, that war was hell.

He made a friend there, a kid from Texas called Jo Jo. One day everyone was sitting around playing poker. Waiting to be bombed, Paul guessed. And Jo Jo had joined them and, when it was time to ante, he dumped, in lieu of money, a bag full of human ears out onto the ground. Paul had gasped and turned to the other men. But they did not look impressed or even surprised. To his dismay, they looked distant, bored, stoned. And suddenly Paul had understood something he'd never understood before, that there was indeed evil in the world and that evil was not, as he had presumed, residing only in the enemy. The faces of those men bent over those cards were far more chilling than the bombing, the mine fields or any one of the many wounded or killed he had seen in his short time there.

When he thought of Vietnam at all, he thought of the faces of those men bent over those cards, about to win or lose a handful of dollars and some human ears.

To Annie's dismay, Sammy's friend Bobby whatever-his-name—Sammy never seemed able to recall all of it—started showing up at odd hours. Sometimes it was seven in the morning when Sammy was still in the shower or at night after Sammy had gone to bed. Annie was disgusted with herself for not liking this kid, maybe disgusted with him, too, for not being likable, and with Sammy for befriending him. But she honestly did not like Bobby. He reminded her of the men who'd hung around Jake's when she was a kid. Like them, Bobby had a greasy, unwashed look and Bobby shifted his eyes sneakily around any room he was in. Bobby could stay out too late, ride his bike from East Missoula to the west side of Russell after dark, with no one but Annie to register a complaint. Bobby seemed to drift around anywhere, to sense nobody cared, did not care himself. She saw that Sammy felt sorry for him. She did too—she wanted to put the kid in the shower, trim his uneven hair, buy him some clothes and vitamins, adopt him. But he frightened her, the way he used Sammy, his things too, borrowing them, returning them sometimes, sometimes not. When he did, it was with contempt, and they bore the stamp of his abuse, looking like him, ragged and damaged.

Then Sammy went through a period where he stayed quietly in his room every evening and seemed listless. One night she thought his eyes looked, well funny, like he'd just come out of the dark.

"Oh, no," she cried and ran to his room with him not far behind her.

"Mom, you said you would never go into my room!" he protested.

She opened his door. It had varying-size signs on it—STAY OUT! MEN AT WORK, OFF LIMITS, NO TRESPASSING, A MAN'S CASTLE—and they all swung crookedly on the tacks that held them as she went in. She didn't have to look far, she could smell it. She went to the closet and pulled out dirty laundry and an old sleeping bag. Beneath all this was a box full of paraphernalia.

"Where did you get this stuff?" He had tobacco papers, marijuana and a small dirty-looking bong. She hadn't thought about this stuff for years. How dumb was she? She collected all the things and took them to the kitchen, resisting the temptation to sit down and smoke a joint.

"I have no privacy around here!" Sammy yelled before he slammed his door.

Had she been too worried about money lately to notice anything? Where in the world did kids—children—get drugs? And how should she handle it? The terror she felt for him out there in a troubled world was unexpected. She hadn't considered that there were larger worries than making ends meet. Annie hardly slept that night and dragged herself through the next day.

"Just you wait," her mother had warned her. "Someday you'll have a child yourself, you'll see." This was something her mother said in exasperation right before she cried over something Annie had gotten herself into. Annie had been a reckless sort of teenager, not very bad but not especially good either. She had two friends at the time who brought out her worst. Jimmy and Sherman. What were they like now? Sherman, she knew, taught physical-ed and history at the very high school he had routinely gotten thrown out of. And Jimmy, she heard, had been wounded in Vietnam and lived in Texas.

Sherman had liked beer. "Sneak me into the basement"—he meant at Jake's—"and I'll haul a case to the window. Meet me in the alley and I'll lift it up to you guys."

They weren't old enough to drive then and carrying a case of beer around was a logistical problem. They had to lug it in a shopping bag to the park, a very nice park with trees and flowers, where the boys drank two each and Annie drank half of one—he'd grabbed warm beer. It made her feel nauseated. While she spun dizzily on a bench, they argued about the leftovers.

"Count them," Sherman said.

"I don't have to," Jimmy said drunkenly. It was surprising how sloppy you could get on two beers when you were a kid. "Twenty-four minus five is nineteen."

"Seventeen, eighteen, nineteen." It seemed Sherman would count them all night. Ability with arithmetic was not among his strengths.

They dug a hole under a flowerbed and buried eighteen cans of Rainier beer—Sherman had one more. The next morning when they came back for them, there was one lumpy mound and six pansy plants, limp and lifeless. Annie made an effort to save the flowers. She replanted them, patted the earth back into place and hoped for the best.

Sherman stored the beer at his house in the tank of his family's much-used toilet—there were six kids in his family.

"All of the beer at once?" Annie asked. She didn't see how they'd fit. Wouldn't water slosh over onto the floor?

"No, three at a time."

"And the rest?" Jimmy said. "Where do you keep that?"

"In my room."

"You'll get caught," Annie said.

No, he told them. His mother never came into his room. She was too afraid of finding something like porno.

"You have some?" Jimmy wanted to know.

"Not yet," he said. It wasn't easy to find pornography in Butte, Montana, in those days.

So every night for six nights, they each had one can of beer, surprisingly cold from the toilet tank, at the park. The pansies survived.

The second time they tried it, they were caught pulling Sherman from the window.

"What the hell are you kids doing?" It was Bubba. "Why you're stealing beer!" He seemed amazed. "From your own father, Annie?"

Well who else's basement had she access to? Full of beer, that is. It hardly seemed remarkable to her at the time.

"Annie, Annie, Annie. What am I to do with you?" Now he sounded like her mother, his voice heavy with the weight of disappointment.

He took them all home, lectured them fiercely and never told on them. Just as well too, as Annie got caught doing enough other stuff and her mother attributed her every ache, wrinkle and gray hair to this. Annie did not steal any more liquor from Jake's ever and even lost her taste, acquired over that week, for beer. She baby-sat—a thing she hated doing—and paid her father back (wholesale cost, of course) by slipping the money, mostly fifty-cent pieces, into the till.

Had drugs been available to them then, she, Jimmy and Sherman would have tried them all.

"I want to talk with you," she told Sammy that night. He had courteously avoided her, did the dishes and fed the dog without being reminded. He was trying to escape her notice, so she might take up some other critical problem and forget this one.

They sat in the living room and Sammy, sullen, slumped in a chair, his arms folded over his chest as though protecting something there.

"Should I discuss this with your father?" she asked.

"No," he said and sank deeper into the cushions.

"Why do you want to do drugs? Are you unhappy?"

No answer.

"Don't I give you enough attention?" He appeared to be off somewhere. His bangs were too long and he flipped them like a fly had landed on his forehead.

"Are you even listening?" she asked.

"So you drink. That's a drug."

"But I'm older. I wouldn't want you to drink at your age either."

"You shouldn't knock something until you've tried it," he said. Oh, he could be belligerent.

"I've tried it."

"When?" This with disbelief.

"I was nineteen or twenty."

"What?"

"Pot, hash, speed." Annie hadn't liked it all that much. On speed, she went through the day wired, unable to focus on any one thing. She hated that feeling. Pot made her hungry. Sometimes she'd awaken in the night after everything was closed and go searching the town for a hamburger. And pot often made her laugh, but not the kind of laughter you could connect to things or recall the next day with amusement. Mostly, whatever she had laughed about didn't make sense, was not necessarily funny, left her puzzled. She tried to explain all this to Sammy.

"And I was chubby enough then without being hungry all the time," she said.

Sammy smiled.

"Ever try acid?"

"You haven't tried that, have you!" The idea terrified her.

"No," he said. "Have you?" he asked again.

"Yes," she said, not knowing what to tell him about it. The first time she'd tried it she was with Paul, just a few couples at a friend's house. This guy had these little globs on a piece of paper. LSD. She was afraid and cut her tab as they called it into two pieces with a scissors. Not much was happening as far as she was concerned. One girl lay on the bed talking about things on the ceiling. Everyone else was wandering around staring at something, a plant maybe or the aquarium or stereo. They're experiencing things and I'm not, she'd thought in disappointment. But just then the stove melted and slid across the floor.

Then one time she saw herself in the mirror as an old lady and had stared in fascination at her future self—though the next day the memory of her withered old self frightened and saddened her. Always the next day was like that, depressing, to fall suddenly from some ethereal, energetic state into laborious exhaustion.

The last time she tried it, she'd gone for a walk with Paul. She began to hallucinate. She knew they were moving but they weren't making any progress. It was like being in a picture, there where the road is wide, seeing that it narrows to a dot on the horizon and being stuck in that wide part. She'd blink and try to focus, concentrating on moving and on not being stuck, all the time walking and checking her watch to find only seconds had passed.

Somehow she'd gotten back to the house—she didn't recall where Paul was by now. She called a friend who talked to her for hours as she slipped in and out of this black space, afraid each time that she was never coming back. It was horrifying to slip in and out of touch. What a close call, she'd think on each reentry, only to slide off somewhere again. The next day she felt the same slipping away and it scared her too much to ever do drugs of any kind again. She was afraid of flashbacks for years when she drove at night or looked down any long stretch of highway.

No, LSD was not fun. All those things leaving their boundaries, all those ponderous questions that wore her out, all that paranoia and the terrible day after. She shuddered. "I promise you," she told Sammy, "it was scary stuff."

He sat there flipping his hair, deep in thought.

"All the kids do it," he said. "Smoke grass, I mean."

"Yes, but you're so young." Was this the only point she could make?

"I want the kids to like me," he said in that straightforward manner of his.

"Sammy," she said cautiously. "I'm going to ask you to wait until you're older and to do a little research here. Take a look at people who've done a lot of drugs." She didn't know what more to say.

"I know I can't really stop you. You can refuse me and sneak around but I'm hoping you won't do that."

He said nothing.

"Otherwise, all I can do is discuss it with your father and grandfather."

"Oh, God," he said.

"Please," she said. "Agree to wait a few years."

"Can I think about it?"

"Of course," she said and knew he'd agree and be honest about it, at least for now.

These things, her problems with Sammy, and the fact that they were slowly going broke, made her feel helpless, that she was barely surviving the events around her. She felt like she was holding on to some slippery rock in white water, afraid to let go lest she be dragged by the current over some killing waterfall, a descent into hell.

But at least Bobby disappeared from their life. Sammy, after visiting Bobby's home without permission one Sunday afternoon, came home sad and perhaps a little grateful. He never discussed what he'd seen, but she guessed something there had soured him on Bobby.

Christmas was the worst. Morton wanted Sammy to come home. Annie's folks wanted them both to come.

"I can't," she told her mother. "I have to work Christmas Eve day and the twenty-sixth too." Both days would be busy. First there would be last-minute shoppers, then exchanges and inventory sales.

"We're putting up a big tree at the bar."

"How big?"

"Six feet."

Six feet! Annie didn't believe it. Her first Christmas away and they were putting up a big tree. All her life she'd asked for a big tree but never had they had one larger than two feet high, often not that tall. They usually looked more like limbs than trees and, had her father had his way entirely, a wreath would have been it. She wanted to cry in disappointment; all those years, all those little trees.

Every year since she'd left the apartment behind Jake's, she had dragged home such huge trees that their tops or bottoms always needed trimming.

"Where do you find trees like this?" Morton said every year as he went for a saw.

This year she wouldn't bother. Sammy would be gone a week. What was the point? A tree would only add to the gloom she expected.

As it turned out, it was creepy as well as gloomy. In his absence, noises she had never heard before now greeted her in every room. The refrigerator stopped and started, the furnace emitted some groan, the plumbing and radiator pipes too. The floors moved noisily beneath her feet and the windows rattled. Then the day before Christmas Eve, sometime in the middle of the night, Annie sat straight up in bed. She was sweating and her heart was pounding. She remembered who Bobby reminded her of.

When Annie was a small girl she often roamed the hills where there were old mine shafts. At the time she imagined that all of the old mines were full of gold. Despite signs that said Dangerous and Keep Out, if boards were rotted or broken so she could squeeze through the opening, she would go in. She never stayed long unless it was very hot outside. Then she'd go as far in as she could see to go, to where it would be cool. But even with a flashlight, it was hard to see inside the mines. And it was often dusty or else damp and musty-smelling. One cold and windy day, she had gone in to warm up before heading back over the hill and home. When she came out she saw a boy looking out over the valley, not ten feet or so from where she stood at the entrance to the old mine. He was big, probably in high school, she guessed.

"Hi," she said, startling him.

"What are you doing here?" he said, angrily.

"Nothing," she said.

"Who's with you?" he asked.

"Nobody," she said.

"What did you find in there?" he said and started toward her.

Now she was frightened and started up the hill. He followed her, yelling at her. "Stop! What did you take?" he hollered.

Now she ran. She could hear him behind her but she didn't dare turn to see. Then she was jerked suddenly as he pulled on her knapsack. She held on to it as tight as she could but then she let go, deciding to let him have it if that was all he wanted. There was not much in it—a flashlight, some rocks, half a sandwich, a library book.

And then a surprising thing happened. The large boy began to slide, then to tumble as small rocks almost like sand began pouring down the hill taking him with them. Annie watched in amazement, then screamed as the boy disappeared into the ground. It was as though the ground had opened to swallow him.

She ran the rest of the way home and when she got there, Jake's was full. A celebration of some kind was taking place and all the adults there, including her parents, were glassy-eyed and laughing. No one but her mother had the slightest interest in her.

"Where have you been?" her mother wanted to know. "You should have been home hours ago. I swear, Annie, I'm not going to allow you out the door if this is the way you act."

"But Mom, there was a boy . . ."

"I don't want to hear it. Where's your knapsack?"

"It fell into this hole and this . . ."

"Annie! That's the third one this year. Damn it. Now go take a bath."

"But Mom . . ."

"Go!" And then someone yelled to her and Elsa had turned her attention elsewhere. Annie had then gone into the apartment alone and crawled into a hole behind the closet, terrified that the boy—living or dead—would be after her.

To this day Annie had no idea what became of that boy. She'd imagined him climbing out of the earth, angry and dirty and sore but, nevertheless, alive and safe. Sometimes she saw men pulling up his broken body, trying to figure out who he was. Other times it was wolves dragging him off to some den. Or worse—sometimes she believed his body was still there.

After that first failed attempt to tell her mother what happened, Annie never spoke of it again. Even by the next day she had felt guilty of some terrible wrongdoing. She felt ashamed, yet too frightened of the punishment to confess. Then as the years went by, when the memory would awaken her in the night, she let it become something she had imagined, a bad dream caused by something she had eaten. Then one day when she was in junior high, she went to the police station and confessed.

But to her surprise, they hadn't believed her. They too thought it was something she had imagined. They had nodded at her sympathetically and said they'd look into it.

"Don't you want my phone number?" she'd asked, insulted by their apathy.

"Okay, if you'd like to leave one."

Okay, if you'd like to leave one? Christ Almighty! Didn't they know the courage it had taken her to go there that day? Still she had left relieved, some of the tremendous weight now gone from her heart. But only some.

Now Annie was so angry just thinking about it that she had to get up out of bed. She got dressed and went outside into the snow to walk it off. She had never forgiven Elsa and Nicholas for being too drunk and uninterested that day to assist her when she'd needed them most.

The next night, Christmas Eve, Annie got slightly drunk with other single misplaced people at the store, and Irma, a girl from shoes, drove her home and they had another drink or two. Maybe three. After Irma left, she went to bed.

Christmas morning she had a hangover. Sammy called. He'd

received a watch, a tape deck, a lot of clothes—terrific stuff, he said—and money to spend however he wanted. And thanks for the sweater, yes it fit. Did she like the perfume? Yes, she did. It sounded merry there at Morton's, very merry. She could hear voices and laughter and 'I'm Dreaming of a White Christmas' in the background.

The phone rang again not twenty minutes later. That would be her parents. At Jake's. She didn't answer.

Annie made herself some dip, got out a bag of chips, poured herself some wine. She lit a cigarette from a pack Irma had forgotten on the coffee table. Annie hadn't smoked in five years. Life, her life, was caught on a hook somewhere. She couldn't go back and there seemed no movement forward that she could see. She had been put on hold. That knowledge, not exactly instructive, and the cigarette, made her sick.

Chapter Nine

A couple of months after Annie and Sammy left, Morton went into Jake's to have a drink. He just stopped in to say hello to Nicholas and ended up staying several hours. Then he began stopping in once a week.

"I don't understand," Marge said. "If you've always hated it, why are you suddenly going there now?"

"Just to keep in touch," he said.

"But I thought you didn't particularly like her parents."

He'd thought that too. "For chrissake," he told her, "they are Sammy's grandparents."

But she didn't buy that for a moment and he'd finally had to tell her to leave him alone. He knew she thought he just missed Annie. And he did, but not only that. He missed roots. Marge had so much family that it had made him miss having one of his own. Then he found that he liked Elsa. He liked her softness and the way she took care of everyone. He like the gentle way she made everyone's business her own.

So he'd go in and sit at the bar and talk to Nicholas and Elsa. And though he usually went in on Thursdays, Marge's bowling night, because he was feeling out of sorts, he decided one Tuesday to stop in after work.

The store had been chaotic all day. First one of his largest suppliers had sent the wrong order and he'd been on the phone all morning trying to straighten it out. Then his deliverymen returned with the truck still loaded because of a fight one of them had gotten into with the customer. And in the middle of their side of the story, the customer, Mrs. Jurosky, had called with hers.

"All I asked was that they take off their shoes at the door," she said. "And they refused. One of them had the nerve to swear," she said.

"At you?" he asked. He was appalled.

"Not at me but, still, in front of me," she said. "So I don't want that stuff unless it's delivered by gentlemen."

After some discussion and argument around the store, he and Jardine ended up delivering it. They had to put one end of the couch down and balance it on a narrow stoop while they took off their shoes on the sidewalk, which was wet from melted snow. Then they'd nearly dropped the couch on a miniature dog that ran around barking underfoot. Next they'd been required to move the goddamn thing to three different locations while Mrs. Jurosky thought each one over. All that was annoying enough but while there, Morton had missed an appointment with a representative from the power company who wanted to look at desks for several executives' offices.

By the time Morton left that day, he needed a drink. He closed up the office, leaving a list of customers who hadn't paid on their bills in months. He'd have someone call them because he sure as hell wouldn't. He hated collections. Christ, he thought. Many more days like this and he'd close up and go work for someone else. Let all his creditors go hang themselves and he imagined for a moment a row of vendors hanging from reproduction oak coat racks sold by a wholesaler in San Francisco like the ones he'd recently ordered.

"Bad day?" Elsa said as soon as she saw him. "Can I make you a sandwich?" she asked.

"No thanks," he said. "Just a drink. I have plans for dinner."

Jake's was noisy. Two men, ironworkers, he guessed, were trying to collect money at the bar for some outlandish project to put up a giant monument of some kind. Morton had laughed when he heard.

"You're putting up a ninety-foot iron statue of the Virgin Mary on top of Saddle Rock?"

"That's right," a large, burly man said, grinning good-naturedly.

"Whatever for?"

"To honor mothers, of course," he said. "How about it?" He held out a hard hat to Morton.

"This is a joke, right?"

"Hell no. This is for real."

"How the hell you going to get it up there?" Now Morton was intrigued. He knew that area. There was nothing up there but a rocky, steep trail with grades probably at 20 to 30 percent.

"We're going to build a road."

"It'll have to be all switchbacks," Morton said.

"Maybe," the man answered.

"You'll need cranes and bulldozers, probably a helicopter," Morton said.

"Yeah, so dig deep," the man said, holding out the hard hat to him again.

"I think you're crazy," Morton said. "You're going to tear up the mountain and destroy a bunch of trees just to put up some god-damn piece of iron that will rust all over the place."

"What's your problem, buddy?" the cheerful-looking guy now said threateningly. "Don't you think it can be done?"

"No, I don't," Morton said. "And even if it could, I don't think it should." He saw Elsa now, staring, frozen. He guessed she thought there was going to be a skull-bashing. Maybe the father of her only grandchild would be killed.

"You got something against mothers?" the burly man's friend, a short stout man, asked, sticking his face close to Morton's.

"Leave him alone, Charlie," the big man said, stepping between them.

"Then tell him to put his money where his mouth is," the short man said.

"Fine," Morton said.

"A hundred bucks says you're full of shit," the short man said getting out his wallet.

"We'll see," Morton said taking cash out of his own wallet now.

"Nick can hold the bet," the tall man said, taking the money from Morton and handing it across the bar to Nicholas.

"And if I lose, I'll give you another hundred bucks for your fund," Morton said.

"Great!" Nicholas said, intervening. "Let me buy you fellows a drink. Elsa, where's those sandwiches?"

"Who is that asshole?" Morton heard someone say as he went out the door. He wondered how Nicholas would answer that inquiry.

When he got home, Marge was gone. She was mad, he guessed. He was several hours late for dinner. Or had they planned to go out? Oh, hell, he thought and rummaged around the freezer for a TV dinner.

Now and then Morton came to Missoula to visit. He'd drive over for the weekend and sleep on the couch even though Sammy always generously offered his room. Annie liked Morton's visits. His anal disposition, or whatever you might call that compulsion he had for symmetry and ordinances, didn't bother her anymore. It was sort of, oh, nice. She saw that life with Morton had been comfortable, directed, reasonable, and that she had been a space-off—his words—only because he kept everything of real concern from her. In consequence of his own everlasting tendency to worry, she had been free not to.

Sammy liked these visits, too. Morton did things with him, took him to movies and ball games, helped him with projects. For instance, they built a doghouse and fixed the fence so the dog wouldn't get caught by the pound again. He'd already been im-pounded three times and it had cost Annie over a hundred dollars, half of which she'd made Sammy pay.

Morton included her, too, sometimes, and once took them to a Chinese restaurant.

"I saw your folks the other day," he said, unfolding his napkin. He had a precise way of fitting napkins to his lap and he always spent several minutes at this.

"Your mom thinks she's getting arthritis," he said. Annie's

mother always thought she was getting something, yet she cheerfully overworked herself and was never sick.

"So I heard," she said. "Where did you see them?" she asked politely. She felt so polite around Morton now.

"At the bar."

"Jake's?"

"Yeah, I stop in there now and then."

"Why? You hate the place." She'd forgotten her new manners.

"Oh, you know. Just to check on things. Bubba, by the way, doesn't look too good. I think he's drinking too much."

That night after Sammy went to bed she asked Morton to increase his child support payments. Well, he didn't think he could, he had more expenses now, he had increased his inventory, he was helping out a friend. He'd see.

Annie's feelings were hurt. She was too disappointed in him to protest, though she thought after he left she could have handled it better. Why hadn't she showed him on paper the cost of raising one child and demanded—well, appealed for—half that amount, as his support payments were certainly small enough. But then on his next visit he gave her a few hundred dollars, to help with Sammy's dental bills, he said.

Annie's parents visited too, usually staying a week or so at a time.

"You'll never guess," her mother said when she thought Annie's father was out of earshot. "Morton stops in at the bar about once a week, imagine that. After all these years, what a surprise."

Yes, wasn't it. Morton, of late, confounded her.

"What a man does is his own business," her father said from the dining room.

Annie loved her parents' visits. She saw permanent allegiance here, perhaps for the first time, and for a few days didn't worry so much about Sammy. Her father took him to his soccer games, to movies, shopping for clothes. Her mother caught up all her laundry and ironing, filled the freezer with homemade bread and casseroles and, oddly enough, didn't insist that she move back home.

"You've established a nice place here, Annie," her father said. "How much is your rent?"

"My God," he said when he heard.

"Sweetheart," her mother added. "You've got to talk to Morton. Get him to give you a settlement. He should sell the house and divide the money with you."

"He lives there," Annie said.

"But he doesn't need all that room. Let him get an apartment," her mother said. "And what about the place at the lake? That's worth something."

"Are you thinking of going back to him?" her father wanted to know.

"No."

"Well, then? Your mother's right." This might have been the first time Annie had ever heard him say those words—"your mother's right." Not that they fought or disagreed all the time, they just didn't share a mutual perspective.

"It's just that it was the money he earned that paid for everything. I don't see where I . . ." Annie didn't complete her sentence. She could see the looks on their faces, looks of annoyed astonishment.

"But you kept house all those years; you think he doesn't owe you for all that?" her mother said.

"Well, no."

"You have peculiar views, Annie," her father said. "But I'd think about this if I were you."

Was she wrong to feel this way? That she and Morton had already closed some deal, that they were both paid up, that nothing more was due—except, of course, for Sammy.

"I could help out, Annie," her father said. "But remember who it was who had to run off to a big town with fancy rents."

"Nicholas!" her mother cried.

"I don't need any help." Annie said.

Once Bubba sent a present along with them for her.

"It's here somewhere," her mother called from the bedroom. She always unpacked immediately after arriving and Annie's father went directly to the kitchen table for a drink, explaining every hazard he had suffered on the drive.

"Take a look at this," her mother said, bringing in a package. Annie unwrapped a dark brown leather purse that resembled a small saddle bag. It had zippered pockets inside and a long strap.

"It's beautiful," Annie said.

"Hasn't lost his touch, has he?" her father said, appraising the heavy cowhide. After Fern died, Bubba had given up working with leather, gone into retirement, and though he sometimes complained about the state of someone's shoes or boots at the bar, he refused to fix them. "Take them to the kids," he'd say, referring to the young couple who'd bought him out. He worried that they were going broke.

"But he's not so good anymore," her father said, meaning his health. "We're a little worried about him. You know he's seventy-eight now." Her father was drinking a beer at the kitchen table and set it down rather sharply to show that it was now empty.

"You want another beer?" Annie said, getting up.

"Annie," he said. "Come home for a visit before he dies. You're like a daughter or granddaughter to him."

Annie couldn't do it. She felt that even one visit to Butte and Jake's might pull her into some ring of safety, some paralyzing security that was sure to be a trap—an easy way out of the dismaying uncertainty she lived with. For some unknown reason, surely it didn't make sense the way Morton and her parents saw good sense, she had to push even further into peril. She had in mind to apply for an opening in the Spokane store, assistant to the designer who did the displays. It was a bigger, more sophisticated store where she could learn. The job paid well too and the cost of living was reported to be less there. Moreover, Sammy liked the idea.

"The kids at school are jerks," he said. "Let's go."

In this, he took after her, always anticipating the next bend in a road, the view over the hill. But his comment worried her. Was this facility for change merely running?

"Make your peace with them," she told him. "You'll find kids are the same everywhere."

Annie didn't think it was wanderlust entirely. It was also that she hated Missoula's inversions, those days when smoke and fog would hang in the valley floor between mountain ranges. She was too accustomed to Butte, where even cloud-covered skies reflected brightly on snow in the clean air and she could see for miles.

"You're just homesick," her mother told her. "Come home and stay for a week or so."

Nevertheless, vast, bright winter sky and an old man she hardly knew anymore were not reasons enough to visit Butte.

But then Bubba died. Her mother called her one Wednesday evening and Annie agreed to go back for the funeral. They drove over after work the next night, taking the route by Phillipsburg and Flint Creek. She stopped at Georgetown Lake and drove by the old place where Morton still kept the trailer on a lot. She left the headlights on and got out of the car. The small, old trailer was more rusty than she remembered and looked like it had not been used in some time. By now Sammy and the dog were down at the water and she had to call them. It was a moonless night and the sound of water slapping the shore was the only reason to believe that a lake was there at all.

Sammy slept the rest of the way and Annie had to buy coffee when she stopped for gas to keep herself awake.

She dropped Sammy off at Morton's and went on to her folks. She'd seen lights going on in Morton's house as she pulled out of the drive, a trail through her old home, from the kitchen up the stairs to the bathroom and then to Sammy's bedroom. She was too tired to care, though she knew under different circumstances she might very well feel emotional about it.

The next day, they all went to a high mass for Bubba in the large church he'd taken her to as a young girl. It was morning and bright sun lit the purples, reds and yellows of the old stained-glass windows. It was too hot in here. Somehow the place in daylight held no mystery for her, the light exposed things: the frayed velvet seats, the thinness of the aisle carpet, splinters on the back of the oak pew in front of her. Even the priest appeared faded and chipped by the years, maybe near death himself. And no rose petals floated on top of the holy water—Annie checked. It seemed stale too. Dead. Leftover from some happier occasion. In contrast, Bubba's coffin stood out alarmingly new and bright, a metal thing, garish in this scant context. It might have been the shiniest thing he'd ever had, the newest thing anyone would ever connect to him. She didn't look at the body and hung back while everyone else passed by the coffin, covered where it opened with dark crimson satin. She didn't want to see him with his hair slicked back or in some suit that he would never have worn living.

They buried him that afternoon, a cold, windy day, in recently thawed ground next to Fern, in a graveyard where hearty weeds and tulips were now rising from a skiff of snow.

Afterward, everybody went to Jake's. Surely it was the most likely place to mark Bubba's passing. She knew almost everyone there and she and her mother received the gifts of casseroles and cakes. It seemed all sympathy was directed to them.

Jake's, like the church, was hot and stuffy. It was as though a fear of chill for the old people had made both her father and the church reluctant to turn off their furnaces entirely. There was a tiredness here, too, the sense that concessions had been made, a passivity and depletion of spirit. Deference. As if each person here, in contemplating his friend's death, was now making funeral arrangements of his own. Everyone sat quietly, eating and drinking, breaking silence with anecdotal comments from time to time, loud comments as most of these people seemed hard of hearing or thought everyone else was.

It was hardly the celebration Bubba might have enjoyed.

"He was getting senile," someone said. "It's for the best."

"He could sure tell a story."

"Couldn't he, though."

"The man drank himself to death." This comment from an old man Annie didn't know. He was drunk.

She saw Morton over in the corner talking to her mother. "Morton," she asked, "will you give me a ride home?"

"Are you all right?" he asked.

"Of course. I'm just tired." She hadn't gotten to bed until very late the night before and then hadn't slept well.

The next morning at breakfast her father handed her an envelope. "Something Bubba wanted you to have," he said.

There was a note inside. "Annie, I'm leaving my cabin up

Pipestone to you," it read. "It's something Fern and I always wanted for you ever since you were a kid. I know you never liked Jake's and I want this to be one place you can come home to. Your friend, Bubba."

Everyone else apparently already knew about this. Her parents looked across the breakfast table expectantly and Sammy called from Morton's and said he wanted to go see the cabin.

"How did you know about it?" she said.

"Dad said Bubba told him a couple weeks ago."

She didn't know what to say. She didn't even know what to think about it. Why had he done it? Why had he made claims on her no matter how aloof she kept herself? What connection had that old man presumed to have with her; why had he loved her?

She and Sammy drove up early that afternoon before leaving for Missoula. It had been so long since she'd been to Bubba's cabin that she hoped she could remember where the turnoff was. Then she saw a sign that said 'cabins' and thought she would stop there for directions. She hoped it wasn't an old sign someone had forgotten to take down. Sometimes you saw signs along roads like this—Harry's Bar or Clara's Grill—that only left you to wonder, when you got to some broken-down remains sagging in the weeds, what had happened to Harry or Clara.

But then she recognized the turnoff. Of course! The old rusty car door with a faded arrow propped at the edge of the ditch marked the turn.

It was warmer now and she unzipped her wool jacket. The sun was melting off patches of snow along the edges of the timber and in the yard. The cabin looked bereft of all life, sloping crookedly along its roof down to a huge pile of firewood covered by canvas. An ancient hand plow stuck jauntily from a snowdrift beside the door.

Inside everything was clean, the sofa and chairs neatly covered by sheets. On the kitchen table there was a blue-and-white flowered oilcloth that looked familiar, stiff and cracking from the temperature here. It was cold, bitterly so, the way only old log walls can become cold. It used to take hours to heat them up, she recalled, those times Bubba and Fern drove her up on Friday nights. Only by morning would the woodstove's heat have penetrated the logs, transforming the place finally into something alive and friendly. How she used to shiver in a down comforter, waiting for morning and the thaw of walls. She shivered now.

"It's great," Sammy said. "Can we come here for vacations?"

"Oh, sometime," she said. The embroidered cloth that Fern had framed and hung once with great ceremony was tilted on the wall and Sammy straightened it. It said, *Make this your home.*

"Are you ready to go?" she asked him.

Well, not yet. First he had to look in all the cupboards. Everything was there. Hills Brothers coffee cans full of oatmeal, sugar, flour, even coffee. There were mismatched enamel dishes she remembered, large coffee mugs, icy to touch, old kerosene lamps, iron pots. The bookcase was full of old newspapers and magazines, mostly *National Geographics.*

"Can I take these?" Sammy asked.

"I guess so," she told him reluctantly. "Well, next time," she said, changing her mind. She dreaded anything being wrested from its place here. Why, she wasn't sure.

Sammy went down to see the creek and she locked up and waited outside in the sun. She was troubled. She no longer knew how to examine herself, how to give credit or place blame. She had not allowed herself, in the pace she now ran at, any time for introspection. Would she recognize what she searched for if she found it?

She knew only that it wasn't here.

"Let's go," she yelled to Sammy. She wanted to start home.

"Dad has a girlfriend," Sammy told her when they stopped in Anaconda to eat.

"Oh, yeah," she said.

"Uh huh. She's real nice. She made waffles with strawberries for breakfast."

"She lives there?"

"I guess so," he said.

Confirmation: The woman, some woman, had assumed Annie's life, was now governess of her juicer and blender and comfortable pillows, her charge cards and a hundred other luxuries. This woman did not have to hand-squeeze oranges, go to the laundromat, read by a broken-down lamp with a short in it. And whose fault was this? Annie's own.

Nonetheless, for the moment, Annie felt sorry for herself.

The next week was busy and on Friday night Annie came home from work after a drink with a co-worker, tired. She kicked off her shoes and lay on the couch with her feet on a pillow to watch the news.

"Mom, don't forget we're going to the movie," Sammy hollered from the kitchen.

Good Lord, she had forgotten she'd promised him. Could she beg off, talk him into sending out for pizza and going tomorrow night?

"Don't tell me you're too tired," he said, seeing her there limp on the couch.

You've been to the movies three times this month, for God's sake, she wanted to say. "Could we go tomorrow night?" she asked instead. "Don't forget you have an early soccer game."

"Yuk," he said and slammed himself into a chair.

"Yuk what?" she asked, trying to catch the weather report.

"Did you know they put three girls on our team and now we'll always lose?" Sammy's team was not the greatest in town, not even close.

"Aren't they any good?" she said.

"Terrible. Why do they let girls play, anyway?"

"Don't the other teams have them? If all of them had girls, it wouldn't be so bad, would it?"

"The other teams aren't that dumb," he said.

"You want to order a pizza?" she asked.

"No. Cook something," he said angrily. "Why don't women stay home and cook and girls stay home and . . ." He seemed at a loss to describe what girls should stay home and do.

"Sammy," she said. "I'm not going to argue women's rights with you tonight." He had such sexist views; she didn't understand where he got them. Once he told her he wouldn't scrub the kitchen floor, that it was women's work. She made it a permanent assignment. Another time she'd tried to explain to him how sexism affected him—how angry she was that men, single men without a family to support, who did the same work as she did, for the same length of time, often made more money.

"Well, why didn't you stay married?" he'd said. "And we could have a VCR and a microwave oven like everyone else."

"Are you unhappy?" she'd said, almost in tears.

"No," he said, a little sheepishly, she thought.

"Do you miss your dad? Is that it?"

"Well . . . ," he admitted, actually he probably saw more of him now. "It's just that I hate being poor," he said. After that she'd called Morton to ask if he couldn't bring over some things the next time he came.

"What things?" he asked.

"Oh, maybe one of the color TVs"—he had two—"or the stereo, if you're not using it, that is." She was sure he wasn't, he only liked TV.

"What's up?" he asked.

"Oh, nothing really," she said. "Sammy's feeling a little deprived, is all."

It had still worried her all the same.

"What are you hungry for?" she asked Sammy now. "How about spaghetti?"

"Meat," he said.

"Go look in the freezer then. I think there's some pork chops." By now only the sports news was left and she still was no better informed on the state of the world then she'd been before lying down. She reached over to the coffee table for the *TV Guide.*

"There's no meat in there," he said, returning. "When's the last time you went to the store?"

"Now, listen, Sammy. I've heard about enough. First of all you're old enough to do some cooking too and you could go to the grocery store yourself sometimes."

"Sure, on my bike," he said and went to the kitchen to find something else.

The last thing she was in the mood for was a smart-ass kid complaining about his dinner. Did males naturally have tendencies like that, grow up with some intrinsic conviction that women were inferior? The doorbell was ringing. She hoped it was one of his more pleasant friends who might want to ask him to a movie or like the idea of pizza. "Sammy, will you answer the door?" She was reading the newspaper now and didn't feel like getting up.

"Can't you get it?" he yelled.

Annie sighed. She got up on the third ring and went to the hallway and turned on the porch light. She opened the door to a man who stood there grinning at her.

"May I come in?" he said.

"Mom, who is it?" Sammy yelled.

"It's your uncle Paul," she said quietly, thoroughly amazed.

It was an awkward visit. Paul could see that Sammy was puzzled. He was trying to recall anything he might have heard about him, this uncle that he had never seen before.

It was not surprising that Annie and Morton didn't talk about him. But you'd think the boy's grandmother Miriam, Paul's own mother, might have mentioned him over the years. But probably not. News extraneous to what involved Miriam directly and in the moment was not passed on to her sons. Those rare times she called or flew out from Chicago to Montana—in summer, when she could tolerate such wilderness—her conversations centered mostly on her bridge scores, her frequent trips abroad, on how little she could count on anyone—maids, doormen, bell boys.

Paul didn't know what to say. No one did. Finally Annie invited him in and he followed her into the living room. It was charming and cozy, full of odds and ends of things—Oriental rugs, old pine pieces, wooden shutters, and he had looked around as though he were in a shop. He especially liked a floor lamp with a silk shade that had long fringe.

Annie had to clear him a chair. She hurriedly swept through the cluttered room, apologizing for shoes, jackets, newspapers and Sammy's school books. She threw it all into the closet.

"Would you like a drink?" she asked.

"Scotch and soda," he said.

He got up again and followed her to the kitchen. She had to wash glasses, was out of Scotch, soda too, and ended up pouring them both some wine and spilling a bit of it. Why was she so nervous? He didn't know how to put her at ease. She looked great, he thought.

"So what brings you to our door?" she asked on the way back to the living room. It sounded slightly sarcastic.

"I called Morton the other day. He said you and he had . . . had split up and so I just thought it'd be nice to stop by to see you and meet my nephew." He looked over at Sammy and smiled. Sammy was nice-looking, healthy and clean-cut. He looked a lot like Morton used to when he was a kid.

"Oh," she said. Sammy sat in a chair nearby and smiled back politely.

Actually what had happened was that a few weeks before, one Saturday afternoon late, he had been in the Mercantile and thought he saw Annie going into the employee lounge. He was shocked and puzzled too. It was almost closing time so he hung around until she came out—to see if it really was her. When she did she was with some woman. They were talking and walked past him and down the stairs. He followed them out the door and down the street. They parted at the corner and Annie went into the drugstore. So now Paul waited near the curb for her, expecting that she would see him and recognize him and that they would talk or something. But she didn't. She went on by him, up the street to a parking lot where she got into a car and drove away.

The next Monday, he left work early and waited in his car until he saw her come out of the store. He followed her to the same parking lot and then to the grocery store and finally to her house. He watched from across the street as she juggled the groceries, unlocked the door and went in. It was then that he went home and called Morton. Morton, not surprisingly, had not expected to hear from him. Paul did not mention Annie and they talked for some time before Morton told him he and Annie were divorced. Good old Morton did not offer the information that she and the boy now lived in Missoula.

"So do you like Missoula?" Paul asked Sammy now.

"Yes, sir," he said cordially enough.

The boy had perfect manners, manners no doubt learned from Morton. It was painful and Paul got up to leave. Then suddenly he blurted out an invitation.

"Could you, both of you, that is, join me for dinner tomorrow evening?" My God, he was nervous too.

And to his surprise the boy wanted to. Annie agreed halfheartedly and with relief, he thought, to have the visit done with.

He would pick them up at seven-thirty, he said, and she shut the door.

Paul wanted to take them to a nice place but not one so gourmet or foreign that the boy couldn't order easily from the menu and so he asked everyone at the garage for recommendations. But ordering from a menu was no problem for the boy and he ordered the best steak on it. He ordered it just like he was accustomed to doing so, which made Paul think again of Morton. Annie started to protest.

"Oh, no," Paul said smiling at her. "I hear it's quite good here. I'll have it too."

Annie was more relaxed tonight, maybe because of the considerable amount of wine they drank.

"Annie," Paul said. "You haven't changed."

"Oh, but I have," she said.

He detected a double meaning here and, ignoring it, turned to Sammy. "You look a lot like your dad."

"My dad looks like you," the boy said shyly. "So I must too," he added. That seemed to be all right with Sammy, to look like him, and Paul didn't mind the fact either.

"How come you never came to visit before this?" Sammy asked him, poking a bread stick into butter.

"Sammy," Annie interceded quickly. "That's a very personal thing to ask."

"No, it's all right," Paul said. "A fair question." He smiled at Annie, who was now biting her lip.

"Well, your father and I had a falling-out years ago. And adults sometimes stupidly hold grudges," he said, frowning. "I hope when you grow up you're not that stupid."

"I hope not," Sammy said. "It's enough being a stupid kid." He said it so seriously, as though he had given the matter a great deal of thought, that Paul and Annie laughed.

After dinner, Paul drove them home and saw them to the door. "I

123

want to stay in touch," he told Sammy. "I'll call you," he said to Annie.

Paul was restless when he got home and changed a washer in the sink, a job he'd been putting off doing, and swept the kitchen. Had they had a good time? It was too strained, he thought. Still, he would like to see them again, though he wasn't sure why. Maybe because he was lonely and in all these years he'd never met anyone quite like Annie. He'd met plenty of women, of course. But the only ones he liked were married to his friends or employees. These were serious, thoughtful women who fussed over children and their husbands. He envied his friends these women. The kind he met either wanted a perpetual good time or else had careers on their mind and had no time. He did meet two, however, that he thought he could get serious about. But it so happened that their interests were not the same and when, for instance, he suggested camping to Rose, she gasped. "You mean sleep outside?" Joy said simply, "I'll do practically anything for you, sweetie, but camping isn't one of them." After that if a girl had long, painted fingernails—it was the one thing Joy and Rose had in common— he didn't even bother.

"It's where you meet them," Rod, his foreman, told him. "What do you expect at the Cowboy Saloon?" The saloon was a country-western bar outside of town where you could dance to a live band. "Why don't you take a class at the U or join the Sierra Club?"

But Paul wasn't interested in finding some mountain climber, which is all he could imagine meeting at the Sierra Club. He just wanted some nice practical woman who wasn't afraid of oil and grease-stained hands or his dirty kitchen. He would like someone who might be able to bait her own hook, make a fire or sleep in a tent. Someone he could talk to, someone who would listen, some-one around his age who knew what she wanted and how to get it. He hoped she might have a sense of humor and good sense in general. He wanted someone who might like him and . . .

What the hell. He could list things forever and it wouldn't matter. The someone he wanted was Annie.

Chapter Ten

"Dad," Sammy said the next day when Morton called. It was Sunday and Morton always called on Sundays. "You'll never guess who came to our house." Annie imagined Morton trying to guess from his end of the line.

"Paul," Sammy said finally.

"Your brother. Uncle Paul." There was another pause and she guessed that as usual Morton had said, No kidding.

"Yeah, and he took us out to dinner. Steak and everything." Then, "Uh huh," Sammy said. "Uh huh."

Would Morton be as surprised as she was by Paul's visit? Paul had looked pretty good. He was suntanned and his hair, now a little thinner, was much lighter around his temples. And he was a few pounds heavier than Morton, who tended to be too thin. He was Morton's brother still, the confident carriage and disarming dark eyes. He was wearing clean jeans that looked like they'd been pressed.

In comparison, Annie had been a mess, hadn't combed her hair since her lunch break, was rumpled, probably had no makeup left—or had it been smeared? She felt fat.

And how, she wondered, had he seen this place? What she had thought of as nice now all seemed rather shopworn and cluttered.

The room had needed vacuuming and she thought she finally smelled the musty odor Sammy often complained about.

Then she'd spilled the wine but, thank God, not on him. Why had she gotten so flustered? It had made her angry that he could pop in on her like that after heaven knows how many years and get her to fuss around, startled, embarrassed and apologetic. And then to agree to dinner! Immediately she had started worrying over what to wear. She'd wanted to wear something dark and slimming, something appealing. How on earth had she gotten so out-of-shape, overweight and unsexy?

She'd insisted Sammy put on a dress shirt. In this way, Sammy was not the least like Morton, who would have worn slacks or a suit to clean out the garage and thought nothing of it.

"Put on one of those shirts Grandma Miriam bought you," she'd said. Miriam always sent him preppy sort of dress clothes, anything but practical, that hung unworn in his closet. But the shirts were nice.

After Annie had showered, dressed and perfumed, she'd felt better. Her excitement had put color in her cheeks. She had applied makeup carefully, deciding, all in all, she looked rather nice. She'd felt beautiful. They had all been beautiful as far as she was concerned, in that elegant, candlelit room.

Sammy was still on the phone. "We lost, 8–2." Morton must have changed the subject to soccer. "It's those idiot girls they put on our team. You should see them stumble around the field."

Would Morton be jealous—not of her, of course not, but because Sammy had obviously enjoyed seeing Paul?

"I like him," Sammy had told her when they had gotten home that night from dinner. "He's not as serious as Dad, do you think?"

"What do you mean?"

"Aw, he jokes more, he's more relaxed."

Yes, she thought so too. She had seen Sammy taking on Paul's easy manner, his composure, slipping easily into an adult world.

"Funny, though," Sammy had said, "he and dad not seeing each other all those years. If I had a brother, I'd never do that."

On Tuesday night Paul called. "I can't tell you how much I enjoyed seeing you both," he said. "I'd like to see you again."

"Sure," she said.

"Sometime over the Easter weekend?"

"Fine," she said. "We'll plan on it." Her voice, she hoped, was casual.

"Good-bye," she said and hung up. She hadn't even thought to ask what he had in mind. A schoolgirl might have been more poised.

Morton arrived Friday night. He was tired, had gotten a speeding ticket and was not in a great mood.

"Anything around here to drink?" he said. She poured him the last of her cheap California wine.

"I'll run to the liquor store," she said. There was one still open nearby.

"No, I'll go," he said. "Sammy, you want to come along? Should we bring back hamburgers?"

"Not for me," she said. Suddenly, she had been able to stick to a diet.

They returned with sandwiches, fries, Scotch, soda and a better California wine.

"Have you seen my folks?" she asked him.

"No," he said. He'd been too busy this week. His mother had called though and wanted to know how they were and how Sammy was doing in school. Annie could imagine the conversation. And how is Samuel progressing with his studies? That would be how Miriam would put it. And Annie has a job, you say? How unfortunate, she'd tell him. Can't you give her more money? Though Annie didn't think Miriam liked her particularly—she didn't like anyone particularly—she always maintained that women who tied themselves down to a man, the richer the man the better, should be rewarded handsomely, in sickness, in health, and most of all, in death and divorce.

"How is she?" Annie asked, trying to extract a few ice cubes from a tray.

"Here, let me do that," he said, taking the cold, stiff tray from her. "About the same, who can tell. She's going to London.

"Do you have a soccer game tomorrow?" he asked Sammy.

"At nine."

"I can't wait to see those girls play," he said.

"It's not funny, Dad," Sammy said.

She made up the couch for Morton while they ate, then joined him in the kitchen for a drink. Her diet would allow one. Sammy went to bed.

"Sammy says Paul's coming over on Easter," Morton said.

"I guess so," she said, keeping all enthusiasm out of her voice. After all.

"What do you think that son-of-a-bitch is up to?" he asked frankly.

She didn't answer. She shrugged.

"Maybe he's still in love with you," he said. "Or maybe . . . Do you suppose—?" Morton didn't finish the sentence and, though she knew what he was thinking, she didn't, as she might have normally, finish it for him.

But Morton had made a point. What good could there be in letting Paul into their life? Would his attention to Sammy, even to her, make it harder for the two brothers to ever be friends? They did have that chance now that she and Morton were divorced.

"Tell him when he comes to leave my Scotch alone," Morton said. Annie smiled.

But she couldn't have put a stop to this visit if she'd wanted to. Sammy expected it, looked forward to it, would have thought Morton had interfered somehow. That would puzzle him and he'd ask questions and want satisfactory answers. Sammy, truthful in most things, expected the same in others.

Paul called one day when she wasn't home and told Sammy he'd pick them up for dinner at seven o'clock on Easter Sunday.

They went to an Italian restaurant that Sammy chose from the yellow pages. It wasn't especially good, the prices were high, and it was back to awkward silences. Paul was distracted by something, Sammy didn't like his lasagna and Annie worried. The magic was gone, he didn't like her. But why should she care? He took them home and did not come in.

The following Saturday when she got home from work, she was surprised to find Paul there. He and Sammy were playing cards on the dining room table. He had gone to Sammy's soccer game,

Sammy had made them bologna sandwiches for lunch, then they had gone fishing on the Blackfoot.

"Let me take those," Paul said, noticing she had groceries in her arms. "But don't put your apron on."

"Yeah, tonight we're going to do something special," Sammy said.

"What's that," she asked.

"We're going to cook," Sammy said.

"Oh, no," she said. "We're out of corned beef hash."

"Don't start, woman," Paul said. "I'm a chef now."

"Corned beef?" Sammy asked, realizing something of interest had been alluded to.

"Yes, your mother and father used to give me a bad time because sometimes I liked to add corned beef to things."

"To everything," she said. "To meat loaf, to chicken stew, to pizza."

"Not tonight," Paul said. "I'm showing Sammy how to make fettucine with clam sauce."

"I'm impressed," she said.

"You should be," he said. "I read cookbooks to relax."

She could see Sammy assessing something here. Did he wonder, Oh, so the three of them at one time were all friends.

Annie went to shower and change. When she returned to the kitchen they were hovering over the counter, assembling ingredients. There was something familiar about the scene, something a little overwhelming about it. She wished Morton could be a part of it. He'd like that, had things been different.

About nine-thirty after they'd cleaned up the mess—there was indeed a mess—Paul threw the dish towel over Sammy's shoulder. "Do you mind if I take your mother out for a drink?"

"No," he said. But was he disappointed? She couldn't tell, he seemed to be considering something. She felt a little uneasy about going and didn't really want to desert him after such a good time. Wouldn't he be confused, wonder about things?

"Mom, could I talk to you a minute?" he said as she got her coat from the hall closet.

"What's wrong?" she said, expecting the worst.

"Your hair's sticking out a little in back. And, Mom," he said, to her relief, "why don't you put on some perfume?"

Paul took her to his house. He didn't make any pretense, did not ask her to a bar first, just drove straight home and guided her from the car, into the house and to the bed. He didn't even say anything, just sighed deeply as he held and touched her and slipped off her clothes.

That evening, she decided, was one of those priceless, fragile gifts life sometimes, without warning, throws your way. It was as though she'd been pulled out of a dark place into something rare and needed, an intimacy she had never before allowed herself, not even with him. It was not just sexual closeness but one that broke through some thick obstruction that had formed around her.

They lay together in silence for some time. Annie could hear traffic from the street and light from street lamps down the block shone across the wall and ceiling.

She asked Paul to take her home.

"Spend the night," he said.

"No, Sammy will worry."

"Call him."

"I'd be too embarrassed," she said.

"You mean you haven't done anything like this before—I mean since leaving Morton?"

"No."

"A virtuous woman," he said. "I'm playing around with a virtuous woman." He made a grab for her from the bed. She was getting dressed.

"Is that what you're doing? Playing around?"

Paul became serious and leaned back on the pillows thoughtfully. She sat on the edge of the bed. "I've known all kinds of women," he said, "but I never forgot you, Annie."

"I know," she said. "I was fun."

He didn't get her joke. "No, I'm serious," he said. "I knew if I looked you up it had to be for something more than . . . well, I knew if there was nothing left for us we'd know right away."

Annie couldn't think of anything to say.

"But there's a lot left."

She still couldn't think of anything. This was all so . . . she didn't know what.

"I'll have you home before Sammy gets up. I just want to sleep beside you."

"Paul," she said. "I can't. If Sammy woke up in the night, he'd worry, he'd think . . ."

"He'd think his mother and uncle were off playing around, getting into trouble."

"Exactly. And that would worry him."

"All right," he said. "I'll buy you a drink on the way home."

Before Annie was out of the shower the next morning, she heard the doorbell. She dressed and went to the kitchen. Paul and Sammy were making ham and cheese omelets.

Later that morning, Paul suggested an outing.

"Any ideas?" he asked.

"The Farmers Market," Annie said. She wanted to buy some dried flowers for a window display she had in mind.

"Yuk," Sammy said. "That place is boring." Annie wished Sammy would adopt a replacement word for *yuk*. It was his favorite expression.

"We'll make it fun," Paul said.

"Why don't you invite Todd along?" Annie said. Todd was a boy from the soccer team whom Sammy seemed to like.

They stopped by Todd's house and headed downtown. The market was on the riverbank by the Higgins Avenue Bridge. It was popular and they had to park several blocks away.

Everything, handcrafted leather and furniture, works by local artists, photography, pottery, weavings, tapestries, handmade rugs, acid-etched mirrors and stained, leaded glass was for sale. There were even cheap Mexican imports that a young couple was unloading from a truck. Some booths had local honey, fresh flowers, and one, handmade cosmetics. This booth offered a miracle cream that would fix anything according to your belief in it, the man there explained. He talked rapidly, excitedly, about its powers.

"I have to have this," she told Paul.

There were food booths, too, and they tried tacos and Swedish meatballs and barbecued ribs. There was homemade wine at another stand and she and Paul sat there in the shade while the boys went off for corn dogs. There were clowns and acrobats and musicians, kids with boxes full of puppies and kittens, tables of pamphlets that protested nuclear power plants and the arms race and advocated the ERA and gay rights.

The boys came back with homemade root beer and they all wandered aimlessly again, silly in the festive atmosphere and fresh spring air.

A local ice cream company had set up a block of ice cream and two girls were scooping portions into paper cups and handing them out. Annie told them all to meet her there, she would find the dried flowers.

There was one display under the bridge that she might not have noticed except for the smell. Annie stopped. It was full of leather, luggage, satchels, purses and wallets and handmade attaché cases. Bubba, she knew, would have loved this. It might have been his own shop set up in a tent. Besides all the things for sale, there was a collection of old shoes, antique calf-length high heels that laced, dancing slippers and old work boots, handsome cowboy boots, even old skates and leather hats. Bubba had had a collection like this, too, that he displayed on shelves around his shop and this is what it had smelled like there. The smell of leather.

Something significant, of consequence, had been taken from her life. That knowledge was contained here, painfully, in her appreciation of the smell of leather. She had not properly mourned the fact before. Was this how she'd do it, in small patches of sorrow that would overcome her from time to time as she found things to remind her? Couldn't she just cry like everyone else and get it over with? No, her guilt for not giving the man the attention he deserved and never asked for was too much. She would be punished.

"Annie," Paul said. "What's wrong?" He'd come back to find her and must have seen her stricken expression. He pulled her away from where she stood, obstructing the flow of shoppers. "What is it?"

"Nothing," she said. "The wine must have gone to my head."

"They're flying kites on the riverbank," he said, guiding her through the crowd.

The next weekend was rainy. They cancelled their plans to go hiking and drove out to Fort Missoula to see the air force bombers from the airbase in Great Falls on exhibit. There was something a little frightening about them, massive collections of metal and rivets and wings, silver and shining in the rain. What, she wondered, did their lives have to do with these menacing structures that had been to war and back? She wanted to leave but Todd and Sammy and Paul were fascinated. They got all wet and didn't care, were trying to take pictures. War was a male interest, she decided.

Afterward they went into the museum to get out of the rain. On one wall was a huge blown-up photograph of Columbia Gardens, a large dance hall and amusement park in Butte, torn down years before, the land now a casualty of the Anaconda Company's ever expanding copper pit. In the photo were people in old-fashioned hats and holiday attire, walking along boardwalks beneath a huge roller-coaster. The photo might have been taken around the turn of the century.

"I used to love this place," she told Paul. Sometimes—in old buildings, especially—she felt like she had been thrown into the future, had arrived ahead of her time, and had actually been scheduled for somewhere else. Rightfully, she should already have lived her life, or perhaps, already had, and had not quite forgotten it—like feeling sure she was the woman in the picture above the piano at Jake's—she, Annie, that harlot. She might even be that bag lady by the river, someone who had already used up her life and now pulled its remnants behind her in a box. Or the old woman she had seen in the mirror at twenty on one-half tab of LSD. It was as though she could live several lives at once, maybe one almost finished, maybe one that hadn't quite started, simultaneous, overlapping, confusing lives.

"See that woman there?" Annie said to Paul. She pointed out a girl in the photograph who was wearing a long filmy sort of dress, holding a parasol. The woman looked sad, almost in tears. Had she misplaced her child or lover?

"I feel like that," she said.

"My God, but you're morbid today."

"It's the rain," she said. "This town on a gray day does that to me."

"Good," he said. "Because I want to buy a place in the country and you can move there."

Men, she decided, sometimes came up with the most simple and practical of solutions, which in the long run were not real answers to anything after all.

Oh well, she was just depressed, still seeing things in terms of drizzle and fog.

The next two weeks were busy ones. Annie's folks were coming around the fifteenth, staying about five days and taking Sammy home to Butte for spring break. Then Morton would bring him back.

Annie had a lot to do. First of all, she had to complete her portfolio, which she had recently decided was awful. She had sent in an application to the Spokane store and, if they were interested, they would interview her around the first of June. That didn't leave her much time. But Bernard's girlfriend Lucille, who was a photographer, had agreed to help her.

"Bernard would just as soon you get this job," she said. "You're in his hair, you know."

Annie often had lunch with Lucille. They had become friends somehow, maybe because when Lucille waited for Bernard she often visited with Annie from the doorway of the display windows, where after hours Annie would still be fussing over some detail.

"I'll make you a trade," Annie offered. "I'll do your laundry and ironing, clean your apartment."

"Oh, nothing as loathsome as that," Lucille said frowning. "I do need help, though, with some guests I have coming. You're a retired housewife, aren't you? Surely you can cook."

Annie agreed to cater two dinner parties for her the weekend of the seventeenth. Annie's mother, arriving the fifteenth, offered to help.

Lucille, for her part, followed her around the store every night that week, photographing displays. If Annie wasn't pleased with what was there, she made a new one on the spot, Lucille helping her to move and place things.

"You have an eye for composition," Lucille told her one night. "You may have more talent than Bernard," she said. "It's good he's getting rid of you."

Annie sent Sammy and her folks off on a sunny Sunday morning. For the first time in years, she now had time to herself—time she wasted, for the most part, worrying about bills. Annie had to admit it. Like Sammy, she hated being poor. Like now, when Sammy needed shoes and she needed something to wear to the interview. It made her feel at the mercy of some inexplicable force in the universe that on a whim could give or take away. How, she wanted to know, did *really* poor people manage? Just one year of scrambling for everything had beaten her down. People were not in charge of their own destinies when they were broke.

Annie had always thought the universe had plenty to go around, and that impartial distribution of it was possible. There was obviously a flaw in her logic. She spread all the bills out on the kitchen table in order of most and least overdue. Annie was writing checks when Lucille stopped by with the photographs for the portfolio. They were just right, Annie thought, dramatic, simple, professional. She'd get this job, she knew it.

"What's all this?" Lucille said.

"I'm trying to find some money here for an interview suit, you know, in case. But I guess I'll have to make do."

"Darling," she said. "You can't possibly wear anything you have." She peered over at the bills like she might peer at something in the garbage.

"Don't depress me," Annie said.

"Listen, I'll lend you some things—a silk blouse, a silk suit, a silk scarf. They'll be marvelous on you, now that you've dropped some fat." Lucille did not beat around the bush.

She doubted that Lucille's clothes would look good on her, but

Lucille was making a supreme effort in her behalf and Annie was grateful.

"Here," Lucille said, handing Annie some money. "I'll take it out in catering sometime."

"Lucille, I appreciate this but I can't," Annie said.

"Yes, you can. It's not for bills, it's for shoes or perfume or underwear. I want you to get that job or at least land this guy you're seeing. It's a favor to Bernard. You're driving him crazy."

"I don't know what to say," Annie said.

"One more thing. I don't want to be picky but I'm going to have my friend cut your hair. Something soft and sexy."

Annie had just gotten back into the bills when Paul stopped by. He wanted to show her a house that he was thinking of renting with an option to buy.

"Maybe I'll even buy some furniture from Morton," he said in the car. He winked at her.

"Hey," she said. "What happened to the person whose idea of decorating was to hang Janis Joplin posters and rusty Coca-Cola signs all over?"

He turned onto the highway that followed the Blackfoot east of town and then turned off the pavement onto a gravel road that wound through the trees into a yard above the river.

"Step this way," he said. "I'll show you the bedrooms."

It was a cloudless day, the water so blue it appeared unreal, like the blue on a Pepsi logo, and the sky, brilliant and sharp, differed only in chromatic tone, a perfect matching shade lighter.

She thought she liked the view best from the porch where she could see the river at a distance, in clear perspective, grounded. From here one could study the changing sky, watch clouds or mist rolling off the riverbank and contemplate the never-ending flow of water.

Now Paul was checking out the basement and the heating system and Annie followed a path down to the water. It was still early spring and the sun wasn't too hot. She loved sitting on a riverbank. Everything in her mind became clearer then. She liked to sit very still and imagine that her thoughts were physical things that she could cast into the water to be washed and sorted by the current. She saw that she needed to love Sammy in a less desperate, fearful way, allowing him to grow up and apart from her without running interference against the mistakes he might make, the opinions he might have.

She was trying to decide things, too. "We'll all move here," Paul had said moments before. "Or somewhere else if you don't like this."

She didn't think so, she'd said. So far she'd had two long-term relationships, one with Paul, one with Morton. For some reason she did not want them to be the extent of her experience.

"Why not try it?" he'd said. "It can't be moving you're worried about if you're thinking of going to Spokane."

But moving to the river with him was not the same as moving to Spokane for a better job. For one thing this place was quite a ways out from town, hardly a neighbor closer than a mile. But that was the least of it. Her greatest concern was Sammy.

No matter what the change in today's mores, parents wanted the adults living in the homes of their children's friends to be married. Teachers no doubt preferred it that way too. And for good reasons. Living with someone was a complicated undertaking when children were involved. You did not just jump into your car and go down the road if it didn't work out. You had to withdraw the kid from school and register him elsewhere, for one thing. And what if the kid got attached to the guy? Then what?

And there were finances to consider. How would she know whether she really wanted to live with Paul or whether she was just worried about money? Or for that matter loneliness, or managing a young boy by herself? It would be easy to think that isolating Sammy out here would somehow keep him off drugs and out of trouble.

She didn't want to turn to Paul out of weariness and misplaced financial or emotional need. She did not want something she had to assign value to or place conditions on.

And what if she decided she didn't like sex again? What about that? Sure she liked it at the moment but who wouldn't after almost a year without? Besides this was romantic now; what would happen after routines were established? She could honestly say she hadn't missed sex, had scarcely given it a thought until Paul turned up. Of course, that could be attributed to how busy she'd been and to other worries.

And this time she had to be absolutely sure she could face certain possibilities—infidelity, that love might wear itself out, or that Paul might simply abandon her again. She didn't want a repeat of the paranoia she'd once felt. Her fear at that time had to be as forbidding to Paul as her mother's threat to burn down Jake's had been to Nicholas. Perhaps Paul's unfaithfulness then had been a predictable reaction, an automatic response to entrapment. A self-fulfilling prophecy.

Then with Morton, because her fear was still there, she withheld something, had not given enough, guarded herself too closely against hurt and rejection. She had not allowed herself to feel much of anything, not even sexually. And Morton's unfaithfulness finally? Was that her fault too, or was there just some propensity in men to play around, an eventual need for someone else?

Bubba had once said as much. Not to her exactly, but to his friend, a woman named Hilge, who had sat at the bar one snowy afternoon where she and Bubba were playing chess at a nearby table. The woman had been sad and quiet for some time, watching them, finally joining them. Annie might have been sixteen at the time.

Annie's father sat down with them too from time to time and made attempts to cheer Hilge up. He could tell a woman about to cry in his bar and he hated that. But Hilge just sat there.

"Bubba," Hilge said finally, in tears at last, choking a little on her words, "why does Harold do this to me?"

"Hilge," he said, giving up the game for the moment, "it's not an easy thing to understand. But I think," he said, "that it's not something you should take personally. Look at it this way." Bubba emptied his drink. "In the process of evolution, at some important point in it, they say there was a great need to populate the earth with people." (Bubba never identified the *they* who said every-thing.) "Well, in that need of the time, the men had their work cut out for them. We'll call this man's bull stage where he ran around, you know, being the bull.

"Then the women were the cows. Pardon that, but the ones to carry the offspring for long months, then to nurse and take care of them." Hilge looked puzzled.

"Actually," he said, "I think what happened is that, because they were the burdened ones, it must have been the women who put down the first stakes and discouraged nomadic wanderings."

"Bubba, this means nothing to me!" Hilge said.

"What I'm saying is, man has never quite gotten over the bull, nomadic stage. And women, maybe, because they became the caretakers for everything, they took on a much different view of sex and resented the mens' freedom."

Annoyed now, Hilge said, "Well, I think I just need a new boyfriend."

"I think you just need a sandwich and coffee," Annie's father said from the bar.

If she had been Hilge, or older at the time, Annie would have asked, But how do woman handle their resentment? That's what she wanted to know. How did you allow men their freedom and forgo resentment? Could you merely let go, walk away, if infidelity didn't feel good? Without anger?

"Don't take it so personally," Bubba had said. What kind of advice was that?

"It's been a wonderful day," she told Paul. They had walked up the river and hiked up an old creek bed that led into some hills. And they had sat in soft grass to eat the sandwiches she had brought.

"Then let's camp out here next weekend," he said.

"I can't. Next weekend is Sammy's birthday."

"His birthday?"

"Yeah, so Morton's coming."

"Ah, to be twelve again."

"He'll be thirteen."

"Thirteen?"

"Yes." She was certain he was counting up the months in his head.

"There's something I should say about that," she said.

"It doesn't matter, the past is past."

What didn't matter? Whether Sammy was his son or Morton's?

"Listen, Annie. I love you. I love Sammy too. Isn't that the important thing?"

Chapter Eleven

After leaving Annie, Paul drove out along the river. He stopped at Clearwater Junction, several miles east of town, and had a beer. Then he headed north until he got to Seeley Lake. It was already dark by now and he parked along the east side of the lake and walked. It was still early in the year and none of the summer residents were around yet.

Even in the dark, he could see the tops of sailboats anchored all around. They were in rows in the marina, bouncing gently, and it made him a little dizzy—the waves slapping against each one rhythmically, hypnotically. It gave him the feeling that he was far away from the action, watching himself from some great distance, displaced and floating.

He took off his shoes so he could feel ground beneath him but the sand was cold and the wind-driven water sprayed his jeans, which chilled him further. So he sat down to put his shoes back on and the receding tide, shimmering in little drifts across the sand, caused another floating sort of disorientation.

It was not hard to figure. If Sammy was born in April, he was either damn premature or Annie was pregnant the day she left. He remembered that day clearly because it was Halloween. He was headed home when a sign in front of a florist caught his eye. BUY

THE WITCH SOME FLOWERS, it said, and he'd darted across the traffic and pulled in and did just that, bought a rather spectacular bouquet of orange mums and white roses. There were pussy willows and some kind of bent twigs that had been painted black in the arrangement too.

But when he got home, Annie was already gone. He was stunned.

"What do you mean gone?" he said to Morton. "When?"

"Early this morning."

"She'll be back," he said.

Morton just looked at him and shook his head. "Why the hell don't you call her when you disappear like that. So she doesn't worry?"

"Mind your own goddamn business," he'd said. He wasn't about to start checking in and out like he owed her that.

The bouquet sat on the dining table and the candy Annie had bought for trick-or-treaters lay untouched, on the hall table near the door, for months and months. He had not answered the bell that Halloween night. He had sat in his bedroom drinking beer in the dark.

He'd known at the time that Annie would be mad that he hadn't come home all night. She probably wouldn't believe that he'd driven out to the river and fished, then fell asleep in the van. He'd trudged up and down the banks to keep warm in the late fall cold because he needed to be close to the water, needed to hold his fly rod in his hand and to cast it again and again across the water. He couldn't explain it but when he got depressed, it was one of the few activities that could snap him out of it. He never told Annie but he feared mental illness.

Everyone gets depressed, she'd say. But he was not just anyone. He was a person whose family had a history of mental illness. Because of some papers he'd found, he was pretty sure that his own uncle, when a boy, had gone crazy. Then the boy, Paul suspected, was secretly shuffled off to a place where he was kept restrained and drugged for reasons no one any longer knew.

Paul had tried to find out more about it not long before leaving Chicago. He'd gone to this strange place on the edge of Highland Park, not far from their home. As far as Paul could see from the entryway, the place was like a rest home. It was very quiet there and the atmosphere was somber, not unlike a funeral home. The receptionist almost whispered, as though giants or monsters slept there, too dangerous to disturb. Then after several minutes she ushered him into an office where a fat, ruddy-complexioned man talked quietly too and explained that there were no records that could help him. They didn't know why his uncle had been there, why he would have been restrained or anything else. He appeared to doubt that Paul knew what he was talking about. "How do you know he was kept here?"

"Because I found receipts for payment up until 1958."

"Perhaps he was moved to another facility then," the man said, smiling.

"No, he died."

"1958, you say," the man said, going to the filing cabinet. "Sorry our records do not go back that far."

Paul went home and reread the journal he had found written in a boyish handwriting that he recognized as his father's. After his father died, Paul had found the journal wrapped in a silk kerchief in the large pocket of the old Packard stored in the carriage house. Perhaps his father hid it there or even sat in the large backseat on its stiff upholstery to write the few entries.

The first one said: "Mother had Arthur admitted to the home today. She said he'll be happy there but we can't see him because it upsets him and he gets depressed then like Aunt Agnes used to. But Mama says he won't be like her. He'll get well."

Another entry said: "I hid in the bushes and looked in Arthur's window at the home last night. I saw him in a chair asleep and so I tapped on the window to wake him. But when he woke up, I saw that something held his wrists to the arms of the chair. He looked right at me once but his eyes were funny and he didn't know me, his own brother. Or maybe he couldn't see me in the dark through the bars."

A few years after discovering the journal Paul found a bill for cremation and hundreds of other bills from the home. "For Arthur P. Tomlin, patient care," they said. Did the *P* stand for Paul? Had he been named Paul Arthur after this man? He'd taken the bills to his mother.

"Who's Arthur P. Tomlin?" he asked her. But she said she didn't know and looked so perplexed when she studied the bills that he believed her. She seemed as mystified by them as he was. He never showed her the journal though. He simply put it back where he found it and left it there—at first because he didn't want to disclose his own hideout in the carriage house; and when he was older, because he guessed that his father had gone to some trouble to keep this from his mother. Paul decided to respect that. He even understood it.

Paul got up now and walked along the lake shore. He ended up walking most of the night until dawn, when he drove back to Missoula. He didn't bother going home. He slept in the car in front of the garage until it opened up.

Everyone who came in to work could see that he wanted to be left alone. Finally, about noon, Paul told his shop foreman that he was leaving.

He went home, showered and got into bed. He slept the rest of the afternoon and night and woke up the next morning late for work. He felt a need to hurry, to get going, after all that sleep. He felt uncomfortable. Life would no longer be the same for him. Alterations had been made. Because if Annie had been pregnant that day she left, and it was pretty clear she had been, then he was Sammy's father.

And like most everything else that had gone on in his life, he was the last to know. It was bad enough that his own brother married his girl and didn't tell him for almost a year. But for neither one to tell him that she was pregnant at the time was really pushing it.

It was so ironic. He'd avoided committing himself to Annie for just that reason, that he did not want to be a father. He intended never to marry anyone because of the mental illness business for one thing—though his mysterious depressions had disappeared years before. What's more, he didn't want to bring any more unwanted children, like himself and Morton, into the world. Whenever he thought about parents he thought of his own. Or those people who used to hang out at all the big keggers around town.

For several years in Missoula there had been keggers that Paul had never seen the likes of before or since. They were huge organized bashes, sometimes up Pattee Canyon or on Miller Creek or the Bitterroot River, where thousands of people, mostly university students, drank from hundreds of kegs of beer. There were always bands and drugs and craziness. He remembered that some big-name band was even brought in by helicopter one year. Another year, a hang glider tripped a power line and crashed. And because of the great traffic jams such a kegger occasioned, it was hours before an ambulance could get through or before the utility company could restore the power. That year, without music and dancing, and because of that awful, sobering moment when the hang glider came crashing to the ground, everyone got unthinkably drunk. And to these extraordinary events some people even brought children. Paul remembered the children, how they wandered around the crowds amusing themselves, sometimes playing with the dogs that came too, sometimes sleeping right in the middle of the deafening electronic sounds of hard rock. They were pitiful children, dirty, slightly ragged and too thin. But they didn't cause any trouble; they just waited patiently for their parents, there somewhere, doing acid or getting drunk or, more like it, both.

So when Paul had seen Annie with Sammy, he'd been amazed, fascinated, relieved. He liked the way she looked at the boy or sometimes scolded him or touched his cheek. She had such regard for him, such a tender respect for him that Paul was moved. But then, unexpectedly, he'd had to turn away, distressed by this sudden evidence of what he himself had missed.

It was almost nine o'clock and he'd have a lot of things at the garage to take care of after being gone most of the day before. Finally Paul got out of bed. He stepped with trepidation onto a cold, bare floor, realizing that he was unwilling after all these years, especially after all these years, to assume the belated and unfamiliar posture of father.

Annie was in the front yard raking up dead leaves and old grass when Lucille pulled up.

"So what did you think of the house on the river?" she said as she slammed the car door.

Annie shrugged.

"Did he propose?"

"Not marriage," she said.

"Oh well, move in on him, make him utterly dependent and then he will."

"Lucille," she said. "What makes you think I want to get married?"

"All women do." This from a woman who lived only for her latest affair.

"Say, darling," she went on, "could you do me a favor? I'm having guests Friday evening. Nothing fancy, a barbecue. But could you make me some canapés, something elegant and a nice dessert? Maybe some sort of potato dish and salad too?"

"I guess," Annie said, stooping over for a dog bone. She needed the money but she wasn't crazy about catering all Lucille's parties.

"How about small popovers, the kind used for cream puffs?" Lucille suggested. "Maybe fill some with crab salad and the rest with berries and whipped cream."

"I guess," Annie said again. As she recalled, the only time she'd made popovers they had collapsed into little soggy mounds.

"A few hors d'oeuvres, some dips, maybe clam and anchovy."

Annie nodded.

"Or whatever you think," she said. "I'll stop by tomorrow night. I have to run."

The store was busy the next day. There was a sale in the furniture department and Annie waited on couples who argued with each other, on people who didn't want a couch, or love seat, or bedroom set unless the rug or lamps or bedspreads were on sale too. They weren't. She waited on one woman who told her she didn't know why she was there, usually only inferior things were on sale, and that she hated sales. Then she spent a thousand dollars. Annie watched while mothers, typically in sets of two, dickered over colors and styles while their children ran between displays and tried to jump on the beds—nasty little kids usually with something in their mouths, chewing gum or drooling suckers.

"Have you heard anything from Spokane?" she asked on her lunch break.

"No," Mr. Perry told her. "Don't worry, it's only been a few weeks."

"Three," she said. She wanted that job now more than ever.

"Annie," he said. "If you think the customers are obnoxious now, wait until you're doing their whole living room. Then they're really touchy. Ask Bernard."

She sat down wearily at a table across from him. "I suppose," she said.

"So are you moving in with Paul?" Lucille asked her that night.

"I don't think so," she said. "Too many problems."

"What does Sammy think of all this?"

"I don't know." She poured Lucille a glass of wine.

"Such a peasant's wine," Lucille said.

"Isn't it?"

"I was poor once," she said. "It was ugly."

Annie laughed.

"Say, why don't you come to the barbecue? It won't be all old married couples," she said. "There will be a few singles."

"Sammy's coming home that night," she said.

"So leave early."

Annie had a miserable week. Monday she ran out of gas and Thursday she had a flat and, between the two incidents, she misplaced her AAA card. The phone company had threatened her with a shut-off notice if she didn't pay immediately and then the store put a new salesman in furniture, a real jerk. What's more, Lucille had come by the store three times and made a nuisance of herself. She had taken to stopping by to chat lately, bringing her a greasy lunch or butter cookies.

"She's spying on me," Bernard said.

"What?" Annie asked.

"She's a jealous woman."

"I don't wonder with all the women you see," she said.

"She docsn't know about them. She's worried about you."

"Hah! Frankly, I don't know what she sees in you," she teased.

"I'm not without my charms," he said.

On top of all that Paul was moody most of the week but Annie ignored him. They went shopping for Sammy's birthday and Annie planned a party.

"Is it all right with you if Morton's there?" she asked him.

He frowned. "I guess so," he said. "If it's awkward, I'll go home."

There were about thirty people at Lucille's barbecue Friday. Annie unloaded a car full of food, popovers not included. Bernard was there—of course, he lived with Lucille most of the time.

"Must I see you socially, too?" Bernard said, winking at her as he passed by.

It was a strange evening. Annie heard couples arguing with each other, jealous of one another, accusing the other of flirting—and she kept coming upon them unexpectedly in the hallway or kitchen. The first chance she got, she sneaked out the back door.

Annie turned on the television when she got home and tried to get into a movie, but she was too tired and her mind raced wildly over the day, too exhausted to settle down or concentrate on any one thing. She had just turned it off when Sammy and Morton arrived.

Morton said he was tired too, that it had been a grueling drive in the heat. "A million semis," he said. "I hope the traffic's better in the morning."

"You're leaving so soon. What about the birthday party?"

"We already had one in Butte," he said. "But I'll take you both out for breakfast. Okay?"

Annie was disappointed for Sammy but too tired to protest. Sammy, however, was full of energy. He unloaded the car, brought in the luggage and ran out back to see the dog.

"I think he had a good time," Morton said.

It turned out he had. She heard all about it the next morning after Morton left.

"Grandma had us over for dinner one night," he said.

"Your dad went too?"

"I said *us,* didn't I?"

"Well, that's nice," she said.

"And there was a fire at Jake's."

"What!"

"Just a little one. An electrical fire but Grandpa put it out."

"Geezus," she said.

"Dad might get married," he said.

"Really?" That was certainly interesting. "Who to?"

"The girlfriend. Marge, the one I told you about."

"So how do you feel about that?"

"I don't care. She's real nice to me. She said I could come live with them if I want."

Annie let that one pass.

"She changed all the furniture."

"She what?"

"Yeah, it's all modern now."

That wasn't all. Sammy had gotten sick one night because he ate too much fudge—and drank a little beer. "How much beer?" "One bottle." Marge had a niece in high school who was going to work the summer in Yellowstone Park. Marge had a job at the Montana Power Company but was going to quit it when they got married. Grandma Miriam was in Montreal visiting a friend. Sammy's old friend Clifford was going to a basketball camp in Arizona. His parents were getting a divorce. Morton had an Atari game and a new VCR. Marge bought a dishwasher. (There seemed no end to the information Sammy had brought home.) The copper mine was filling up with water because the company didn't pump it out anymore—it was closed down. Maybe it would be a lake soon, she should see it. What did she think about him living there with dad the school year?

"Can I think about that?" she said. Morton had brought it up the night before after Sammy went to bed.

"Think about what?" Paul asked, peeking in the back door. "Happy birthday," he said and held out a package for Sammy.

· · ·

"You're quiet, everything okay?" Paul asked on the way to the store for ice cream.

"I had a fight with Morton last night," she told him. "He wants Sammy to live with him during the school year."

"What did you say?"

" 'No.' So he said, 'Let Sammy choose.' I said, 'I don't think you should make Sammy make a decision like that. Either way he chooses, he'll feel guilty.' "

"Good," Paul said. "Because I plan on both of you living with me."

"Guess what?" she said to change the subject. "We have the house to ourselves. All the kids are camping out in Todd's yard tonight after the party. They have this huge tent." She had made them promise not to run around the neighborhood all night. She could just imagine them taking a ghetto blaster out there, raiding gardens, ringing doorbells—or were they too old for that?

"Great," Paul said. "Does that mean I don't have to go home tonight?"

"I don't know," she said. "After all, Morton's living with someone. But I feel so weird about it."

"Why don't we just be honest with him. I'll talk to him the first chance I get," he said.

When they got home, Paul lit the barbecue and Annie marinated the spareribs that Sammy wanted for dinner. The boys were playing Frisbee and Paul joined them.

After dinner, when she came in from the backyard to the kitchen, she heard Sammy and Todd talking in the dining room.

"Your mom's not so crabby like mine," Todd said.

"Sometimes she is," Sammy said.

"Your uncle's nice too."

"I think they're having an affair."

"You mean doing it?"

"Yeah."

"How do you know?" Todd asked eagerly.

"They act funny."

At seven-thirty the next morning, without knocking, Sammy came barreling through her bedroom door.

"Mom," he said, "Can I . . ."

Annie sat up, pulling the sheets up around her. She felt Paul move beside her.

"I thought . . . ," Sammy said. He sort of backed out of the room, amazed it seemed.

"I'll go talk to him," Paul said and put on his pants.

Annie waited. She was worried. She couldn't help it. She could not recall ever walking in on her parents. In fact, she and her friend Mary Lou had once sat outside her parents' room for an hour hoping to hear something sexual. But they gave up on it when her father began to snore.

"What did he say?" she asked Paul when he came back twenty minutes later—she timed it.

"I couldn't find him," he said.

"I'll make coffee," Annie said and got up in a daze.

She should have told Paul right then, it was the perfect time. The rest of the day was too hectic—they took Sammy and the rest of the kids to a street fair downtown. Nothing appeared to be bothering Sammy. Annie was the only one with something on her mind.

"Paul," she said as she walked him to the car that night. "We have to talk."

"Okay."

"About Sammy. There's something I have . . ."

"Don't," he said. "I don't want to hear it." He said this angrily. "Annie," he said, more gently now. "I'm not ready to be a father."

That infuriated her. "Don't worry," she said walking back toward the house. "Sammy already has a father."

"Aren't you going to say good-bye?" he asked.

"Good-bye."

"I'll call you," he said and drove away.

Annie was furious all evening. Wasn't that just like him? He hadn't changed. He would never be ready for anything, not for her, not for marriage, not for Sammy. The big jerk couldn't handle anything, not even what he thought—that Sammy was his son.

When she got home, much to Sammy's surprise, Annie slammed doors, refused to take a phone call from Lucille and took a bath.

If Paul couldn't deal with what he thought, she wondered in the tub with some of Morton's Scotch, how could he deal with the truth?

The truth was that Annie didn't know, could not be certain herself, which of the two brothers was the father of her son.

Some of those evenings, years before, when Paul hadn't come home, Morton had understood what she was going through. Several times he'd coaxed her from her bedroom, made a fire, brought her a glass of wine, listened to her, held her as she cried. And things happened. Tender, caring things to comfort her because Morton loved her then, even though, more than anyone in the world, he loved his brother Paul.

The first time anything happened she had been crying, literally on his shoulder, and to their surprise the cot they were sitting on collapsed beneath them, dumping them onto the floor. They had begun laughing then and quite unexpectedly Morton caught her by the shoulders and kissed her gently, then passionately. There occurred then an inevitable struggle, a push-pull, a wanting and an allowing though she herself for any number of practical or moral reasons had forbidden it. For Morton too. What happened between them was his only deviation ever from the straight way he saw the world, his only step over the ethical boundaries he had constructed for himself and always maintained.

"I know you love him," he told her one night. "And I can never come between you. I've betrayed my brother's trust but I can't help it. I can't stand to see you hurt. He acts like an asshole sometimes but I honestly believe he loves you. If I thought he didn't, I'd fight for you."

Annie always appreciated that breach he'd consented to for her sake and it may have been the reason she could marry him in spite of everything. She loved him, too, though perhaps in a more brotherly way than she'd loved Paul. But maybe that kind of love outlasted the other and was why they were good friends now.

Chapter Twelve

Paul went home. He had left a window open in the kitchen and now there were moths and mosquitoes all over the place. He shut the window and made a note to get screens and bug spray and put it on the refrigerator. He took out some ice and started to make a drink. He changed his mind and got out a pop, still thinking about Annie. It had been a nice weekend and he was glad that Morton hadn't stayed for the party. He doubted that he'd have gone then. He would have felt too out of place.

Paul was worried about Sammy, worried because Sammy had burst in on him and Annie like that, though they were only sleeping. Paul wished he had found him. He wanted to explain his intentions and tell him how much he and his mother meant to him. He didn't want that scene to be what Sammy thought about when, years later, he looked back on the various relationships of his life. Though he didn't want to compare Sammy to himself, he did anyway.

Was he making a mistake getting involved here? Was this just one more way to compete with Morton? Were there things he still hadn't forgiven him for? Paul ran through a list in his head. No, all that was petty stuff he didn't care about. He thought they had managed, whenever possible, to settle their disputes as they occurred.

Paul, as the second child, might have had it easier than Morton had. Perhaps to his advantage, Paul was less visible to Miriam, and less favored. In any case, after their father died, their mother made Morton their father's replacement.

Often when there were other boys in the backyard playing catch or keepaway, Miriam would come out on the verandah. "Morty," she'd call. "Could I borrow him for a few minutes?" she'd ask the other kids. And sometimes the boys would be gone before Miriam let him go.

"Where's everyone?" Morton would ask on a dead run for the backyard.

"They left," Paul would tell him.

Morton would look so disappointed that Paul would feel sorry for him. Sometimes Paul would sneak in to see what was keeping him, probably out of jealousy because she never called *him* in. What on earth did his mother have Morton doing in there? he'd wonder as he looked about the large house. And he'd find Morton at the piano playing a sonata for old lady friends of Miriam's, or at a French lesson with some tutor that had a crush on Miriam, or worse, the poor kid would be up in her bedroom with a tailor getting measured for some suits he'd have to wear to the opera. After Father died, it was Morton, never Paul, who had to accompany her to a play or opera.

Paul could still see the look on Morton's face one day when Miriam had them with her on some errand in the car. Martha, the housekeeper, was driving and they were in the backseat. Martha had to slow way down because a group of boys were playing baseball in the street.

"Look!" Morton had said to Paul, pointing to the boys. Mother looked too and said, "Those poor boys." But Paul knew by the way Morton looked at them, then turned and watched them until they were out of sight, that Morton thought as he did, *Poor boys, my ass.*

Morton then, maybe in rebellion for being made the little man of the house, became the ruler of it, the dictator over a whole kingdom. He became bossy, opinionated and domineering.

When Paul was thirteen, it was Morton who had pounded on him for skipping school; then at fourteen it was Morton who had punished him for getting drunk.

"You little idiot," Morton had said. He had stood above Paul as he knelt over the toilet throwing up generous portions of vodka and sloe gin. Morton then brought in his radio and played Sousa marches at full volume. He didn't stop until Paul, furious, his head splitting, grabbed the radio from Morton, ran to the window and tossed it through the glass down into the garden.

And it was Morton who objected when Paul had not wanted to sell furniture down at the store.

"But that's the reason I'm working so hard down there, to secure you a future. You're just a lazy, selfish brat and always have been," he said.

"Morton, go fuck yourself," Paul told him.

And poor Miriam. She had expected and groomed Morton to be always by her side if need be. But, like Paul, he ran off to live in an area of the country where most people could give a diddly-shit about what your father did for a living or where your grandfather went to school. And like Paul, he fell for the first really unpretentious girl he'd ever met. What a comedy life was. He and Morton liked Annie because they hated the type of woman they had grown up around and likewise Annie was drawn to them because they were different from the men around Jake's.

Paul wanted to be a better role model than Morton or Miriam had been to him or, he feared, than Morton now was for Sammy. Paul wanted Sammy's memories of growing up to be happier than his own.

When he was nine Paul had gone to Camp Potawatamee. Camp Lobotomy they called it. It was the summer after his father died and he had come down with something. While all the other boys swam and hiked and played ball, he had hung out in the tent with stomach cramps and an aching head. When they finally broke camp and loaded everything into trucks and returned to town, his mother was not there to pick him up. He sighed and walked over to someone else's mother to ask for a ride. They let him off at the gates on the edge of the driveway and by now he was so tired that he dragged his backpack and sleeping bag behind him through the gravel, not caring whether they tore or not.

The house was dark except for a small light in the living room that they usually left on when they went out. He wondered where Morton and his mother had gone, where Martha and the maid were.

He went around to the side and dropped his stuff on the patio and went in through the breezeway to the back door. Once in the kitchen, still in the dark, he opened the refrigerator. He could see a dried-up piece of steak, an opened bottle of pop, moldy cheese and a carton of milk. Oh, yeah, he remembered, the help were on vacation. He grabbed the Pepto-Bismol and took a large sip.

Paul closed the door to the refrigerator and went down the hall toward the stairs. But something caught his attention; he heard sounds from the living room. His stomach was still queasy as he tiptoed to the end of the hall and stood in the entrance to the large living room. Across its breadth he saw something on the couch in the almost-dark room. First he stood there trying to focus, then in wonder, as the shadow against the drapes became his mother, moving ungracefully up and down, as she sat over the penis of the unidentified guest beneath her.

Paul ran up to his room where he threw up the last meal from Camp Lobotomy and cried himself to sleep.

The next day at work, there was news.

"Annie," Mr. Perry said. "Spokane called. They want you to call back on your break."

"We would like to interview you," a Ms. Irving told her. "We'll be in Missoula on the fifth, if that's convenient for you."

"What's the matter with you?" Mr. Perry asked her later. "I thought you'd be thrilled."

The news was not enough to cheer her up. She'd have welcomed it the night before when she was angry but today it didn't seem to make any difference. Now she just had the feeling that her life was out of her hands, that it would run its course with or without her participation.

Paul did not call all week. She expected him to, he had said he would. She alternately refused to stay home in case he did or hung by the phone so as not to miss him. He'd changed his mind. So would she. Better to have it end now than later—that's what her mother would say. Her mother had answers for any puzzle life might put forth. When one door closes, a better one opens. If you let a thing go, it will come back to you—if it's really yours.

Philosophy obviously acquired after the days of threatening to burn down Jake's.

Sammy sensed Annie's mood. He was thoughtful and quiet, as though she were sick and noise might disturb her. Her heart went out to him. What a nice kid he was. Didn't he wonder what was going on? He made no mention of Paul. Did he feel implicated?

"You want to talk about it?" Lucille asked her one night on the phone.

"Talk about what?" Annie regretted the irritation in her voice.

"When you're ready, let me know." Lucille hung up. No doubt her feelings were hurt.

But what could Annie say? That she'd made a huge error, gotten burned again by the same guy or that she was at the same time, all at once, every moment, feeling ten things.

Annie tried to keep her mind on the interview coming up. She went shopping for a new suit, tried to envision herself happy and excited in Spokane.

Her mind was not an easy one to manage. It was too full. This week, her brain wandered around aimlessly, sent off in indiscriminate directions by such innocuous things as a gasoline spill, coffee boiling, a child singing and she would at once be lifted to a scene of her past.

Only today a church bell on her way home from work made her remember sitting in damp moss years ago up at Southern Cross, a place on the mountain above Georgetown Lake. She could feel that moss against her hands, smell the pine trees behind her, see every detail of early sunlight hitting that smooth, calm lake. Not an hour later, wet, fresh-mowed lawn made her recall a Girl Scout camp-out, where in the night she woke to the smell of clover and the faraway, haunting sound of cowbells echoing through the mountains in the dark. There wasn't a star in sight.

By the time Paul did get around to calling, eight days later, she was dismayed. Where had he been four days ago, five days ago when she needed him? By now she had moved on, and owing to the great distance she had gone, he'd never be able to catch up to her. That was how she felt.

"No," she told him. "We can't go camping next weekend. I have to get some things ready for a job interview Monday."

"So you're really serious about that job in Spokane?"

"Yes, and if I get it," she said, "I'm taking it." There was silence on his end.

"Paul," she said. "I don't think we can go back. Please understand."

"Wait," he said. "Let me see you for dinner so we can talk."

"No," she said. She did not want Sammy to think they were back together again.

"I just want to talk to you. Then I promise, if you want, to leave you alone."

"No," she said.

"Have dinner with me after your interview, at least. Just one last time. Please."

"All right," she said. She made arrangements to meet him and hung up.

Her mood, after that, improved remarkably. She took Lucille out for a drink and apologized. "I don't know what got into me," she said. "I'm sorry I was so bitchy." Lucille eyed her suspiciously.

Sammy, seeing the change, must have decided it was his turn to be bitchy, that she owed him.

"I have to wear this shirt," he declared.

She'd just finished the week's laundry. "I'm not going to the laundromat for one shirt."

"Wash it out by hand then," he demanded.

"Sammy, if it's really important to you, I can do that. But you'd better ask me, not tell me." What was so special about this shirt anyway? It said 'Sex Wax' across the back, had a skier on its front. She didn't know where he'd gotten it.

He stomped off to his room, not ready to yield to reason yet. The next day, she noticed, he wore it dirty.

He groaned every night about doing the dishes, spent all of two minutes at it, aggressively taking out hostility on them, breaking a few, leaving them spotted and half rinsed in the drainer, soap suds all over the floor. He neglected to feed the dog or water the plants, disappeared without a clue to his whereabouts and was generally a snot for three days.

"You know I have an interview this afternoon," she reminded him on Monday. He was playing catch in the living room.

"I know," he said. "Don't forget I'm going out for pizza tonight after my game."

"I won't," she said. "Will you please go outside with that ball?"

"Criminy," he said, getting up.

"Aren't you going to wish me good luck?"

"Good luck," he said halfheartedly and went out the back door.

Annie was nervous and decided to walk to the store. When she got there, she was early. Her interview was at three o'clock. She found a ladies' room where she touched up her makeup, combed her hair, smoothed out her suit, made sure her blouse was neatly tucked inside her skirt and gave herself a pep talk. She took off her running shoes and put on dress pumps.

Annie was directed to sit at the end of a conference table in a small room with three interviewers, Ms. Irving and two men. They were serious, cautious people who resembled each other—the suits, the posture, the glasses—and who seemed more concerned about why she wanted this job than whether she might be good at it. How did you begin to answer a question like that? Because it gets smoggy in Missoula. I have wanderlust. The new guy in furniture is hustling me. My lover . . . All that raced through her mind, but surely she hadn't said any of it.

Then Ms. Irving turned off the lights and showed slides of different window displays they'd had over the year in the Spokane and Seattle stores. She pointed to different details on the screen, explaining how each neatly augmented the overall appeal of the display. Annie found most of them either crowded and lavish or stark and spare.

One had a totally black background and one white mannequin, hairless and in a ballet posture perhaps, adorned only by gray pearls at her neck and waist.

Another had a whole corner window of broken umbrellas. The tattered, damaged umbrellas—some had been inverted by wind— were draped along the floor, flung against the walls, hung from the ceiling. In their midst a figure stood wearing only a trench coat,

suggesting with her bare head and feet that she was nude under-
neath and, by the way she held one edge of the coat, perhaps also a
flasher.

They hardly glanced at Annie's portfolio. The woman, all business and good manners, was the first to shake her hand courteously. They would call her soon. Annie was now dismissed and
she left, still thinking about the umbrellas.

There was plenty of time before she was to meet Paul. Annie
pulled her running shoes out of the small bag she'd brought for her
portfolio, makeup and shoes. She spent the rest of the afternoon
walking along the streets downtown, then along the river. She saw
tourists taking pictures, children in Little League uniforms walking in groups of twos or threes, and older kids playing Frisbee. A
businessman with a briefcase whizzed by her on a skateboard,
jumping off it at the curb, crossing the street, only to hop back on
at the opposite side and disappear down the block. The man on the
skateboard cheered her up. She was taking life too seriously, she
decided, and stopped at a little bar for a drink.

When she got to the riverfront park, the sun was still bright
across the water. Birds nearby were fighting soundlessly over leftovers a young couple were throwing to them across the grass.
Annie was tired and sweaty and her feet hurt. But she was ready for
whatever Paul might say and the decision the interviewers would
come to.

She saw him pull up to the curb now and wave. When she got
into the car, he kissed her cheek. He was unusually quiet as he
drove through town and across the bridge. He pulled into the old
train depot on the other side of the river, now a restaurant, and
parked.

Evidently he'd made reservations. There was a table ready for
them by the window, with a bucket of champagne chilling. A
waiter filled their glasses. The sun went behind the mountains and
a rosy glow remained at the horizon. They could see across the
river, lights from downtown shimmered in the current.

Paul made a toast. "Here's to this evening, a celebration of many
things."

What did he mean? Did he assume she had turned down the job,
would make up with him, take him home?

They ordered. There was an uncomfortable silence then and she sipped her drink and he smiled at her.

"How was the interview?" he asked.

"I don't know. I'm awful at that kind of thing. My mind goes blank."

He understood, he said, and began to tell her about some awful interviews he'd had. This was all very odd, to be sitting here discussing interviews with an estranged lover. He had not even asked about Sammy, nor had he referred to the past week and a half.

Their food came and they began to eat. Paul seemed preoccupied.

Then he put down his fork and pushed his plate aside.

"Okay, so we'll get married," he said.

She was too surprised for the moment to say anything.

"Don't you want to?" he asked.

"Listen, Paul, you don't understand about Sammy."

"Yes, I do," he said. "He's my son. I'm ready for that now. It just took time."

"No," she said sadly, realizing how hard this would be for him. "You don't understand. I wanted to tell you from the beginning but you wouldn't listen. Sammy could be Morton's son."

"He was premature?"

"No, full-term."

"You mean you slept with my brother before you left me? My own brother went to bed with you?"

"Yes," she said.

Paul slammed down his drink angrily.

"I admit it was a terrible thing but listen to me."

He didn't answer and she thought, perhaps, it was best to leave.

"I can't talk to your back," she said. "Look at me."

When he didn't, she threw her napkin into her half-eaten salad, grabbed her things and walked out. She was running across the parking lot when he caught up to her.

"But why?" he said. "Tell me why." He had hold of her shoulders now, was white with indignation.

"What did you expect? You just took off without a word any-time you were in the mood. You were too arrogant even to consider you might be throwing us together." She pulled away and started walking again. She wanted to get to the street and find a cab.

"But my brother," he said, almost in tears.

"Don't blame him," she said. "I was certain you were seeing that Joannie."

"No, I swear it," he said. "Did Morton tell you that?" They were on the street now.

"No. Later, after we were married, he told me you weren't. But at the time, maybe he thought you had someone else too."

"I loved you, Annie. I admit I was playing around then. But I loved you."

She stopped walking. She saw a cab down the block and she waved at it.

"So you were playing around. Yet you can't see any connection between that and what happened between Morton and me." The cab pulled up to the curb.

"And here I felt guilty all those years because I thought it was something I'd imagined."

Annie got into the backseat of the cab. "Good-bye, Paul," she said.

She thought she heard him say something else as the cab pulled away. She did not look back.

Early the next morning, Paul was at her door.

"Where's Sammy?" he asked.

"He just left for ball practice," she said.

"I couldn't sleep all night. I had to see you. Can I come in?" They were still standing in the doorway.

She let him pass.

"I've been a bastard," he said. "It was all my fault. Morton even tried to warn me. He said I didn't appreciate you, that if I didn't start, I'd lose you. I was too selfish then to see what I had."

He sat down on a chair. Annie sat on the couch. "But I do now," he said. "I don't care who Sammy's father is, I love him. And I see now that Morton and I've wasted the years. We all have." He made no move toward her, just sat there.

He seemed embarrassed now. "Does Morton think Sammy's his son?"

"Of course not. I told him when he asked me to marry him that I was pregnant and it could be yours."

"And he's lived with that all these years?"

"Yes."

"What a bastard I am," he said again. "Will you forgive me?"

"Yes," she said.

"And marry me?"

"I have to talk to Sammy first. He comes first."

"Right," he said. He had now joined her on the couch and he pulled her to his side.

"There's something else."

"What?" he said, kissing her ear.

"Remember that I told you how I felt about sex with Morton, that I just reached a point where I hated it?"

"I remember," he said. "You like it now, don't you?"

"So far," she said. "But what if after a few years I feel that way again?"

"I guarantee you," he said, taking her blouse off. "You will never get tired of sex with me."

"See how arrogant you are," she said and threw the blouse at him. The phone was ringing.

"Hello," Annie said.

"Annie, this is Ms. Irving," The word *Ms.* hung there on the phone wire like static.

"Welcome to the team," she said. "We voted unanimously to offer you the position."

"Oh, dear," Annie said.

Chapter Thirteen

"You're going to give up a swanky job like that for a guy?" Lucille asked. She was sitting in the kitchen shelling peas. She'd come for dinner.

"Maybe it's not as swanky as I thought," Annie said. "I want to go back to school."

"How come?"

"I don't know. When I saw the kind of window displays they have in Spokane and Seattle, I realized I was in over my head."

"What does Sammy say?"

"About what?"

"About you getting married?"

"I'm not."

"What?"

"I decided to just give it a year."

"Why?"

"Well, I want to try it out first." When she'd told Paul she sensed . . . relief maybe.

"Try it out, huh?" Lucille looked amused.

Annie just grinned at her. She was basting a chicken that needed another fifteen minutes or so in the oven.

"So what does Sammy think about all this?"

"He says it's okay."

Paul had taken them out to dinner. All the momentous occasions of her life, it seemed, took place in restaurants. "I love your mother," Paul told Sammy. "I want to marry her." He'd paused here and looked at Annie. "She says no, but that she'll live with me and decide later, that is, if you'll come too." Sammy took it very seriously. He might have been a father giving away the bride.

"It's okay with me, Mom," he said, acknowledging her presence there finally. They had all toasted then. "To us," Paul said. Then began a flurry of plan-making. Paul wanted to move them right away so Sammy could enjoy the river and woods before school started again, that is, if they all agreed on that place. They had to decide soon, he said, and he wanted Sammy to see it first. Annie had to give notice at the store, take out a student loan and enroll in classes. She had to tell Morton, her folks, decide what to do with her furniture. Paul said leave it, they could both start over with whatever she liked. Sammy groaned. "She likes junk," he said.

"It was a very nice evening," she told Lucille.

"I'll set the table," Lucille said, unimpressed.

After Lucille left, she called Morton. A woman answered. Marge. "Who's calling, please?"

"This is Annie," she said.

"I'm sorry, Morton's in the shower now."

At this hour? Annie wondered. Morton always took his shower at 7:35 A.M.

"Will you please ask him to call me back?" she asked.

"Is anything wrong?"

"Oh, no, but it is important."

"What's up?" he said when he called her back ten minutes later.

"A lot. Do you think you could come for the weekend? We need to talk."

"What's wrong?"

"Nothing," she said. She didn't want to discuss this on the phone. She also wanted him to spend time with Sammy before the move. Besides, she not only didn't want to go there, she didn't have time. She wondered if he'd bring Marge.

It wasn't easy getting Morton alone. She waited up the night he arrived until midnight, when Sammy finally went to bed. By this time, naturally, Sammy had told him they were moving in with Paul, that Annie wasn't ready to get married yet, that she was going to go to school, that Paul was taking him to a football game, and everything else he could think of. Morton took it all in with an air of restrained astonishment and three Scotch and sodas.

"I just want you both to be happy, Annie," he said after Sammy went to bed. She supposed he meant her and Sammy, not her and Paul.

"I know you do."

"Will Paul try to replace me with Sammy?"

"He can never do that."

"I was an ass," he said. "I didn't give him any attention. I regret it."

Annie passed him ice cubes for his drink.

"But I'm doing better," he said. "You won't believe this but I spend quality time with him now."

"I know," she said. "I can tell, it makes Sammy happy." She smiled across the table at him. She planned to tell Morton that she'd told Paul everything. She didn't know quite how to bring it up.

"Does Paul think he's Sammy's father?" Morton asked after a long pause, as though reading her mind.

"No, I told him all that."

"How'd he take it?"

"Not too good at first," she said and they both laughed.

"I'll bet," Morton said.

"Don't let him hurt you again, Annie," he said, suddenly serious now.

"I won't."

Morton was quiet, he seemed to be contemplating his now-empty glass. "Annie," he said, "please let Sammy live with me."

Annie sighed. "Let me think about it, okay? Maybe next summer."

"Thanks," he said.

She got up to go to bed. He rose too.

"Friends always?" he asked and hugged her.

"Absolutely," she said.

Sunday night Annie called her folks.

"What?" her mother said. "What's going on? Now you're in love with Morton's brother? Isn't that a little awkward?"

"It's none of our business, Elsa," her father said on the extension. Annie knew he was pacing back and forth as he talked.

"Nicholas," her mother said coldly, "if it's not our business, whose is it?" That began a typical argument that always failed to place blame where either wanted it.

"Do you have to interfere in everything?" her father said.

"Stick your head in the sand, as usual," her mother said.

"Mom, Dad, did you forget this is long distance?"

"Oh, my God," her mother said. "We're sorry. Well, write us all about it and we'll hang up now."

Her father said good-bye. "Just a minute," her mother said, agitated, starting to cry. "How's Sammy taking it?"

"Elsa!" her father said.

Annie sort of enjoyed her parents' reactions to things, it was one of the more predictable occurrences still available to her. She hadn't always felt like that. At one time she probably hadn't even gotten along well with them. Her teen years she recalled with mixed feelings—jumbled up, unidentified strong emotion. Had she been ashamed of these nice people, Elsa and Nicholas, this rather beer-bellied man and his opinionated but good-hearted wife? Not exactly ashamed. It was just that the strangeness of their life always brought her an embarrassing kind of attention.

Nicholas was, on the whole, rather uninterested in her. Around the bar he was a personality, a jovial barkeep who kept things moving, knew when to listen and when to disarm with harmless chatter. He was a kind man who guessed correctly when trouble was coming, knew who could drink, who could not, who might require coffee and food soon or a ride home. Elsa often had to get up out of a sound sleep to close up while he delivered the inebriated to their doorsteps.

Around the apartment he was silent and disgruntled. He sat in a vinyl BarcaLounger for hours and read the newspaper, watched television or surveyed things, anything there, with disapproval. He always acted like Annie was a phase of life that with patience might pass, much like mortgage payments or an illness. Annie was certain that he had never really taken her into account until she was old enough to sit legally across the bar from him and drink. Her status changed at once. Now he had a thousand ideas to share with her, needed her opinion, was proud of her.

Elsa, on the other hand, had overwhelmed Annie with her attention, especially to the little details.

"You have a spot on your nose," she might say and, wetting her handkerchief with anything handy—beer, coffee, melting ice cubes, a drink someone might have left on the bar, try to rub it off.

"Wait a minute," she'd call out as Annie left for school. "Let me fix that hem, it's loose in the back." Annie would feel obligated to return and stand in the kitchen while her mother hastily kneeled beside her with thread and needle.

Then her mother got into health. Long before it was smart to do so, Elsa ordered from newsprint circulars anything available that might make them the happy, healthy specimens of humanity they were meant to be. She talked constantly about someday opening her own health food store. Creamy gravies, cinnamon buns, Cocoa Crispies, pop-tarts, to mention a few items, all mysteriously disappeared from their diet. A coarse, golden stuff now filled the sugar bowl, strong dark honeys that made Annie's throat tighten were always on the table, herbal teas took over the coffee tin and some grainy, dark loaves of bread that had to be kept frozen lay in rows over the ice cube trays.

They had meatless meat loaf and seven-grain cereal. Elsa bought a blender and made healthy drinks. One particularly disgusting combination called Lion's Milk required grape juice, unhydrogenated oil, blackstrap molasses, powdered milk and the miracle product, brewer's yeast. Annie threw this mixture up three times before Elsa conceded that, because of her stubbornness, Annie could just forgo the benefits of blackstrap and brewer's yeast for all she cared.

Maybe Nicholas feared Elsa would turn Jake's into a health food restaurant. Elsa, enthusiastic as any missionary, told glowing tales at the bar about the cure-all effects of alfalfa sprouts, vitamins, soy beans.

"Elsa, for chrissake, do you have to talk about the chemicals and sugar in beer at the bar? This is how we make a living, you know."

Nicholas needn't have worried. His clientele was hardly the type to trade whiskey and beer chasers for ginseng tea.

Elsa read everything she could get her hands on concerning health. She eagerly awaited the postman, who delivered a variety of mail-order books: *Getting Younger, Living Longer. Yoga for Westerners. Eat Right to Keep Fit. Stories the Feet Can Tell.* This information then produced an upswell of activity in Elsa—a large slant board appeared in the small living room, she kept a yoga mat under the couch and she always wanted to get at your feet, a world of their own, she said, full of nerve endings and little knots that must be worked out. Never mind the pain. Elsa would slant for twenty minutes a day, do yoga for an hour and practice foot massage any time she found a volunteer.

Looking back on all this, Annie admired the way her mother embraced this new religion, meeting all derisive laughter with calm superiority. Hers was certainly not a popular view at the time. Certainly not with Annie.

Once a date picked her up at the apartment. Usually Annie met her friends at Gamer's, an old and popular cafe uptown. But for some reason, Sidney insisted on meeting her folks. Annie knew she was in trouble as soon as Sidney complained of a headache. Elsa walked over to the couch, took off his shoe and sock and went right to work on the nerve ending to his sinus. Sidney was startled and laughed nervously. But it seemed to take his mind off his headache. "Yes, I feel fine now," he said as they went out the door. Annie was too mortified to ask if that were true. His misery and hers, the embarrassing silence of the rest of the evening, was surely worse than any headache he might have had. They had been too unsure and immature at the time to appreciate the tenacious quality of Elsa's enthusiasm.

Annie, in those days, would have gladly traded her parents for any of her friends'. Mary Lou Haggerty, for one, had a slim, pretty kind of mother who would lie on the floor in her pedal pushers reading *Better Homes and Gardens*. Their home was a sprawling, modern ranch, carpeted and equipped with every convenience and appliance, even colored telephones. Mary Lou had one in her bedroom, her own line. Annie envied that, as anyone calling *her* was answered by "Jake's Place, just a minute"—which meant five or ten because her father invariably was too busy to leave the bar to holler for her. Only patient friends got calls through to Annie. Annie had never tied up the phone for hours. Who could hear over the jukebox and other activity at Jake's?

A simple walk to Hennesey's Department Store from Wool- worth's might embarrass her. She knew every bum in town and they did not hesitate to call out to her even from across the street. Well, they weren't really bums. They were just old miners and railroaders who kept certain hours at Jake's, men who impressed her friends the wrong way, she felt. Bubba, too. He was so large and bulky, so menacing-looking in a way, in the dark work suits of green, gray or black that he always bought at JCPenney, usually greasy and disheveled from his hobbies—tinkering with engines and appliances, and broken-down pinball machines. He usually needed a haircut and shave—or half of one anyway. Twice she met him on the street with one side of his face scraped pink and the other still covered with two days' growth of stiff, white beard. Had he been interrupted at the sink or was he just absentminded? He wore his hair, wiry as his beard, a little too long, too, and it stuck out around his head wildly. "The old shoe-shop man," her friends called him when they spotted him, and Annie wished anything now that she had said once—even once might have been enough to absolve her—His name is Bubba.

Morton wished he had brought Marge along. He could have used her support. Of course Sammy had not known that the news about Annie and Paul would be unwelcome to him. To Sammy it was something new and exciting.

Morton had known that one day Annie would get involved with

someone again and that it would affect Sammy. He just never imagined it would be Paul . . . again.

"Well, honey, aren't you at least glad it's with your brother?" Marge asked. She thought it was great. "You know, the influence on him will still be a family one."

Morton groaned. He had not yet had the heart to tell Marge how really complicated all this was. She didn't know that Paul and Annie had ever been together before, that Paul was more likely to be Sammy's father than he was. But it was all so tacky, he hated to talk about it.

And, too, Morton was jealous of Paul. No matter what, Paul always won out, always got his own way. Even as a kid, Paul was brighter, better-looking, and girls liked him more. Once Morton said as much to his mother. They were watching Paul as he backed his car out of the drive. He had a date.

"Girls always like Paul," Morton said and sighed.

"Oh, but Morty," his mother had said, putting her arm around him. "You'll always be my boy."

"Stop saying that!" he said, pulling away. "No wonder no one likes me and Paul hates me. Leave me alone," he'd cried and run off.

And it had been Paul who had had the good sense to leave Chicago first. That had amazed Morton. He thought about it after Paul left every time he got upset with Miriam or the store, which was often. His mother clung to him even more, and maybe for a short, sick period, he clung to her too. Neither had guessed how much they had counted on Paul, even needed him. He wasn't responsible or dependable, he didn't like to work, hardly ever showed up for meals and fought with most of the help but Martha. He stayed out late, barely graduated from high school and wasn't the least bit interested in either going to college or working at the furniture store. But he could see through to the heart of most matters and didn't mind telling you what he saw. He was down to earth and often rude. This shocked Mother and secretly pleased them both. Morton would have liked to have been such a smart-ass himself.

Then Morton began to think of leaving too. His mother still traveled a lot. She had a life, she didn't need him. And the store was

losing money. He had never told his mother or Paul, but his dad
had taken a lot of money out of the business over the years. That
fact was neatly hidden in the books but nonetheless, there it was.
Morton and an auditor had spent days trying to figure it out.

"I hate to tell you this but your father embezzled money from
this business."

"You must mean the man who managed it after Father died."

"No, I mean your father."

"But that doesn't make any sense at all. It was his own money,
his own business, his father's in fact. He inherited it."

"I don't know what to tell you but there it is in black and white,"
the auditor said, slapping his hand across the pile of ledgers on the
desk. "Maybe he gambled," he said at the door.

So while there were funds in trust to support his mother and the
house and her usual high standard of living and traveling, there
was no money at the store to pay creditors or to buy new inventory.
All the cushion money remaining after his dad died had been used
up by the time Morton was old enough to take over. It had not been
stolen, just mismanaged by help who didn't really care. And business had not been great either. Morton would have had to borrow
from the bank or ask his mother for funds, and he would not do
that.

Then too, the girl Morton was seeing was getting serious about
him or rather, he guessed, serious about the money she thought he
had. So instead of taking her hints to marry, instead of using his
connections in Chicago to borrow money for the store, he sold it
and decided to follow Paul to Montana.

"I wasn't that surprised when Paul left but I never expected you,
of all people, to desert me," his mother cried as he prepared to
leave. "Who'll take care of me?" she said. She meant financially, of
course.

"You'll be well taken care of, as always," he told her, explaining
that she still had her inheritance and that, in addition, after selling
the store and paying off the debts, he'd turned all profit over to her.

Typically, that went right over her head. "Just take all the money
and go," she said.

"Go talk to your accountant, he'll explain," Morton said.

Everyone, not just his mother, had thought Morton had put that money into the store in Butte. Not even Annie knew where the money to reopen had come from. Morton had borrowed it from Nicholas, her father. It was money Nicholas had saved over the years from Jake's.

Annie decided to leave everything behind except the silk lamp shade and small mahogany box. They meant something now, would remind her of the past year, of her struggle to develop what she hoped was an independent spirit. Her car wasn't in great condition anymore, but she knew it would at least be a good second car.

Mr. Perry was nice. "I'm surprised you didn't take that job," he said looking at her curiously. She smiled.

"But if things don't work out for you there on the river, I'll hire you back. How's that?"

"Thanks," she said.

Bernard congratulated her. "You landed them both," he said. "Quite a snag." Bernard, Lucille too, always made it sound like she had just come from a fishing trip.

"It's important to have a choice," he said. "Although, you probably made the wrong one." He looked grave.

Lucille came over to say good-bye. "Where is this Paul?" she wanted to know.

"He had to go to Boise and pick up an old car he's buying. He'll be back in a couple of days."

"Then why are you moving in now?"

"I don't know," Annie said. "I just sort of want to feel the space before he comes."

"You want to claim it, you mean. You want to make it yours." She laughed now.

Is that what she wanted to do? Annie felt confused and a little embarrassed. Was she so transparent to others about things she couldn't see herself?

"Here, help me with this thing," she told Lucille. She was trying to get behind a buffet so she could vacuum the baseboard. Maybe if Lucille thought her fingernails were at risk she would leave.

"Sorry, my chiropractor says no lifting. Anyway, I've got to run."

"Good-bye," Annie said and hugged her.

"Don't forget to call when you get bored with him," Lucille said. Annie just smiled.

It was good to be packed up and ready to go. Annie would have liked it better without a dog along, but at least he'd had a bath. "If we're taking that dog," she'd told Sammy, "you better make him smell like fresh flowers."

"So what did your dad have to say?" she asked Sammy. Morton had called the night before to say good-bye.

"The usual."

"What's usual?"

"You know—'How's everything, what's new, be good, have a nice trip, call when you get there.'"

"That's it?"

"'And think about living with us.'"

"Living with *us?*"

"Yeah, but I don't want to."

"How come?"

"Because Marge doesn't like dogs."

"Oh," she said, stunned for a moment. A decision, based not on a preference for his mother, but for his dog. And what's more, *she* didn't like dogs either. Annie turned to look at Pal, who insisted on putting all he could fit of himself between the bucket seats, which, thank God, wasn't much. Just as she thought, he was sneering at her. It wasn't the first time either.

They'd never become friends, not even when Sammy went to Morton's. Then the dog hadn't let her out of his sight, and would lie at a distance of eight feet from wherever she happened to be—on the couch, in the backyard, at the kitchen table—watching her, not to engage her attention, but as if to catch her in some violation. Watching her and measuring her. Sizing her up.

One evening after work when she turned the corner about ten blocks from home, she noticed him running along the street with a couple other dogs. She hadn't been home long when she heard him at the back door—Pal had taken to jumping over the fence, coming and going as he liked.

"Listen, Pal," she said. "Let's have a little talk." He'd hung his head, not in shame but to ignore her properly. "Pay attention," she told him. "Now, if you get caught by the pound even once while Sammy's gone, it's all over. Because I refuse to bail you out. I'll tell him a semi ran over you or that you got rabies or that a neighbor poisoned you. You hear? And quit scratching at this door, you're ruining it." He raised his head then and sneered.

He didn't get caught by the pound again but he didn't give up scratching at the door either.

After stopping for a few groceries, Annie turned onto the highway. It was a dark night and the moon was not out yet. She had never driven out here after dark and hoped she could see the turnoff.

A quarter of a mile farther a narrow drive led into the trees. Out of the car, Annie could feel the crisp, dry chill of a late summer night in high altitude.

"Be a good dog now," Sammy said to Pal beside the entrance to the house. Inside were a few pieces of furniture the last occupants had left and a bed Paul had set up in the bedroom. In the living room there was only a coffee table leaning against the large stone fireplace. It was a big room with exposed beams, log walls and the comforting, homey smell of old wood smoke and seasoned logs. There was no power on yet and the pilot to the furnace was out. She used a flashlight to light an old kerosene lamp. There was indoor plumbing, she was thankful for that, a woodstove in the corner of a big bedroom, a kitchen, two smaller bedrooms and the bathroom. The walls in these rooms were of plaster.

"We'll warm up the big bedroom and sleep in there," she said. "Are you hungry?"

"Starved."

So was she, though they'd eaten at six and it was now only ten-thirty. There was something about the woods and the river that made her hungry. She started fires in the woodstoves in the kitchen and large bedroom.

She warmed up by the fire while Sammy went to get the cooler and some dog food out of the car. When he returned, she got out sandwiches she had made and a soft drink. They moved a table close to the woodstove and sat there to eat. The warmth made her sleepy and after they ate, she used the flashlight to find her way to the bathroom.

Sammy brought in his sleeping bag and he and Pal settled down next to the stove, which was popping peacefully and flashing light across the room from its little window as its flames rose and fell. There was a handsewn quilt on the bed and matching curtains. She smiled at the thought of Paul making the bed and hanging curtains. On the oak dresser was a decanter of sherry with two small liqueur glasses. She poured some and got into bed with it. Goodness, she marveled, even feather pillows. This was such a change from her little house. She blew out the lamp.

She could hear the river—or was it just the trees—and the hoot of an owl. This forest, for some reason, frightened her. Inside everything seemed cozy and protected, but there was nothing cozy outside.

"Mom, are you asleep?"

"Not yet."

"Hear the owl?"

"Yeah."

"I think there's two of them. They're calling to each other."

They listened but the owls had quit hooting.

"Once I got lost in the woods," she said.

"When?"

"When I was a kid."

"My age?"

"Younger."

"What happened?"

"I guess I wandered off from Bubba's and couldn't find my way back." She'd panicked and ran. The underbrush was thick and scratched her face and arms and caught on her clothes. It was getting dark and cold and the forest had suddenly gotten quiet. No birds sang, no friendly chipmunks scampered past, there was nothing but a terrible quiet. Everything had abandoned her to the night, even the battered wildflowers in her hand had closed up rather than face the black dark that began at the forest floor and moved up the tree trunks to fill the sky.

"So what'd you do?"

"Sat down and cried. Finally someone found me, a fisherman."

"Did you get in trouble?"

She laughed. "No. My mother said it was so smart of me to stay put like that. I never told her I was too scared to do anything else."

"There it is," Sammy said. The hooting was faint now. The owls had moved away.

"Will Paul be home tomorrow?"

"Tomorrow or the day after," she said. "Better get to sleep."

Annie woke up several hours later. Sammy was tapping her shoulder.

"Mom," he said. "The fire went out and I'm cold."

"Can you get it started?" She could hear him rummaging around in the wood box.

"There's no more kindling."

"Get in with me," she said. Her nose and ears were cold now too.

"Your feet are freezing," she said when he did. "I'll warm you up," she said and snuggled up to his chilled back.

"Mom?"

"Yeah?"

"Are there grizzlies around here?"

"I don't know. Why?"

"Before you woke up the dog was growling."

"Probably a mountain lion. Go to sleep."

"Do you think we'll live here long?"

"Why? Don't you like it?"

"Not so far," he said. "Do you?"

"I think it will be okay," she said.

She sure hoped so. She hadn't liked living with Nicholas and Elsa and she left. She didn't like life with Paul the first time and she left that. Same thing with Morton. Now this. What if she didn't like it either? Sometimes she worried that she didn't belong anywhere, that there was no place where she, Annie, would ever be at home. Then too, she worried that there really was such a place, that she might locate it and in doing so, find herself stuck. Permanently stuck.

Part Three

THE BLACKFOOT

Chapter Fourteen

Life now had what might be called shape. At least Annie saw everything in those terms—days were circular, the household triangular, and she and Paul reminded her of a parallelogram, that is their lives ran parallel to each other, except for frequent, maddening collisions at odd angles.

They were soon accustomed to the location in the woods, to the river, to the quiet. Weekdays Sammy rode a school bus to junior high, Paul drove to town in the early morning and she left a few hours later to attend classes at the university.

These were held in an old building without elevators. She took courses in design—history of, principles of, practical application of—and in business procedures. Afternoons, she went to a class where they worked entirely with color. This was the one she liked best.

Annie found herself sitting for hours by the window on a high stool where she could look up from her palette and see the buildings nearby, odds and ends of different styles, brick and stone and, of course, the campus. Intrigued by the potential of color, she lost track of time here. She was learning to duplicate any shade, could guess correctly how much blue or yellow or red another hue might need, to tell when one mixture would complement another, when and why it wouldn't. She began to understand chroma, hue, tonality, shading, complementary accents.

The instructor was a thin, short man in his sixties. He was very high-strung and had tantrums. He often stamped his foot when agitated or cried out in exasperation over what he said was a stupid question or a bad mistake. Annie didn't exactly admire these outbursts but she was certainly in awe of them. She appreciated how spontaneous and heartfelt they were and what shock appeal they initially had. But how quickly the tirades came to be ignored by everyone. Everyone but her. She liked to think that one day she would stomp her feet and yell at everyone too.

Annie sometimes felt she could spend a lifetime here, quietly mixing paint, designing space, looking up now and then to other heads bent over their own work or at that intricate web of dark buildings outside. She wished she could spend her life combining color, pattern and texture in some place without customers slamming in and out of doors with their charge cards and endless demands for bargains and service and immediate delivery.

This class was held in the late afternoon and afterward Annie had to hurry through errands to the library, to xerox something for a class or to the grocery store and rush home to start dinner.

Sammy and Paul usually showed up around six, home now an inconvenient log house at the end of a muddy road.

"When are you going to redo it?" Paul asked Annie.

"When I have some time," she said.

"I hope that's soon," he said the day his furniture arrived. He had not bought it from Morton after all and there was a quality about Paul's things that made the eye wander to the old logs, the dirty, fading wall paint, and the worn spots in the carpet.

"I thought you'd rush right out for wallpaper and area rugs," he said a couple of months later.

"Maybe you and Sammy should do it. It could be a lot of fun. I'll help."

"What's the deal here?" he said, looking up from the mail he was going through. They were in the kitchen, one of the three rooms with access to the large porch and backyard. He or Sammy or both usually sat at the counter talking to her while she cooked.

She didn't know what the deal was.

"Anything special?" she asked him. He had sorted the mail into two piles.

"Not much," he said and laid the piles aside. "I had hoped to have the house repainted, at least, by now. I'd like to have some people over from the garage, maybe ask some of the neighbors on this road. In fact," he said, "on Sunday, if you don't mind."

"Uh huh," she said, chopping vegetables for a salad. A party. Morton loved them too. She didn't like them. She always found herself wandering around even when the party was in her own home. And now Annie could not be considered a wife exactly—she would occupy some other position, "friend of host" maybe.

Paul had lived with women before, alliances no one had seen as either binding or noteworthy. Though his friends did seem impressed that he'd moved—with a woman—to a house and that the woman had a son. It was a complicating element, a gold star for her. Had they known, too, that Paul and the woman and son shared a common last name, there was no telling what the impact might be. Impact was what Paul's women had in common. His welder or shop foreman or their wives didn't hesitate to refer to Penny or Dorothy, to the chip dip one might have served or to the size of Brenda somebody's breasts. Annie wandered off from these conversations to find less personal ones—sports in the kitchen, politics in the backyard. One night several weeks before, after passing up several groupings of people at a party Paul's bookkeeper was giving, she had sat down wearily on the couch next to a man someone had brought along. She was trying to figure out if there were patterns to how groups formed. He and the other people there, gathered in a circle around the coffee table, were discussing a book about cloning that someone from Missoula had written.

The man next to her said, "If such a thing is possible, any madman could clone an array of children in his own image."

"What do you think?" a woman with thick glasses asked Annie.

"Well," she said shyly, "maybe souls select the vehicle of existence. If so, they'll likely choose clones, too."

"I don't follow," said the woman. Nor did it appear anyone else did either.

"I'm just saying that, perhaps the superiority of the soul using the cells—not the hereditary genes or environment—may be what determines the greatness of any person. So maybe no matter what the circumstances of the birth, two-cell or one-cell, the proportion of advanced to less advanced people might end up being the same. So, say Gadhafi prototypes were produced in wombs but advanced souls chose to inhabit those fetuses, then this army of babies could conceivably turn out to be humanitarian, non-Gadhafi types anyway."

No one, it seemed, knew what to say. They had looked at her in disbelief. She was not popular at all at parties, it seemed.

"What kind of party did you have in mind?" she asked Paul. Now he was balancing his checkbook.

"Just a regular old party," he said. "I want to ask the real estate guy and that neighbor I met the other day."

Sammy came in with a load of books he flung down on the counter. "Hi," he said.

"Your books will smell like garlic," Annie told him.

He shrugged. "Can you go to a parent-teacher conference on Monday at four-thirty," he asked her.

"Of course," Paul said, looking over the slip Sammy had brought home to be signed.

Sunday morning Paul set up a keg of beer and small cartons of red and white wines with dripping spigots. He lit the barbecue and rummaged around for paper plates. Annie studied until eleven o'clock when Paul called to her. Then she showered and found clean clothes suitable for a hostess of a home kegger. By noon, there were people circulating through the house. The party was not unlike ones she and Paul had given years before.

Annie was in the living room when a pretty girl, maybe twenty-five, in floppy pants and tight halter came in through the porch with a dog, one with the proportions of a Great Dane.

"Do you mind leaving the dog outside?" Annie asked her.

"Just who are you?" the girl said.

For a moment Annie was startled. "I live here," she said. "Who are you?"

The girl didn't answer, just flounced out, her floppy pant legs swinging on the way. Even the dog flounced.

In a minute or so she returned with Paul, who was now slightly drunk and in high spirits.

"Annie," he said, "Cynthia."

Cynthia and her dog ignored the introduction and followed him out to the kitchen, Cynthia now radiantly the victor.

Rather than doing any of the mean things it occurred to her to do, Annie went outside. She didn't recognize anyone and awkwardly detoured around the lines for drinks and food and slipped through the garage. By the other door, just at the edge of the woods lay Sammy's dog, Pal, his chin flat against the grass. He looked disgusted.

"You're no hero yourself," she said. "C'mon."

He appeared to think better of it and stayed put. But by the time she got very far down the path to the river, the dog, who must have trailed her, showed up suddenly beside her.

When it started to rain, they crawled though a space in the underbrush and sat. Besides the company of a half-wet, smelly dog, she really had no reason to complain, Annie decided from where she sat beneath the bushes. What with much of the world ravaged by war, starvation, oppression, what would her complaint be? Still, no matter how good things were, there seemed always an empty space to fill, some internal wasteland where nothing flowered.

Paul dipped the rag in turpentine and then wiped off the last traces of stripper, old paint and the dark gummy finish from the dresser he was refinishing. He did the same with an old toothbrush—dipped it in the tin and splashed it on the drawers so that he could brush out the small olive leaf pattern around the keyholes. He liked working with wood, felt there was still something of life in it, something of the forest from where it had come and of the earth that once held its roots. Even something of the sap that had run through its grain. So to him, stripping off decades of old paint and varnish was a small act of discovery and liberation—finding life, and freeing it. He could feel it beneath his hands as he washed the wood carefully with clear water. And he would feel that life again when he finally applied a coat of finish—equal parts of turpentine, low-luster varnish and linseed oil. This was an old recipe given to him by a cabinet maker who had worked for his father, a mixture that, when rubbed in carefully with a soft rag, left the wood glowing and nourished and kept it from drying out. Paul worked slowly, humming to himself, enjoying the sunlight filtering through the hedgerow at the side of the yard.

"Paul, your mother's on the phone," he heard Annie call.

The sound startled him and he knocked over the turpentine and splashed one side of the dresser.

"Goddamn it," he said and kicked the can across the garage. "Tell her I'll call her back," he yelled toward the house. He was irritated, his former mood shattered by the rippled pattern of turpentine glowing in puddles across the dirt floor. He stooped for his wash rag and carefully wiped the side of the dresser.

What did his mother want now? he wondered. Was she on her way somewhere or was she about to descend on them? He was annoyed by the feelings she sometimes evoked, maybe the obligation to love her and the fact that he usually didn't. It was not even obligation. It was more a desire to love her, a need to and the belief that by his inability to do so, he had somehow missed out. He felt that the doors to some great mystery and treasure had been snapped shut on him. He was lonely for the mother his was not. Such a fool.

Paul slammed the last drawer into place and put away his tools.

It had been a long time since he'd felt this way. This was more something he'd felt as a kid when he had watched his mother absentmindedly stroking his brother's hair. The tone of her voice softened for Morton as though he reminded her of somebody or something. But Paul could never get her attention in that way. He was never a clear picture to her and she sometimes got him mixed up with Benny, the kid next door.

"Come in for dinner," she once called to Benny across the yard, thinking it was Paul. And she once handed movie money to Benny by mistake and then laughed. "Why, you're not Paul," she'd said surprised. "Give that back," she said rudely as though he'd stolen it.

And though Paul knew she liked Morton more, he didn't seem to have any better luck with her than Paul did. Morton was a nervous wreck around her, even worse than Paul. When she was with Morton, he would actually wince, or worse, whine. Paul attributed Morton's nervousness to his belief that Morton had not confronted the fact that he, Morton, did not like her either.

Now Paul moved the dresser to the shady side so it could dry out of the sun. Annie wanted to put it in the front entryway. Like him, she appreciated old furniture. This trait of his had always exasperated his mother and Morton. Paul had enjoyed annoying them about it, especially at the old store. Sometimes, when he'd stopped to pick up Morton there, he'd grow impatient and bored. To amuse himself, or maybe just to irritate Morton, he'd advised customers to go home and fix up what they had and to save their money.

"Be a smart-ass," Morton would say. "But it's the purchases of new furniture that pay the bills."

But Paul and Morton hadn't always fought. They often went for months without a quarrel. And there had been a time when Morton would have never thought of taking out a girl Paul had gone with. And certainly he would not have slept with one Paul had ever slept with. Not then.

Paul threw the rag and toothbrush he had used in the turpentine into the garbage; he didn't feel like cleaning them as he usually did. Paul guessed he was still angry that Morton had gone to bed with Annie those many years ago. Or maybe he was still angry that he'd just found out. And he couldn't help wonder who had seduced whom.

Paul closed the window in the garage, then the large doors. He did not want dust to get on the wood. The only good thing about what happened was that Annie would not dare to throw up *his* past to him again. And the worst thing, of course, was that Annie and Morton weren't positive who Sammy's father was. But Paul was.

First of all, how many times could the two of them have gotten together then? Morton was only there for part of the summer and fall. And Paul hadn't been away overnight that often that he could recall. Maybe three or four times at the most.

Then, too, Sammy was more like him than Morton. He had mechanical ability, liked to work with his hands, preferred fishing to watching football or basketball, hated carrots and beets as he did, and arched his right eyebrow the same way when he smiled. Annie had caught that about him.

No, Paul was willing to bet that Sammy was his. "Don't you agree?" he said aloud to the dog, stopping to pet him on his way in to call his mother.

Parent-teacher conferences went much smoother when you took along a guy with the same last name.

"Sammy's parents," the homeroom teacher said, looking at his appointment calendar on the desk at the front of the classroom. "Come in."

"Sorry we're late," Paul said.

"I'm George Stotts," the man said, reaching to shake their hands, directing them to chairs.

"Nice to meet you," Paul said. Annie smiled.

"Now, then."

In similar fashion, they met three more teachers and none of them said, You're probably not home much or You don't spend enough time with your son. Instead they said, "Sammy might be underachieving" (he was) and "He doesn't put forth the effort he could" (he didn't).

Paul was the one to act like Annie had failed Sammy. "He didn't get the right background in math," he insisted. "We have to push him."

She wished him luck. Annie didn't know how you could make a scholar out of someone who didn't want to be one.

Paul started helping Sammy with all his homework. There were now miserable sessions every night in the dining room.

"Sammy, don't you understand the differences between *their, they're, there? They're* is a contraction meaning 'they are,' *their* is a . . ." Annie always found something else to do in another room at these times.

Maybe Paul was right. Maybe she should have pushed Sammy more. The only trouble with that was she didn't know how to motivate him. They argued about it.

"He has to go to college! My God, Annie, what would his life be like without an education. What do you want for him anyway?"

"But we don't have educations."

"My point exactly. We didn't need them. He will. Now life is all computers and technology. Don't you want him to be prepared?"

"Well, I don't want him to become neurotic or get an ulcer doing it," she said.

She wanted him to be a kind, honest, gentle adult who might go out to lunch with her twice a week and discuss, well, anything. An adult who might have sweet children she could take to movies and on little trips, ones she could more or less fuss over. It hadn't occurred to her to worry about how he might support a life like this.

"Of course, I want him to have a good education," she said.

"Well, babying him won't help him get one."

"Well, badgering him won't accomplish anything either," she said.

"Just what kind of career does he want?"

She didn't want to say.

"I don't know," she said.

Last year he'd wanted to be a truck driver. He wanted an air-conditioned Kenworth with a stereo system and a CB. He planned to drive back and forth across the U.S. hauling cargo between Canada and Mexico. Sammy had tacked up pictures of eighteen-wheelers on his walls and took to drawing pictures of them in full detail, front, back, sides, putting in chrome wheels and mud flaps that said in small print, SAMMY'S TRUCKING. She'd supposed correctly that it was a phase he'd grow out of. But, if he didn't, well, it was his life, wasn't it?

"Mom," Sammy said to her one night when Paul was at the garage. He lifted his head wearily from his books. "I hate school. I'm not good at it."

She sighed. "Try to think of it as a job you have to work at for the present and do the best you can," she said. "Because the better you do, the more options you'll have later."

"Options for what?"

"You know. To get the kind of job you want."

"I want to work outside."

"How about forestry," she said. "Or geology, oceanography," she suggested.

"How about logging? Or oil rigs?" he said.

"Aw well," she said. "There's plenty of time to decide."

He looked at her accusingly.

"Whatever you decide," she couldn't help adding, "is okay with me."

"Thanks," he said, smiling now, relieved maybe, or just pleased by her response. For she was guilty. She had taken sides, had undermined Paul's effort to push him and Sammy knew it as well as she did.

Random damp leaves about the yard and partly cloudy skies mornings suggested that summer had run its course, that autumn was on its way. Annie longed suddenly for that dramatic admission in nature that things did change. She felt almost desperate for crisp orange leaves beneath her feet and the approach of the first snowfall and chilly air. But it turned warm again and the balmy weather appeared to invite company. The first to arrive was Miriam.

"Mom," Sammy said one Saturday afternoon from the door to the porch where Annie was studying. "Grandma Miriam called. She's at the Florence Hotel and wants someone to come get her."

It was not what she needed. Three chapters to read by Monday and Miriam in town.

"Sammy, didn't she ask why you answered the phone . . . you know, why you're here instead of where, you know, where you usually are?" My God, how she put a question sometimes.

"I don't think she noticed. Why?" he said. "Hasn't anyone told her what's going on?"

"I don't know," Annie said. She doubted it.

"Don't you think that's strange?" He seemed to be thinking it over. "Maybe," he said, "it's because Grandma Miriam is a little weird."

Weird was not the right word. Miriam was a little, primpy woman, not without elegance, who commanded great attention.

She negotiated it quietly, by some surreptitious manipulation, by her appearance of helplessness. But she was scarcely a helpless person. This woman once made her way across India unattended. She once moved from Chicago to New Orleans and then back when she found Creole food and the humidity distasteful. Annie pictured these treks in her mind. The little woman—that's how she always thought of her—in wool tailored suits, twenty feet ahead of big porters unable to keep up, lugging her cartons of bone china and silver tea services.

Miriam probably didn't know Annie lived with Paul, or that she ever had, years before. It was Annie's belief that Morton and Paul kept personal matters hidden from their mother because they felt her too delicate and superior to face common realities. It was true that Miriam seemed to transcend the common and ordinary: poverty, late notices, dentists, public restrooms. Had this woman, Annie wondered, ever cleaned a toilet?

But on her brief, unexpected visits, it was Annie who felt help-less. Helpless, large, and yet, nearly invisible. Morton always dropped everything to wait on his mother, wouldn't even let Annie serve her an hors d'oeuvre. Had he been afraid she'd spill wine on Miriam or stumble, maybe fall on her lap? By way of anxious administrations to his mother, Morton conveyed to Annie that she should just sit it out, that he would see to it that this vulnerable (he thought)—invincible (Annie thought)—little matriarch was pre-served and guarded from anything base or ugly. Morton consid-ered the simple mechanics of a kitchen too harsh and unthinkable to expose Miriam to. But he needn't have been concerned that his mother would come into the kitchen and stick her hands in dish-water. She was content to take the largest seat in the living room— Annie thought that was so she could look even smaller, more frail somehow. She preferred the center of the couch, accepting Mor-ton's lavish, nervous service there, doing nothing to put him at ease. Annie might have been hurt had Morton not always col-lapsed after these visits, into some relief/despair-mixed weariness.

Annie called Paul at the garage.

"Your mother's in town. She wants someone to pick her up."

"Geezus," he said. "You never know if that means for dinner or what. Well, don't bother cooking. I'll make a reservation somewhere. Oh God," he said, "my mother's . . ." He sounded rattled. "I'm sorry, Annie. I guess you know all this."

"Paul, does your mother know *we're* here?"

"No," he said.

Paul, too, hovered protectively nearby Miriam all night. Not waiting on her exactly, but in a way doing just that. He orchestrated the conversation, kept it moving above the surface of the obvious facts. But Miriam didn't mind, seemed to prefer not to notice that the same woman and grandson who once resided with Morton now made their home with Paul, or that there was anything very interesting or extraordinary about it.

When they went out for dinner, Miriam took them to her hotel despite Paul's insistence that he'd already made reservations somewhere else. There was a waiting list but Miriam, looking fragile, mysteriously and immediately got them a table with a view of the pianist. She seemed not to notice Sammy at all until the end of the evening. Perhaps he was unrecognizable to her out of context. But then before they left, she said, "Sammy, does your grandfather still own that exquisite little place in Butte?"

He didn't know what she was talking about and looked at Annie for a clue. She nodded "yes" to him. "Yes, he does," he said.

"Fine," she said. "Excellent."

"What was all that about a place in Butte?" Paul asked once they were in the car.

"Miriam was talking about Jake's. She went there once."

They all started laughing.

"Grandma Miriam in Jake's?" Sammy said in wonder. He could see the humor in that.

"Geezus," Paul said. "How did that happen? She's such . . . such a prima donna," he said.

"She was in town and wanted to go."

"I can't imagine Mother anywhere but the Ritz," he said.

"Me neither," Sammy added.

"Well, you two have no imagination," she said.

Actually, what had happened was that Annie had invited her

parents to dinner during one of Miriam's pop-in visits. At the time, Morton was frantic.

"You invited your folks? You shouldn't have done that, Annie. Mother sometimes snubs people."

"Oh, Morton, don't be such a snob," she said. "You're just worried she'll see what a commoner you married." Annie was in a rush and Morton was tagging after her as she set places, found napkin rings, stirred the gravy. She was just as afraid as Morton but she refused to insult her folks by not inviting them. She and Morton had been married three years and her parents had not yet met Miriam. That was because, so far, Miriam's visits had been infrequent, at busy times, and brief.

However, Miriam seemed to like them and insisted on serving them imported sherry, which she ran up to the guest room to get out of her luggage. But what amazed them all was that Miriam asked to be taken to Jake's.

"Nicholas, Annie tells me you run a local establishment," she said to Annie's father.

"Yes, a bar," he said and winked at Miriam.

God, Annie thought, did he have to wink?

"Will you take me there, you and Elsa? Why, we can all go after dinner." She'd clapped her hands gaily and Annie saw that Morton was mortified.

"Do something," he told Annie in the kitchen.

"What can I do?" she said. It was funny in a way. "Relax, honey, it will be an eye-opener for her, an experience she missed in Paris."

"Damn it," he said and returned to the dining room, hoping it would be forgotten.

But Miriam brought it up again after dinner. "Let's go now, shall we?" she said.

"Mother, Annie's prepared a beautiful flan," Morton protested.

"Listen, Mrs. Tomlin," Nicholas said. "You might not like the place. You see," he said, "it's a little rough around the edges."

"Rough around the edges," she repeated. "Such a pleasing expression."

"Miriam," Annie said, "We don't have a baby-sitter. It's impossible to get one on such short notice."

"Oh, I forgot about him," Miriam said, looking perplexed. It was true, she forgot Sammy until he was about six. By then he was big enough to acknowledge. Then Miriam, aware of his existence suddenly, even made an effort to charm him.

"Well then, wrap him up and bring him along," Miriam said.

They finally agreed that Annie and Morton would stay home and when the three returned, they'd have dessert.

Morton paced the house, expecting elegant Miriam to arrive, collapsing, any minute. At ten-thirty, he finally called the bar.

"We're just leaving," Nicholas told him. "Soon as your mother finishes this dance."

"Christ almighty," Morton said to Annie. "She must have gotten bombed."

But Miriam came in the door quite sober and happy.

"It's a marvelous place," she said. "Divine. Why Annie, I never realized you came from such pioneer stock."

Annie didn't know whether to be pleased or insulted. So you thought Jake's was delightful, she'd wanted to say. You drop in from your glamorous life to the provinces and get a kick out of seeing something seedy—another interesting experience like riding an elephant. Miriam, she wanted to say, if you think it's special now, you should study the place as long as I have. You should have grown up there, Miriam. That would've been something different for you, Miriam dear.

All she had said was, "I'll get the flan."

Miriam came by cab, unannounced naturally, for brunch the next morning. They'd just finished breakfast but everyone stayed at the table with Miriam while Annie poached her some eggs. Miriam thought she might stay a week, she said, give up her hotel room and move in here.

"It's time to get to know you all better. See what kind of people will inherit my money."

"Mother!" Paul said. "Have you gone crazy?"

Annie thought she'd missed something in his train of thought.

· · ·

Miriam had a way of changing schedules. Dinner was now at eight o'clock, a more appropriate hour for it. They had cocktails at seven now and Annie always went to the table a little dizzy. (She and Sammy took to meeting in the kitchen at five o'clock during Miriam's nap for a snack "to tide them over" (to give them strength to face the ordeal would have been more accurate).

After dinner, Annie had to drink strong coffee to keep awake to study. She and Sammy usually went off to bed long before Paul and Miriam. They left the two of them deep in some discussion, usually current events significant to Miriam—an oil spill in the Caribbean, the strength of the dollar in Europe, the effects of terrorism on travel.

When Paul came to bed hours later, he patiently removed the books Annie had fallen asleep over from his side of the bed.

Annie was running out of ideas for interesting eight o'clock dinners. Miriam had already been there a week. On Thursday, always Annie's busiest day, she didn't have time to stop at the store. When she got home, Sammy had already snacked and left a mess. Miriam, already up from her nap, was in the den watching the news. Annie sat down to think. She didn't have the heart to make another cheese sauce for asparagus or broccoli, or face another complicated salad, grill one more lamb chop, get out one more pot.

There had been something simple about single life in town that she'd overlooked; the freedom to eat something junky from a sack at the coffee table, to fill up on nachos and avocado dip or fried egg roll. Some nights when too tired Annie had lain in the bathtub and let Sammy make sandwiches and soup. So carefree, they'd been. What random, last-minute meals they'd taken together, disorderly, informal banquets.

"Sammy, please go out to the freezer in the garage and see what you can find," she asked now. He returned with enchiladas and tamales.

Annie baked it all in the oven, served it on china.

Paul frowned.

"Splendid," Miriam said. "This is so, so American, don't you think?"

"American?" Paul said.

"Yes, you know, packaged, frozen. American." Miriam was fascinated. Paul, however, was not.

"Why don't *you* cook tomorrow night, Paul?" Annie said.

He seemed confused.

"You can cook, dear?" his mother asked.

"Real good," Sammy said. "Except he never does anymore."

Annie gathered Paul was embarrassed, not by the fact he never did anymore, but that he could.

"I'm really not very good at it," he finally said, pushing away his barely touched plate of enchiladas.

"That's too bad, dear," Miriam said.

Miriam stayed for three weeks in all. And in that time, she managed to spend a little of each day alone with each of them. Paul's time was after dinner, Annie's, at lunch. While Annie sat, Miriam made her fresh coffee that she ground from beans she kept in the freezer. She poured hot water, not quite boiling, over an x-shaped glass pot that held a filter in its top. She'd brought the pot with her in her luggage. Then she made a salad and popped two fresh croissants into the oven. Annie always wished Paul and Morton could see their mother now.

Sammy's time was at breakfast. At his grandmother's insistence, he now ate with her before leaving for school. Of course, he made *her* bacon and eggs.

"Doesn't she ever make anything for you?" Annie asked him.

"No, she just talks while I do it."

"What about?"

"Everything," he said.

Miriam's conversations with Annie stuck more to certain topics.

"Why do you want to take all these courses?" she asked.

"I want to get a job in design."

"Whatever for? Doesn't Paul make enough money?"

"Yes, but, well, I want something to do."

"Isn't being a mother and wife enough? Couldn't you decorate some of your friends' houses?"

"Miriam, you do know we're not married, don't you?"

This was news to Miriam.

"My dear!" Miriam said, quite alarmed now. "You're putting yourself in a precarious position. You're not protected at all. You'll have no security. Why would you do that?"

Annie wasn't about to try to explain.

"That man is getting all of the benefits and none of the responsibility," she said looking utterly confused. She might have been talking about some stranger. "You're an odd woman," she said and sighed. "Funny both of my sons should take to you so."

Miriam announced her exit from the household in the same sudden way she had made her entrance.

"Tomorrow morning," she said at dinner, "I'm going to Morton's." Her bags, she said, were packed.

"Mother, are you crazy?" Paul said. Again Annie wondered at Paul's choice of phrase. It occurred any time Miriam surprised him.

The next morning, Miriam did not make coffee. She acted a little flustered. Paul was putting her on an early flight and they sat in the kitchen waiting for him.

"Dear, aren't you curious as to why I stayed so long?"

"Well," Annie said. "Since you never have before, I guess I am."

"A psychic told me to. He said, 'Get to know your children before you die.'"

"My goodness," Annie said.

"Now I know enough," she said and gave Annie a good-bye kiss on the cheek. "There you are," she said to Paul, who'd loaded up her luggage, eight pieces of it, all leather, into the car. Annie couldn't help wondering what Marge would think of the visitor she was about to receive.

"You seem quite content with Morton's wife," Miriam said to Paul on the way to the airport.

"Good God, Mother! Annie is no longer Morton's wife. Besides I went with her long before Morton even knew her," he added defensively.

"Oh, dear," she said, evidently not hearing him correctly. "You always did want what Morton had."

"For God's sake, I have never wanted what Morton wanted.

That's why he's in furniture and I'm a mechanic." It was so lame but then he was too exasperated to think.

Now Miriam was quiet. He supposed he'd spoken too harshly. She wasn't used to that from him anymore. It had been a few years since he'd even bothered. "Sorry," he said finally.

"Do you still hate me?" she asked next.

"No, I've never hated you," he said, suddenly feeling sorry for her.

"You were always so your father's son," she said. "I guess that left Morton to me," she added.

Paul had nothing to say about that. How could he? Everyone in the household had known that she'd like Morton more.

"You know your father and I were always mismatched. I suppose people think I married him for his money but I didn't. It was my family that had all the money."

"The Cunninghams?" Paul said.

"Yes."

"How did you two get together?"

"I was attracted to him because he was different from the boys I knew and so we had this big fling. I guess I was rebelling against all that high society business." Now she laughed.

"My parents were pretty strict, you know. The times too. So, because we were having this big affair, we were expected to marry. And, like fools, we did."

"Were you ever happy together?"

"Oh, maybe a few months." They both laughed at that, maybe, Paul thought, because it was so pitiful.

"And I was spoiled, I admit it. I was used to getting my own way." Now to Paul's surprise, his mother started to cry. "Martha once accused me of breaking both your father's heart and his spirit."

Paul could imagine it easily. Martha could become very vocal about her complaints. She ran the house as though it were more hers than Mother's. Paul reached over and touched Miriam's shoulder gently.

"Well, Martha regularly accused me of things," he said and his mother smiled. Paul wondered what had ever happened to Martha but this, he decided, was not the time to ask.

"I often wondered if they weren't in love."

"Who?"

"Your father and Martha."

"No way."

"Why not?"

"I don't know." He had never thought about it before but now, as he did, it was not so incredible an idea after all.

"Knowing Martha," Paul said, "had they been, she'd have kept it on the up and up." Now Miriam laughed.

"Yes, she was just the type that would have loved a platonic affair," Miriam said. "Straighter than my own mother ever thought of being."

"Mother," Paul asked unexpectedly, "how come you never remarried?"

"Honestly, I don't know. Probably because I don't want to share anything. Not my freedom, my time, my money."

Paul nodded and they were silent. One thing about Miriam he had to admire, she always knew what she couldn't give—or didn't want to give—and never allowed guilt to push her into trying, as most people did.

He was at Johnson Field now and slowed to make the next left into the airport.

"So do you think Morton still hates me?"

This question took him by surprise. "Mother, you amaze me. I doubt he ever hated you, any more than I did." If anything they were both angry at her most of the time and didn't know how to handle that anger. But he wasn't about to say that. "But you might want to ask him," Paul couldn't resist adding. He'd like to hear Morton answer that question. It was his belief that Morton never knew his own feelings about Miriam.

"Morton was always angry because he thought my attention to him made you hate him. He told me that once."

"He did?" Paul could not imagine it. He'd never given Morton credit for being aware of that much before.

"He sure did."

Now Paul pulled into the passenger departure zone and parked.

"Aren't you going to see me off?" his mother said.

"Of course. But I'm not going to carry eight pieces of luggage from the parking lot."

"I guess not," she said.

"You sit still while I unload it." He smiled at her. She looked a little done in.

When he had it all on a baggage cart inside, he opened the car door and helped her out. She had regained herself by now and took his arm and he walked her to the line to check in. She was incredible, nodding regally to everyone as though she was a celebrity.

"Paul, dear," she said when her flight was announced, "don't try to take that boy from Morton."

"Good God," he said. "Where did you get an idea like that? Is that what Morton told you?"

"Of course not. Any fool can see what's going on," she said. "And I'm telling you, your father wouldn't have liked it one bit."

"How would you know what he'd like?" he said angrily.

"About this, I know. And if he could, he'd tell you himself. Believe me, he would."

"You better go now or you'll miss your flight."

She kissed him on the cheek. "Did you hear me?" she asked. "That boy will do fine if you leave him alone."

"Good-bye, Mother," he said. She waved and disappeared through the gate.

Christ Almighty, he thought as he walked back out to the car. Half the time he didn't know how to feel about that woman. He alternated between loving and hating her, between being charmed and annoyed. But one thing he did know—which ever way he felt about her, it always managed to make him squirm.

Chapter Fifteen

It wasn't long before Annie heard all about Miriam's visit to Morton.

Morton and Marge had gone to Kalispell. They stopped in Missoula on their way home and Morton called Annie on the telephone.

"Why, Morton," she said. "Where are you?"

"At a gas station," he said. He wanted to see Sammy.

"He's not here right now," she told him, trying to remember where Sammy had said he was going. "Morton," she said as an afterthought, "come on over for dinner."

"I don't know," he said.

"I'll expect you and Marge at eight o'clock," she said and hung up. Miriam had left her mark on the household. They had continued to have late dinners, sometimes they ate as late as 9:00. Tonight would likely be one of those nights.

The four adults were a little ill at ease. Not Sammy, though. He acted like everyone was here on his behalf, uncomfortable to be sure, but the very strength of that discomfort, a commentary on his value. Accordingly, he became a gracious host, finding an ashtray for Marge, turning down the oven for Annie, running out to the car for the wine Morton had forgotten to bring in.

"Morton," Annie said, trying to revive conversation when things got too quiet, "How are the Pinskis?" (They were fine.) She tried other areas. "How's everything at Jake's?" (Morton didn't jump at the chance to talk about that.) Had he seen Martha and Henry? (They were fine, too.) Did the neighbors ever sell their house? (Yes, they lost money but no details were forthcoming.) Marge and Paul had even less to contribute.

"Have you been up to Georgetown?" Annie asked during one particular awkward lull.

"Not much," Morton said. "You know how it is this time of year."

"Yes," she said. It would be getting cold now and soon fishermen would be out, hauling little shelters onto the frozen lake where they would wait for the jerk of a line through holes cut in the ice. On good days, the winter sun might appear at the crest of the highest mountain ridge, permitting light to sweep the lake and valley floor, a day's journey on up to the westernmost ridge. Then darkness, unbelievable, sudden darkness. And on a good night, stars, a sky full, their brilliance exaggerated by clear, dry air and deep black canyons. My God. She was homesick.

"Annie," Paul said. He always knew when her mind was wandering. "Morton says Mother was at his place for a visit."

"So how did it go?" She directed the question to Marge. But it was the wrong thing to do, she realized from the look on her face. Maybe Marge thought it was a trick question.

"She's very nice," Marge said quickly.

"Very nice, but eccentric," Paul said. A son was the only one who could safely make a statement like that.

"Yes, she's odd," Morton said as though it was the first time it had occurred to him.

"That's exactly what Miriam said about me," Annie told them. Everyone laughed at this admission. No one, she noticed, disagreed.

"We have dessert," Annie said and Sammy offered to get it.

"How about some Kahlúa with our coffee?" Morton asked, and Sammy went back out to the car to get that too.

Miriam now became a safe subject. "Now she's going to stay put awhile, she says," Morton told them.

"She always says that," Paul said. "She traveled so much when we were kids, the help used to take turns reading us her postcards. Remember that?" he asked Morton.

"Right. Remember that one maid who loved those cards?"

"Harriet! She got the biggest kick out of them," Paul said. "'Dear Boys,'" he mimicked. "'I'm having the time of my life in Cairo. It's pretty as a picture here—this postcard hardly conveys anything of its splendor.'" Now he held up an imaginary card and pointed, perhaps to Cairo.

Morton laughed. "'So keep up your studies and be good to the help,'" he added. "'I know what nuisances you can be. Sincerely, your mother, Miriam.'"

Everyone laughed now. "Sincerely, your mother, Miriam?" Annie heard Marge say to Morton in wonder.

"Let me clear this table and we can all go into the living room," Annie said.

"Let me help," Marge offered.

Marge followed Annie out to the kitchen. "How long did Miriam stay here?" she inquired as she rinsed dishes.

"Three weeks or so."

"She was with us a month," Marge said in that same wondering tone. Annie laughed and Marge smiled back shyly.

How it came about that Morton and Marge stayed the weekend, Annie wasn't sure. Well, they'd had a lot to drink after dinner and that undoubtedly had much to do with it. By morning it appeared established in everyone's mind that they were, after all, only normal couples in abnormal circumstances. They could make the best of it.

Paul and Morton took their coffee outside. She and Marge fried sausages, squeezed oranges and scrambled eggs.

Marge, she guessed was around thirty-five. She obviously went to a gym, she was in shape. She wore her light hair in a bob and had perfect white teeth.

"I like your house," Marge said. For a minute Annie thought she meant the one in Butte.

"I, myself, like something a little older," Annie said.

"Yes, but old houses always need repairs and they're drafty." Annie knew that now she was referring to the one in Butte, to the gush of air that came up from the basement and the radiator pipes that had to be wrapped and primed, to any number of things wrong with Annie's former residence.

"Why don't you move?" Annie said. It couldn't be easy to occupy a house with a recent past.

"I haven't felt like I could suggest it," Marge said.

"Well, you should," Annie said. She doubted that Morton ever liked the house anyway.

After breakfast, Sammy planned to go with Marge and Morton on a drive up the Bitterroot Valley. He did not need directions, he said, he knew the way everywhere. It was true; Sammy had, even as a toddler, an uncanny ability to locate himself. He had homing instincts that had gotten Annie back on the right mountain road, for instance, more than once.

"You'd better take a map," Paul said.

"No, Sammy will know," Morton said. He was a nervous driver himself who'd come to depend on Sammy for directions too.

There was a silence now, as though the two brothers were considering the strength of the other's authority here.

Marge interrupted skillfully. "We plan to take you all to dinner tonight," she said. "Right?" This question to Morton.

"Right," he said. "We'll return at six, how's that?"

"Thanks for everything," Marge said.

"See you later," Sammy said and the three left. Without the map.

"Well . . . ," Paul said.

"More coffee?" Annie asked.

Annie worked most of the afternoon at the kitchen table. It looked out over the porch and the light was perfect. She'd appropriated this space and the table was usually cluttered with T squares, rulers, drafting pencils, graph paper. Wads of discarded ideas, having not made it to the wastebasket, were piled in the left corner.

202

Paul always looked curiously at what might be lying there, maybe to see if she was getting her money's worth at school.

"What are you doing?" he asked. She'd noticed he was a little moody today, didn't seem to know what to do with himself. She'd heard him slam books shut in the living room, open a beer in the kitchen, saw him walking thoughtfully around the yard.

"I'm designing a ten-room house for people with the following needs: The husband is a poet, the wife plays the harp, the oldest son is handicapped and the other son, a baby. They don't like dark colors, they entertain often, want privacy . . ."

"Where do you find these people?" he said.

"It's hypothetical," she said. "Just practice."

"Annie, I don't know how you can spend so much time solving problems that aren't real," he said and went on back to the living room.

At the restaurant that night, Paul was in a better mood. He talked at length with Morton about whether it was still advantageous to buy stock in IBM. They discussed going in together to play the market a bit. Sammy listened intently, which pleased both men.

Marge told Annie her impressions of the new mall. There was nothing Marge did not care for in that mall except the high prices.

Sammy waved to someone. The someone, at further glance, turned out to be his homeroom teacher, Mr. Stotts. He came over, nodding to Paul and Annie.

"You know my mother and uncle," Sammy said. "And this is my father, Morton, and my stepmother, Margaret.

Stepmother. It was a word that had a certain holding quality; it seemed stuck there physically in the air. The homeroom teacher appeared confused. "Aw, well . . ." he mumbled. "My wife . . . our dinner. Nice meeting you," he said, backing away. Did I get that all straight? he must have asked his wife.

Deviation, all right in private, can seem subversive when it smacks up against convention. After that they all agreed they were tired and went home.

In the morning, after breakfast, Morton and Marge packed and they all went out to the driveway. No one seemed to know the etiquette for saying good-bye appropriate to this situation. Annie finally hugged them both, Marge first. Sammy did the same. Paul shook hands with them.

"We'll see you over Thanksgiving vacation," Morton said to Sammy.

"And you'll have to visit sometime too," Marge said to Annie.

"Move first," Annie said and winked at her. Marge appeared taken back for an instant but then smiled and waved.

That night Paul was restless.

"Let's go for a ride. Just the two of us."

"Okay," she said. "I'll tell Sammy." He was in his room studying. Paul drove toward town.

"Did you enjoy their visit?" she asked.

"It was awkward," he said.

"I guess," she said.

He pulled off the road near where the river forked and parked. They walked along the bank and sat on some pilings by an old bridge. It was chilly and Annie wished she had put on a heavier jacket. They could hear the voices of campers across the river and see figures moving about the cliffs above. Cleaning fish, she guessed, or making camp, or maybe eating their catch and drinking a beer after a day on the water. Whatever they were doing, it appealed to her: the voices in the dark, the smoke from their fire, the flashlight or lantern no brighter than shimmery ripples across the water. She could smell fish.

"I know Sammy is my son," Paul said, taking Annie by surprise. Her attention made a sudden leap from a small fishing boat across the river to the pilings where they sat.

She didn't answer. She had seen this coming. Nonetheless, she was unprepared.

"I want so badly to tell him," he said.

"You can't," she said in a whisper. Still the words echoed hoarsely across the water.

"Would it be so bad?" he asked. "Would it?" He had his hands on her shoulders now. The smell of fish was for the moment overwhelming, as if Paul and not the river was the source of its odor.

"You can't."

"Why not?" He was upset now and she thought he might cry. Or was it she who might?

"I don't know why, but you can't," she sobbed.

He held her without speaking; at some point they had stood up. The current was slapping at the pilings now and the voices, men's, could now be heard clearly. It was agitation, she heard, an argument, there would likely be a fight.

"I want to go home," she said.

After Paul went to sleep, Annie got up. She went to Sammy's room and opened his door quietly. She could see his jeans draped over the chair in the moonlight, its light pointing toward the silver on his belt buckle, which dangled from a frayed belt still looped at the waist of his jeans. She went over to the bed, her feet brushing things still warm, a T-shirt, maybe his underwear. She turned off his stereo and gently took the earphones from his head. He moved a little but did not wake up. He probably went to sleep like this every night. Couldn't he strangle himself in the midst of tossing in the night with those headphone wires?

Annie went to the kitchen and made herself a drink. She would have enjoyed a cigarette now. She took the drink to the porch.

What if, she wondered, her mother came to her and said that Bubba was her real father? How would she feel? She would likely be too sick at heart to hear the whole dramatic story and her mother might go on trying to explain. But Annie would be grief-stricken, shattered, busy wondering who she was after all. Annie could imagine a scene like that. Then she might turn against her mother for living a sloppy life where such a thing could happen. Your soul chose this, her mother might argue. But that had to be impossible, why would it choose that? (Her mother was not religious in any developed sense, she just liked to explain things in terms of soul choice—among them, cripples, insanity, addictions.)

She didn't need a revelation of this kind and neither did Sammy.

Annie woke up at dawn stiff and lined from the lawn chair she had slept on.

. . .

Morton dropped Marge at the beauty shop and Sammy got in the front seat.

"We'll meet you at Barsotti's at six o'clock," Morton told her. He turned the corner then and drove downtown. "Mind dropping by the store for a minute?" he asked Sammy.

"No, sir," Sammy said but Morton knew he was disappointed. They had plans to run up to the lake to see if the road was open, to make sure the water was turned off and to get some firewood. But he'd just remembered the payroll checks. They needed to be made out by tomorrow even though payday wasn't until Wednesday. By now his employees were so accustomed to getting paid late Tuesday afternoons that they all hung around the store after work or, if it was their day off, they dropped in. And this week they'd be even more anxious because of Thanksgiving.

When they got there, two of his salesman were squabbling over a commission and Morton gave Sammy some change for a Coke and told him to run next door where there was a soft drink machine. Morton took the salesmen into his office to straighten things out so customers couldn't hear from the floor.

When they came out of his office, Sammy was sitting on the edge of a large couch that had floral-print upholstery on white background, a very expensive special order. Sammy's foot was swinging as he sipped the Coke, his heel striking the fabric as he talked with the secretary.

"Sammy!" Morton yelled. It was the wrong thing to do. Sammy jumped up and spilled his Coke, then hastily wiped at it with his sleeve.

"Sorry," he said, and looked miserable.

Morton sighed. He just hoped the spot would come out. He went back into his office and called a rug-and-upholstery cleaner.

"Ready?" he said to Sammy, who was now standing outside the door.

"Yes, sir," the boy said and followed behind him out the back door to the alley.

By now it was late and they would have to hurry if they were going to be back in time to meet Marge by six. Morton stopped at a gas station on the way out of town and then at a drive-in for some hamburgers. The roads were clear though it had snowed the night before. There was little traffic.

"How about a little music?" he said to please Sammy, and turned on the radio. Evidently Marge had changed stations because there was some church music on. Morton put it on a country-western station thinking Sammy would prefer that.

When they got near the lake, it began to snow again. The road around the lake was open. It looked like the county snowplow had been there just that morning. The snow piled alongside the shoulders was clean and the remaining snow pack showed no evidence of traffic. The lane to his property, however, had not been plowed. They left the car at the gate and walked in. There were animal tracks, most likely deer and rabbit, and urine stains along the fence where a dog had peed. Otherwise snow in neat, white drifts covered everything including the lake. The trailer looked like a stack of hay and the woodpile beside it like a staircase leading to its top. Across the lake the forest and mountains, now a dark shade of blue, rose into a low ceiling of heavy clouds.

Morton and Sammy stood in silence at the edge of the lake. It was getting colder and Morton guessed the temperature had dropped ten degrees just since they had arrived.

"Paul's teaching me to fly-fish," Sammy said.

"Oh yeah?" Morton said. He'd forgotten that Paul used to like to fish. Evidently, he still did. "Isn't it a little cold to go fishing now?"

"We haven't gone yet. I'm still learning to cast. I practice in the backyard."

In the backyard, of course. Morton now recalled Paul as a kid practicing on the grounds and that the gardener had a fit and complained that the boy was always snagging the hedge and trellis with fish hooks though Paul insisted he never used anything on his line but dry flies. Morton could imagine Paul and Sammy in the backyard. Paul would explain how to hold the pole, how to snap it back to just the right angle behind him and to then release the line to an imaginary spot far in front of them. Then he would show the boy how to tie flies and they probably set up a room in the basement or, more like Paul, took over half the house for their sport. There would be a table, probably the dining table, with little plastic cases on it that would hold all this shit, little pieces of thread and fish line and tackle and little tools, probably pictures of flies beside them and then books on fly-fishing and then boxes beside the table full of smelly fishing boots and old hats and nets and other junk. And anyone walking by would trip over piles of other fishing poles on the floor. And the two would be bent over this stuff for hours and . . .

"Dad, do you think we should go? I'm getting cold," Sammy said now.

"Oh, yeah, sure," he said. The snow was coming down pretty heavily and Morton pulled up his collar and trudged behind Sammy up the lane to the car.

There was already a skiff of snow on the highway as they came down the hill into Anaconda. The car was warm now and Morton turned off the heat. It dawned on him that he hadn't checked the water tank or the trailer. Nor had he filled the trunk with wood as Marge had asked him to. She wanted it for a fire on Thanksgiving.

"Dad," Sammy asked unexpectedly. "How come you and Paul haven't been friends all these years?"

"Who said we weren't friends?"

"No one. But you never talk about him. He never came around until we moved to Missoula. I just figured you weren't exactly close."

"Oh well, that. I guess we grew apart over the years."

"You mean you used to be close?"

"I don't know that we were ever *that* close. Well, maybe we were."

Suddenly Morton felt undecided: Were they or weren't they? And how did you ever know? They spent a lot of time together because they were so isolated in that big mausoleum they had lived in. Neither one of them had many friends . . . well, maybe Paul did. And they had some good times. He had many fond memories of the two of them trying to entertain themselves, getting away with anything they could like hiding themselves or other things from the maids and housekeeper when they were very young— once they'd kept a dog hidden for several months before anyone in the house knew. Then when they got older, instead of sneaking things in, they began sneaking out. Usually they'd head down the street to catch a bus to more interesting neighborhoods. That was a favorite. They liked to walk around busy areas where doorways opened to odd little shops though they seldom bought anything. Morton could practically smell the meats and sausages that hung from big hooks in a little butcher shop next to a newsstand full of comic books where they liked to hang out. They spent a lot of time watching older guys at the billiard tables in a place called Smokey's. And sometimes they tried to sneak into peep shows but a man would chase them back out to the street. Nevertheless they noted every marquee, every suggestive poster and promise on it— LOLA, LIVE ON STAGE FOR YOUR PLEASURE. XXX. MASSAGES. GUARANTEED NOT TO RELAX YOU. MUST BE OVER 18. Then when they got older, instead of taking the bus, they would sneak the car out and go for rides around the various neighborhoods, avoiding busy streets by parking blocks away from where the action was and walking over.

Morton had some bad memories too. When they were small he would always hide Paul somewhere when Mother got drunk, warn him when Father got morose, lie for him when the gardener or some other household help went on a rampage about him. And then, of course, there was their father's death.

"Did you two fight?" Sammy wanted to know.

"Oh sure, brothers always fight."

"You mean knock each other down or just do a lot of yelling?"

Morton laughed. "I guess we did some of both." Indeed he could remember several fights that he'd just as soon forget.

"Boy, if I had a brother I'd never do that."

"Do what?"

"Fight."

"Don't be too sure about that," Morton said. "So what else is new?" he said to change the subject.

"Not much," Sammy said. "Paul wants to teach me to weld this spring. And he says I can come down to the garage if I want and watch the mechanics too."

Christ Almighty, Morton thought. Paul was just like a kid showing another kid all his favorite toys!

By the time they got to Butte and Barsotti's, it had quit snowing.

Marge, her sister Alice and Alice's three kids were already seated at a big table. Alice's husband came in and stamped off wet snow from his boots and looked around. Marge waved to him and he came over and sat across from Morton. Sammy was seated down at the other end of the table with Marge's nephew.

Now two large pizzas showed up at the table. "The double cheese with mushrooms goes at that end with the kids," Alice told the waitress. The waitress put the other pizza in front of him, then returned with a pitcher of beer and another of pop. There was a large television on the wall closest to where the kids were sitting and a football game was on and everyone was pretty much occupied with that. The Denver Broncos had just scored a touchdown. Morton's mind was still on the conversation he and Sammy had had. The beer was awful and he walked up to the counter to the bar and ordered a Scotch.

When he got back, Marge frowned and reached across him for a piece of pizza that she handed to Sammy.

Morton watched absentmindedly as Sammy studied this piece of pizza, then proceeded to take off all the pepperoni and mushrooms and pile them on his napkin. Suddenly Morton was angry.

"What the hell are you doing?" he asked Sammy rather loudly.

"Taking off all the stuff," he said.

"Don't you have a pizza in front of you without stuff?" he asked.

"It has mushrooms."

"So you take a piece of ours that has mushrooms and pepperoni so you can remove two things? Why didn't you just take off the mushrooms from your own?" Now everyone was glaring at him and he ignored them.

"Sorry, I thought yours didn't have mushrooms," Sammy said.

"Hand me a piece," Morton said, indicating with his hand the pizza in front of Sammy, now the only pizza left. "And all that crap you took off your piece," he added. Everyone pretended to concentrate on the football game.

"Look, Sammy," Morton said over the game as he slapped at the pizza with Sammy's discards. "See. Now I have to just put all this crap back on."

"Morton, you're being ridiculous," Marge said. "It's my fault, I didn't know he didn't like mushrooms."

"Mind your own goddamn business," he said.

Now she had tears in her eyes, her sister and brother-in-law were glaring at him again, and Sammy was sulking. But he couldn't help it, he just felt irritable. When he went out for dinner he wanted a tablecloth and real food. He didn't want to sit on some goddamn bench at a picnic table with a lousy pizza and watered-down beer.

Chapter Sixteen

Not long after Sammy returned from Morton and Marge's, Morton began to write long letters to Annie. At first they were to everyone but as the job of answering them fell to her, the correspondence became personal. No one appeared to care. Paul would say, "When you write Morton, tell him hello," or, "Tell him he still owes me ten bucks on that Charger game." Sammy, too: "Mom, don't forget to tell Dad I'm going out for basketball." If either one ever thought the letters Morton wrote were unusual, they never said.

"Dear Annie," he'd begin. "To continue our discussion, I think that men have a worse time of it, basically because they don't really relate to each other as good friends. Their competitive natures have developed a certain distrust and aloofness. Now women, it seems, can discuss at length their most intimate feelings with each other. They cry, get it all out, take advice and feel better. Men's conversations, on the other hand, stick primarily to sports issues, the economy, their mechanics, etc. You know what I mean, impersonal topics that get around what they feel or worry about."

He'd go on to elaborate his position, maybe include an article he had just snipped from *Psychology Today* to support his view. (When had he begun reading magazines like that?)

Then in the next letter he'd continue his train of thought.

"So maybe that's why men need women—actually *need* them. They're really the only ones men can talk to, that is, if men have the good sense to. But it's usually the case that men are so accustomed to hiding their real feelings that they become unable to open up even to a receptive, understanding woman."

Once he wrote: "I think that's why men chase around. Their basic ego structures require constant reaffirmation and support. A sexual conquest then becomes a means to assure them that they are still alive, still worthwhile, that they still have *it*, if you know what I mean. And having it is everything to a man. Our culture instills that."

Then a surprising thing happened.

He wrote, "Marge left me. I think by opening up to her, I scared her. Maybe she thought I had no strength. What do you think?"

Annie didn't know what to think.

"He's just going through a midlife crisis," Paul told her. "All that stuff he reads. He takes life too seriously." This from a man who drank beer every night to relax. This from a man who had recently developed impotence.

"I don't know what's wrong with me," Paul said. "Maybe I'm tired."

"Maybe it's the beer," Annie said.

"Are you counting my drinks now?" he asked, glaring at her. Even in the dark she knew he was glaring. She could only glare back. She wished he'd try reading a little of the stuff Morton did.

She was once again putting too much energy into a relationship, energy that was not reciprocated. Fulfillment in life was probably to be found elsewhere: self-expression, careers, religions, maybe long-term goals. More and more she thought that the only thing keeping them in place was Paul's need for a son. Or worse, some need to prove that his sperm count, at some point, had been consequential.

"You're thinking mean things," he said to her.

"You can tell?" she said, feeling on the floor for her robe.

"Yes, I can hear the spin of discontent," he said.

"Do you want something from the kitchen?" she asked, finally locating the robe without falling off the bed.

"No, wait. Don't go. Hold me," he said.

Not a week later, Morton dropped in. There he was asleep on the couch one afternoon when she arrived home, his luggage on the porch, ransacked and spilling over where he'd gone through it for a change of clothes. The clothes he'd had on were in a messy pile nearby. A messy pile, that is, for Morton. She knew they were all in for trouble: Morton was changing his basic personality and maybe Paul was too. Two men in the midst of midlife trauma in one household was going to require . . . well, something.

Sammy, who arrived a few minutes later, of course, was delighted. Paul, when he got there, for the moment, was too. Annie sat in the kitchen too discouraged to cook. Where had Morton gotten the idea that women all had close friends they could run to with problems? From Marge? Because Annie had never had a close woman friend. That was likely the reason she was such a . . . she didn't know what. But it was on the tip of her tongue. Except for her mother, her life had been spent basically in whiplash response to male viewpoint. Annie needed to talk to someone female, her mother wouldn't do.

She thought of calling her old friend Mary Lou Haggerty. But that was not a good idea. Mary Lou would have her own life, and that life, if she remembered Mary Lou at all, would be described to her at length, eloquently, humorously—imposing tales of complication and enviable affairs that would make anything Annie said sound thin and whiny. The last time she had heard from her, Mary Lou was living in San Francisco, had never married, had three daughters with names like Gypsy, Sunshine and Ocean. Mary Lou, from the photograph she sent, looked like Cher.

Annie called Lucille.

"Annie, darling. How are you?"

"Just fine." Now she felt a little silly.

"Let me guess. The river is wonderful and the sun always shines?"

"Not exactly, but hold the thought."

"Oh, no, you're miserable, aren't you?"

"Of course not." What a terrible idea to think you could talk to someone by phone.

"So how's Sammy?"

"He's doing okay."

"Bernard's here. We're having a little party."

"I'm sorry, let me call you back."

"No, wait. Annie, what's wrong?" There was real concern in her voice.

"Oh, well, everything."

"What, for God's sake? Tell me."

"I guess I'm not too good at this—on the phone and all."

"Listen, Bernard's going to be out of town this week and I hate staying by myself. How about I come out there?"

"Oh, no, I didn't mean that."

"Why not? Right now you need someone to talk to and I need some diversion."

Annie didn't know what to say.

"I'll have Bernard drop me off."

"Lucille, don't come if this is a hassle for you . . ."

"Hell, no. It's no hassle at all. Here's Bernard."

Now what had she done?

Before Lucille arrived, Paul and Morton were at each other's throats and had been for several days. Paul put vinegar in Morton's bottle of beer and, in the morning, blended egg whites and switched shaving mugs on him. Morton left messages from the IRS with Paul's bookkeeper at the garage, then mailed him a certified letter that Paul had to worry about all night before he could pick it up at the post office. That kind of thing. Then every chance they got, one pushed the other in the river. Sammy seemed to think the house had suddenly come to life and it was great fun.

When Lucille arrived, things settled down. Morton and Paul

composed themselves and now gallantly deferred to each other in her presence. It was a welcome calm evening.

The next day, Annie made Lucille lunch and it was warm enough to eat on the porch.

"How's Bernard?"

"He's great and sends his love. He said to tell you, these are his exact words—'There's no mistake so great that you have to live with it forever.'"

"He still assumes I made a mistake?"

"Didn't you?"

"Maybe. But not for the reason you think."

"Then what?"

Annie sighed and pushed back her plate. The river was full of activity and Lucille was photographing it. Annie watched as Lucille got out her zoom lens. There was an elderly couple putting on hip boots upstream from the house and a young couple were climbing rocks on the opposite bank. "Did you know I lived with Paul years ago? In fact, that's how I met Morton."

"Tell me," Lucille said and pulled her chair up, as though waiting for the punch line to a great joke.

"It turned out I got pregnant."

"And Paul is Sammy's father."

"Well, maybe."

"Oh, no. You mean you don't know which one is?"

"Right."

"My God, Annie. Only someone like you could complicate life like this." She sounded quite pleased to point that out.

"And no one knows?"

"Paul and Morton do, of course. My parents don't. Sammy doesn't."

"So what's the problem? Everyone seems to get along together just fine.

"You see . . ."

"I get it! You're having an affair with Morton and Paul's about to find out."

"No." She wished Lucille would quit guessing and let her explain. "Paul's certain that Sammy's his son and wants to tell him everything."

"Hmmm," she said. "Bernard's wrong. Some mistakes are for keeps."

The young couple who were rock climbing now reached the top of the hill and disappeared from view.

"What you have to do now," Lucille said, "is face the worst thing that could happen."

Annie didn't answer. What she had to do now was prevent the worst thing that could happen from happening, though she hadn't the least idea how.

The elderly pair in hip boots had walked downstream holding their fishing poles in the air. How far would those people go, Annie wondered, before casting?

"Smile," Lucille said and snapped her picture.

Later that afternoon, Annie tried to give Lucille some idea of Paul and Morton's recent behavior. "It's ridiculous," she explained. "So just in case they start up again, you'll know what to expect."

But they didn't. And surprisingly, Lucille liked them both and Annie thought that they liked her too. Lucille and Morton spent some time together. They went for a walk one morning and, the next afternoon, drove to town to shop and to pick Sammy up after school. In the evenings, everyone had dinner together. Annie wasn't getting much work done, but she thought she'd catch up later.

On Friday, there were no classes and Annie fixed Lucille breakfast—Paul was at the office and Morton had gone to visit Sammy's school.

"Annie, do you ever feel bad about what happened, you know, about quitting your job with Bernard and all?" She was smoking the longest cigarette Annie had ever seen.

"No, why?"

"I don't know. You seem a little distant. There's no hang-up at all?"

"Nope."

"Well, I feel bad. I know you're the guilty type who worries about things like that."

"Things like what?"

"Like getting involved with a co-worker."

"What are you talking about?"

"Your affair."

"What affair?"

"With Bernard."

"What! Who told you that?"

"Someone at the store. She said that's why you wanted that job in Spokane, because you were embarrassed."

"Didn't you ask Bernard, for God's sake?"

"Of course. And he didn't deny it." Lucille was angry and pounded out her cigarette.

"I don't understand. We were just friends. *Just* friends," she repeated.

"Bernard is never just friends with anyone unless he's attracted to them. And as long as there's sexual attraction, there's no friendship. It's something else. Usually sex."

Annie was shocked. And she felt suddenly foolish. She should have known Lucille had had something on her mind to have come here. "Well, think what you like but we were friends," Annie said.

"Hah!" Lucille said, "No women expects a guy to be her friend."

Annie did, at least she'd expected that of Morton. She'd even written him to ask whether he thought men and women could be close friends.

"As I've said," he wrote back, "it's my opinion that men need women. But not just sexually. They need someone they can open up to. And many men, so I've read (he'd included some statistics), are finding out that women make good friends. Of course, it helps if there's no attraction. Attraction equals distraction," he said.

Lucille had no more to say and neither did she. Lucille was now courteous, cold and otherwise preoccupied. Annie couldn't believe that Lucille had worried about this. Annie had hardly given Bernard a thought. He liked the sensual type anyway. He was always off with some sexy woman.

If Annie were to admit to herself how she felt about this, she guessed she would have liked to try it—being a tramp—as a lifestyle. She would have liked being this outrageous, sexy woman who drove men crazy. Because being sexy, she had noticed, had little to do with how attractive you were. It had to do with something you did, with some signals you sent out. And she would have liked to have sent them out to Bernard. She would have liked, for that matter, to have had an affair with him, to have been one of those woman he drooled over instead of . . . well, the way she was. What is more, Annie now liked the idea of betraying Lucille!

But something stopped her and not just this threat of AIDS you heard so much about lately. It was something else. Annie could only compare it to a time she was at a revival in the high school gym when she was seventeen or so. There was music, startling in the emotional response it evoked. There was this tremendous energy, the energy of a thousand or more people, no doubt feeling the same. And there was some truth in what the evangelist said, she recognized intuitively. There was everything that night that might inspire someone to forget him- or herself and come forward at the right cues, to confess his sins and to be saved. She wanted more than she could say to go up there and have that happen. But she was immobile. Why was that? Even if that had not been her chance at salvation, shouldn't she have at least made the effort—tried it out? But she was prevented by some shadow self that said, *You are not that*. Annie got this feeling anytime she tried to step out of herself, to cross the imaginary line she felt in front of her. *You are not that* was the message she got when she thought of either being a born-again or suggestive or a hundred other things.

Immediately after that conversation with Lucille in the kitchen, Lucille changed. And the whole household changed with her.

Lucille became a little sarcastic and flirted with Paul, Sammy and Morton. They all flirted back. Annie suspected she had never been her friend. She'd just been keeping an eye on Bernard.

Paul became a little sarcastic too. And so did Morton and Sammy.

Annie found herself in the kitchen alone the rest of the day. She could hear laughter from the living room and occasionally a request: "Annie, would you grab three more beers," or, "Annie, could you bring out some ice?"

"What's so funny?" she asked, making one such delivery.

"Oh, nothing," Paul said. And for some reason that was funny too and they laughed.

When *she* joined them, all laughter stopped. They became sullen. They had little to say until Sammy, who'd been on the phone in his room, came out to ask if he could go to Lolo Hot Springs with his friend Sean.

"Are his folks taking you?" Annie asked.

"No, his older brother."

"I don't think so," she said. Everyone listened.

"You think he wants to go with parents? Annie, this is the eighties," Lucille said.

"Let him grow up," Morton said.

"Geezus, Annie. Give him some space," Paul said.

With this encouragement, Sammy became fierce. He could see who the enemy was. "All the other guys can go."

"No," she said.

What had come over them? Three adults pushing for a fourteen-year-old to go out of town, on that highway, with other teenagers. Didn't they read the papers? Annie had the feeling if she'd said, Yes, go ahead, they'd have opposed that too.

Sammy huffed back off to his room and the others started up where they had left off an earlier conversation. It had to do with heart transplants.

"I guess I'll go study for a while," she said.

"Yeah, Annie's got to hit those books," Lucille said mockingly.

"She's going to be the big decorator," Paul laughed.

"No, she's just going to go to school all her life and pretend to be one," Morton said.

More laughter.

Annie went to her bedroom. Was she getting paranoid?

That night, because Lucille had announced she was leaving in the morning, Morton wanted to take them all out for dinner. It was time he left too, he said. Annie was relieved.

The evening began well enough but degenerated early.

"Annie, you're quiet tonight," Lucille said.

"She's always quiet," Sammy said.

"It's distancing phenomenon," Paul said. "She thinks we're drinking too much." They were (except for Sammy, of course).

"No, I think it's more that Annie doesn't exactly live in this world," Morton said.

"Yeah," Lucille said. "Her philosophy is, Analyze but don't participate."

"Insulation, immunity," Paul said.

Then Lucille said something quietly that Annie couldn't hear and Paul and Morton laughed.

"What did she say?" Sammy asked over the hilarity. He hadn't heard either.

Now Lucille was singing something in French and Sammy was looking puzzled.

Annie got up. "Please excuse me," she said.

"Should I go with you?" Lucille asked. "Or can you make it alone?"

"No, no, I'm fine."

When Annie came out of the restroom she could see all of them were laughing. Paul seemed to be the director of the entertainment. She said good-night to the hostess and walked out the door wondering how to get a cab. But why should she when Paul's car was in the parking lot and keys to it in her purse? Besides, she reasoned, none of them should be driving in the condition they were in.

Annie backed out and drove down the street looking for a place to get some coffee. She felt disconnected, fast floating as though skimming across the top of something. Instead of a café, she pulled into a tavern. She sat at the bar for a long time, stirring her margarita, which was too sour to drink. A man seated next to her was talking to the bartender about wind chill factor. There was something she wanted to add to what he said, but there seemed no entrance into the conversation. She knew a lot about wind chill.

A good north wind could freeze anything in sight: water pipes, gas lines, chimneys. She'd seen smoke going up a chimney reverse its direction, back up and fill a room, as if the air at the top of the chimney had frozen and blocked its exit. Sometimes the wind would suddenly die down, leaving the route it had taken absolutely solid and still. Now, human breath could shatter the glassy air, making a crackling sound in a dreadful silence, and footsteps, a further disturbance on the crust of wind-packed snow.

But now the man was saying something else, that his mother-in-law was crazy. Annie wanted to comment on that too, though it was unlikely anyone would believe her *entire* family could be crazy. *She* could hardly believe it. It was as though they had all gone into the same state of anger, clever and animated, mutually reinforcing each other, joyful over the prospect of getting even. What if, in this frame of mind, Paul decided to tell Sammy that he could be—and likely was—his father? What if Lucille decided to tell Paul or Morton or Sammy—or all three—that Annie had an affair with Bernard? Might they abandon her, leave her suddenly alone?

In any case, their behavior led her to discover her own loneliness, a discovery all the more terrifying for having occurred in such close proximity to intimacy.

"She's got no balls," the man next to her said suddenly, startling Annie.

Apparently he was talking about his wife and Annie caught a little of his litany of all the things wrong with her. Annie had heard complaints like these before at Jake's. She'd heard men go on for years about their wives, saw them take advantage of their good natures and forgiving spirits. Annie knew these wives, they were gentle, nurturing women. Who, she wondered, had these caring women turned to when they'd needed care?

Then, when one of these women died or perhaps simply left in defeat, the husband, now lonely, became appreciative of all things soft and tender gone from his life. He would berate himself for hours at the bar. Why, he'd wonder, hadn't he appreciated his wife before?

"Well, you're certainly no conversationalist," the man seated next to her said.

When she got home, Sammy was in bed and the other three in the living room.

"How could you be so selfish?" Paul inquired.

"Do you know we had to wait an hour for a cab?" Morton complained.

Lucille said nothing. She was on the couch, her arms folded across her chest, her jaw tight and protruding. Now, when she saw her that way, Lucille did look like, well, a bitch. Where had the impression come from, that she could be counted on?

"You should have called. We thought you had a wreck or something," Morton said.

"Hey, I was the only one sober enough to drive."

"The hell she was," Paul said to Lucille.

"Then it was inconsiderate to leave us," Morton said.

"I'm sorry," Annie said.

"Helluva lot of good that does," Morton said.

"Annie, what's gotten into you?" This from Paul.

Annie didn't answer. She did not know what had gotten into her.

"I asked you a question!"

"Don't bully me, Paul," she said.

"Or what?"

"Or I'll—I'll throw something," Annie said.

"She wouldn't dare," Paul said, turning to the others.

Had he addressed her directly, she might not have.

She not only threw a nearby ashtray at the mirror but she knocked a pile of reference books off the desk to the floor and heaved an encyclopedia at the coffee table, which scattered their drinks like bowling pins.

To her surprise, the mirror didn't splinter as she'd hoped or fall off the wall. She had only extracted a small chip, which left a tiny blunt fracture, a dark spot, against the shiny surface. Perhaps that surprised them too because when she left the room, they were still gaping at it.

She felt their disappointment. They were thinking, Is that it— just that little bitty scene—after all our goading? But this was the best she could do. She might never get more assertive than this. Whether anyone accepted her this way or not, no longer mattered.

She felt great. Absolutely great. Everyone was angry at her and she not only did not care, she felt wonderful.

Annie awoke early and alone. She'd had a very pleasant dream. She had been floating down a river—was it the Blackfoot?—with Paul and Sammy and Morton. Just the four of them, floating between overhanging trees. She recalled the trees especially and the shadows they cast across the clear, deep water. Yet, they were in the sun, not the shadows, on some unhurried journey. They were toasting something. They raised their drinks, beer she thought, and clinked them all together. They kept on toasting, but what? She didn't remember words, no one seemed to talk in this dream. There was just an impression that they had drunk to the years that had passed between them, to a history of mistakes and indulgences that now, amused and tolerant, they all admitted to and toasted on their way somewhere.

Annie got dressed and went downstairs. Paul was on the fold-out couch with Morton. It was hard to tell the two sleeping figures apart. Was it because, in her mind, they had become more or less identical? Didn't they both depend on her in the same way, fault her for the same misconduct, appreciate her by the same measurement? And didn't they both do it with similar enthusiasm? Because of Sammy, there were lasting connections here and she had better resign herself to that fact. And, in consideration of her own deep attachment to them both, it was just as well. She sighed and went out to the kitchen to make coffee.

The spell on the household was broken. One by one, everyone got up and joined her on the patio. Over the morning she accepted everybody's comments cheerfully, if not smugly. They were:

Sammy—"Mom, I hope you're in a better mood today."

Lucille—"I always knew you could get violent."

Morton—"Annie, I've never seen you get so upset before. I hope Paul isn't driving you crazy."

Paul—"Glad to see you're still here. I half-expected you to take off in the night or something."

Four individual responses to her behavior. It was such a relief.

"Morton's going to give me a ride home." Lucille said about noon. Annie helped her pack. She didn't have a lot to say, she seemed to be thinking. Finally she patted Annie's shoulder. "Sorry," she said.

They went out to the kitchen then where everyone waited. Paul and Sammy helped Lucille carry her things to the car.

"Annie," Morton said watching from the kitchen window, "your friend's real nice and all, but isn't she a little weird?"

"How do you mean?"

"Oh, I don't know," he said. "Say, you haven't forgotten that Sammy's spending the summer with me, have you?"

"No, I haven't," she said.

"Good," he said. "I'll be in touch." He kissed her cheek and then as an afterthought, hugged her. "I'm sorry we didn't get a chance to talk much this trip, but I'll write," he said sadly. She walked him to the car and waved good-bye to Lucille. She stood outside with Sammy and Paul until Morton turned onto the highway and drove out of sight.

Annie felt sorry for Morton; she knew what he was going through now. He was thinking about the empty house waiting for him, about the modern furniture Marge had left, or worse, taken. He was recalling with alarm that his home was no longer familiar, that the old and enduring things were gone and that someone had swept in and out recently, briefly, with shiny replacements, now either out-of-place or missing.

Morton had not gotten to the highway before Lucille had her hand on his knee. She moved over so quickly that he veered suddenly left.

"Relax, sweetheart," she said. "Let's stop somewhere and take a shower," she said. "I'm hot." Then she laughed and unzipped his pants.

They stopped then at a roadside cabin. After they had made love, Lucille became talkative. She'd showered and was drying her hair. She was still naked. "So what's it like to have your brother trying to get your son away from you?"

"What!"

"Yeah, Paul wants to tell Sammy that he's the father."

"Who told you that?"

"Annie. That's right. In fact she's a nervous wreck worrying about it. You must be too," Lucille said and tweaked his stomach. He was laying on the bed watching her.

"Poor Annie," he said.

Evidently this wasn't the response that Lucille had anticipated because she became angry.

"Poor Annie, my ass! What the hell are you talking about. Poor Annie. That's all I hear. That what Bernard says. Everyone feels sorry for her but I don't." Now she rifled through her bag and brought out a hairbrush.

"I know she's been to bed with Bernard. You didn't know that, did you?"

Morton didn't answer. Lucille's anger was a little scary for some reason. She was brushing her hair and turned back to him again.

"What are you going to do when Paul tells Sammy?"

"Nothing," he said. What could he do? After all it could be true.

"Doesn't it upset you?" She seemed amazed.

"Of course it upsets me." Surprisingly though, not as much as it might have. He thought that over while Lucille put her bra on and then continued brushing her hair. She used quick, hard strokes.

When he really thought about it, it was probably the best thing for Sammy—to have two fathers. If they all put the boy first, it could be a blessing. If they were generous, that is, and shared him. Otherwise, he would certainly lose out and, he liked to think, so would Sammy. Because since his divorce from Annie, Morton had made a real effort to be a good father. He had come to see that he had missed something as a child. He used to think that since he had not had a father, not really, he had therefore probably not needed one. He hadn't stopped to consider that a father had real functions outside of the usual financial one. It was the divorce that had made him see this.

Now Lucille stepped into her panties, the left leg first. Then she sat down at the mirror to do her makeup.

"So what if you never get to see him again?"

My, but this woman was hard. "I doubt that will ever happen."

"Why not?" she said turning to him, her lipstick on only her top lip.

"I don't know. I guess because Paul's my brother and Annie's fair."

"Annie's fair! Hah! A lot you know about women."

She went back to her makeup, smiling at him in the mirror. Then for some reason, she slammed the lipstick down and turned towards him.

"What's wrong?" he said, alarmed.

"Everyone always takes Annie's side. Sometimes I just get sick of it." She paused now, beginning to cry. "She's not even pretty." She came over to the bed now.

Morton felt sorry for her and he held her. "It's all right," he said. "Everyone likes Paul better than me and, besides that, I'm going bald."

But she didn't appreciate his joke and continued to cry softly. Finally she got up and finished dressing without comment. She put her blouse on, then her pants and shoes. She looked at the door. "I guess I better get home. Bernard will be worried." She bit her lip.

Lucille said nothing more on the way home but she patted Morton's knee when he pulled up to her house.

"You're a nice guy," she said and got out.

She waved at him and smiled now.

Wow, what a weird woman, he thought as he drove away.

Chapter Seventeen

Everything that first week after Lucille and Morton left was anticlimactic. Some dynamic had gone with them. Paul and Sammy tended to wander around the house every night in search of some lingering effect of it, disappointed that nothing remained. There was tension all right, not the energizing kind Morton and Lucille had fostered, but the dulling, depleting sort that indicated worried minds.

What Sammy's worries were she didn't know. But her speculations about them were part of what was unsettling her. There wasn't any trouble at school that she knew of, no signs of drugs. Was it just puberty or was Sammy feeling the pressure of his position, that is, his disputed sonship?

"What's bothering you?" she asked him finally.

"Nothing," he said. That's all he said.

Paul, she supposed, had the same old problem on his mind—beating his brother out of a son. As for her, you'd think she'd limit her worries to theirs, but she had acquired a new one all her own, and she self-indulgently gave it more than its share of attention. She had come to the conclusion that Bubba had been her real father. It explained everything, and in particular, why Nicholas—

lately she thought of him as Nicholas—hadn't liked her as he might have.

Annie, over the years, had accommodated two notions of her father—one, that he was a fair, just man who liked her, and the other, that he was a fair, just man who did not. Simultaneous, contrary, fixed opinions that she had failed to see before. Enlightenment twenty, maybe thirty, years late of being some assistance.

Nicholas was always critical of her, studying her.

"Well, now," he'd say. "Let me take a good look at you."

It had made Annie uneasy. He could look at her in a way that made her want to know what he was seeing. From what she could tell it was something directly behind her and off in the distance. Once, she had looked quickly over her shoulder to see it herself. Nicholas had complained, "Stand still," he said. "Stop bouncing around when I'm talking to you!"

Sometimes she thought he came to her room nights and stared at her there too—or had that been her imagination? If he had, it wasn't in the way she often looked in at Sammy, inspired somehow by how life had ignited itself in cells inside her womb, a spontaneous combustion that then took direction, bigger, more defined bones, curly hair, personality, a changing voice, even acne. Life that needed her, yet excluded and denied her too. There was mystery here, confusion, awe, but always appreciation when she looked in on him. But that was not how Nicholas had looked in at her. He had stood at the doorway, never coming quite in, the light behind him, his face dark and troubled with something that made her feel older than him, a little sorry for him. Could she have dreamed that? Did Sammy have dreams like that? Alerted by her entrance into his room, did he see her in distorted dreams as an ominous presence in the dark? Yet, she was certain her father at the door was no dream.

No, Nicholas never really liked her. He was embarrassed to rediscover her each day playing in the bar. It was with dismay that he'd yank the sheet off one of the tables she'd made a tent of or kick through a pile of playthings she might have collected in a corner.

"Get your stuff out of here," he'd say. "It's time to open."

"Does she have to play out here?" he'd ask Elsa, who might not

answer or who might give a weather report, for that had everything to do with it.

Annie either played outside or in the bar, never in the apartment.
But outside, on the busy downtown sidewalk, people stepped on
your jacks, or your hopscotch lines, or your ball rolled into the
street and down the hill. Annie settled on walks around the block.
She knew every frost heave on it, every empty lot, every peeling
hydrant, the doorways old vagrants preferred.

"Give me a nickel, kid," one old wino called Avery routinely
asked. The man was said to have been a magician and to have had
certain abilities. (In that neighborhood, every panhandler had a
name and a past, one someone at Jake's would be familiar with.)

"Do me a trick," she asked him back, a request he would only
blink at. She never gave him money, he never did a trick, but
sometimes she shared her cookies or lunch with him.

Annie always carried food. She was an explorer—out to see the
world, her knapsack full, a change of clothes ready. (She actually
carried along clean underwear and another shirt in case she didn't
go back. She always did.) Saturdays, a day her mother was too busy
to call down the block after her, she'd cross the street and walk
around another block, then another, careful to return to her own
every so often, linger out front of Jake's, yell in at the door or get
more supplies. In her mind, it was just another outpost she was
forced to stop at along her route. When she was old enough to have
gained permission to go to the library, she went instead to the train
station or to the viewing stand over the huge copper pit where from
the top activity below seemed merely Tonka trucks on a sand hill.
Here the mountains adjacent leaned down to her, menacing, in-
clining granite that warned her to measure up. But at the train
station, there were fellow travelers with knapsacks too, and like
them, she could find an empty bench, lay her head on her bundle
and contemplate the next stop on her journey. She was looking for
something, treasure, she thought, gold, an abandoned fortune,
buried money, any valuable that she could recover and claim for
herself.

Sometimes people told on her at the bar. "I saw Annie today way
over on Colorado Avenue." "No," her mother would say, "she was

at the library." Once someone reported seeing her at the train station. "She said she was going to her grandmother's."

"Her grandmother's dead," Nicholas said, looking uncomfortable.

Elsa would call it mistaken identity—all children looked alike— and Nicholas would not credit her with having gone so far.

Often Annie stopped at Bubba's shoe shop.

"Little one, what brings you so far from home today?"

"My shoes need repair," she'd say. Often they did.

"Let me see," he'd say and make a minor adjustment to her buckles or provide new laces. Or if they were falling apart, he'd replace the heels or the soles or stitch up the sides. Annie's parents had no idea what she had saved them over the years on shoes.

"Do you have time for a root beer?" Then he'd take her next door to the drugstore fountain.

"Where all have you been today?" he'd ask while she drank her chocolate soda—she never did have root beer. It was always somewhere over the mountains or across the wide Missouri, as the song said, or somewhere not far behind Lewis and Clark on an expedition of which she had a tattered map. Her destination, the place where the Columbia River meets the Pacific. She never let her imagination take her that far, was perhaps afraid to. And after the incident where the boy who'd chased her fell into what she later suspected was an abandoned mine shaft, Annie never ventured out too far from Jake's and never into those hills again. She began actually going to the library, letting her adventures now take place safely between book covers. Still she continued her visits to Bubba's.

"Well, you better run along home now," Bubba said sooner or later. "Before the fort thinks you've met with trouble and sends out troops."

Then she'd return to Jake's, to intrude once more on her father's otherwise carefree day.

"Go watch television," he'd say. "Practically the first to have television in the whole town and you never watch it."

"That kid's spooky," she heard him tell Elsa once. Spooky. What did a word like that have to do with her?

Her folks would have been kinder to have just told her the truth then. Had they told her then, she could have gone to Bubba's for root beer and stayed, adjusting her outlook to include shoes. Shouldn't she tell Sammy the truth now? No. Sammy was happier than she had been, he did not wander the world Saturday afternoons, he was not spooky. Besides, there was nothing conclusive to tell him.

"Is something bothering you?" Paul asked her Friday night. (Each of them now asked the others this question.)

"No, I just have a lot of work to finish." (And no one answered truthfully.)

"Maybe you should quit school."

"Why?"

"It's making a nervous wreck out of you. You toss and turn all night and last night you cried out in your sleep."

"What did I say?"

"Nothing coherent, just garble."

"I can't quit school, I like it."

But he was right. She was worrying too much about everything. She might just as well come right out and ask her parents. And for now, get her mind on her work.

That morning she left the house early. She decided to go down and sit on the riverbank. She had a project she had to turn in and she put the assignment in her bag, though she knew it by heart: Redo the interior of a two-bedroom apartment, it said, keeping in mind a large, rather awkward gun cabinet the client insists on keeping as it is a gift he inherited from his father. He also has an extensive stamp collection he wants displayed on the east wall. This client also complains of a very drab, cheerless office and wishes his apartment to be a warmer, more exciting environment to come home to. He has recently joined a singles club and intends to start having intimate suppers in the location of his view window. However, he doesn't want the apartment too colorful as his aging mother is a highly excitable woman who visits often from Fresno. Finally, he wants the kitchen hidden from view, without sacrificing the light from its large window. He hates kitchens.

"Geezus, Annie," Paul had said when he read all that. "Who makes these things up?"

Though Annie usually enjoyed these assignments, she was having trouble recently. She had begun three different solutions here, and after hours of work, each one had lost direction. Maybe she needed to just think it through.

The river was quiet. There were only a few people hiking on the opposite bank. It was too late in the year now for rafters. This was the time she liked the beach. There was a slight breeze now and she welcomed the fine spray from the current that hit her face and back and the low, but still warm, sun. Later on, in the spring and summer, the entire river would fill up with rafts and canoes with ghetto blasters, and its banks with campers, beer parties and sunbathers. The now-soft sun would become a blinding glare across the water and make the sand along the riverbanks hot enough to burn the soles of bare feet.

There was something alienating and hazardous about a river. It was an edge to something frightening and sad. Even the birds knew this and cried out warnings or roamed disagreeably, picking at each other over a piece of garbage on the sand. Sand, the transformation of rock, beaten down now into powder simply by water. Water that turned treacherous.

Annie knew what it was to drown. How she knew, she wasn't sure. She just knew. She knew with unqualified certainty what it was to be caught helplessly by the tide, to be rolled and tumbled and taken down into deep water, to fight ineffectively and to die. From time to time, she knew other things too. Not so much anymore, but often when she was young she could look at something or pass somewhere and trigger an entire emotional response she did not comprehend.

So, the first time she'd seen the picture of the girl that hung over the piano at Jake's, she'd felt a mixture of shame and sadness, unfamiliar feelings, unrelated to what was occurring in her own life. At the time, Annie was at the player piano, trying to pump it hard enough to make it play. She could put in the rollers but she was too short to reach the pedals from the bench. So she'd stand up and pump with one foot, a system that didn't work too well. But this day she climbed up on the piano bench to get another roller and, while she was at it, looked closely at the picture. There was recognition first of all and fascination, though the girl only stood, unsmiling, one hand resting on something, maybe a chair. The background was blurry, but Annie knew it was a parlor. Then suddenly, Annie was the girl, an occurrence beyond *déjà vu*. She was really her, coming home to that same room to find the picture, not in the trash or missing, but turned to the wall and her name a forbidden word. Annie, a five-year-old, relived the scorn and shame and anguish of that fifteen-year-old who later, before Annie's birth, came to be a popular and well-known figure around Jake's, her name apparently still forbidden, as no one around Jake's, at least this generation, ever recalled what it was.

Of course, Annie never explained her experience to anyone—the people she knew were satisfied and relieved to think life began mysteriously and ended mercifully, and that short season between was its entirety. Only her mother knew something of how she felt.

She had found Annie at the piano bench crying, holding the picture.

"It's me, it's me," she had insisted when her mother tried to take the picture away.

"No, it's not you, Annie. It's a girl who's been . . . who's been gone from here a long time." Elsa never could say *dead*. But on the day she'd taken down the picture, Annie knew she had been that girl, and too, that the girl's father then hadn't liked *her* either.

So here she was now, one hundred or so years later, still trying to figure out something about fathers.

Life, she guessed, really was eternal, but not as a reward, just unstoppable. In which case, there was just so much she could hold any father responsible for. Just so much failure or success she could attribute to genetic or environmental contributions a father did or didn't make, to attention he could or couldn't give. More likely it all had to do with what you brought to the world with you each time—what you learned, what you needed to learn—and like carry-on luggage (an old valise maybe) its contents were sortable, replaceable, to some extent discardable. Then this carry-on, this valise full of things—that for better or worse improved or not over the lifetime—you got to take with you when you died. The only thing you got to take. That was probably exactly how it worked.

So, what did it matter then, who your father was? For no good reason she could think of, it just did.

When Annie got back to the house, Paul had lunch prepared. He and Sammy had cut fresh flowers and the table was set in the dining room. It was too hot now to eat outside. "This is very nice," she said.

"How was your brainstorming session?" Paul asked.

"Aw, that. Not so good."

"No ideas, huh?"

"No," she said. "I think I'll tell the client to get another decorator."

Paul laughed.

"Just give him large, splashy paintings he can hang when his mother's not around," Sammy suggested. "Then put boring ones on the other side and he can turn the pictures around when she comes."

Annie smiled at him. Really, he could be so sweet.

"I've been thinking," she said. "I'd like to ask my folks to come visit."

"Hey," Sammy said, "tell them to come for my first soccer game."

"You're ready for more company?" Paul said. "You're behind in your classes now. You want more distractions?"

"They could come next weekend. I'll be caught up by then."

Paul was frowning.

"You're not looking forward to meeting them, are you?"

"It's not that," he said. "Having company all the time gets to be . . . well, tedious."

"I promise you, my folks are just normal people." Maybe she shouldn't have said normal. Maybe she should have said nice or interesting. She wasn't sure they were normal at all. Her mother still massaged feet and had recently taken up Tai Chi, which, she said, she practiced early every morning in the living room. And Nicholas was always a little disoriented when away from home. He didn't like any town over a certain, very small, size. And the fact that I-90 went through Butte didn't mean he liked driving it.

. . .

"You want us to drive all the way?" her father said when she called.

"You could take the bus," Annie said.

"Well, Nick, we really ought to go meet Morton's brother," Elsa said on the extension.

"Paul," Annie said. "His name is Paul."

"You know, in case they get married," Elsa said.

Nicholas, unconvinced, clicked his teeth.

"Sammy would like you to come for his first soccer game," Annie said.

"Oh, of course, dear," Elsa said. "We'll be there."

"Tell Morton's brother we're looking forward to this," Elsa said before hanging up.

Annie finally handed in her project. She'd done the apartment in a soft shade of salmon, parquet floors, the furniture in navy blue, and accessories—using Sammy's suggestion—something high-tech and bright but easily put in a closet when mother visited. She put sliding panels of stained glass across the kitchen (everyone else put shutters) and, in the guest room where the mother slept, she carried through the navy blue but only in accessories on calm light gray-blue walls and carpet. She used white as the accent color.

"Yes," her teacher said. "Uh huh."

Annie wondered sometimes if the assignments he came up with weren't his real clients after all. And if so, maybe he used the class to do his work for him.

Chapter Eighteen

The morning of Annie's parents' arrival, fog moved in over the river and settled there in plump rounds that resembled polar bears on ice caps. Within the hour, the shapes had collapsed into others more like lumpy bedclothes. The fog was dirty gray and engulfed the horizon, spreading quickly to include what was left of visible sky. Annie watched the fog all morning, felt its movement up the hill, its entrance into the house, now chilly. It was as though the fog had permeated her brain too and she found herself falling asleep on the couch while resting from a few sweeps of a dust cloth, then again after dragging out the entire contents of a closet when she'd only meant to put away the vacuum. Now there were boat oars and soccer balls, umbrellas, gym shoes and jackets all over the floor. She had made more mess than she had cleaned up. How had she managed that? And on the one day she wanted everything in order.

Bringing together the important factions of one's life for the first time was no pleasure unless it turned out a lot better than you expected. She wasn't expecting much. It had taken Morton and her parents all of ten years to get used to each other. And in this case, there wasn't time. Her folks would rush in and out just long enough for everyone to add first impressions to preconceptions.

And they all would have them—ideas of each other based on something they believed about Annie. Knowing her, as they thought they did, they would carefully allow for surprises, for strangeness, and then when no one extraordinary turned up, they would be more disappointed than relieved. For each one of them liked to think of herself or himself as the only normal influence on Annie's life.

Sammy shared none of her concern.

"Do you think Grandma and Grandpa will like Paul?" she asked him. She had picked him up after school.

"Sure," he said. He was moving the dial on the radio.

"Can't you just leave that in one spot?" she asked. It was irritating to hear it jump around like that, to news and rock stations and advertisements, then onto classical music and easy listening.

"Find a station and leave it," she said.

He settled for a rock station.

"Well, do you think Paul will like them?" she said.

"Why not?" he said drumming on the dashboard.

"Mom," he said a few minutes later. "I want to get a perm."

"A what?"

"A perm."

"But your hair is curly."

"I want to straighten it."

"Whatever for?"

"It looks too faggy."

"It does not."

"You can't say no."

"Why not?"

"That would be sexist."

Annie changed lanes to the right. "It's your hair," she said.

"Will you do it?"

"I don't know how to do that stuff. Go to a shop."

"I can't."

"Why not?"

"I'd feel too weird."

It made no sense to her. Ruining curly hair. The men she'd grown up with didn't fool around with what genes and heredity had dealt them. They accepted it without question. To do otherwise would be a declaration, something others could interpret and use against you. Just the way you dressed made a difference around Jake's in those days. Suspenders or a belt. Leather shoes or white bucks. Everything had its significance and denunciation was easy to come by. Tamperings with nature were left to the women, though these were more definitive and women paid for excesses. Makeup meant a certain thing; too much—more of that thing. Bleached or dyed hair, fingernail polish, hair nets, permanents, girdles, no girdles, pedal pushers, long hair after the age of thirty, shorts after the age of eighteen, every choice was telling.

Annie was about thirteen the day she came home with a permanent. There was a moment of hushed surprise while everyone at the bar looked to Nicholas.

"What happened to your hair?" He seemed unable to see that it was curly, must have mistaken it for something else, because then he said, "It wouldn't be a wig now, would it?" Had she been older this might have brought a laugh. But on account of her youth, no one dared. This was serious. They seemed to see it as an end to something, the beginning of something else.

But this was nothing compared to the day her father discovered her without eyebrows, well, that is without her own real ones. She had spent the afternoon at Mary Lou's experimenting with Mrs. Haggerty's rather extensive collection of cosmetics. Her dressing table was a mélange of colors and smells, an artist's palette that promised entry into womanhood. There were paints and brushes, perfumes, creams, polishes, things of extraordinary detail and complicated procedures. To become beautiful, Mary Lou explained, some things required removal and others, application, and some just readjustment. Everything was here to accomplish all of this. Available were eyelashes and plastic fingernails, foamy little cups for bras, shoulder pads and something similar that fit in the armpit. There were deodorants, and removers for polishes, makeup and facial hair, and powders and rouges and lipsticks of all descriptions. Besides all that, there were little tools—clippers and scissors, files, eyelash curlers and more significantly, as it turned out for Annie, tweezers. First, Mary Lou said, you started *here*.

But after having evened here and there several plucks too

much—this took the better part of an hour—two jagged, thin, impossible lines were all that remained. Annie, in great frustration, shaved off that limp bit and drew in two curves, bold and unalike, on her now raw, exposed brow. There was a special pencil for this emergency and Annie thought how much easier it would have been to just use the razor in the first place, saving painful pulling and a lot of time.

When he saw her, her father gave a startled shudder and said nothing at all. Nor did anyone else. The customers of Jake's concurred in a silent reproach. Her shame was aggravated further by the fact she could never draw the eyebrows the same no matter how she tried. One was always higher or fatter or longer than the other, or worse, she forgot to draw them on at all! Or they dripped down into her eyes when she perspired, which was often. To have no eyebrows at all and then to have prickly little newly grown hairs made her sweat. It was probably the reason she still wore long bangs and never plucked. Some memories do not fade with time.

Annie just hoped Sammy had better luck with his perm. But why shouldn't he? No one looked twice these days at purple hair, spiked hair or at an entirely shaved head. But shaving off your eyebrows, in her lifetime so far, had never become stylish.

They stopped at the grocery store and picked up everything she had forgotten the day before. They were still early for the bus. They sat down to wait.

Annie hated bus stations. They were all somehow alike, drab, barren expanses of space in need of scrubbing and paint, furnished with long rows of plastic seating and vending machines that never worked for her. And music. Depressing, obnoxious, assaultive music. She always felt weary at bus stations and train stations, as though she had just returned from some extended trip, had come a great distance with nothing to show for it, no snapshots, no suntan, no souvenirs. Just a feeling of exhaustion and of having misplaced her luggage.

Passengers were starting to come in the door behind a rope and she and Sammy stood up to watch for two familiar faces.

She saw her mother's first, identifiable even far off in a crowd. It brought to mind a piece from a newspaper Morton had shown her once called "The Montana Face." It was a careless condemnation suggesting stupidity, ignorance, blankness, a people with faces conditioned not by emotion or struggle but by facing too long into wind. Morton, being from Chicago, thought it was funny.

"Ah," he'd said, "the faces at Jake's. This writer, no doubt, has been there."

"Go to hell," she told him.

But what Morton and the writer had failed to see here was that amazing ability to refuse to register every detail of one's history and circumstance in lines and creases or glance of the eye. These were private people, their faces not so much blank as they were anonymous, and that by choice. You could not glean from these faces more than the occupants would allow. What you might wish to know about Elsa, for instance, she would have to tell you.

Annie's father appeared to have lost Elsa in the crowd and was several people behind her, trying to catch up.

Nicholas, always ill at ease when it came to travel, discussed every bump and curve of the road. He didn't like being driven any better than driving. "It's so unnatural to go whizzing across the earth like this," he said. "My ears still hurt."

"Well, this is a city," he said twice on the way through town as if he'd never been there before. He sat straight and alert in the front seat as Annie entered and exited traffic, then got on the river road. He finally let go of the door handle when they reached the turnoff to the house.

Paul was home. He came out to meet them.

"He looks an awful lot like Morton," her mother whispered on the way into the house.

"What happened here?" Paul asked at the front closet where stuff still lay in the hallway. She'd forgotten about it.

"Could you put it back for me?" she asked him and led her parents, wondering, through to the porch. Without Annie noticing it, the fog had disappeared. The sun was setting over the water, creating a red blaze of light where it glanced off the current and the bend in the river.

"Do you get bears here?" her mother asked, looking not in the direction of the woods but over the porch as if one were below.

"We're not in the wilderness," her father said.

"I know that," her mother said. "It makes me a little dizzy being so close to the river, though." She did seem a bit dizzy and she sat down on a lawn chair.

"So you're Morton's brother," Nicholas said to Paul at dinner.

"Yes, I am." Having come to agreement on this, they both fell silent.

Elsa talked though. She guessed for them the chemical content of the snack pudding she'd bought when they'd stopped at the bus station in Deer Lodge: 65 percent nitrites, the balance, nitrates—no, she said, changing her mind, 20 percent incidental preservatives, 10 percent sodium, probably the rest nitrites and nitrates. She had saved a nondairy creamer and promised to read them the label later—it was in her overnight bag and truly amazing. She gave them her own diagnosis, as well as those from the medical arts, of most of the customers of Jake's. "Claire's doctor told her she has heart trouble but she just smokes too much," she said. "Harry's doctor says it's the gallbladder but I think he's simply not digesting his food. He needs papaya enzymes." She concluded all that by naming those who'd failed therapy and "passed on." She then gave a weather summary of Montana, east of the Continental Divide, then west, for most of the last month. Then, tired maybe, she went on to ask Sammy about school.

Annie tried to read Paul's face. He was listening politely. Her father too. He heard Elsa's weather report as though it was an analysis of some mystery he hadn't experienced himself.

Only Sammy was relaxed. He had nothing of his usual smirk tonight. Having become more insecure (or confident) about being a teenager, whichever, he could become rather obnoxious at times. He now held critical views, administered stern judgments of his peers—for example, Eric Adams was bucktoothed and sloppy, Carrie somebody was fat and also sloppy and Scott McLaughlan, a real punk in Annie's opinion, was declared "ultimate." But tonight, he was more agreeable, she thought, all because of Elsa.

What did he think of his grandmother? Would she become a point of reference in his life, a reminder that he'd known a good woman? Would he recall the details, like playing in an old tub of water on her back porch hot summer days while Elsa sang songs to him as she pared fruit to be canned later that evening when it would be cooler? Could Sammy remember how much time she'd given him?

"Children need a good rocking," Elsa would say, pulling a chubby Sammy onto her large breasts to rock when anything upset him. Morton had always looked on this event with curiosity and confusion. Possibly that was what had gone wrong with Morton and Paul—Annie was certain something had gone wrong with both of them. They had never had a large bosom to curl against when things went bad. Annie couldn't imagine Miriam providing that. First of all her bosom wasn't large, it looked bony and sharp, and rocking chairs were too small a space for Miriam.

Annie's own childhood, she feared, predated Elsa being a rocker. She imagined Elsa had been too busy then at Jake's, holding together a double life—with Bubba and Nicholas—to have done much rocking.

"Mom, you didn't breast-feed me, did you?" Annie asked suddenly, realizing after she spoke that she had just interrupted Sammy's explanation of computer-assisted instruction.

"You interrupted," Paul said.

Sammy snickered self-consciously and her father narrowed his eyes at her. He could narrow his eyes farther than anyone she knew without them actually closing.

"It wasn't the style then, no," Elsa said. "Too bad, too. All that sugar they put in formulas." There was real regret in her voice.

"But I learned better by the time you had Sammy," she said. "I told her," she said to Sammy, "breast-feed."

Sammy now looked flushed.

Mother's guilt. Annie had her own assortment of regrets. She had bottlefed (she and Sammy had likely missed bonding), she'd had anesthesia (that created a potential for drug addiction she'd read), she'd given birth under fluorescent lighting with a crabby doctor who used forceps, impatient because her delivery had interrupted a crucial inning of a baseball game. (The article said births of this kind, led to insecurity, alienation, to God-knows-what-all.)

"Were you breast-fed?" she asked her father.

"Hell if I know," he said.

"What's all this?" Paul asked.

Annie shrugged. This subject brought dinner to an end and everyone went off to watch television. All her loved ones, departing for the living room, unconcerned that they had failed bonding, were unknowingly alienated, insecure people who'd had tortured births, and what's more, had been denied real comfort because breasts, at the time, as a medium of nourishment, had gone out of style.

As soon as the news came on, Sammy said good-night to everyone and went to bed. Annie was sitting on the couch between her parents. Paul watched them. He saw that Annie turned to each of them as they talked, that she gestured in the same way that her mother did, and that both women let Nicholas interrupt them.

"Annie, did I tell you they finally got that statue . . . ," Elsa began.

"These guys put up this statue on top of the mountain," Nicholas said, turning to Paul. "It weighs fifty-one tons. They took it up by helicopter in six sections."

"Right before Christmas," Elsa said. "Our Lady of the Rockies. You should see it. They have a spotlight on it at night and they're going to have a tour bus and . . ."

"Morton lost two hundred bucks on that one," Nicholas said to Paul. "He bet it couldn't be done."

Now the news caught their attention and they all turned to watch. An armed and dangerous felon had escaped from the state prison at Deer Lodge. It seemed like there was always someone armed and dangerous escaping from there.

"Whatever happened to Andy Petty?" Annie asked her father. "Wasn't his brother-in-law always escaping from Deer Lodge?"

"Yes, Jack Moriarity," her mother said. "Mad Jack. Andy thought he had it in for him for some reason."

"Yeah, probably a good reason," Nicholas said.

"He always hid out when Mad Jack escaped," her mother said.

"He said Mad Jack was going to kill him," Nicholas said to Paul.

"So what happened?" Annie asked.

"Ummmh, let's see, he escaped about five times . . . ," her mother said, now pausing to think.

"I saw an escaped convict once," Paul said abruptly and everyone turned to him. "It was years ago up by Echo Lake. I was driving by just as the radio told about him. A few minutes later I was walking along and there he was."

Paul had completely forgotten the incident until now. Apparently Elsa and Nicholas were reminding him of a lot of things. He'd seen that convict the time he'd gone to find Annie not long after she'd left him. He was on his way home from Butte after going there to Jake's, the only time he'd ever gone to Jake's.

Paul had driven back to Missoula then through Anaconda and, on impulse, turned off the road by Georgetown onto a gravel one when he saw a sign with an arrow that said Echo Lake. He thought he'd drive up there and spend the night, maybe try to do some fishing. Going home alone, after his big plan to get Annie, wasn't going to be easy.

A news bulletin had broken through the music on the radio. He didn't remember the details but the newsman said a convict had escaped earlier that day, was thought to have walked over the mountain, and was considered armed and dangerous. The newscaster was just describing him when Paul pulled off the road and parked. He got out of the car and walked toward the lake. He came out of the woods and there, close enough to touch, was the guy still in prison uniform. His pant legs were rolled up as though he'd been wading in water. The man was as startled as Paul was and jumped into the brush. But for a moment their eyes met in a fast accounting of each other's fear. Yet it was more than that.

It was the same thing Paul had seen in Vietnam on the faces of men on both sides of the war. Eyes that looked angry, betrayed, puzzled—no doubt wanting to know how life, their lives, had come to this.

"You see that kind of despair in some of the vets around town," Paul said now. He saw it sometimes in Bounlieng too. Bounlieng was the Vietnamese mechanic he had hired several months before.

"That's because all the goddamn war protesters raised such a stink that the vets got a bum deal," Nicholas said.

"No, it's because it was a stupid war and everyone knows it," Annie said.

"They always fight about this," Elsa said to Paul.

Paul wondered if Nicholas and Elsa had any idea that both he and Annie had been war protesters. He hadn't thought about Vietnam in a long time, not until hiring Bounlieng. "How come your people generally favored the Vietcong and communism?" he'd asked him one day. He was helping Bounlieng pull an engine.

Bounlieng had looked at him. "To us war was not about communism, it was about religion."

"Religion?"

"Yes, you see many Buddhists became Catholic because of the French missionaries. Catholics received benefits from the French and later from the Americans. Even President Diem and Madame Nhu supported Catholicism and everyone was required to carry ID cards with a cross on them—the Catholic symbol. So many Buddhists, my parents too, threw the cards away. When they were stopped by the authorities and told to show their cards, they couldn't and were punished. Some Buddhists were even killed."

"I didn't know," Paul said.

"Not many people do," Bounlieng said. "You see we believed in the freedom to determine our own future just like Americans. But most people did not understand American interest in our country."

"But the Russians were interested too."

"Yes, but we saw no Russians. We saw only Americans with plenty of supplies and equipment. 'What do they want?' we said. 'To die for us?'" Bounlieng shook his head. "But the Vietcong we understood. They received no pay, they had no fancy weapons. They travelled by foot or canoe and they lived on what the villagers gave them. They did not destroy our crops or villages and they respected our customs. For the Vietcong, there was no future unless they won.

"Look at this crank shaft," Bounlieng said then.

Paul nodded and handed him a rag to wipe his hands.

"But most of the time there was no choice," Bounlieng said. "We had to help whoever was holding the gun."

Now Nicholas brought in two beers and handed one to Paul. Annie and Elsa had both gone to bed.

"So what ever happened to Mad Jack?" Paul asked him.

"Died peacefully in his sleep two days after climbing over the wall."

"His last big escape, huh?" Paul said.

"The funny thing is that he was found that time not a block away from where Andy was hiding out. Thought Andy was never going to get over that."

"Too close a call, huh?"

"Nah, I doubt that. Mad Jack never planned to get him. He got more pleasure out of worrying him."

"You think so?"

"Hell yes. Why, before he ever went to prison, he and Andy used to fight at Jake's. If Jack wanted to kill him, he would have done it then."

"I'll be damned," Paul said, trying to imagine something as active as that taking place in the Jake's he'd seen.

The next morning Elsa, of course, did Tai Chi in the living room at dawn. Then they all had breakfast outside and it was wonderfully clear and sunny. Annie made Paul and Sammy a lunch to take, cleaned up the house and made beds, ran to the store. When she got home her mother was baking cookies. The kitchen smelled of cinnamon and chocolate and fresh-brewed coffee. Annie knew she should go shower but she sat down and watched her mother drop little buds of dough onto a stainless steel cookie sheet.

"Where's Nicholas?" she asked.

"He went for a walk," Elsa said. "Since when do you call your father Nicholas?" Elsa asked, smoothing shortening onto another cookie sheet with a wad of paper towel.

"Mom," Annie said. "We don't have any family secrets, do we?"

Her mother laughed.

"It's just that I don't want to find out twenty years from now that I was adopted or something."

Her mother stopped what she was doing and stared at her. "How on earth does your mind work?"

Annie said nothing for a while.

Her mother went back to the cookie dough. A timer rang and she removed a sheet from the oven, replacing it with one she'd just filled.

She brought a plate of them and coffee over to Annie.

"Honey," her mother said, sitting down at the table, "do you get enough exercise?"

"Oh, probably not," Annie said.

Elsa had several suggestions, including one Annie had never heard of—exercises under water. "When you're done, you feel marvelous," Elsa said. Obviously she had tried it.

Annie nodded. "You know," she said, "I've always wondered something."

"What's that?"

"I've always wanted to know why Bubba took such an interest in me all those years. Why he left me his cabin."

"Oh, that," her mother said. "Well, he always liked you, from the day you were born."

"What!" Annie said.

"No, let me see, I guess you were about six months or so. You see, when he came back from the war, he had trouble with shrapnel he took in his back. But worse, he was depressed. He used to come into Jake's and drink a lot. Then when you were about six or seven months, I got pregnant again. Did I ever tell you that?"

"You told me once you miscarried."

"Yes, and in trying not to, I had to go to the hospital for a week or so. I had to leave you with your father and the neighbor girl. Well, your father wasn't too handy with babies, so when the girl didn't show up, Bubba offered to help. I said, 'I don't want some drunk baby-sitting!' But there was no one else, so Bubba, I guess, washed diapers, made your food—you were on solids then, and I imagine he fed you and even changed your diapers. I was worried sick but your father said everything was under control. And when I got home there you were asleep in a basket on top of the bar with a pink ribbon in your hair. I suppose Bubba's interest in you brought him out of his depression a little. Then a few months later he met Fern—she used to cook at a café down the street." Elsa paused.

"So then what?"

"They got married." The timer went off again and Elsa got up.

"Aren't these good?" she said. "I put wheat germ and rice flour in them." (Staples she'd taken from her suitcase.)

"Yes," Annie said. "So after that did Bubba, well, did he see me much?"

"I suppose he did, dear. I remember he made your shoes when you were little. But when you got older, you wouldn't wear them and he stopped."

"Oh," Annie said, trying to recall.

"By the way," Elsa said. "I don't like to bring this up, but . . ." She paused again, maybe for encouragement.

"But what?"

"Are you going to marry this guy or not?"

"Paul," Annie said. "I don't know."

"What's the problem here, dear?"

"Who has a problem now?" Nicholas said coming in the back door.

"I was just asking Annie why she doesn't get married."

"Women these days don't like to get married," he said.

"What do you know?" Elsa asked.

"I go to the dentist," he said. "I read those magazines," he said. Annie laughed.

"When are we going shopping?" Elsa said putting the cookies into Tupperware.

They picked Sammy up from school. Elsa had cookies for him in her purse, which he bit into suspiciously. He was not fond of healthy cookies. These had enough unhealthy chocolate chips in them, however, and he ate them.

They wandered around the various shops. Sammy was looking for running shoes and her mother was just looking.

"Let's go back and get those high-tops," Elsa said to Sammy. Annie frowned. They were expensive.

"All right!" Sammy said.

"You two go," Nicholas said. "We're going to get a beer." He had spotted a café-bar some time ago and led Annie to it.

"I hate shopping," he said and sat down.

"Well, here's to a happy life," he said, tapping her glass.

"So you don't want to get married," he said.

"I didn't say that exactly."

"All these brothers, all these houses," he said as though Paul and Morton were a half-dozen men with real estate. "Ah," he said. "It's too bad."

"What's too bad?"

"What's in it for you, Annie?"

"I don't think . . ."

"Did you ever settle with Morton?"

"No, I guess not."

"You guess not?"

"Not yet."

"Ah," he said again. "You see what I mean. You're not taking care of yourself."

Annie felt flattened. The beer, the conversation, the whole day was weight.

"You're worried, aren't you?" he said with sudden tenderness and took her hand.

She hadn't expected softness from him and it made her feel like crying. She felt a lifetime of tears just at the edge of her throat.

"Something's bothering you," he said.

She knew if she talked, she'd cry. Her chin was already starting to tremble. How had he known anything was bothering her? Annie blinked through moist eyes at him.

"Bubba left you some money, Annie. Actually he left it to me for you. You know, to invest for you."

Now she really did cry.

"Damn it, I thought this was good news."

"Why did he?" she managed to ask.

"What do you mean, 'Why did he'? After Fern died, there was no one else, but me and you. Your mother and I talked it over. We thought you should know. She's worried about you." He seemed flustered.

"Come on, don't cry now. If something goes wrong here, you at least have security."

She nodded. It was a comforting thought.

"Another thing," he said. "When I die, I'm leaving Jake's to you."

"To me!" She was amazed. It occurred to her that it would have been the best thing for all of them had her mother actually burned Jake's to the ground those many years ago. They would all have been better off. Because Jake's had flavored everything, it had narrowed their outlooks, brought them to limiting conclusions.

"Sure," he said. "You could do well there. Real well."

"My God," she said. What more surprises did this man have? This man who might not even be her father. She thought to ask him, as this was the time, if there ever was a time to ask. But this was as far as she cared to go with it. She was finding, in the long run, it wasn't as important as she thought. She sort of liked the idea of not knowing. And whether Nicholas was her father or not, Bubba had filled in where Nicholas failed. He'd substituted something she was grateful for. She only wished she'd realized it before and told him so. But maybe he'd known. Why else would a little kid seek him out at Jake's or at a shoe shop across town? Surely he'd known. It made her feel better to think that an old, kind man had known.

Chapter Nineteen

If Paul had liked anything at all about her folks it was that they'd said, "Fish, like guests, stink in three days," and left. If they liked anything about him, they weren't telling.

Spring was taking place in a general fog, dense and pale gray, that sometimes lifted and often didn't. Annie went alone afternoons to the river wearing a down jacket or wrapped up in a blanket.

Annie needed sun. It wasn't that life had become depressing as much as she wanted to think there was something to be gained by taking the trouble. Her enthusiasm, all at once for no apparent reason, was as gray as this scene before her.

Her classes were coming to an end, Sammy's too. He was now looking forward to summer at Morton's, wanted keys to the cabin Bubba had left her, prepared what he would take as if he was going to a distant country on safari judging by all the footwear and gear he thought he'd need.

Paul was fretfully helpful with these preparations, adding his own plans for the fall to the ones for the summer. One day he took Sammy to buy a round-trip plane ticket, and then marked the calendar that night with great ceremony—an X on departure day, a check on Sundays for calling home collect and an X on a day in August for return.

"What if I'm at the lake or Mom's cabin on weekends? There's no phone." (*Mom's cabin* was an unnatural and rather startling thing to overhear.)

"Oh then, I suppose you call before you go and when you get back. That's it, just call Fridays and Mondays."

"But I'll leave on Fridays."

"Thursdays then. Call every Thursday and Monday and if you don't go, on Sundays." By now the calendar looked like a dartboard.

"I'll pack this weekend."

"What's your hurry?" Annie asked. Sammy wasn't leaving for almost a month. Like Paul, she was unsettled about his going. She tried to have a positive attitude—she would job-hunt and get one and adjust to it and spend more time with Paul, so that on that X-marked day in August, Sammy would return to some order and a new stability.

"You can take my luggage," Paul offered. There was the general clatter as Sammy ransacked the hall closet. Annie went outside to the porch.

Sammy finally appeared at the door. "Good-night, Mom," he said and went off to his room with Paul's expensive leather bags, a gift from Miriam.

"Are you sure you want him to take those?" Annie asked Paul. "There's no telling what he could do to them."

"Of course," he said handing her a drink before sitting down. In those bags, there was assurance even for her, that Sammy would at last come back.

There was a slight chill that night though no breeze. She had a sweater around her shoulders and now she put it on and buttoned it. She was so sleepy that she ought to go to bed.

"Did Morton tell you he's thinking of relocating?"

"No." She could not imagine Morton changing bedrooms even. "Where?"

"Here."

"Here?"

"Yes."

"But what about the store?"

"He wants to open one here."

"When?"

"September maybe."

"When did he tell you that?"

"When he was here."

"Why didn't you say something?"

"It's not exactly for sure."

Annie couldn't think of anything to say.

"So what do you think?" he asked.

"I don't know."

"Does it bother you?"

"Why should it?" That was a dumb thing to say. Actually it did. Enormously. Somehow it brought the future into a sharp, new focus. Like a slide show, it flashed before her in silent, clear little scenes. Morton leaving Butte—she saw him loading a U-Haul with furniture and filing cabinets and office supplies. Her parents' death—in this scene, she was at a grave site utterly alone. Where was everybody? Then she saw a FOR SALE sign on Jake's, then Jake's was a failing boutique, then a parking lot. FOR SALE signs went up on Morton's house too—her house—and at his trailer at the lake—her trailer at the lake. Strangers were sitting on her porch there, looking out at water she had swum in, at mountains she had hiked. Then under the WELCOME TO BUTTE sign on the old road from Boulder was a gate and another sign that said BUTTE IS NOW CLOSED. There was to be conclusion to all she had loved there, to all she had hated. No chance to collect anything she might have left or misplaced.

"Well, it bothers me," Paul said.

"What?" For a moment she'd forgotten about Paul there.

"The thought of Morton living here."

Oh, yes, that too. Then she'd have the two of them here, always in some desperate, noisy struggle, each trying to gain an edge over the other. She sighed.

"You're quiet," Paul said after turning out the light.

"Hold me," she said. She would have liked to have made love but knew from the way Paul stiffened that he didn't want to. She pulled away then and he turned over on his side.

Sex. It was not a simple thing. She knew only that she enjoyed it with Paul and hadn't with Morton. Paul was less intent on it than Morton had been. More than anything else, Morton's fervor had worn her out.

Ironically though, Paul, not Annie, was the one now having problems. And while he didn't exactly blame his condition on her, he thought she should be able to cure it.

"You could help," he'd said one night several weeks before.

"Meaning what?"

"You know."

"You mean you don't think there's an underlying problem here?"

"Like what?" he asked.

"Let's see, ummmh, do you hate your mother?"

"No, of course not. Who could hate Miriam?"

He was right. She was exasperating maybe, but not hateable.

"Are you having an affair?"

"Of course not."

"Do you want to make love to me?"

"Of course."

Paul was going to answer everything with *of course* or *of course not.*

"Are you afraid I'll stop liking sex with you like I did with Morton?"

"Will you?"

"No." Morton took it too seriously, she started to say, and changed her mind—because he might ask her to explain and she wasn't sure she could.

"So what's my problem?"

"Well . . . do you feel that some things are out of your control?"

"For instance?"

"This situation with Sammy. Is all this struggle about him the cause?"

"Of course not."

"Well then, take vitamin E."

"That's malarkey."

"Get a physical, see if something's wrong. Quit drinking."

"And if all that doesn't work?"

"Then maybe you just don't like it anymore."

"That's bullshit."

"I suggest, then, that for now you quit trying so hard. Relax."

"Is that all you've got to say?"

"That's all."

"That's all the expert on the subject has to say?"

"That's it," she said, ignoring his sarcasm. He was referring to a party they'd gone to a few weeks before at a neighbor's home. A guest that night, a visiting uncle of the host, brought up the subject of sex, sex as recreational sport.

"That," the man had said, "is how it should be enjoyed."

He was a handsome older man, distinguished-looking in the way handsome men seem to age. This man, Howard, had been telling stories about Alaska and South America, and was generally the center of attention all evening. The women, Annie noticed, were interested in what he had to say about sex. The hostess Meridith, though, was embarrassed and nervous. A younger woman was angry, ready to fight, others were curious and one woman, a student at the university, asked him to explain.

"Recreation," he said, "meaning just for fun. No emotional ties, no guilt, no pressure, no hassles."

"It seems to me men already have that," one woman said. Her husband looked uncomfortably at his drink. He was notorious for chasing around, the hostess whispered to Annie.

"But Howard," intervened the host, who was called R. J. He paused to light his pipe. "What of the emotional aspects? The deep feelings of love and caring. Don't you think that's what makes sex meaningful?" The women smiled at R. J.

"No. That's what makes relationships meaningful, that's what makes a marriage work, that's what makes a hug warm. I'm talking about sex as something aside from that, divorced from all that. Sex as something free, standing on its own as another kind of pleasure, unattached from responsibility and the old ways of thinking about it." He might have said more but he was interrupted.

"What about the institution of the family?" Meridith asked.

"What I'm talking about would make the family stronger. There wouldn't be all that jealousy and emotional struggle going on."

"So you see sex devoid of meaning, as something . . ." By now several people were talking at once and Annie missed the end of the woman's sentence. She was in her late twenties and pregnant.

"But what's in it for women?" someone else asked.

"Everything," Howard said. "If women really want equality, they must free themselves of all the romantic and emotional garbage that they have put on sex."

"I see what you're saying, Howard," Annie said. "For example, what if there were places a woman could go, let's say, to get a massage and additional services, a place where she didn't expect love or romance, just a certain attention in terms of quality, service, time." All the women and some of the men laughed. Paul was not among them.

"A whorehouse for women!" the university student said.

"I guess so," Annie said. "But think about it. A woman might enjoy it for several reasons." (More laughter.) "No, really," she said. "First of all she wouldn't be trying to please anyone in return, or even in the first place. It would be entirely selfish. She'd be paying and could expect, well . . ."

"Satisfaction," the pregnant woman said.

"Exactly," Annie said. "What's more important, she wouldn't feel like she was the one being paid, she wouldn't be the prostitute here—the masseur isn't buying her dinner, isn't supporting her emotionally or financially, and doesn't get anything out of it but his pay."

"And tips if he's good," Meridith said. She had overcome her embarrassment and was now enjoying this.

"You've got the right idea," Howard said. "This is what I'm talking about. Equality. Recreation."

"But would the male ego be able to handle this?" the university student asked.

"I say it couldn't," the pregnant woman said. "Men just couldn't accept it. Could you?" she asked her husband, who looked rather amused by the question.

"Could any of you?" she said, looking around the table.

"I admit," R. J. said, "I wouldn't like it."

"What it boils down to then," the student said, "is that for equality to exist, men either have to move up to attitudes on sex more like those women have always had, or women have to lower themselves to how men act."

"Let's not talk higher and lower level here. That presupposes that one attitude is better than the other," Howard said.

"But that's exactly what you've been saying," several women said at once. "That recreational sex is better."

"They have you there, Howard," R. J. said.

"So do you really advocate whorehouses for women?" the pregnant woman asked Annie.

"I don't know," she said. "I really think that there's more to it than this and that most women couldn't do it—go to a whorehouse—and maybe they shouldn't want to."

"Why not?" Meredith wanted to know.

"Well, maybe . . ." She didn't know how to put this.

"Maybe what?" the chaser's wife said.

"Maybe in trying to become equal in all things, women lose out, and humanity too."

"You mean you don't believe in equality for women?" the pregnant woman asked. Everyone looked at Annie in disbelief.

"Of course. We should all have equal rights, but we don't have to exercise them all. For instance, I don't want to go to war, not because I'm a woman but because I don't believe in war. Yet, I probably don't believe in war because historically women haven't. I guess I'm saying I don't want women to give up not believing in war."

"In other words, women shouldn't drop down to a man's level," the woman married to the chaser said.

"That's a sexist attitude," her husband said.

"I think what Annie is saying, is that once women give up a certain belief about sex, it's gone for all time and we're back to the cave," the pregnant woman said.

"Paul, you've been quiet all night, what do you think?" Meredith asked.

"I think this conversation, on the whole, is extremely interesting but really bizarre. I, for one, am going to watch the checkbook to make sure there's no money going out for 'additional services.'" Everyone laughed at this.

On the way home Paul had been quiet. But in bed, he'd said, "Did you have to jump into the conversation like that, all that whorehouse-for-women crap?"

"Hey, this is the eighties."

"What's that supposed to mean?"

"You say what you feel."

"That's what you think. Not at the neighbor's house, you don't."

"Sorry."

"Just forget it," he had said and turned away.

The sight of his mother, clearly involved in and enjoying the act of sex, had occasioned many a sleepless night for Paul over the years of his youth. It was one of the things he hated her for most. It wasn't until he was thirty that he saw some advantage there for him in that one revealing act of passion he'd seen as a child. He could thank a few of the women he slept with for pointing it out.

First there was Pamela Harrison. "You know what I like about you," she'd said. They had just made love.

"No, what?" he said. He was exhausted.

"You like sex," she said.

"All men do," he said, wanting to sleep.

"No, all men think they do. They need it, sure, but usually they're all hung up about it. You know, like their mothers were about to catch them at it. But you like it."

"Great," he said. "Aren't you tired?"

But then Christine Lander really got him to thinking.

"I love making it with you," she'd said, lying beside him one night.

"'Cause I'm good, right?" he joked.

"Because you give the woman permission to like it."

"Now you're putting me on."

"No, what I mean is you communicate something. You know like—Come on, girl, abandon yourself and enjoy."

"What?" Now he'd sat up, interested.

"Yeah. I feel like I can get right into it and you won't be shocked."

"That's unusual?"

"You better believe it. Most guys think they want you to really like it but if you do, it scares them."

"Why?"

"Then they think you're a whore."

It was sometime after that that Paul came up with his Virgin/ Whore theory. His friend Dean said it was nothing new to psychologists and anthropologists and so on but it was new to Paul and he thought of it as his discovery.

It was simple. Men, he decided, believed—because in some respects they were taught this or, on their own, surmised it—that women were of two varieties. The first was the pure, wholesome type, which included mothers, sisters, grandmothers and, of course, daughters. Also other women of influence like some teachers, friends and so on. Then there was that group of women who were neither pure nor wholesome, like prostitutes and those fast girls everyone knew. They were easy to spot. But this group also included those tricky types not so easy to spot. You found out about that kind just about the time you'd decided to marry one of them. These were the type who, despite how clean-cut they were, went wild during sex. This type, for most men, Paul could see, held special terror.

He'd tried to explain it to Annie. "Why do you think you didn't like sex with Morton?"

"No chemistry?"

"Wrong. The reason you couldn't like sex with Morton is because he wouldn't allow it."

"What?" she said.

"Hear me out. See, you weren't free to like it because then that would have scared him. It would have confused him. He wouldn't have known if you were a nice girl or a whore. And no guy wants a whore to be the mother of his children."

"What the hell are you saying?" she asked. She was getting angry now.

"I'm talking about what was going on subconsciously," he explained. He went over the whole theory again.

"And that's why Morton went looking for sex with someone else. He still wants that kind of passion so he looks for someone he can allow to be a whore. Maybe that's why so many men play around."

Annie frowned. "You're telling me you don't see women as one or the other?"

"Right. They're both. Women are all Virgin Marys with the potential to be real whores."

"So, if this is so simple how come you know this and other men don't?"

"They just haven't figured it out," he said. Having missed certain experiences, they had not learned this. Morton, for example, having missed that spectacle of their mother fearlessly riding some man's penis one summer night on the horsehair sofa, had not learned early, as Paul had, that mothers like sex too.

Of course, why he was having trouble himself lately, he didn't know. It had to do with just being tired he guessed. Just goddamn tired. Of what?—he didn't know that either.

Chapter Twenty

Paul and Annie had finished dinner hours ago and were now having a drink on the porch. They were quiet for some time. There was a heaviness to the air. Humidity, evidently, had weight. Annie could barely make out the yard light at the edge of the driveway. If she stared at it just right, one moment it was far away and the next, at the edge of the porch.

"You know, Annie. I think we should get blood tests."

"What?"

"Blood tests."

"Whatever for?"

"I mean Morton and me. That way we'd know which of us is Sammy's father. Settle it once and for all."

"Absolutely not."

"I think this is Morton's and my decision to make."

"Wrong," she said. "It's mine. I've thought about this a great deal. I don't think . . ."

"This way we'll know. We wouldn't have to say we *just* figured it out."

"You want to tell him only part of the truth?"

"Well, then he wouldn't, you know, think that you were promiscuous."

"What!"

"I didn't mean that the way it sounds."

They fell silent again. Annie felt tired. No weak. Not only was it hard to see in humidity, it made her weak. What's more it seemed to raise the volume of a person's voice, probably carried it to every porch on the river or back to Sammy's open window. She couldn't even think in it.

"This is something I have to do," he said firmly.

"If you should dare," she said, "I will leave you and take Sammy with me. What's more I will deny anything you tell Sammy. I will even say there was a third person—the real father."

"You wouldn't." (No, she probably wouldn't.)

"I would," she said. "Think it over," she said. "Selfishly disrupt a kid's life, not to mention your own brother's, but be prepared to pay." She got up to go inside. "Give it some real thought," she said, "because you're taking a gamble. Maybe those blood tests will show Morton's his father or maybe . . . ," she couldn't help adding, "a third person after all."

"You didn't!"

"Why not? Think of how many women you slept with when you were living with me back then. Then think of a good reason why I shouldn't have slept with half that number."

Well, he apparently had no more to say tonight. She went to bed.

Now she was wide awake. Everything inside her was racing. She felt enough adrenaline was circulating to fight a battle when only enough for a brief skirmish had been required. She tried to calm down.

After this nothing would be the same between them. She had done exactly what her mother had done, delivered an outrageous ultimatum, only her own was worse.

First of all, her mother's had been more straightforward and carried the message that Elsa cared enough to fight for Nicholas. This one, on the contrary, meant Annie was not fighting for Paul, but against him. That fact had likely already destroyed something in him. And that she'd had to make it at all had done another kind of damage to her.

Could they salvage anything from this wreckage? She didn't know.

Why was it that Sammy, the innocent party Paul and Morton both professed to love, wasn't just *loved* instead of being a thing to stake a claim on? Did men really have this need to find immortality through their children?

"It's easy for you to say that," Paul had once told her. "You're the mother, you'll always have him."

It wasn't true. Both Morton and Paul could have him all their lives. *They* could go into business with him, lend him money, help him through college, meet him at a bar after work. They could bet on horse races, discuss stocks and bonds, compare gas mileage. But mothers lost sons. They grew up and left home, had their own families, sat stolidly at their mothers' holiday table if they still lived in the vicinity (and hadn't gone to their mother-in-law's), kissed Mom on the cheek and retired after dinner to the football game in the living room with other men. You only knew your sons through the women they might marry or the children they might have. If you allowed them to be independent at all, and you had to allow that, you lost them to careers and indifference and to things even mothers didn't understand. Or worse, you lost them entirely to other men's wars, brutal, meaningless wars.

At best, she had a few more years to live with Sammy. Then it would be over. He might search for her in every woman he met, regard her fondly, send her flowers, but it wouldn't matter.

Women lost sons.

Ten days, Annie counted them, had passed in slow, painful estrangement. Paul spoke cordially to her if Sammy was around and not at all if he wasn't. She did the same. He slept stiffly at his edge of the bed or on the couch after falling asleep there with a book or newspaper. Of course, he didn't come near her, but it was just as well. Thus far sex, when not boring, cost too much. So far she had paid with a pregnancy of questionable paternity, and sadly, Sammy paid also. She'd paid further with an ill-begotten marriage, a miserably failing relationship—a second time—and the costs were still mounting. Pay she might but she refused to feel guilty, if for no other reason than this—if sex were ever sinful, it was also, coincidentally, very hard work, that is, everything that went along with it was. Otherwise, she had no clearer idea what to think about it than she'd had at sixteen.

Annie had finally become neurotic; she knew it. She had an anxiety neurosis. "An anxiety neurosis," she read, "is a nervous disorder characterized by persistent anxiety. Symptoms range from mild to chronic tension, timidity, fatigue, apprehension and indecision to more intense states of restlessness and instability." She couldn't read any further. She had enough symptoms already. She had begun to wake up in the night from dreams she couldn't remember and then couldn't get back to sleep. Then in the middle of anything she might be doing the next day, something would remind her of those dreams—brief snatches would occur to her and she'd make every effort to recall the dreams but nothing would come. It was like having a known but forgotten word just at the tip of your tongue. This might happen five or six times a day. And she couldn't think anymore without horrible foreboding about everything. Worry did not just occupy electrical-chemical waves in her brain, or however that works, it became a physical presence that chose a location, the region of her heart and solar plexus and stomach, a terrible disturbance to her inner landscape. It was a combination of things—an extreme case of butterflies, a bad headache, the dread of something, an aching sensation—and all of it in her chest. Add to that powerlessness. She felt an absolute lack of personal power, physical energy, or will—no doubt the long-range effects of sin, moments of passion, and evil thoughts—a punishment to exceed all crime. Perhaps she was paying in advance for sins she hadn't thought of yet. Often when Paul and Sammy left the house, she went back to bed. Sleep, except for those dreams, had become an escape.

Sammy, if he noticed her strange behavior or Paul's, didn't notice it much. He had come to the conclusion that abnormal behavior was now more normal than former normal behavior had been. He saw most things as odd, or ill-fitting.

Teenagers, Annie thought, despite any of their own anxieties, had remarkable restorative energy. She envied that.

On the sixteenth morning of hostilities, Morton called.

"Morton," she said, "you just missed everyone."

"That's all right," he said. "I wanted to talk to you."

"What's wrong?" she asked.

"Nothing. Do me a favor, will you? I'm in Helena. Drive up and meet me at my hotel. We'll have lunch."

"That's a long way to go for lunch, don't you think?"

"I know but I need to talk to you."

"All right," she said. Maybe getting out of the house would do her good.

"Hey," she said. "What are you doing in Helena?"

"I'll tell you later."

She tried to guess what Morton wanted to talk about. It could be he wanted full custody of Sammy or wanted to tell her he was moving to Missoula or that he was getting married again. Or maybe Paul had written about the blood tests.

The traffic was heavy with farm trucks and semis until she got to the cutoff for McDonald Pass. She had written down his directions to the hotel and had them on the seat beside her. It was a small, modest, old hotel on Last Chance Gulch, not Morton's taste at all.

Morton was pacing the lobby waiting for her.

"Annie," he said and kissed her cheek. "You look marvelous."

"God," she said, "neurosis must agree with me."

"Pardon?"

"Nothing," she said. "You look good too." He didn't. He looked rather distraught, in fact.

He guided her into a clanky, gated elevator that required them to first shut the gate, then to shut a sort of chicken-wire door encased in glass. She hadn't seen an elevator like this in years. They got off on the third floor and went into an old, rather charming room, a little faded but clean. She sat in the only chair. He sat on the edge of the bed.

"So what's up?" she said.

"What would you think," he said, "if I sold everything and opened a new place close to you?"

"How close?"

"About an hour or so up the Bitterroot. There would be more business there and it'd be a change for me."

Well, it was some relief, she supposed, to have him half-an-hour away. Somehow she'd imagined him moving in with them or maybe next door.

"Give me a minute," she said and tried to think. There was something to be admired here. Morton, of the three of them, had changed more over the years than she and Paul. He had managed to overcome himself somehow, his fear of change, his idiosyncratic restrictions, his demands for predictability. She had to give him credit. However . . .

"Morton, here's my best advice. Take a month off and go somewhere. Take your time thinking this over. And think about doing it without selling the lot at the lake."

"Why?"

"I want it."

He laughed. "Well, I know you are entitled to something," he said. "I plan to give you half of everything anyway."

"Just give me that."

"I thought you'd rather have the money. You already have a cabin."

"I know," she said, "but someday Sammy might want it. Someday, you might even want it—particularly if you move up the Bitterroot. You could drive right over Skalkaho Pass and on to the lake."

He smiled.

"One more thing," she said. "Don't move there just on account of Sammy—I mean, that we live nearby. What if things don't work out between me and Paul? What if we move away?"

"Oh, my God, Annie. You're not thinking of running off with that Bernard, are you?"

"What?" Annie was flabbergasted.

"She told me."

"Who told you what?"

"Lucille said that you and Bernard, you know . . ."

"When did she tell you that?"

"The day I took her home."

"No, Morton. You don't have to worry about that. If we moved from Missoula, it wouldn't have anything to do with Bernard."

"Are you and Paul in trouble?"

She didn't answer. She didn't want to talk about anything or

Morton might squeeze out of her Paul's plans for Sammy. He was good at prying things loose.

"I'm so sorry," he said.

She got up to go so she wouldn't cry. Morton's kindness always got to her. In fact that had started all her trouble in the first place, going to bed with him because he could be so damn kind.

"Where's lunch?" she said wiping her eyes.

"Geezus, I'm sorry. I forgot," he said.

"It's all right, I'm not hungry." She smiled at him, he looked so worried.

"But give it some time, okay? And a lot of thought." She didn't want to be responsible for him moving when things collapsed and she and Sammy went somewhere like Brazil.

"By the way," she asked as she went out the door, "why did you want to meet here in Helena?"

"Because I'm also meeting this guy here who has the property I might buy."

She shook her head at him. "So much for giving this some time."

He laughed.

By the time she got back on the road, it was three o'clock. It had been cool up on the pass but the closer she'd gotten to the floor of the valley, the hotter it got. She felt weak and traffic was barely moving. Annie couldn't get her mind off Lucille. Why had she told Morton that stuff about Bernard? Why did she think it in the first place? Had she told Paul the same thing? That was probably why he'd become impotent and so paranoid about losing Sammy.

Now her mind moved to Paul, the impossibility of their situation. With every stop in the flow of traffic her mind jumped subjects. Morton would be hurt too by all this. It was hot now and carbon monoxide hung above the road.

Sammy was the one she worried about most. He was so vulnerable these days, she thought, picturing the way he strutted and criticized and became aggressive, then shy and soft or self-defensive, all in a matter of minutes. She hardly knew him anymore. In giving Paul, and Morton too, a place in Sammy's life, she had sacrificed her own time with him. Rarely did they have a moment to talk anymore, or to go out to eat by themselves, or to play cards or Scrabble. Or even argue. There used to be intimacy in their arguments and fights. He used to run in all the time with something to share with her, something she had to listen to, or for help choosing a shirt or a movie or a subject for an essay. Now if Paul was around, he never came to her room to sit on the end of the bed and tell her every inane thing any person at school had said, to complain of teachers or to list who he hated that day.

Annie was sweating. She could see patterns in the vapors rising upward around the car. Ripples and wavy lines of noxious fumes rose in layers in the dirty, yellow air. Her eyes stung and her throat hurt. Soon it was dusty, too. The highway had narrowed to one lane of dirt that blew across the road construction crew in the other lane and the large equipment parked along the shoulder.

"They're dynamiting up ahead, sorry for the wait," an old man holding a stop sign explained to each car down the line. He was sweating too and it ran down into dust that had already caked in creases across his face.

She'd give anything she had now to be sitting on some creek bank high in the mountains where she could drink cold, clear water, take her shoes off and put her feet on soft moss. To look up to blue sky and pine-scented air, to hear water running swiftly over rocks, to see fish jump from deep, shaded pools. She wanted a green meadow and the rush of breeze through tall trees. She longed for the creaking of cottonwoods in strong wind and the smell of a river.

Cars honked again and she jammed the accelerator. Now it was start and stop. It had taken her an hour and a half to go twenty miles. At last traffic began moving again.

Annie saw water through the trees up ahead and at the next turnoff got off the highway. She drove along a gravel road and across a small wooden bridge. She parked and got out.

She walked through a meadow until she found a clearing in the brush along the creek. Then she sat on the bank and took off her shoes and put her feet in the water. You could have all the lakes and rivers you wanted but there was nothing, nothing like sitting with your feet in a cold, fast running creek. She sighed. What she really wanted, all she needed, she decided, was so simple she had missed it. She wanted nothing more than to feel safe—that is, to be unafraid and to know that no matter who was or wasn't in her life, including Sammy, that she would be all right, that she could somehow provide anything she needed for herself. Maybe even love.

Suddenly she looked at her watch. She had a strong intuition that something dire was now pending, that it had to do with Sammy, and that she must hurry home.

Paul was in the kitchen when Sammy got home.

"Hi," he said. "Where's Mom?"

"I don't know. She didn't leave a note."

"Man, I'm hot," he said throwing down his books. "Three more days until school's out."

"Let's do a little fishing," Paul said.

"Right now?"

"Right now. Look," he said and pointed to the corner. "I found my father's—your grandfather's—fly rod out in the garage. It's the one I learned to fly-fish with."

Sammy picked it up and looked it over appreciatively.

"I'm going to put that new reel on it," Paul said. "And you can have it."

"Thanks," Sammy said and grinned.

"Better take a jacket though, it'll cool off soon." Paul took out a can of beer from the refrigerator. "Want to take a Coke?"

"Sure," Sammy said, grabbing a jacket from the closet.

"Take that red one of mine," Paul told him. "It has pockets for flies and anything else we'll need."

"Okay," Sammy said and stuffed cookies into one of the pockets.

They stopped first at the garage, where they put on hip boots. Paul took a net, fish basket, his rod and the reel for Sammy. Paul fastened the shiny reel to the old rod and handed it to him.

Sammy led the way down the narrow path to the river bank. The dog followed right behind him and Paul followed the dog. There was a breeze now and the water was in the shade of the tall pines behind them. They walked east, headed for a favorite pool where the river forked and where large brown trout could be found. Paul watched Sammy cast into the dark, deep water. The boy had his grandfather's talent for it, Paul knew. He made it look easy. Sammy was reeling in now and soon he plucked a large speckled trout from the water and gracefully scooped it up with the net. The dog got up from where he lay and sniffed it gingerly, trying to grab it with a paw as it thrashed around on the grass.

Paul went further upstream and waded out into the current to a sand bar. He looked back to see Sammy bringing in another fish. His own luck was not so good. There was a hatch on now and the fish were not biting at anything he had with him. Paul looked up at the hill above him. Maybe he'd go up and get some dry flies and leave Annie a note, get some more beer. He left his rod and basket on the grass opposite Sammy, who was now out trying the current too, apparently having no more luck than Paul.

The breeze had gone down and the mosquitoes were out now. He'd get more repellant at the house, too, he thought.

When he reached the house, there was still no sign of Annie. He scribbled a note and put it on the kitchen table, used the bathroom and had to look in several drawers before he found an empty container of repellant. "Hell," he said aloud and threw it into the wastebasket. Back in the kitchen he got out a couple of beers and another Coke for Sammy and put them in a canvas bag.

By the time he got back down to the river the sun was just at the bald spot on the ridge behind him. They hadn't much more time to fish. Once the sun cleared that ridge, the woods shut out most of the remaining daylight unless you walked down the middle of the river. But that was nice too. It seemed that no matter what else was wrong about a man's life, there was something about the woods and the river that made it right. Everything was cooling off now and he could smell pine, cottonwoods, fish. He hurried.

Paul stumbled once on the path and caught himself on the limb of a small cottonwood that hung over the trail toward the water. "Goddamn it," he said. When he got to the pool Sammy was not there so he continued east along the bank expecting to find him around the bend. But Sammy was nowhere to be seen. Hell, he thought, he's walked up to the old bridge or to the big hole upstream from it.

Paul climbed down the bank and walked in the river where it was rocky and fairly shallow. The sun had cleared the ridge and it was getting harder to see. The river looked extraordinary in this light, he thought. Silver and shiny.

But Sammy was not at the bridge either. "Goddamn it," he said again. What he ought to do was to sit down and drink a beer and throw a line in before it got too dark. He could wait for Sammy just as easily fishing as not. He turned then, thinking he'd heard someone call, but the falls beyond the bridge muffled everything.

"Over here," he yelled. There was no response though he didn't expect one. It would be difficult to cast in this light and the narrow ledge he stood on butted up against large boulders and trees that hung low over the bank of the river. Paul decided not to even bother and he sat down and pulled out a beer.

He finished the first beer and got out the second. Again he heard something. This time it was thrashing in the brush.

"Sammy?" he called. But it was the dog. He began whining when he saw Paul and headed back into the brush he'd just come out of. And suddenly Paul knew the dog wasn't just after a skunk. He got up and ran along the bank after the dog, now darting in and out of the shadows of the woods. The dog stopped up ahead at the hole Paul thought Sammy had probably gone to. The dog cried and nervously ran back and forth across the bank as though pacing. Paul tripped on something that rolled slightly under his foot. "What the hell?" he said and knelt down to see. It was his father's fly rod. And now Paul saw what the dog saw in the water, material—a jacket maybe, puffed up and bloated with air, floating atop the water like a buoy at sea. And the body beneath it, Paul saw with horror, was face down in the water, prevented from being swept downstream by a large limb that had fallen into the river.

Paul scrambled down the bank, jumped into the water and walked through the current until he could grab on to the same limb. Here the river was deep. Then he swam awkwardly, struggling with the weight of his hip boots. Finally, holding on to the limb, he pulled himself over to the body. He could see before he got to it what he had feared most: it was his own jacket that floated in the silver dusk.

. . .

Soon after Annie turned onto the river road, a sheriff's car passed her, then an ambulance. Her stomach gave a sudden leap. The sight of them out here heightened her earlier feelings of fear and dread. She accelerated, slowing only for the curves. Before long she saw the emergency vehicles in the distance. When she got closer she realized that they were not far past the turnoff to her own driveway, parked on the shoulder of the road. The vehicles' lights were still going but there were no people or other cars about, no indications of a car wreck that she could see. Had a car gone over the side of the road and down the hill? When she turned off the road onto the gravel, there were no lights on in the house, no signs that anyone was home. Had they heard the accident and gone to help?

She sighed with relief to see Paul's car in the driveway when she pulled into the yard. Wherever they were, the dog must be with them.

Now her heart was racing and she ran into the house. Sure enough there was a note. *Down at the fishing hole.* She grabbed a flashlight and ran out the door to the path that led down to the river. Again she felt a strong sense of foreboding, of fear for Sammy.

She fell once and tumbled several feet before she stopped herself and could get up. She felt blood on her hands and one knee where branches had scratched her and now her back and shoulder felt bruised. The flashlight would not work and she had to step carefully along the path though she knew it well. The sky was clear yet it was a dark night. Soon she was in a heavily wooded area so dark that she could barely see the trees. But she could feel them, immense and rather sinister, inches from the path.

She had a swift and clear sense, as she chose her steps along the now narrow ledge of river bank, of the insignificance of all her worries when matched against the chance that something had happened to her son.

Chapter Twenty-one

Paul was frantic now. He grabbed at the body in the water and pulled it up, hoping for some sign of life. He held the lifeless body in his arms and looked down at its face in that cold, gray light in amazement. It was an old man he held, with the face of his own father. For a moment he was startled, confused, disoriented. And he was suddenly cold and aware of his own heart beating loudly and haphazardly. He stared at the face for some time, until voices along the bank interrupted him. Then someone was beside him in the water, someone who took the old man from him, someone who was prying his fingers from where they gripped the body.

"Let go now. Easy," the person said.

"Where's the boy?" Paul cried.

"He'll be along," another man now at his shoulder said. Apparently they thought Paul was in danger too and one pushed him from behind, guiding him back across the water to the bank. The man got out of the river and helped him up.

"Where's the boy?" he asked again.

"He's coming with the sheriff," the man who had the body said. He was covering it now with a blanket.

"Do you know this man?" he asked Paul.

"No—Yes—No," he said. His mind, for some reason, had imagined the face of his father, though his father had been a much younger man when he died.

"What?"

"No, but he looks like someone I knew," he said to no one because they had turned their attention to still other men coming out of the woods. And among them, Paul saw, was Sammy.

"Sammy," he called. Sammy was staring at the still figure on the ground under the blanket. Even in the dark Paul could see the unmistakable look of horror in the boy's eyes. When Sammy saw him, tears began to fall soundlessly down his face. Paul held him realizing that Sammy was as wet and cold as he was. Now words tumbled out too.

"I found him sitting on the bank and he was shivering and I gave him the jacket. I told him to wait there while I went for you. But I couldn't find you so I went back to where I left him. But he'd disappeared. And then I saw the red jacket in the water. When I got to him he wasn't breathing and I tried to pull him out but he was snagged on that limb so I propped his face out of the water." Now his voice broke into sobs. "Then I ran up the bank and to the highway and stopped a car but it was too late and . . ." Now Sammy wept and Paul let him. He wanted to cry with him—for him and for himself. In relief. In gratitude.

The men had the old man in a body bag and Paul was suddenly aware of a dispatcher's voice and others, coming in and out on the walkie-talkie the sheriff wore at his belt. And light from a flashlight now caught the familiar line of his father's fishing rod still on the ground not far from the body. Paul picked it up and handed it to Sammy.

"Let's go home now," he said gently. He put his arm around the boy and whistled for the dog.

Now Annie could hear voices on the river, men's voices, different from the usual voices that were often heard in the woods at night: campers settling in, or lovers, or the more intense sounds of children or drunks.

Annie stopped; she could hear movement in the trees. But it was only the dog. He ran up to her excitedly and bounded back the way he'd come, disappearing into the dark.

"Wait," she cried, trying to catch him. But now there were two shapes emerging from the trees, figures that even in darkness were familiar.

"Sammy," she cried and ran to him. She held the wet, cold boy to her breast just as a slight line of moonlight rose from the water.

She, Paul and Sammy then walked in the direction of home, in the direction of the full moon lifting upward, out of the river at its bend, into the sky.

After Sammy got out of the shower and into bed, Annie went to her room. She was exhausted. This experience had taken all her energy. Paul woke her when he came in.

"Here," he said. He had sleeping pills and brandy.

"I'm too tired now," she said. "Put them there and if I can't sleep, I'll take them."

"Where were you today?" he asked. He had forgotten he wasn't speaking to her.

"Helena."

He might have said more but she was too tired to answer or turn off the light or hear his next question.

The next day, for most of it, she felt spaced out, unconnected to her body or brain. She might forget what she was doing or thinking right in the middle of it. Had she concentrated so hard last night that the faculty had worn out? It was so taxing to worry. She imagined this was how drug overdose felt. It appeared that Sammy was feeling the same way.

Paul was concerned and attended to both of them.

"Annie, I'm sorry about, well, everything," he told her that afternoon. She was lying on the couch.

"I am too," she said. "All those threats."

He laughed.

"Do whatever you have to do," she said.

It didn't matter any longer who told who what. She believed Sammy had whatever it took to cope with two fathers, might even appreciate the effort the two brothers had put into this. And as for Lucille telling everyone on earth anything she wanted, Annie didn't care. It had lost urgency. It was probably better for a son to know up front that his mother wasn't the Virgin Mary type anyway. And Morton could live where he wanted, it was neither her fault nor her responsibility. But what was really amazing to her was why any of it had ever overwhelmed her in the first place. How easily life got out of hand. If it were all going to fall down on top of her, the sooner the better. The way she felt now was that she wouldn't take any measure, not the smallest, to prevent that from happening.

"Why did you go to Helena?" Paul asked. He'd stayed home from work and Sammy had stayed home from school.

"To meet Morton."

"Morton!"

"Yes, he wanted to talk about moving here."

"Why didn't you tell me you were going?"

"You weren't talking to me."

"Oh, well, that." He paused now. "Did you tell him anything about the blood tests?"

"No."

"That's good."

Annie didn't even care why that might be good. She felt as if she was falling asleep again.

The next week, Annie had only to attend one class, pick up her projects and go to a party her teacher was giving. She spent much of the week, though, shopping with Sammy for underwear, wool socks, jeans, tape cassettes, a flashlight, a first-aid kit with a tourniquet for snakebite, a canteen, a new backpack, freeze-dried food, sunscreen, sunglasses and insect repellant. Also a mousetrap for her cabin. He'd obviously thought it all out.

"You won't need this many clothes," she told him. "You're going to end up wearing one pair of jeans, cutoffs and an old shirt. And if you recall," she said, wondering how he would get on the plane with all of this, "they have shops in Butte too." She didn't think he could hear her, he was so excited.

He was going through things in his drawer and she was sitting on his bed.

"Hey, what's going on in here?" Paul asked. He was standing in the doorway.

"I'm getting organized," Sammy said, going through a pile of paper. "Look," he said, now staring at a picture. "This is the man who drowned."

"What the hell? Where did you get that?" Paul said, coming over to the bed now too. Something in his voice made both her and Sammy stop their sorting. Paul was upset.

"It was in this stuff," Sammy said.

Now Paul held the picture, frowning.

"Who is he?" Sammy asked, alarmed.

"This is a picture of my father, your grandfather, Hammond Tomlin."

"Oh, that. Your mother left it for Sammy," Annie explained. "I just remembered it this morning and put it on the dresser."

"But," Sammy said, "it looks like the man . . ."

"I know," Paul said.

Annie looked at him in amazement. She had seen a picture of the drowning victim in the newspaper and he had looked nothing like Hammond Tomlin. She had even shown it to Paul and he had curiously studied it. She was about to remind him of that but she caught the look of wonder and questioning that passed between him and Sammy and she said nothing.

One day Annie found herself getting her own things together. She dug out jeans and sweatshirts and tennis shoes. At some unknown point in that week she became aware that, without having made a conscious decision, she was going too. She would drive Sammy to Morton's, go up to Bubba's cabin and spend some time there. She'd open it up, air it out, take an inventory. She would chop her own kindling and haul her own water from the creek. She thought she might take some books, her drafting table, maybe the typewriter. Then having her fill of that, she'd pack up and drive up to Georgetown Lake, sit on the little porch off the trailer evenings and watch the sun set over the water. She could row across the lake every morning to Denton's Point for breakfast. She would simply alternate between the two places, have dinners with her parents, see if anyone she went to school with ever came home summers—like Mary Lou Haggerty or Jimmy or Sherman.

Annie's life, for the time being, would have no fixed course.

"Drive him?" Paul said. "What about his plane ticket, it's already paid for."

"You use it," she said. "Come visit. That is, if you want." Dinner was almost ready and she got out vegetables for a salad.

"Christ Almighty," he said. "How long are you planning to stay?"

"I don't know."

"I thought you were going to look for a job."

"Not right away."

"You won't find it there, Annie."

"Find what?"

"Whatever it is you're looking for."

"I know."

"If you can't find it here, you won't find it there." Apparently, he intended to go on.

"I know all that. But I want to go anyway, just for a while."

"How long is a while?"

"Maybe a few weeks, maybe a month." (Maybe the summer if she liked it.)

He sat down, exasperated or perhaps just tired.

"What you're doing is going through a crisis of philosophy. You're questioning the tenets of your existence, the premises upon which you've established yourself."

She supposed he meant she was trying to get out of a rut. "I don't know about that," she said. "I just want to go home." She was at the sink, washing lettuce and tomatoes.

"Now everyone goes through these things from time to time. It's nothing to worry about."

"Good," she said, trying to remember if her hiking boots were in the closet or the garage.

She thought there was more he wanted to say but he put his head back and closed his eyes as if entering meditation. Suddenly he sat up straight. "Tell me the real reason you're going, Annie."

She sighed and dried her hands. She went over and sat beside him, took his hand. How would she explain it to him? Would he see that for the first time in her life she looked forward to home, looked forward to Elsa and Nicholas, to blue mountains, a silver lake, to alpine tundra? Moreover, to a cabin someone, for whatever reason, had left her, an inheritance she now had to claim.

Would he understand a sudden need for things like the way sun falls on a certain ridge or over a town decaying against a hill? Not that she might care to stare at a view like that forever but for a while, yes.

But more than that, Annie wanted to see a picture above a piano and to find out a name. She wanted to spend some time at a bar lined with old men and women sure who they were, where they had been. She wanted to take her son there and buy the house a drink—because home, despite every objection she could commit to memory, now included that bar. Life, her life, now could admit a rundown place called Jake's.

"So that's it?" he said.

"Yes."

He was quiet and watched her now as she broke lettuce into a bowl and cut up an avocado.

"Well then, can I come too? I don't mean for Sammy," he quickly added. "I think Morton should have his summer alone with him."

"There's one thing," she said. "I'm not coming straight home."

"You're not?"

"No, I thought I'd take a side trip through Yellowstone, go into Wyoming, see the Tetons."

"Great," he said. "I'll keep you company."

She looked up at him and saw that he was in earnest. Why not? she wondered. No one ever said crossing a state line was something you had to do alone.

"Okay," she said. "Maybe I'll even take you to Jake's."

"Lucky me," he said and smiled.